Love, Look Away

SAGE EARTH GIFTS

LISETTE BRODEY

SABERLEE BOOKS

Published by:

SABERLEE BOOKS
Los Angeles, CA
United States of America

Copy editing: Chryse Wymer
Cover illustration: Charles M. Roth

ISBN-13: 978-1-7340894-0-0 (paperback)
ISBN-13: 978-0-9909606-9-0 (e-book)

To Charles Roth

Thank you for everything you have done for me, from one year to another, to the next ... and on and on ...

"Grief can be the garden of compassion. If you keep your heart open through everything, your pain can become your greatest ally in your life's search for love and wisdom." —*Rumi*

ACKNOWLEDGMENTS

To Chryse Wymer, for being such a great editor and never losing sight of my vision

To Charles Roth, for his devotion to creating this cover

To Lisa Wentworth, for being supportive in more ways than I can count

To Alexandria II (Pasadena, CA) for helping me with my research to bring this book alive

To: Talatha Allen, Shykia Bell, Kenneth Brodey, Dody Cox, PattiAnn Cutter, Laura Daly, D.L. Savvides, Ruth Nina Welsh, and Sheri A. Wilkinson for their ongoing support and kindness.

There are so many people who have supported me in so many ways. I wish it were possible to thank each and every one of you. I hope you all know who you are. And last, but not least, thank you to my fellow authors for your support, advice, inspiration, and friendship. You all mean so much to me.

Love, Look Away

CHAPTER ONE

"I want my money back!"

The angry voice startled Margie, the frazzled employee sorting through the chakra healing crystals on the counter at Sage Earth Gifts. She looked up to see a thirty-something-year-old woman with frizzy red hair and wild, scowling eyes. In the redhead's hand was a vanilla ice-cream cone, dripping onto the floor. Margie screamed out for her boss. "Sage, are you around?"

"Need backup just to talk to me?" the redhead said with a sneer.

"What the holy … you're dripping all over the floor!" Reaching below, Margie grabbed a roll of paper towels and a bottle of spray cleaner, then hurried to clean the disaster in progress. Rufus, a forty-pound brown-and-white terrier mix, had already woken from his nap on a nearby mat and rushed over to clean up the mess with his tongue.

"That dog is an opportunist," the woman barked. "And pets don't belong in stores."

Margie glared at her before kneeling to clean the sticky remains of the melting dessert off the floor. "You must be thinking of customers with messy food; they don't belong in stores at all."

She looked at the dog. "Go find your mom, boy. Go on."

Rufus hurried back around the counter and disappeared behind the orange, red, and purple Indian tapestry curtains that separated the store from the back room. The woman glowered at Margie. "Like I said, I want my money back. And I'm not a customer."

"Right. You're not. So money back for what? You haven't bought anything here, and we clearly don't sell ice-cream cones."

The redhead scanned the store. "You sell everything else in here. The sixties are over, just in case you haven't noticed. Like over a half century ago."

"If you don't like the store, don't shop here. And stop dripping that thing!"

"Don't lecture me!" The woman stomped her foot on the floor so hard that the melting ball fell to the floor. "I want my money back!"

Margie screamed as the ball splattered onto her gray slacks. She stood and faced the woman. "Look what you've done! How dare you?" She huffed in disgust. "And again, money back for what?"

"For this cone. What else? I stopped to look at that stacked rock water fountain you have in the window. I was watching the water trickle over the rocks, and it's like the thing hypnotized me. It's eighty-five degrees outside and just standing there watching its hypnotic flow made my ice cream melt."

Margie looked down at the ice cream she was wearing. "Maybe you've noticed that my pants need dry cleaning now. Do you want to pay for that? Well, do you? At least it's a legitimate request."

Sage Gordon, the store's owner, in her late twenties, wearing a denim dress, ankle-high fringed brown boots, and a blue headband on top of her flowing brown hair appeared from behind the curtains with Rufus at her side. She hurried over to the two women. Rufus, who got there first, immediately started to lick the ball of ice cream. "Sorry, Margie. I was on a business call. What's going on?"

"This nut ball wants to be 'reimbursed,'" Margie said, making air quotes, "for her cone, because she was allegedly hypnotized by the fountain in the window, thereby causing her ice cream to melt in the sun. You know the sun, that big fiery yellow ball in the sky that we control by remote." Margie groaned.

"I'm not a nut ball! And don't talk about me like I'm not here," the woman snapped. "I should call the Better Business Bureau on this place."

Margie refused to acknowledge her. "I love you, Sage. But I quit! I'm a wreck. And this is the thanks I get for coming in on a Monday to cover for your aunt. I bend over backwards to help and get a swift kick in the butt for it." She sighed. "Remember I was going to leave that day the crazy old lady started singing 'Ohm on the range' and then screamed at me to turn *our* music off? That was really the last straw, but I stayed because I didn't want to leave you high and dry. I know you're dealing with a lot, but sorry. No can stay. As you are well aware, I have a surplus of nuts in my own family — a large assorted can of them. I thought working here would be peaceful, but it's too reminiscent of the genetically related life forms who rankle me with appalling regularity." She looked remorsefully at the floor. "Again, sorry, but no way I'm cleaning this sticky slop up, either. I'm just leaving—"

"The sooner the better," the woman chimed in.

"Can't you just stay until I find someone to replace you? Just give me a couple of days. You know I'm going through a rough patch."

"Oh, boo frickin' hoo," the redhead spat.

Margie stiffened with anger as she continued to address Sage. "I wish I could, but I refuse to sacrifice my sanity a second longer. You're a really good person, but I'm outta here. I have to do what's best for me. Nobody else will. Bye, Sage. Bye, Rufus." She looked at the redhead. "Good riddance!"

Margie thrust the roll of towels and the spray cleaner into Sage's hands, ran behind the counter to grab her purse, then hurried out the door, the bells above clanging as she made her exit.

"Good riddance to you too!" the woman called after her.

Before Sage knew what was happening, a customer, an elegant African American woman in her late forties, dressed in black pants and a satin teal blouse adorned by a silver pendant, took the towels and spray bottle from her, kneeled and quickly cleaned up the mess. With a smile, she stood and addressed Sage. "I'll just throw this in the trash can out on the street. Be back in a jiff."

Sage watched curiously as the kind stranger hurried outside to dispose of the melting mess. Within moments, she returned to the store, where Rufus immediately greeted her with sloppy kisses before Sage motioned for him to sit.

"Who's she?" the redhead asked Sage, nodding in the stranger's direction. "Your savior?"

"Godiva Genevieve Jones. Don't you remember me, *Sandra*?"

The redhead stared. Her lips parted as if to speak but got stuck midway.

"Surely you haven't forgotten this face." Godiva smiled cheerfully and put one palm on either side of her chin. "I was the manager at the Swansea Health Club for three years. The first time we met, you had all but one mouthful of your smoothie left, when you dropped it because 'some hot guy made you all tingly,' and you thought that warranted management giving you a free refill. I gave you a big fat no on that. You became loud and disruptive. Remember me now?"

"No, I—"

"I didn't have these then," Godiva said, flipping the ends of her long braids. "My hair was shorter. I've changed. But you haven't. Still trying to get something for nothing. And from what I heard, you pulled similar stunts at the club before I ever worked there. And everywhere else in town."

Uncomfortably, Sandra turned to Sage. "I take it you're the owner of this place." She glanced over the counter at an old wooden sign that said Private Property. "Not a very welcoming message. But then again, it's totally appropriate for this unfriendly so-called business establishment."

"It's for decoration," Sage said. "I think that's pretty obvious."

"It is to me," Godiva said with a smile. "I love relics from the past."

"Love thyself," Sandra said, snickering at her.

Godiva put her hands on her hips and glared at Sandra. "Honey, if calling me a relic rings your chimes, let that mighty clang wake the dead. I don't care. But since you don't like this store, and you're not getting any money for another cone, maybe this would be a prime opportunity for you to skedaddle, freckle cheeks." She twiddled her fingers to emulate a person walking quickly.

Sandra looked her dead in the eye. "Still can't remember you. I wouldn't forget the name Godiva if we'd met. It's so … uh … chocolate …."

"And so am I, honey," Godiva said with a spoonful of sass. "Folks often call me Gigi. Maybe that name will tickle your memory."

A look of horror swept Sandra's face. "Oh! Um, uh, yeah." She cleared her throat. "I'm late for an appointment!"

Rufus growled at Sandra as she left the store with a flourish, just as Margie had done. The two women and the dog stood in the middle of the shop together, listening as the bells clanged.

Within seconds, Sandra made a U-turn and stuck her head in the doorway. "I'm suing that dog for intimidation." She growled at Rufus, then left.

"Grrr."

"It's okay, boy," Sage said, rubbing the dog's neck. "The bad lady is gone."

"She is," Godiva said.

"Um, thank you. I really wasn't in the mood for that. Not that anyone is ever in the mood for an angry customer — or non-customer, but I really appreciate your intervention. I'm the owner, Sage Gordon. I should have stepped in, but you were handling her so beautifully."

"Trust me, it was my pleasure. I've been working with the public for over twenty-five years. I really am the nicest person," Godiva explained with a wink. "Most of the time. I just don't suffer fools gladly. And I was more than happy to have a go at that fraudster again. People like her irk me to no end. I should be thanking you for *letting* me take over." She smiled. "I do feel so much better."

"I think we both do."

"You wouldn't by any chance be looking for someone to fill your very recent job opening, would you?"

Sage smiled. "I very well might be." She nodded to her left. "You want to go sit over there and talk about it?"

Godiva looked over at the wicker-framed purple and red beanbag chairs in the corner by the bookshelves. "I would love to. But if I get too comfy and don't want to leave, I give you permission to yank me up. Gently. But you can yank. Deal?"

"Deal," Sage said, laughing, as the two women made themselves comfortable on the chairs, and Rufus curled up on the floor nearby. "Would you tell me something about yourself?"

"As I told 'Sandra the Mooch,' as she is known around town,

my name is Godiva Genevieve Jones. Some people call me Gigi. Easier for them. You know how it is. Why say a three-syllable word when you can get away with two?"

"Having a monosyllabic name—that's one particular issue I haven't had. Of course, people still mess up my name. Royally! I'm constantly having to say, 'It's Sage, you know, like the herb or like wisdom.' And sometimes this empty face just looks back at me, and I just say, 'Sage. It's Sage. Rhymes with page.' Then, either they get it or they don't, but I'm done trying to explain. I don't know what it is with people and names. I've had two people actually think my name was Sergio! And I've gotten Sadge a whole bunch of times as well. How crazy is that? Anyway, I'd like to call you Godiva if that's your preference."

"It is. Thank you. I've actually come to love my name. My grandmother's name was Genevieve, my middle name, and that was originally going to be my first name. But at the last minute, my parents decided on Godiva." She made a face. "Did they even *think* about Lady Godiva, who supposedly rode her horse naked in the streets back in the thirteenth century? Did they ever consider that yours truly would get teased unmercifully in the hallowed halls of learning? Of course not."

Sage laughed. "Glad it all worked out. So, tell me about your work background. Are you really sure you want to work here?"

"Are you kidding? I love this place," Godiva said. "I think this is the hippest shop in Swansea. I've bought a couple things in here before, but you and I never really met. Three months ago I bought a set of wind chimes for my back porch. The brass bells with red balls and dragons."

"Oh, I loved those," Sage said. "I think you bought the last set. Can't get anymore, either."

"Good. I like having things that are special."

"I heard you say you managed the Swansea Health Club for

three years," Sage said. "Why did you leave?"

"A man." Godiva groaned. "A very fine man who I thought was my soul mate. Freddie Lamar. The finest man I've ever …."

"May I ask what happened?" Sage said.

"We were going to move in together, and work together, so I quit my job to help him manage the online part of his sportswear business. That's when I found out he was married. Separated. Close to filing for divorce, but he'd never told me any of that. And I felt so betrayed. Couldn't help but wonder what else I didn't know about him. I told him to call me if he ever actually got divorced; then, two seconds later, I told him not to bother, ever, because that wouldn't change the fact that he lied to me big time. And I hate liars. And that's the very simple version of an extraordinarily long and painful saga. But as far as my job went, Jada had already hired a new manager, and I needed a break."

"You still love him," Sage said, looking into her eyes.

"Girl," Godiva said, putting a hand on Sage's wrist, "you're not supposed to be able to tell. Nobody is. I'm too tough to let my feelings show."

"I'll bet you hide them well when you have to," Sage said. "But you're safe with me."

"I know that, honey. I see the same pain in your eyes."

Sage bit her lip. "So what did you do before you worked at the health club?"

"Lots. About a decade ago, I worked in a boutique on Columbus Avenue in Manhattan for five years. The commute eventually wore me out, so I took a job as a bank teller in Swansea. That definitely wasn't my thing. Money is boring when it's not yours, and there's nothing for a person like me who loves looking at the world through a kaleidoscope and embracing life's colorful and crazy ways. Luckily, I found a position in a local boutique, so I left the bank and sold clothing and accessories for several years.

Everything was cool, but when my cousin, Jada Porter, opened the health club and asked me to manage it, I couldn't refuse."

Sage brushed a lock of her brown hair out of her eyes. "How long have you been unemployed?"

"Five months and change too long," Godiva said. "I thought it would be healthy to take a mental vacation, but all I'm doing is letting that man live rent free in my head. And I need to work. I *want* to work."

Extending her hand, Sage smiled as the women shook. "You've got a job. We're open six days, closed Sundays, except for the month before Christmas. So your days off are Sunday and Monday. My aunt Ruth looks after the shop on Mondays. And when she can, her daughter, my cousin Robin, works too. And sometimes one or both of them come in to work if we get swamped, but that's usually more around the holidays." She exhaled. "Anyway, the day is almost over, and I don't feel like talking business minutiae now, but if you come in tomorrow morning at eight thirty, we can discuss everything. The store opens at ten. I think you'll be the perfect person for me, Godiva." Sage petted Rufus's head. "Margie was competent. However … she has too much crazy stuff in her personal life, and most days, her nerves were rattled before she even opened the store every morning. I tried to be supportive, often to no avail. I'm sure you got a wee glimpse of how overwhelming she can be. We all have problems, but most days, you've got to lay your stuff aside and do the job. Especially working in a place where people come to empower themselves and leave negative energy outside.

"I opened this store for people who need peaceful ways to move through life, whether it be through meditation, working with crystals, or anything that frees them up to look at life from a different angle." Sage sighed. "I really try to keep a mellow atmosphere, but Margie was the antithesis of mellow. I always figured someone would tweak her last nerve, and she'd quit on the spot. Guess I was right. But no matter who you are, or what lengths you go to maintain a calm existence, life can throw curveballs and knock the stuffing right out of you. I know. And sometimes life is just too ginormous to lay it aside and work. I get it. But still."

Godiva frowned sympathetically. "I heard you mention a 'rough patch.' Something tells me I'm not the only one with a broken heart."

"Nope," Sage said.

"I don't want to pry. But are you comfortable sharing just a little? No pressure."

Sage paused. "I guess. Sure. Why not? We'll be getting to know one another soon enough anyway." She resettled herself in the chair. "I had a best friend since high school, Carrie, who spent a long time trying to pressure me to go out with a coworker of hers, Caleb Dunlap, in the marketing company where she works in Manhattan. I despise being set up, but I finally gave in, and to my amazement, he turned out to be what I thought was this incredibly thoughtful, funny, gorgeous, and fantastic man. So, I was grateful to her for being such a persistent pain in my butt." Sage looked embarrassed. "I'm actually kind of a shy person, so I don't meet men as easily as some women do. Anyway, I thanked Carrie every day and told her how happy we were and how wonderful she was for jumping through so many hoops to get us together." She exhaled. "Me and my big mouth. A year later, Carrie's boyfriend dumped her, and here I'd made the unwitting mistake of telling her, *consistently,* how amazing her coworker Caleb was."

"Oh, no you didn't! Oh no *she* didn't! Oh no *they* didn't."

"All of the above. And did I mention Caleb and I were engaged? And that we had a date set and a venue picked? I had literally just mailed those stupid 'Save the Date' cards when I found out my two closest friends had betrayed me. With each other! Did I mention he has the most gorgeous turquoise eyes? Wandering, but gorgeous all the same."

"I'm so sorry," Godiva said. "How long ago did this happen?"

"About four months, two days, and three hours ago," Sage said. "Roughly."

Godiva laughed. "You're a beautiful soul. You'll find someone else. Someone much better."

"Not gonna happen."

"Don't say that," Godiva told her. "It will happen. You'll see."

"No. Actually it won't, because I won't let it. I never want to date another man again. Ever."

"You will, honey," Godiva said, placing a comforting hand on top of hers.

"Nope," Sage said, turning her head so Godiva couldn't see the lonesome tear that fell. "No, I really won't."

CHAPTER TWO

"I think you're going to pick this up really quickly," Sage said to Godiva as she straightened the bookshelf display. "And it sounds like you know more about tarot cards and crystals than I do."

"My grandmother, the one I was named for, was really into these kinds of things. She's the one who taught me all about the different crystals and what they mean. When I was seven, she gave me a piece of amazonite after a school friend had done something to hurt me. She told me that the stone would help get rid of bad thoughts and feelings. It worked, too. The next day, my friend apologized. Maybe I believed in the power of the crystal because I idolized my grandmother." Godiva grinned. "I think the teacher relaying the unfortunate incident to my friend's parents had everything to do with the apology. But to this day, I still credit the amazonite. My grandmother also told me that it brings an enhanced capacity to communicate the wisdom in our hearts. Of course, at such a tender age, I didn't understand that the way I do now ... at a ripe *old* age."

"What an amazing grandmother you had."

"I did. I miss her terribly. As I grew up, naturally, she taught me even more. When I was twelve, she gave me a gorgeous apatite pendant. She said it was perfect for people like me with a passion for life and creativity. It also helps to develop one's psychic gifts. To this day, I wear teal and turquoise a lot because it reminds me of the stone and how its colors just exude my life spirit. But even more so, the colors remind me of my grandmother. Sometimes I could swear I hear her talking to me … guiding me." Choked up by her own words, Godiva scanned the different boxes of cards and books, carefully examining the titles. "She'd love all of this: *Shamanic Healing, Love's Power, Spirit Animals.* I'm telling you, if my grandmother were still alive, she'd have bought out this entire section of your store."

Sage laughed. "I wish I'd known her."

"She was wonderful. She created a world that was filled with interesting things and people, rather than just existing in the world outside her door. She always wanted to be different. Me too. That's why I was happy I got the last of your dragon chimes."

"Come to think of it, those dragon chimes were the only set I got in. I remember they were sold the next day. I just didn't know who had bought them."

"Even better!" Godiva looked around admiringly. "So, tell me, what made you open this store?"

"Well," Sage said as they walked behind the counter, "I thought this old-money town could use a jolt of something new and different … at least new and different for Swansea. I wanted to sell merchandise that made people happy and would appeal to many types of people … especially those who seek peace, love, healing, and psychic insight. It's hard to explain, but I saw a store like this in New York, and it just felt right. I didn't copy it, but I used it as a template to create something that was right for me."

"You found such a great location."

"Oh, that part was sheer good fortune," Sage explained. "I inherited this building from my grandfather. My grandparents lived upstairs, where I live now, and for many years they ran an upscale kitchenware store. After my grandmother passed away, he gave up the business and rented out this storefront as office space. Three years ago, when he died, the building became mine. He knew I had always wanted my own business, and he thought being a business owner would bring me great fulfillment. Anyway, I'm very blessed that this store and home now belong to me."

"No doubt your grandparents would be proud. Sage Earth Gifts is quite popular in this town."

She smiled. "I took a gamble, and it seems to have paid off. When I first opened two years ago, a lot of people came in here expecting a freak show. I had one socialite, Naomi Hall-Benchley, try to stop my store from even opening. She said it was 'incompatible with the essence of Swansea.'" Sage twisted her face at the memory. "But I think a fair number of people on the town council disliked her way more than they disliked the idea of my store. Still, there were lots of Swansea-ites who expressed their disdain more quietly. Ironically, many of them ended up being some of my best customers. They buy jewelry, scarves, candles, and greeting cards on a regular basis. Other things too."

"I know all about Naomi. It's tough to live and work in Swansea and *not* know her." Godiva looked into the jewelry case under the glass counter. "Your taste is exquisite, Sage."

"Thank you." Sage picked up a key with a small string of chakra crystals attached.

"This opens the jewelry case below and the ones against the wall. As you can see, the cheaper costume jewelry just hangs on the hooks over there. The yin-yang designs are big sellers. The steampunk jewelry too."

Godiva took in everything. "Gotcha. I'll get to know this gorgeous merchandise as best I can. Looking forward to it." Seeing the register, she smiled. "Hallelujah! Same machine I used at the boutique. I just have to learn the particulars of your business, and

I'm good to go. I'm fascinated by all of it, so what I don't know, I expect to learn quickly."

Sage took a cleaning cloth and began polishing the countertop. "I think the universe brought that crazy Sandra in here yesterday so Margie could finally quit, and I'd find the perfect person for the job."

Godiva laughed. "Clearly, the sun goddess, or solar deity if you like, melted that ice-cream cone with precise synchronicity!"

"It made both Rufus and me happy," Sage said. "For different reasons, of course."

"Hey, where is that sweet boy?" Godiva asked, taking the cloth from Sage and finishing the job.

"He's upstairs. I thought I'd keep him out of the way while I showed you around. I'm going to take him for his morning walk soon. By the way, I should tell you: once in a while I foster animals. Rufus was my first foster. Five years ago." She laughed. "You see how that worked out. I have two cats of my own, Finlay and Babaloo, but occasionally, when I can, I foster animals when the shelters are too full. I keep them until they find their forever home. One day, I'd love to have an animal sanctuary, but that's a dream for way down the road."

"What a beautiful dream. I'm an animal lover too."

"I like you even more," Sage said, smiling. "Anyway, I'm sure you'll learn everything as we go along, but there's one thing I need to tell you before the first customer comes in," she said as she stacked some product catalogs lying on the counter.

Godiva looked curiously at her. "What's that?"

Sage nodded toward the old Private Property sign hanging on the wall above. "No doubt you remember this sign from yesterday when that cone woman made a nasty remark about it."

"I do. And I meant what I said. I love old relics."

"Me too," Sage said. "But this sign is more than decoration

to me. It's a personal memento from my childhood. And people try to buy it from me *all the time*. I don't care how much they offer; it's not for sale. Never. Ever. Okay?"

"Understood. Sounds like it has very special meaning to you."

"It does," Sage said, her eyes filling with sadness.

"Do you want to tell me about it?" Godiva asked. "And if you don't, feel free to tell me to mind my own beeswax."

"I could never say that to you," Sage said, attempting to smile. "I know we've just met, but there's something about you I really trust."

Godiva put her hand over her heart. "Thank you, Sage. I'm really touched. And that goes two ways."

Sage pulled up two purple barstools that had been shoved in a corner. "Have a seat. We have a little bit of time before we open."

Godiva sat. "Ooh, I like this. It's comfy. But don't worry; my butt won't get too attached to it. Now, tell me about the sign."

Laughing, Sage sat opposite her. "Well, truth be told, my childhood sweetheart, my soul mate, kind of stole it for me."

"Whoa," Godiva said. "So, should I be more interested in the sign or the boy?"

Sage frowned. "The sign is all I have left of the boy." She stood and reached into a carved wooden bowl of stones that sat on the counter. Each stone was engraved with words, and Sage meticulously pulled out one that read, "Love You Forever." As she sat down again, she caressed the stone in her hand and spoke. "His name was Jimmy Cole. He made me laugh like nobody else could. He used to do crazy voices and imitate cartoon characters and actors from the shows we watched. The first time I learned he could do that, I had my head turned and totally freaked, thinking Bugs Bunny was behind me. The look on my face sent him into fits of laughter, and within minutes, we both had tears running down our faces. Such great memories." She paused to reflect. "He and his family lived two doors down from me until we were both eleven."

"Did you grow up here in Swansea?"

"Not too far away," Sage said. "In Bancroft. About fifteen minutes north of here."

"I know it," Godiva said. "Definitely a quieter lifestyle than Swansea. A lot of farmland too, if I remember correctly."

"You do," Sage said. "I grew up in a farmhouse, as did Jimmy, but neither of us lived on a farm. The land behind our homes had been bought by this grouchy old man, Chester Simmons, before we were born." She paused. "I guess he wasn't old then, and come to think of it, he wasn't that old when we knew him, but being mean can make people seem old. Especially to kids."

"Don't I know it," Godiva said. "And Chester is a grouchy name."

Sage laughed. "Anyway, he had these fields, which were just a small portion of his property, that weren't used for anything. So, most every chance we got, Jimmy and I would escape to them. We had our own fantasy world there. It was really special. He was the king and I was his queen. Sometimes, when my mother wasn't looking, I'd borrow this rhinestone tiara she had, along with one of her sparkly evening wraps, and dress up like a queen. Of course, a ten-year-old's version of a queen is quite different from the real thing, but Jimmy always promised that no matter what, one day he'd get me a real crown with multicolored jewels. But as a young girl in love, a rhinestone tiara did the job just fine."

"And no doubt you had to be creative with what was available to you."

"Exactly," Sage said. "You understand me."

"I do. Heck, I'm still trying to make miracles with what I've got lying around. Go on. Tell me more."

"Okay, but just the abridged version." Realizing she was still caressing the stone, Sage put it back in the basket. "One day, Simmons discovered us on the property and went ballistic. He started screaming, saying that it was no longer a part of our family's land, and we needed to stay away. Jimmy pleaded with him. He pointed out that we weren't hurting anything and that we never left any trash behind. But Simmons didn't care. He got even angrier and told us that if there were ever a next time, he'd call the police and have us arrested."

"How awful!"

"Yeah. And the next day, he put up a stupid fence and attached about ten Private Property and No Trespassing signs to it. It was ridiculous."

"Sounds like the dude needed to get a life," Godiva said.

"You think?" Sage giggled. "A week later, Jimmy called me at night and told me to look under my bed."

Godiva raised her eyebrows. "No he didn't!"

"He did," Sage said. "He had stolen one of the signs for me and snuck it under there when he came over to see me after school. We were working on a science project, and he managed to hide the sign between two poster boards. Even though I found it a bit strange when he went upstairs to use the bathroom and took the posters with him, I didn't question him. In the back of my mind, I wondered why he carried them in such a weird kind of possessive way, but that's all of the thought I gave it."

"We're blind to a lot when we're in love," Godiva said. "Guess that's true even in childhood." She paused to reflect. "Tell me more about the sign."

"Well, I loved having it, despite being constantly afraid that Simmons was going to come knocking at our door with the police by his side. But that never happened. I think he had put up so many of them in a fit of anger that he didn't even notice one had gone missing. I loved the sign. I was only ten, but it was like the boy of my dreams had given me the Hope Diamond or something, not a piece of wood that had Private Property painted on it."

"That's so sweet. True love."

"It was," Sage said with a self-conscious smile. "And the next time I saw him, I thanked him with a kiss. And he kissed me back. Then we vowed that when we grew up, we'd be king and queen of our own castle and live happily after ever."

"And ...." Godiva asked.

"Despite our young ages, we really loved each other. Our friendship went on for another year, and then, one day, Jimmy and his family just disappeared. I mean, they literally moved out in the middle of the night. My first thought was that Chester Simmons murdered them and buried their bodies in his field. I was going to take my dog, Tuffy, out into the field to sniff around, but my parents would have chained me to my bed before they let that happen. Hmm. Maybe they thought I might find something." Sage paused to consider what she'd just said. "I had all kinds of crazy ideas. Another one was that space aliens abducted or vaporized them. I had just turned eleven. My worst birthday ever. I was about as inconsolable and distraught as a kid can get. My parents were distraught for me. That was so many years ago, and I've never given up searching for him. I've looked on the Internet a million times, every which way. It won't surprise you to know I've found absolutely nothing. Which kind of makes me think that my theories weren't so crazy." Sage looked down sorrowfully. "I'm kidding, but I've never stopped wondering why there's no trace."

"How odd. And how very sad." Godiva frowned. "May I ask how old you are?"

"I'm twenty-nine. People never believe me. I can't tell you how many people wink at me when I tell them my age. It's like twenty-nine is some mythical age, and all twenty-eight-year-olds skip it and go directly to thirty."

"I have to chuckle," Godiva said. "I'm forty-eight, but I do like telling people I'm twenty-nine when they're nosy enough to ask … like I just did."

"You look way younger. You do. But I hear you. I'm actually forty-eight as well."

Godiva looked stunned, then burst out laughing. "You're funny. I wasn't expecting that. You have a very dry delivery."

"My secret weapon," Sage said with a wriggle of the eyebrows. "One of them. But seriously, I am twenty-nine and you do look amazing."

"Thanks, honey. Now tell me a bit more. Am I to understand that you haven't seen this boy for eighteen or nineteen years?"

"That's right. Honestly, and I am so insanely embarrassed to admit this, I think the reason I've never been gung ho on meeting men is because I've been waiting for Jimmy to come home." Sage stopped to replay her own words. "Wow. That's a revelation … to myself. I think just now … I've learned something about what makes me tick. Maybe that's why Carrie tried so hard to break me out of my shell to meet Caleb … before she decided she wanted him for herself." Sage's face reddened. "And apparently, he agreed with her."

"I take it she knew all about your childhood romance."

"She did. I shared everything with her." Sage sighed. "Even when I didn't know I was doing it."

"I'm so sorry they both hurt you, honey. And I'm even more sorry you never found Jimmy."

Sage fiddled with the leather-studded bracelet on her wrist. "It doesn't seem logical that we can meet people that we love so much, only to find out that it's not meant to be. It's happened to me twice. I just don't understand. I've been 'in like' several times, but that's not the same. It doesn't tear your heart into pieces when you part ways."

"Please don't let the past stop you from finding love again. Jimmy and Caleb may have come into your life just to let you know that it's possible to love someone with your whole heart. They may have been messengers from the universe. Sometimes things aren't what they seem, and messages can be tough to decipher, especially where the heart is involved. Don't be afraid to fall in love again. Especially now. You're just beginning to understand how your past has affected your present. Give yourself time to learn. It doesn't happen overnight. I have no doubt that if you're introspective and honest, you'll have even more clarity in the days to come. I think you're going to find that it will be easier to give your heart to a new man. You'll see."

Sage picked up her phone that was sitting on the counter. "Oh, look. It's nine fifty-three. Almost time to open the doors."

℘   ℘   ℘

As Godiva straightened the scarf display, she looked up to see the man who had just entered the shop. Close to six feet, he was bald with a closely trimmed beard, a few extra pounds around the middle, smartly dressed, and wearing a huge smile. He looked down as if speaking to an imaginary dog by his side. "My, my, Toto. Looks like we're not in Bed, Bath, and Beyonce anymore." No sooner had he spoken than Rufus had pushed aside the tapestry curtains and eagerly greeted him. "Hey, boy! I know you. Rufus the doofus. It's been a while. Meet Toto."

Rufus paid no attention to the invisible dog. "Okay, don't meet Toto," he said, shrugging with a smile.

"Hello there," Godiva said to him, chuckling. "I know you from somewhere. And I recognize that sense of humor."

"From the health club, I'm sure." He patted his stomach.

"I'm forever trying to get rid of these and keep trying to convince myself that it will happen. But I have lost fourteen pounds and kept them off. So there's hope for me yet."

"There's always hope." Godiva smiled. "I'm embarrassed. I can't recall your name. It's right on the tip of my tongue."

"Adam!" Sage said, coming from behind the counter to give him a hug. "I'm so happy to see you. It's been nearly a year." He happily returned Sage's hug, then scanned the store as Rufus went back around the corner. "This place looks even better than I remember it. I never really got a chance to look around and inspect your fine wares. Probably because Jameson Clothier kept the same hours as you did, and I was imprisoned there most days. They didn't even like it when I went out for lunch. They wanted me nearby in case it got busy. You know, because of the high probability that a bus might stop in front of the store, carrying stuffed shirts from far and wide, each desperate for a custom suit or a polo shirt in every color and style Ralph makes, and they'd rush, en masse, into Jameson." He sighed. "I was so happy to get out of that clink."

Sage laughed. "I do remember they were sticklers of some sort. I thought you might have left Swansea for good after enduring all that."

"No such luck. I'm still here. But I've been going into New York a lot," he said. "Scoping out the men's clothing stores and doing a bit of buying and such." Adam stepped back to take a look at her. "You look fantastic! You wear that dress and those boots like a superstar. I love the rhinestones in your headband that match your earrings. You look like a queen."

"Thank you," Sage said. She tried to maintain a smile as childhood memories came back to her.

"Did I say something I shouldn't have said?" Adam asked.

"No, not at all." She smiled and gripped the sides of Adam's shoulders. "So tell me about you. Have you really been shopping for nearly a year?"

"Not exactly," he said, laughing. "I'm opening up my own men's clothing store in just under three weeks. I've been taking my time getting it together because I need to do it right. I definitely don't want to be a carbon copy of Jameson Clothier. I want my store to be hip. No multicolored plaid shorts for weekend golfers. I still plan to sell clothing that the staid Swansea crowd will like, but I want my store to be the place where they'll also find something different. I'll be including some big and tall sizes too. It'll be called: Haber Dash: Trendy Apparel for Men on the Move, and Sedentary Dudes Too."

"Best store name ever!" Godiva said. "I love it. And you're Adam! Don't know how I forgot. I'm Godiva Jones. You might remember me as Gigi."

"Gigi! Yes! I'm Adam Canoga. And you look wonderful. I'm sorry I didn't recognize you at first. Your hair was different and so was mine." He paused for dramatic effect. "I had some." Adam walked over and shook her hand. "I had no idea you were working for Sage. What should I call you? Do you prefer Godiva or Gigi?"

"I really do prefer Godiva." She folded a purple scarf and placed it in a basket display. "And I just started here … two hours ago."

"Fantastic!" he exclaimed. "By the way, that part about sedentary dudes is just my unofficial tagline. Though I did actually consider including it for a hot minute. But there are too many serious people in this town … too priggish and proper. Sticks up their … um … you know. But I would've put that on the sign, too." He paused to consider what he'd just said. "I mean the *sedentary thing*—I would have put *that* on the sign, but I figured the town council would have an issue with it, and I didn't need the hassle."

"Town council lives for issues," Sage said. "It's their *raison d'être!*"

"Ah, *oui, madame!*" Adam said.

"Everybody needs to feel relevant," Godiva said. "Some folks just go about it in all the wrong way."

"Oh, yeah," Sage said. "Issues are the specialty of town councils worldwide." She looked at Adam. "Is that your store around the corner on Hudson? I saw someone was moving in, but I didn't know who."

"*C'est moi*," Adam said. "The sign is being made now. I'm having an open house before the official opening, and I'd love for you to come." He looked at Godiva. "Both of you. I'm doing an all-day thing because many of the guests are business owners, and everyone's on a different schedule."

"I'd love to stop by," Godiva said.

"Me too," Sage said.

"Great." Adam looked down at Sage's hand. "Uh … I don't mean to pry, but I can't help but notice that you're not wearing an engagement or a wedding ring."

Sage walked behind the counter to straighten some accounts payable she'd been calculating. "You're very observant." She looked down at the papers. "No, I'm not. Caleb and I broke up."

"I'm sorry," Adam said. "I think. Or is that a good thing?" He followed her to the counter and stood in front of it.

Sage stared at the paperwork and pretended to be examining it. "When someone leaves you for your so-called best friend, who is one and the same as the person who set the two of you up, then I'd say it's a good thing because it means you've dodged a bullet." She swallowed a lump in her throat. "Okay, *I* dodged a bullet." She paused, then looked at Adam. "I just wish Caleb had aimed his metaphorical gun at me before the whole world knew."

Godiva started to speak but thought better of it and moved

on to the votive candle display.

Adam looked sympathetically at her. "You're just about the nicest person I've ever met, Sage Gordon. This may sound old-fashioned, but you're really the salt of the Earth … beautiful inside and out. I always wanted to ask you for a date, but by the time I got my nerve up, well, you were otherwise engaged."

"Um …."

Adam looked more nervous than Sage. "So I can't help but wonder. If I got it up …." He laughed awkwardly. "I mean my *nerve*, if I got up my *nerve* up … gee, how embarrassing … any chance you might say yes?"

"Oh, Adam," Sage said, mindlessly taking the cap off a marker and snapping it back on. "I'm sorry. I'm not in the frame of mind to see anyone. I'm just not." She looked at him and noticed in her peripheral vision that Godiva was shooting a look at her.

Adam tried to hide his disappointment. "I hear you. It's not easy when a relationship breaks up. At least not when you didn't want or expect it to. I've been there." He stepped away from the counter and looked at Godiva. "Well, it's nice seeing you again, Gigi — I mean, Godiva. I hope you'll both come by my open house. It's not for a while yet, and I'll be dropping off flyers, but I wanted to invite you now. You know, sort of a save-the-date kind of thing."

Sage's face dropped.

"Oh, no. Did I say something wrong?"

"No, you're the best, Adam. It's like I told you. I'm just not in the best place … head wise. Lots of triggers. What can I say? That's all. But yes, I'll come to the opening."

Adam smiled and looked down at his side. "Let's go, Toto. These fine ladies have work to do."

Sage and Godiva offered cheerful good-byes as Adam left, both of them noticing that he hung his head the moment he was out of the store.

"Oh, my!" Godiva said. "Curly McBurly likes you. A whole lot."

"How do you know that?" Sage asked, astonished.

"Honey, that invisible dog knows the man has a thing for you."

"No," Sage said. "Sorry. I meant, how did you know people call him Curly McBurly?"

"Oh, he coined that moniker himself when he first joined the health club. Some people were afraid to use it because they thought someone else had made it up to poke fun at his lack of hair and extra pounds. It just occurred to me that's why I couldn't remember his actual name when he walked in."

"I had no idea he'd made up his own nickname," Sage said. "He really is a sweetheart … a funny, self-deprecating guy. One of the nicest people I know."

"He's a big teddy bear. Would it be so terrible to get to know him better?"

Sage cocked her head and looked at her new employee. "I've known you less than twenty-four hours, and you're already my personal life coach and matchmaker."

"Guilty as charged." She paused. "Too much?" Godiva asked with a look of playful remorse on her face.

"I'm flattered that you care. But I'm really trying—"

"To avoid men," Godiva said, finishing her sentence.

"Yeah, that!" Sage said as she looked at the door. "Hey, here come some more customers. See if you can sell our wares to them instead."

"I will do that. Sorry—"

"S'okay," Sage said. "I already know what a romantic you are. I was one in a former life."

"You will be again," Godiva said under her breath.

"I heard that," Sage said. "Behave yourself."

"Welcome to Sage Earth Gifts," Godiva said cheerfully as the bells clanged, and the door opened. "If there's anything I can help you with, just let me know. My name is—"

"Actually, you can. I hear you have a nice selection of Himalayan salt lamps." A blond woman in an expensive gray pantsuit smiled. "I need one for a birthday present. And please … tell me you gift wrap here."

Sage, still at the counter, spoke up. "We do. I can handle that for you."

Godiva looked at her. "No need. I'm a pro at wrapping. I'll take care of anything this lady needs."

"Okay then," Sage said. "Great." She addressed the customer. "You're in good hands with Godiva." She looked at her new employee. "Everything should be marked. If it's not, let me know. I'll be here slaving over hot paperwork if you need me."

Godiva nodded. As she began to lead the customer over to the salt lamps, she noticed the woman's friend, an attractive forty-something African American woman, staring at her, then averting her glance when Godiva noticed. Rattled, she kept walking. "And here are our Himalayan salt lamps. I do hope there's something here to your liking."

"Oh, these are gorgeous," the woman cooed. "I think I'm going to get one for myself. And you have so many sizes and designs. How will I choose?"

"I like this one," her friend said, picking up a medium-sized lamp with a rough surface. It has personality." She looked at Godiva, then at her friend. "But you know, sometimes, when you've got rough edges and a big personality, you're misunderstood. And despite putting yourself out there … in a big old way … you find yourself abandoned. Dropped on the floor and shattered." She looked at Godiva again. "To bits."

The blonde looked oddly at her friend. "Okay … So I take it

you like this lamp? You relate to this lamp? Or maybe it reminds you of a lamp you know ... and don't like so much?"

Godiva suppressed a laugh.

The woman looked a bit miffed. "You buy whatever suits you, Doreen. You're giving the gift, both to your mother-in-law and to yourself. Doesn't matter what I like. I was just making a general observation. Besides, I like my lamps with a little shade."

Doreen smiled. "Okay, then. It's just that you just seemed so, should I say, oddly captivated with what I am buying."

The woman glanced at Godiva before responding. "Not captivated at all. Not by salt lamps anyway. I'm just a keen observer. I don't miss a lot."

Sage and Godiva exchanged looks.

Doreen, addressing Godiva, pointed to two lamps. "These are my choices. The larger one is the gift, so if you'd wrap it, that would be great. This one," she said, looking at her friend, "the smaller one with the rough edges, is for me."

Godiva kneeled and pulled out two boxes from under the display. "Brand new, in the original packaging," she said, still feeling the other woman's eyes on her back. "I'll ring these up and have the gift wrapped in a jiff."

Doreen followed Godiva to the counter, reaching into her purse and pulling out a credit card, while her friend looked around the store, pausing every moment or so to shoot daggers at Godiva.

Five minutes later, Godiva handed her a sage-green shopping bag with the store logo on it. "Please enjoy. And I hope your mother-in-law is pleased with the lamp."

"Oh, she will be. She's wanted one forever ... something about negative ions and fresh air. I just love them for the ambiance they bring to a room. Thank you." Doreen looked over at her friend, who was now casually looking at the scarves. "Are you ready, Sienna?"

"As I'll ever be," she answered. Taking one last look at Godiva, she followed her friend out the door, pulling it closed so the bells clanged extra loud.

CHAPTER THREE

After staring at the door with their mouths agape, Godiva and Sage looked at each other.

"I was going to ask you what that was all about," Sage said. "But you seemed as confused as I am."

"Wow," Godiva said. "Just wow." She looked over her shoulder. "Is my water bottle back there? I need some hydration. I'm drained."

Sage reached around, grabbed Godiva's water bottle, then handed it over the counter to her. "You okay?"

"I will be. I'm just a bit dazed and confused. Maybe 'sucker punched' would more aptly describe it."

"Who was that woman?" Sage asked. "She really seemed to have a wee bit of resentment toward you. But it didn't look like she had any idea who you were until I said your name."

Godiva took a healthy swig from her water bottle. "And I had no idea who she was until her friend said *her* name."

"And she is …?"

"Sienna Lamar-Langsford," Godiva said. "I've never met her, but she's Freddie's sister. She's been living in Los Angeles with her husband for years, and the last time I remember Freddie seeing her, he flew out west." She sighed. "I just don't get the attitude. Seems like she thinks I hurt her brother, not the other way around."

"You gonna do anything about it?" Sage said, twirling her pencil like a baton.

"Not a darn thing, but I'd be lying if I didn't tell you my curiosity was piqued."

"And you're feeling a bit angry," Sage said.

"Am I that transparent?"

"Invisible Toto could see that."

"Touché," Godiva said, straightening the scarf display Sienna had been looking at. "I deserved that. And in case you're wondering, no, I don't even *want* to do anything about it. Let sleeping dogs lie."

"Woof!" came the loud bark from behind the counter.

Sage looked out through the glass window and smiled. "Oh, no. Here comes Trubs!"

As Rufus picked up his squeaky red snake toy and rushed to the door, Sage laughed and looked at Godiva. "That's my word for trouble. And my nickname for—"

The bells on the door clanged loudly as the impeccably dressed man entered with a big smile. "Randy Goodrich is in the *house!*"

Rufus, who could hardly contain his excitement, ran in circles in front of Randy, his snake squeaking loudly as he did so.

Sage walked from around the corner. "I have no idea how he knew you were coming," Sage said. "But I swear, he *always* knows!"

Randy handed Sage a long-stemmed red rose and gave her a kiss on each cheek. "He's got 'Randy radar,' which possibly emanates from my exquisite cologne, or perhaps he's just picking up my vivacious and vampish vibes. Believe me, darling, I'm used to it, especially with some of the men in this town." He paused, then spoke in a faux stage whisper. "Swansea truly has divine architecture, but someone built way too many closets. Bursting wide open! Especially when I'm nearby."

Sage laughed. "You're too much. I'm going to put this floral beauty in my Randy vase. Don't worry—after you leave, I'll add water," she said, laying the rose on the counter as she walked behind it.

"Hi, Randy," Godiva said.

Randy's face lit up. "Godiva Genevieve Jones! Give Randy a kiss!"

They embraced, and Randy kissed her on each cheek as he did with Sage. "Are you working here for the sagacious one?"

"I am," she said. "I just started today."

"That's wonderful," he said, reaching down to pet Rufus, who had dropped the snake in favor of showing more affection to Randy. "I love this dog. He has such exquisite taste." He looked directly at Rufus. "No dirty paws today, I hope. Randy has no time for laundry or ironing. He's only pressed for time."

Sage grabbed a red vase from a side cabinet, put the rose in it, then placed it on the counter next to the bowl of stones. "Come here, boy," Sage said, patting her thighs. "And bring your snake. Time for your nap."

The dog obliged and picked up his toy, taking one last admiring glimpse at Randy as he wagged his tail, then rounded the counter to his bed in the back room.

Sage waited until Rufus went through the curtains, then rejoined Randy and Godiva. "It appears you two are acquainted. How nice."

Randy put an arm around Godiva. "I would have brought two roses, had I known Miss Jones was here. I've known this treasure of a lady for years." He made a sad face. "Pre-Freddie, Freddie, and post-Freddie."

"It's true," Godiva said, playfully tilting her head to rest on his shoulder. "Randy took me to dinner after the breakup to console me, and he was absolutely wonderful afterward. Then I went into hiding for five months to wallow in my misery, so I haven't seen much of anyone."

Randy looked at Sage. "Tsk. Tsk. And whose sad story does that remind you of?"

"Mine, teacher."

"Come here, darling." He stood with one arm around each woman. "Randy is always here for your sorrows, but I hope there will be joy as well. For both of you brokenhearted lovelies."

"You're the best, Trubs," Sage said. "I think Rufus loves you even more because he's seen how many times you made me smile through my tears. Speaking of loved ones, how is Kyle?"

"Dashing, delicious, daring, and dauntless."

Sage smiled. "Dauntless, huh? That's a new one."

"Which brings me to the reason I'm here."

Sage mock frowned. "You mean it wasn't just to see me and Rufus." She laughed. "What can I do for you?"

"Well," he said, looking at both women with mischief in his eyes. "My dauntless man is opening up his own business in the office complex on Bridge Street. He's had enough of working with the Benchley family and enduring their incessant machinations and stuffy gatherings."

Godiva looked at him curiously. "Good for him. And you want to decorate his office with tapestries and other good things from Sage Earth Gifts?"

Randy looked around. "As much as I love this store, darling, no. A trinket or two, most definitely."

Sage looked seriously at him. "But you haven't seen my new furniture showroom. It's filled with gems from the sixties. No doubt Kyle would love a lime green Day-Glo couch."

"Oh, my," Randy said. "Nice try, sagacious girl. But you have to get up much earlier in the morning to fool Randy Goodrich."

"I would," Sage said, laughing. "And that's unlikely to ever happen because I'd linger in dreamland even later than I already do if I didn't have a store to run."

"To sleep in is divine," Randy said, walking over to inspect the Buddha statues. "The early bird may catch the worm, but the late bird enjoys it for lunch, dinner, and dessert." He ran his tongue over his top lip. "Yum."

Sage blushed.

"Watch it," Godiva said to Randy. "You might lose your PG rating ... not that you have one."

"Oh dear," Randy said, feigning innocence as he picked up a Buddha for closer inspection. "Did I say something risqué?"

"What can we do you for, Trubs?" Sage asked, laughing.

Randy struck a serious pose. "I need a white-sage smudge stick." He turned to Sage. "Not you, darling. Just the product that bears your name."

Godiva hurried over to the basket of smudge sticks sitting on a nearby shelf. "We've got them! Two sizes. The larger one is nine inches. Will that work?"

Randy put the Buddha back on the shelf. "Miss Jones is getting very personal," he said playfully. "But if you must know, yes, perfect."

Holding out the basket, Godiva walked over to him. "Would you like to choose your own stick?"

"Of course!" Randy said. "Wouldn't you?"

They all laughed while Randy sorted through the basket and chose a smudge stick to his liking.

"Not to be nosy," Sage asked as Godiva put the basket back on the shelf. "But who or what are you trying to cleanse?"

"Well," Randy said, walking to the counter with the stick. "I told you that Kyle is starting his own business. He's got a beautiful four-room office suite for himself and his two employees, but that dreadful Naomi Hall-Benchley previously occupied said space for foundation work, and Kyle and I both agreed that a cleansing of her negative energy was not only a good idea, but an absolute necessity."

Godiva walked around the counter to ring up the smudge stick while Sage stood by Randy's side.

"If this one doesn't do the trick, I'll give you a second one on the house," Sage said. "That woman's energy is horrendous."

"Times one hundred," Randy said. "Your friend and my BFF, Molly Rose, could write a book on what that woman's done to her. Naomi is worse than ever now that … oh, I don't even want to squander clean air by invoking her foul essence, or you'll have to take a smudge stick to this place as well."

"I hope not," Sage said with a smile. "I really try to keep toxic energy out of my store." She thought for a moment. "I'm not always successful, mind you, but I try."

Randy handed his credit card to Godiva. "I wish I could stay and chat a bit longer, but I've got to get back to the *Herald*. I have a feature to write for the weekend edition. I'll be back another day to purchase some trinkets. I think Kyle will really like that stone Buddha."

Godiva smiled and handed Randy a shopping bag. "Here you go, kind sir."

Randy looked pensively at the bag. "Being one who cares about the environment, I don't think I need this for just one item. I can put this in my side pocket." He pulled the smudge stick out of his bag and looked at it, then cleared this throat. "Ahem. Randy thinks he will need a shopping bag after all." He winked. "But I'll be sure to repurpose."

He leaned over the counter to kiss Godiva on the cheek, then turned to kiss Sage as well. "Wonderful to see you both. Until next time, lovelies."

"Bye, Trubs."

"Take care, Randy."

Sage smiled. "I think Randy is the only man who never ceases to make me laugh. I needed that."

"Me too," Godiva said. "More than you know."

ဆ ဆ ဆ

"Ready for day two?" Sage said as she sat on an upholstered purple barstool and sipped her chamomile tea at the counter. "I couldn't be more pleased that you're here, Godiva. I have to keep reminding myself that yesterday was your first day. And here you are working before the store even opens."

"I've had my coffee and muffin." She winked and tilted her head toward the wall. "Besides, those necklaces are putting out an SOS, and I have to respond."

"You really know what you're doing. And, I should add, you have quite the fan club in Swansea. Which is utterly unsurprising, by the way."

Godiva sighed as she reached for some tangled necklaces hanging on wall hooks. "I suppose I do have a fan club of sorts. With one major exception."

"Sienna."

"Yeah. Her," Godiva said with a soft voice.

"Please tell me you're not letting her get under your skin. That's exactly what she wants."

Godiva settled herself onto a nearby meditation cushion on the floor and began inspecting the necklaces. "I'd be giving you the same advice, Sage." She sighed. "See, the part that I can't shake is not knowing why she acted that way. I keep telling myself that Freddie wouldn't lie about how and why our breakup happened, but then again, he lied about being married. So what do I know? Or more to the point, what *don't* I know?"

Sage squeezed a lemon wedge into her antique floral teacup. "What other advice would you give me if I were in your shoes?"

"I'd tell you not to wear heels when you're likely to do a lot of standing all day."

"And what would you say to me after I made a lame joke to avoid answering the question?" Sage asked with a crooked smile.

Godiva looked up. "You calling my joke lame?"

"I am. Come on. Spill. What advice would you give me?"

Laying one necklace aside on the cushion, Godiva began working on the others. "I'd tell you that if you're at peace with yourself and your actions, that nobody can take that from you, unless you let them. And that second-guessing what other people think will make you so crazy that your good sense will turn into nonsense if you're not careful."

"You're a wise woman," Sage said, looking down at Rufus. "Okay, boy, I hear you."

"How many people do you know that always take their own advice?" Godiva continued as she successfully separated two yin-yang necklaces.

"Hmm," Sage said as she stood. "Point taken. Hey, it's two minutes to ten. I'm going to open the doors and take the boy for a walk."

Godiva looked up from the cushion. "Uh, before you unlock the door and leave, could you do me one favor?"

Sage smiled and walked toward her. "Sure. I'll give you a hand. I've had trouble getting up from that thing too. And I'm only twenty-nine."

ഉ ഉ ഉ

The midmorning sun felt good on Sage's face as she and Rufus headed down Swansea's bustling Main Street. Wearing a white, long-sleeve lace-crocheted dress and a dusty-rose embroidered beanie cap, she felt carefree and almost happy.

Rufus, donning a faded-green vintage bandana and camouflage harness, acknowledged each tree with a back-leg salute, then eagerly wagged his tail at everyone he knew. For Sage, this morning ritual, where she and Rufus greeted the town, felt especially good, knowing that Sage Earth Gifts was in capable and far-less neurotic hands. And it looked to Sage as if she may just have found a new friend, someone much wiser and kinder than Carrie had ever been.

Just as they passed Williker's Cheese Shop, Sage ran smack into Adam, who was just coming out of the store.

A huge grin appeared on his face. "This is my lucky day," he said. "I just came in here to place an order for my open house." He beamed as he admired her outfit. "You look like the angel of summer in that dress, Sage. Like you could just drift up into the sky and float among the clouds."

"Thanks, Adam. You know. I feel kind of good today. How about you?"

"Same. I'm opening my hip new store soon, and better than that, I threw all caution to the Swansea wind and hopped on the scale this morning. I'm two pounds lighter and still a fighter. That's a total of sixteen pounds gone."

"That's such a great feeling," Sage said. "Good for you."

"Thanks." Unaware of what he was doing, he straightened his posture. "I've missed seeing you on your morning perambulations. Of course, working at Jameson, all I could really do is press my nose up against the glass and wish I could actually speak to you. Or wave."

Sage smiled. "You did a lot of waving. Pressing your nose up against the glass? Nah, don't remember that."

"Me either. That was just a metaphor for my frustration."

"I hear you." She looked down at Rufus, then at Adam. "We're headed over to the park so Rufus can do his business in private. Want to join us? I don't have a lot of time, but maybe we could just sit and chat for a few minutes."

Adam's eyes sparkled. "I would love that. I wanted to suggest something of the kind, but after yesterday, saying what I did to you, I felt like you might think I was some pushy guy who wasn't getting the message."

"No," Sage said. "I know who you are. I'm the one who's messed up. I'm feeling kind of happy today, but my heart is still shattered and my head isn't on straight. It may never be, quite honestly."

"Your head is on perfectly straight."

"That was a metaphor for my frustration," Sage said with a smile.

Adam grinned and made a sweeping hand gesture toward the park. "Shall we?"

ᘐ   ᘐ   ᘐ

Ten minutes later, Rufus had taken care of business, chased a squirrel up an oak tree, and was content (fifty percent-ish) to lie on the ground in front of Sage and Adam, who had nicely settled onto a park bench. As Rufus surveyed the wildlife and checked out the other dogs, Sage and Adam enjoyed the momentary solitude.

"This is nice," Sage said. "One of the many good things about having a dog is that you are forced to drag yourself away from the great indoors."

"I hear you. That's the problem with my invisible Toto. He doesn't need to be walked." He chuckled. "Seriously, I could have used a team of huskies during my years at Jameson. That's how I put on these extra pounds. I have only myself to blame, but being a prisoner to the persnickety, I allowed myself to indulge. I can't blame that on anyone else. Not even the Jamesons, much as I'm tempted."

"That's an admirable trait," Sage told him. "You know ... not blaming others when our lives go wrong. Even when they have had a royal hand in our misfortune." She paused. "That sounded a bit Shakespearean, I think. But not necessarily in a good way."

Adam smiled. "I think it was my 'prisoner to the persnickety' that led you down the odd language path."

"I would agree with you," she said, her eyes smiling. She thought for a moment. "You know what? We'd better stop joking about this before we start sounding like Swansea blue bloods."

He laughed. "You're right. We were teetering precariously close to the edge here."

Sage looked at him, smiling.

"I just said 'teetering precariously,' didn't I?" Adam said.

"You definitely did," Sage said. "Not to mention 'perambulations' before that. We'd both better be careful." She smiled. "Anyway, as I was saying before we got swept away by evil language forces, it's admirable not to blame others. I don't want to contradict myself so quickly. Maybe in a few minutes, though."

They laughed as Rufus stood and growled at a Welsh Terrier looking his way.

"That's Spunky," Sage explained. "He and Rufus got into a scrap over the affections of a King Cav at the dog park last year. And, as you can see, they both have long memories."

Rufus growled again and sat as the terrier's owner led him in the opposite direction. "Grrrrrr."

Sage winked. "He has to have the last word. What can I tell you?"

"It's human nature," Adam said. "Wait, that made no sense.

I guess it's canine nature too." He laughed.

As Rufus finally settled, Sage patted him on the head. "Good boy, Ruf." She turned to Adam. "I think it's really wonderful that you got yourself to the health club after putting on weight. I'm always trying to lose a few pounds myself, but I work on that by walking a lot."

"A good reason to be your own boss," Adam said. "Hard work, but worth it."

"Exactly," Sage said. "Speaking of losing weight, I wanted to ask you something. I hope you won't mind."

"Go for it."

"Godiva told me that you were the one who coined the name 'Curly McBurly.' I knew people called you that, but I had no clue it was your brainchild."

Adam bit his bottom lip and thought for a moment. "I needed to be the one to make the jokes. So, I created a nickname for myself before anyone else could. You know, it's a funny thing about health clubs. They're places that a lot of people go to get fit. But I swear, Sage, when I went to work out that first day, every guy in there looked like a male model. I felt as if I was the lone person trying to actually get fit instead of just staying fit. That didn't end up being the case, but it was my initial perception. I didn't want anyone calling me 'the fat guy' behind my back or mocking my hair loss. So I decided to own all of it, and started introducing myself as 'Curly McBurly.'"

"And how did people respond?"

"With laughter and smiles. It was one of the best things I've ever done. The only downer was that a lot of people, like you, didn't know it was my idea, and they felt guilty hearing others call me that." He smirked. "And some, of course, didn't."

"Sometimes people can suck," Sage said.

"They can," Adam said, gently touching her hand. "But the

wonderful people like you make up for a million of them."

"Thank you," Sage said. "I wish we could sit here longer, but I've got to get back to my store and hey … you're opening one."

"Indeed I am. May I walk you back to your place? It's on my way."

"I'd love that."

Rufus, who was already on all fours, started tugging in the direction of a female Maltese who had caught his eye.

Adam looked at Rufus. "Can't blame you, boy. You know what you like."

ॐ   ॐ   ॐ

"Welcome to Sage Earth Gifts. Let me know if I can help you with anything. My name is Godiva."

The dimple-cheeked man with the wavy brown hair flashed a smile as if he and his expensive suit had just caught the notice of the paparazzi. "Godiva. What a pretty name. I don't think I've seen you here before."

She took a few steps over to the counter where she had been unpacking and sorting incense sticks. "I just started. The last employee quit rather unexpectedly the day before yesterday. I happened to be shopping here at the time, I needed a job, and Sage hired me pretty much on the spot."

"Her assistant quit unexpectedly? In a snit?"

"You sound like you know Margie," Godiva said, noticing his very blue eyes.

"We've met, but no, not really. I know Sage, though," he said casually, "and I'm well aware that Margie is on the neurotic side. Sage must be happy to have someone like you." He smiled. "You look very Zen. You know, like you belong here."

"Thanks," Godiva said, sensing he was uneasy. "I'd say Zen

is my middle name, but it's Genevieve." She winked. "Is there anything I can help you with, or are you just browsing?"

He continued to speak. "I'm sure you don't get many men, or women, dressed in business attire, who are just casually browsing in the middle of a workday."

"Like I said," Godiva told him, laying out three shades of purple incense sticks on the counter, "I just started here. But I've worked in Swansea businesses for years, so yes, I'd agree with you there."

"Actually, I don't work in this town," he said. "I have a meeting here later, so I just thought I'd come by and say hi to Sage."

"She's out walking Rufus."

"I can wait. It feels good being here. It's so Zen and all. I'm good."

As he walked away to browse the bookshelf, a stocky man in jeans and a Boston Celtics T-shirt, with a large mixed-breed dog on a leash, walked briskly into the store. Before Godiva could greet him, he introduced himself. "Hi, I'm Bill Kenner. This here is Gordo. I named him for Sage." He vigorously rubbed the dog's neck. "She fostered this boy when his first family abandoned him after only a year. I live outside Lowell, Mass. Two years ago, I was in Swansea on some business and decided to check out the shelter. I'd been in the market for a big dog — you know, one that was hard to place. I have a farm and can give it a proper home and all. The fine people at the shelter told me that Sage Gordon was fostering what might be the perfect dog for me. Sure enough, she was. If that lovely lady hadn't been so kind, well, I don't want to think about it. Gordo's the best dog I ever had. What I do want is to show her how well he's doing and express my thanks again. I'm just passing through, so if she's not about at the moment, I'd like to wait. If she won't be too long."

Get in line. Godiva smiled. "She's expected back shortly."

"Outstanding! Mind if I sit in one of those wicker chairs in the corner? Don't want to be in the way. Especially with Gordo. He's seventy pounds."

"That's fine," Godiva said, noticing the Zen-conscious guy in a suit was carefully listening from a distance.

She walked over to the counter, grabbed the incense sticks, then proceeded to put them in their proper cubbyholes, right under the roll-on perfume oil display. When the shop bells clanged loudly, she nearly dropped them on the floor. *Darn, I thought I was used to those things by now.*

Composing herself, Godiva arranged the sticks in their place, then turned to find Margie glowering at her.

"What are you doing working here?" Margie asked. "You're a customer. I only quit two days ago."

"And I took your place," Godiva said. "Simple."

Margie's nostrils flared as she scrutinized her. "I've been working here almost three years. That crazy woman with the dripping cone pushed me over the edge. Especially after that flippin' ball of ice cream splattered all over my expensive slacks. I was also dealing with PMS and my lunatic mother, not that you need to know any of this, but it was the perfect storm of craziness, and I just snapped. Stuff happens. I'm human. And my husband is furious with me for quitting, which doesn't help anything."

"I'm sorry. I don't know what to say."

"You knew what to say when you helped yourself to my job, didn't you?"

Godiva noticed the two men watching the exchange as if it were a Wimbledon match, but Margie seemed utterly unaware of their presence while she proceeded to take the art of scowling to new heights.

"Well, aren't you going to answer me?" Margie said.

Godiva shifted uneasily as she stood, six human eyes and

two dog eyes watching her. "I availed myself of a job opening. Sage needed an assistant and I was not only here, but I'm extremely qualified."

"Well, sorry for the inconvenience, but I need my job. My husband's not just angry, he's not even speaking to me." She softened. "Can you *please* show some decency and quit so I can have just a modicum of sanity in my life? I believe you're qualified, but I worked here a long time, and that makes me way more qualified."

Godiva walked behind the counter to throw away the incense-stick packaging. "I'm not going to quit my job. I already love it here. If Sage wants to let me go when she returns from walking Rufus, then that's her decision. Okay?"

"No, it's really *not* okay."

"And it's really *not* your decision," Godiva countered as she turned to see a well-dressed woman in a pink floral dress enter the store. "Welcome to Sage Earth Gifts. I'm Godiva. Please let me know if I can help you with anything."

"I hope you can help me. I just came from a company meeting that went off the rails. I need some calm and thought this would be the place. Do you have CDs of crashing waves or falling rain? I need something to soothe my nerves."

Margie walked over to the woman. "Our tropical rainforest CD is a big seller. In addition to the sounds you mentioned, we have the soothing sound of loons with soft music in the back."

You'd be the expert on loons. Godiva glared at Margie, who wasn't the least bit rattled.

Just as Godiva repositioned herself to talk to the customer, Margie gave her a not-so-subtle nudge, pushing Godiva out of her way. "May I also suggest aromatherapy? It can do wonders—"

"Woof. Woof." Gordo, who had been quiet, was now full of excitement.

The customer, who hadn't even realized the dog was in the

store, jumped as Gordo's bark startled her, then jumped again as the front door bells clanged, and Rufus, happy to see his old friend, barked in response.

Sage and Adam just stood there, almost bewildered by the activity. Sage let go of the leash as Bill let go of Gordo's leash, and the two dogs happily reunited in the middle of the store. The customer, now aware of everyone in the store, dropped her jaw in disbelief while commotion swirled around her.

Stunned, Sage was focused only on Margie and Godiva. She then looked directly at Margie. "Did I just see you waiting on this customer?"

"I was trying to help because I need—"

"You don't work here anymore, Margie. You made that perfectly clear when you quit on me the other day."

"I made a mistake, Sage. A huge one. I'm so sorry. Please, it's urgent. I need to talk to you. I need my job back."

The man in the suit, who had been halfway hiding on the side of the bookshelf, stepped out from the shadow. "I made a bigger mistake, Sage. I need to talk to you more. I need *you* back!"

"Caleb!" Sage gasped. "You shouldn't be here."

Godiva looked at Caleb. *She said he had exquisite turquoise eyes. I should have known! And damn, what a looker.*

"I don't think this is the store for me after all," the customer said. "At least not now." She looked at Sage. "Maybe another day when I can figure out who actually works here … and you can too. When dogs aren't boogying, when your love life is settled, and when the full moon is but a crescent in the sky." She shook her head. "This place almost makes my office seem normal."

"We can restore peace to your life," Margie said desperately. "Perhaps you'd like to play one of our crystal bowls or chakra drums!"

The woman rolled her eyes, then rushed out of the store. As

Sage turned to speak to her, she noticed Adam was long gone.

CHAPTER FOUR

As she felt the joy leave her spirit, Sage made a mental note to speak to Adam later. But she wasn't quite sure how she'd do that without giving him mixed signals. First things first.

The tension in the room was palpable. Bill took both dogs by the leash and pulled them to the corner of the store while Caleb retreated to the bookshelf. Godiva, choosing to remain silent, stood next to Margie as Sage addressed her.

"Margie, you quit your job. Not with two weeks' notice, not even two days' notice." She spoke with an uncharacteristic firmness. "You gave me two minutes' notice and told me to clean up the slop on the floor myself. Am I missing anything?"

"Oh, Sage!" Margie said as she flipped the ends of her hair. "With all due respect, you're missing *so* much. You know me, and you know how to read between my crazy lines. That wasn't personal. I know I screwed up, but please, don't punish me by leaving me jobless. Rick isn't even speaking to me. It's miserable in my home."

"I'm sure you two will work it out. And you'll find another job. But just for the record, I didn't hire Godiva, nor am I keeping her, to punish you."

"C'mon," Margie pleaded. "It *is* a punishment! I've been

here for three years, and I know everything inside and out." She nodded in Godiva's direction without looking at her. "*She* doesn't."

"*Godiva*," Sage said, looking at her new employee with a smile, "is probably the best person I could ever find for this job. It fits her like a glove. Things worked out as they were meant to be. I wish you well, but I have no intention of giving you your job back."

"Then how about giving me some part-time hours for when you're super busy? Or if you need to take time off."

"You know I have people for that. But what I really don't think you're getting is that I don't want you working here anymore. Period. Besides, when you find a new job, you likely won't even be available. So take solace in that."

"I've already been looking and there's nothing!" Margie looked at Godiva. "You had some nerve being here when that mess happened the other day."

Godiva furrowed her eyebrows as she laser focused on Margie. "You're kidding, right?" She looked at Sage. "Is she kidding?" She turned to address Margie again. "You're sounding as nutty as Sandra right now."

"Who?"

"The woman with the melting ice-cream cone."

"Oh, are you two friends now?" She grunted. "Well, I'm nothing like her. And don't you be so high and mighty," Margie said to Godiva. "You get my drift."

I wish you'd drift on out of here. Godiva challenged her with a stare.

Sage gently took Margie by the elbow and led her to the door. "You need to go. This kind of nonsense makes my store everything I don't want it to be. I was kind enough to mail you a check for all of the days you worked since last payday. Including the hours before you left me in the lurch. It should be in your mailbox today."

"I appreciate that, but you're making a huge mistake, Sage," Margie said as Sage escorted her to the door.

"No, I'm definitely not," Sage said, opening the door. "And if you're going to cause this kind of commotion again, please don't come back. I hate that you've made me sound so harsh, but it seems like it's the only way you'll get the message. Good-bye now."

Margie shot a look at Godiva, then at Sage, before donning a mask of dejection as she walked away.

Sage turned around. "Bill," she said. "Hello! And Gordo, how's that good boy!" Gordo came rushing over to her, as did Rufus, nuzzling Sage to remind both her and Gordo who was top dog. "I'm so happy to see you both. And I'm so sorry that your visit had to coincide with such craziness."

"No worries," Bill said, his jovial nature filling the store. "I enjoyed the show." He laughed. "Just kidding."

"Kidding not kidding," Godiva added.

"Well, it was more excitement than I see on a typical day at the farm," Bill said.

As Sage kneeled to give Gordo a hug, Rufus stuck his head between them. "Oh my, someone is jealous."

Bill laughed. "They love ya, Sage. Guess you're a woman worth fighting for."

Godiva peeked at Caleb as he became visibly more uncomfortable.

"Anyway," Bill went on, "I just wanted you to see what a happy dog you fostered. My family and I are thankful for your big heart every day. I don't usually bring Gordo along on business trips, but when I knew I'd be coming to Swansea today, I had to bring him with me."

"That's so kind of you," Sage said, petting Gordo as he nuzzled her. "And please thank your wife for the photos she's emailed me. I love getting them. But I must say, it's very special to see Gordo in person … or should I say 'in dog.'" She laughed. "It really warms my heart. Thank you for this." Sage stood. "How is everyone in the family doing?"

Bill looked at Caleb, who was anything but Zen-like as he waited anxiously. "How about we catch up the next time I come through town? I think someone is keen to have your full attention right now."

Sage smiled uncomfortably. "Okay, then, Bill. That's a deal." She petted Gordo on the head, then kissed him good-bye. "I'm so glad you found your forever home, boy. And thank you so much for stopping by with your dad today. You have a very special place in our hearts forever."

As soon as Bill and Gordo left, Rufus walked over to greet Caleb, who uneasily petted him. Not feeling the love, Rufus made his way behind the counter, past the curtains, and into the back room.

"And then there were three," Godiva said, trying to break the tension. "I can … um …."

"You stay where you are," Caleb told her. "Sage and I will go upstairs and talk."

Sage answered him with a hard stare before she spoke. "Sage and Caleb will not go upstairs. No way."

Caleb dusted something off his lapel and walked over to her, a pleading look in his eyes. "Please, honey, I really need to talk to you."

Pressing the palms of her hands against her forehead, Sage took a moment to think. "Okay, Caleb. We'll talk." She took in a deep breath. "In Coffee & Teaz."

He started to protest but knew better than to push his luck. "Okay, babe. Coffee & Teaz it is."

Sage looked at Godiva. They exchanged knowing glances as if they'd been friends forever. "I'll be gone for a bit. You've got this."

I was just going to say the same thing to you. Godiva watched Caleb put his arm around Sage, who flinched in discomfiture as the two walked out of the store.

ஒ   ஒ   ஒ

"Thank our lucky stars for a corner table," Caleb said as he placed two hot drinks down in front of Sage. "Glad you grabbed this spot before someone else did."

"Thank you for the chai latte," Sage said, her face devoid of expression. "Why are you even here?"

"You heard what I said in the store, my Bohemian baby. I want you back."

"Ugh. Don't call me that ever again. And why do I care what you want?"

Caleb put his hand on top of hers, and she pulled it away. "I call you that because it's what attracted me to you in the first place. I may work in Manhattan, and I may play the game, but you know those New York women don't nourish my soul."

"Not my problem," Sage said stoically. "And New York is filled with wonderful women."

"The first time I saw your photo," he pressed on, "Carrie had given me her phone to show me pictures of the town where she grew up. When I saw a photo of you in your store, and found out you two were best friends, I just had to meet you. I could feel your energy and kindness through the photo. It zapped me." Caleb put his hand over his heart. "Right here."

Sage snickered. "I kind of got zapped in the same exact place. But for a very different reason."

"I walked into that one, didn't I?" He took a small sip of his coffee when he realized Sage had no intention of responding. "Drink your chai latte before it gets cold."

"Hot stuff cools down, Caleb. You don't need to explain that to me. The bright side of that is that it doesn't burn as much once it does."

"Please give me a chance." He looked around the room as if the air or the smell of coffee might inspire him. "Carrie never told you this, but I had to work on this horrible research committee with her before she would even try to set us up. And I agreed to stay for six interminable months if she did. I hated that committee; it was futile and tedious. But that's how much I wanted to meet you."

Sage looked at him curiously. "You mean it wasn't her idea to get us together?"

"No way! Not even close. But after you and I finally met, and it was obvious that we clicked, she wanted to take credit. Because she knew she could use it to manipulate both of us when the need arose."

"Wow," Sage said.

"I'll give you some more wow," he said, feeling empowered. "Despite the fact that she was seeing Kevin, she never wanted us together because she wanted me. He was her second choice. I guess he finally figured that out and dumped her."

"Well," Sage said, her voice tinged with sarcasm. "Her persistence paid off. You're together."

"No, no, no, no, no! It did not. Not only are we not together, we don't even speak anymore. And you may or may not know this, but Carrie transferred to the Miami office."

Sage raised her eyebrows. "I didn't know. And now I do. And I don't care."

Caleb took a few more sips of his coffee. "I just want to explain what happened. And I've waited four months to do so because I knew that if I tried to contact you any sooner, you wouldn't even have given me the time of day."

Sage pulled out her phone. "It's eleven thirty-six a.m." She smiled insincerely. "You can leave now."

His deep blue eyes looked mournfully into her brown ones. "You need to know what happened. Even if you never want to see me again, don't you want the truth?"

She took a sip of her chai and thought for a moment. "I guess. Some closure wouldn't be a bad thing. So say whatever you need to before I come to my senses."

Caleb relaxed his shoulders and sighed with relief. "After Kevin left her, she pretended to fall to pieces. She's a good actress too. I was actually convinced that she'd gotten over me and was truly devastated by the breakup." He paused. "I mean, she wasn't okay with it, but she wasn't decimated."

"You mean like I was."

Caleb cursed under his breath. "Yeah, I guess that's right, honey. Can I finish?"

"Might as well," Sage said as she slowly tore a napkin to shreds. "Don't take your sweet time though. I have a store to run. And shouldn't you be in Manhattan dazzling some clients with your charm and BS?"

"I told them at work that I had a couple of doctors' appointments and I'd be a while." He sighed uncomfortably. "Anyway, let me get on with this. See, Carrie had some big family wedding coming up, and she was mortified to go alone."

"Yeah, her cousin Henry's."

"Well, she kind of guilt-tripped me into being her date. You know, like couldn't I just do her this one favor since she'd set us up and we were so happily engaged? Couldn't I just save her from humiliation in front of her family as a thank you?" He looked away for a moment, then back at Sage. "I hated the idea of not telling you, but she told me it was better that you didn't know. And I stupidly agreed."

Sage, taking further frustration out on the napkin, had now

ripped it into little pieces.

"Gee, honey," Caleb said looking at the table, "when did it start snowing?"

"Just finish this story, Caleb. You've got five minutes. If you want to use them for dramatic sighs and pauses or cutesy one-liners, whatever; be my guest." She picked up her phone. "But I'm out of here at eleven forty-five."

"Okay, okay! I'll be quick. We got to the wedding, which was at this five-star hotel in White Plains. As soon as we got our drinks and started mingling, I knew I'd been duped. She was super clingy, touchy-feely, and acting like we were a couple. So, like an idiot, I decided to drink myself into a mellow state where I wouldn't be so upset." He pushed his coffee cup away. "I played right into her plans. The next thing I knew, I woke up in a hotel room, naked in a bed with her, and she was taking selfies of us."

"What the—"

"My words exactly," Caleb said. "And several much stronger ones."

"How did you even get that drunk? You're a couple-of-drinks-and-you're-fine kind of guy."

Caleb pushed back from the table with both hands. "This is so embarrassing."

"Tick tock."

"Okay. You're right. I'm not a heavy drinker. And I knew that there's no way I drank myself into naked oblivion. And I felt really weird. Like I'd been drugged. Hello? That's because I was."

Sage's eyes opened wide. "She roofied you?"

"She did," Caleb said, looking down at the table in shame.

"That's absolutely disgusting," Sage said, showing real anger for the first time since the conversation began. "So I'm confused here. As bad as all of that was, why didn't you just tell me the truth instead of breaking up with me?"

Caleb picked up a napkin. "This seems to have helped you," he said as he started ripping it.

Sage grabbed the napkin from him and started ripping it herself. "Don't you try to steal my coping methods, buddy. And your time is up, but luckily for you, I'm granting you a brief extension. But only if you make it quick."

"This is the hardest conversation I've ever had in my life." He paused to reconsider. "No, it's not. The one where I told you I was leaving you for Carrie was."

"Why did you even do that? You must have hated her at that point!"

"I did, but for months prior to the wedding, she kept telling me that you were still searching the Internet for your soul mate. Some guy named Jimmy who you had been madly in love with in high school until he left for college."

"High school?" Sage asked. "Really? Try grade school. I haven't seen him since I was eleven. His family disappeared in the middle of the night, and it's always haunted me. Call my parents and ask them if you don't believe me. And yes, as a kid, I thought I'd marry him someday. I was going to be the queen to his king. Again, when we were both in grade school. But I was happy with you, and after we met, I'd pretty much stopped looking for him, and I left those fantasies behind for far more realistic ones with you: my grown-up, real-life fiancé. And yeah, once in a while, I *would* do a quick Internet search, because Jimmy *had* been special to me, and a part of me will always want to know what happened to him and his family."

"Oh, honey. I wish I'd known the truth."

"Then why didn't you ask me?"

"Because I was afraid you'd tell me something I couldn't stand to hear. Carrie told me that he stole that Private Property sign for you because it came from some field where the two of you used to go to have sex."

"Are you serious?" Sage bit her lip. "Again, we were in elementary school. That's repulsively untrue and she knows it."

Shame washed over Caleb's face. "I can see that now. But here's the thing. One weekend, when I was in the store, a customer tried to buy that sign, and you were so quick to say no. And so adamant about it." He grabbed both of her hands. "You've got to understand. Carrie had been feeding me lies for months, and when that happened, it just sort of played right into what she'd been saying."

Sage pulled her hands away. "Again, you never thought to ask *me* about *me*? On what planet is Carrie a better source of information about *my* life, *my* feelings, or *my* intentions than I am? Sheesh, Caleb. I thought we had such incredible communication. Clearly not."

"I've had over four months to think about this," Caleb said. "Four lonely, miserable months."

Sage couldn't help but notice that he was squeezing his eyes, hoping for some tears to complement the pain he was trying to demonstrate.

"I feel like such an idiot," he said.

"I still don't understand," Sage said, too angry to match his crying attempt with one of her own. "Was that nonsense about Jimmy all it took for you to break up with me?"

"The naked pictures," he said as his voice weakened. "Before I woke up, she emailed them to herself … to three different accounts. Just to make sure that if I had been somehow able to delete them from her phone, she'd still have them. She told me that if I didn't break up with you, she'd send them to you and to your parents." He cursed again under his breath. "Then, she said she was actually doing me a favor."

"Really? And what convoluted logic did you swallow to

believe that?"

Caleb blanched. "I feel like such a fool, in hindsight."

"Waiting," Sage said, tapping her fingers on the table.

"She said that it would only be a matter of days until you broke up with me because you'd finally found your ex-boyfriend. Oh, yeah, and that she heard you on the phone telling him that you were just looking for the best way to let me down easy, and then you'd be all his. And that he should 'hang in there because it won't be long.'"

"That's a bold-faced disgusting lie," Sage said. "But how do I even know Carrie said that and you're not making it up to defend yourself?"

"Honey, she was your supposed best friend. Did you ever hear from her after this happened? Did she ever try to explain any of it to you?"

"No," Sage said, looking out the window at the passersby. "Never. But really, when you steal your best friend's fiancé, there's not much else to say. Don't you think?"

"Look at me," Caleb said. "She was so jealous of you, baby. You have an amazing sense of self that she covets. You opened your business and made a name for yourself in this town. You don't need designer clothes or big-city friends to feel like you matter. You look like a million bucks dressed in your own style. You have a true heart of gold, and people gravitate to you. It's not an act that you put on; it's just real. It's you. And when someone does you wrong, you stand up for yourself. Like you did today with Margie." He gulped. "And now … with me."

"I still don't get any of this. If I had an ex-boyfriend waiting in the wings, you would have known, Caleb. We were so close. So in love. How could you have let her fool you like that?"

He looked at her uneasily. "Don't take this the wrong way, baby. But again, she fooled you too … for years. Didn't she? You thought she was your very best friend. You thought you could trust her with your secrets."

Sage put her head back and covered her face. "I don't know. I don't know anything anymore. I'm so confused."

"Please look at me."

She took her hands away. "I just don't get why you left me so easily. Or why, after you broke my heart, if you had a sense she had been lying about Jimmy, that you didn't try talking to me sooner. And yeah, maybe I wouldn't have given you the time of day, but you didn't even fight for me, Caleb."

"I thought the damage I'd done to our relationship was far too great to ever be repaired."

"And now you don't? Because—"

"Because now I've had time to think. We've both had time to feel the pain of being apart. And well, you know what they say about time."

"What? That it heals all wounds? Because it doesn't." Sage stood. "And now I'm going back to my store. I've seen more drama in one morning than Broadway sees in an entire season."

"I'm glad you have such a Zen space to retreat to," Caleb said as he stood to look into her eyes one last time. "I've tried to create one in my apartment, but without you, it's just a bunch of stuff."

"Sucks to be you," Sage said, refusing to tear up.

"Can you at least think about everything I've said?" Caleb asked her. "Because whether you like it or not, I am fighting for you. I always was; you just didn't know it. But now you will. I love you with every breath in my body, Bohemian Baby, and I'm never giving up on us."

Sage stopped to study the pain in his eyes that matched her own. "Take care of yourself, Caleb. And stop calling me that!"

He could only watch her as she hurried out the door.

CHAPTER FIVE

"You feeling any better?" Godiva asked, watching Sage come through the tapestry curtains. "I'm happy to report we had a busy afternoon. Right now is pretty much the first quiet moment we've had."

"That's great," Sage said as she stood behind the counter and looked around the store. "But not so great I left you here alone. I hope you weren't overwhelmed."

"Not at all. People were browsing and buying at different times, so I never had any kind of rush at the register. Just need to straighten up a few displays. That's all."

"Thank you. And I'm really sorry. Retreating to my home after coming back from Coffee & Teaz was so unprofessional of me. Ninety percent of the time, I can just put my personal stuff to the side. But Caleb's visit was completely unexpected … as were the charming revelations he shared. I just felt sucker punched, and I wasn't able to put my response on hold, which is exactly what my supposedly enlightened self should have been able to do. I feel ashamed of that."

"Oh, honey, don't be," Godiva said as she put some stray bottles of essential oils back in their place. "I suggested … um … rather strongly … that you should go upstairs, remember? You needed to deal with your feelings … past and present tense. Believe me, I understand. And I'm happy that I had so many customers all at once."

"I'm so grateful for you. I can't say that enough."

Godiva smiled. "Were you asleep the whole time?"

"Right after closing the windows and shouting several words from my extended vocabulary, I laid in bed and cried for an hour," Sage said. "At this point, I'm more angry than sad, but crying is still the best way I know to dilute pain … and anger. So I just let the tears fall and wash away as much of the bad stuff as possible. My sweet boy stayed by my side and tried to cheer me up with kisses. That's the last thing I remember before I fell asleep. I woke up to find both cats sleeping on top of me. My poor boy, obviously displaced, had gone through the doggie door and come down here. I saw that he's asleep in the office now. He almost always wakes up when I come down the stairs, but he's probably worn out from trying to console his angst-ridden mommy. Poor guy."

"He's fine," Godiva said, walking over to the counter. "Did you cry again once you woke up?"

"No way," Sage said, opening the counter display case to straighten some necklace-and-earring sets. "I'm all cried out, believe me … especially over Caleb. I made some tea and had a late lunch. Then, I cuddled with Finlay and Babaloo a bit more before making this inglorious return to the land of the living. And here I am. And yes, I really did say 'inglorious return.'"

Godiva chuckled, then offered a tentative smile. "I love your humor and self-awareness. But don't dis yourself, Sage. You needed to do all of that. I'm really glad you listened to me and went upstairs."

"I am too. When I first came back to the store, I thought I could avoid wimping out like that. But when customers started coming in, I realized I wasn't in a frame of mind to deal with the public. You were right. I needed to be gone for a while." She looked at the label on a recently delivered package sitting on the counter.

"Oh, the UPS guy dropped that off a few minutes ago. I was going to get to it in a hot sec," Godiva said, looking at the crystals in the Lucite display bins. "Just wanted to see what we needed here. Didn't realize we were so low on the garnet and healer's gold. Oh, and earlier today, after I explained to one customer that the rose quartz is the stone for the enhancement of love in all forms, she bought fifty of them. Said she's giving them out to her friends and family."

"Wow," Sage said. "Hope she knows the stones don't come with guarantees."

"She actually saw our disclaimer on the wall. She said it was all in good fun," Godiva said. "But still, I think she's hoping." She pulled a list from her pocket. "Anyway, I've taken inventory; it's all here."

"You're amazing. I'll put some orders in tomorrow," Sage said, picking up the package. "And I'll handle this. It's from a new vendor, and I'm curious to see the craftsmanship of their jewelry. I hear it's extraordinary." She looked at Rufus, who had just come from the back room. He walked over to Sage, stood on his hind legs to give her a kiss, then walked over to have a lie down on his mat by the meditation cushion. "Did you see that? Is he the best or what?" Sage looked at the small clock behind the counter. "Oh my! I lost all track of time. My sweet boy hasn't had a walk in forever."

"Actually, all's good," Godiva said, holding a handful of onyx stones. "He has. Randy came by earlier. When I told him what happened, and that you were upstairs, he offered to walk Rufus. He had him out for a good fifteen minutes."

"Aw," Sage said. "Trubs is the best." She looked curiously at Godiva. "What's with the onyx?"

"Oh, these," Godiva said looking in the palm of her hand.

"Found them mixed in with the obsidian and a few with the hematite." She gave a lopsided smile. "As you know, some folks get the black stones confused with one another. It's all good."

Sage smiled. "Take a break and sit with me. I appreciate how hard you work, but it's okay to chill for a bit, especially after such a busy afternoon by your lonesome."

Godiva put the stones back in their rightful bins, then walked behind the counter. She sat next to Sage and looked at her. "You know Caleb will be back, right? He made it pretty clear that he's prepared to fight for you. Do you want him to?"

"I don't think so," Sage said, twirling the ends of her hair around her index finger. "Right now, I'd say definitely not. He hurt me too much. I'm doubting if what we had was ever real in the first place."

"That's natural, honey. Believe me, I know."

"I didn't tell you this," Sage said, letting her hair go and looking directly at Godiva. "But before Caleb and I got together, he had been seeing this woman named Amanda who works in a high-level job at a pharmaceutical company where her father is the CEO. They'd been together for two years, and Caleb was about to propose. The day before he was going to pop the question, she dropped him … via text!"

"Whoa. That's cold-blooded."

"Yeah," Sage said. "Totally. And the timing was really suspicious. He thinks that someone told her he'd been looking at rings … but *not* the kind of rings that were remotely acceptable to her, and that's when she concluded that Caleb would never be able to keep her in the manner to which she'd always been accustomed."

"But Caleb looks like he does all right," Godiva said.

"Oh, he does very well. That just shows you what a spoiled brat she is."

Godiva rolled her eyes. "How long did it take him to get over her?"

"Who knows," Sage said as she stood, reached for a pair of scissors, then ran them between the two envelope flaps. She paused to think. "Maybe he never did."

"Well, from what I saw," Godiva said, now standing by her side, "he's crazy about you."

"Take a look at these. Tell me what you think," "Sage said, pulling some merchandise out of the box. "And regarding Caleb, I've said everything I needed to say to him."

As Godiva began inspecting the new shipment, Sage gazed mindlessly out the store window.

"I know how you feel," Godiva said, picking up a small Ziploc bag to examine a pair of amber and citrine silver earrings. 'Cause I've got squat to say to Freddie."

"Well," Sage said. "Maybe you ought to think of something pretty quickly, because there's a tall, handsome, and very muscular black man standing outside the window … wearing a tight gray V-neck shirt and black jeans. He's looking past the fountain and … wait for it … directly at you. And I'd bet the store that it's him."

Godiva turned to look out the window. She gasped. "Holy #@$%!"

"Yeah, I figured that was a safe bet."

"What the blazes is he doing?"

"I'd say he's smiling at you."

"Is this 'National-Ex-Come-Back Day' or what? I didn't expect this at all. I have no idea what to do. For one, I'm at work, and for two, I'm not going anywhere with that man."

"Coffee & Teaz maybe?"

"I'm not going *anywhere* now. I'm working."

"Now is a fine time to go somewhere," Sage told her. "Hey, you 'suggested' I go upstairs earlier, so now I'm 'suggesting' you leave. It's only fair. While I was crying and sleeping, you had a busy store, *and* you never got out for lunch. So take it now."

"I brought my salad to work with me. I'm good."

"It's after five. Take your lunch now and come back in the morning."

"But—"

"But your boss is insisting that you go. We'll compare notes tomorrow, and maybe we'll both feel better after a good night's sleep. And if we don't, we can commiserate between customers." Sage grinned. "Get ready, woman. Here he comes."

৯৯ ৯৯ ৯৯

"Tell me I did not see Miss Godiva Jones and Mister Freddie Lamar headed toward the kiosk in the park together," Randy said as he walked through the door. "Only hours after Mister Dunlap came back for you." He looked down at Rufus, who was ecstatic to see him again. "Hello, Mister Rufus. I understand the inability to contain your excitement. Seeing Randy so much breathes new life into the expression 'lucky dog.'" He looked at Sage. "Tell Randy."

"I think Randy has the general idea," Sage said, coming around from behind the counter to get her customary kiss on each cheek. "Yes, Freddie came here about six minutes ago, desperate to speak to Godiva. Oh, and thank you so much for walking my boy earlier. I really should have been here. This is my store and—"

"You did what you needed to do, Miss Sage. And the store was left in capable hands." He smiled. "As for Rufus, it was my pleasure. I was just out for some fresh air." Randy glanced at the crystal display while petting Rufus. "I'm certainly curious as to why so much romantic activity is swirling around this establishment. Perhaps overnight, when you were fast asleep, the rose quartz and the hematite magnets gave birth to a powerful new crystal called 'Lover come back.'" He laughed. "Maybe they had twins!"

"Ha! That might explain it," Sage said. "Come here, Rufus. Go back over to your mat and lie down while Mommy talks to Uncle Randy." She nodded toward the spot. "Go on, boy."

Rufus looked up at Randy, as if he hoped for a different command.

"Obey your mom," Randy said. "She knows best." He winked. "At least when it comes to you."

"What are you saying, Trubs," Sage said, poking him gently in the upper arm. "I'm very sure Godiva didn't tell you that I took Caleb back. Or anything of the sort."

Randy looked at her in mock horror. "She most certainly did not. In fact, she told me almost nothing. Miss Jones said that it was up to you to disseminate such highly personal and perhaps even shocking information." He placed a hand on Sage's shoulder. "Though she did hint that you might want to speak to me about today's traumatic events."

"Traumatic? I don't think I'd go quite that far," Sage said. "And somehow I don't think she phrased any of it as you just did, but yes, I'm very happy to see you, my friend."

Randy smiled as Sage greeted a lone customer who walked in and headed straight to the bookshelves. He lowered his voice. "I'm sorry I couldn't come in later ... after you close the store. I had an early morning at the paper and just now finished my work. I'm meeting Kyle in forty-five minutes, so I've carved out this time for you, if you want it. I know it's awkward with customers milling about."

"They do mill, don't they?" Sage said with a smile. "Well, there's only one person in here now, and we can talk quietly behind the counter."

"Will you be able to tell Randy the events of this morning while maintaining professional decorum at all times?"

"I did a lot of crying and cursing earlier in the day. I've

reached my quota for the day, so I'm good."

"Excellent," he said, following Sage around the counter. "And if we have any time remaining on the clock after dissecting Mister Dunlap's visit, perhaps we can speculate on Miss Jones and Mister Lamar."

ഗ   ഗ   ഗ

The kiosk in the park was a popular place for Swansea's end-of-the-workday crowd. After locating a table not far from the trees, Godiva and Freddie sat across from one another, each with a glass of wine in front of them.

Freddie smiled as he looked at her. "You are insanely beautiful, and I love you more than life itself."

Godiva just stared at him. *I will not cry. I will not cry.*

"You haven't said a word since we left the store," he said, his deep voice giving her goose bumps.

"Everything I needed to say, I said the day we broke up."

"The day *you* broke up with *me*," Freddie corrected her.

"I didn't expect to see you again. Ever."

Freddie reached across the table and took a firm hold of her hand. "Now you know there's not a lick of truth in that, baby. You knew I'd be back." He bit his lip. "I just intended on waiting until my divorce was final. As you well know, circumstances changed all that."

"Your amiable sister," Godiva said flatly. "The lovely Sienna."

He took a slow seductive sip of his Cabernet, then let go of her hand. "Her husband of fifteen years left her. She's on the bitter side, and she took that out on you. You'll be happy to know she'll be going back to Los Angeles soon. She flew east to lick her wounds for a couple of weeks … see family and friends. You know."

Godiva tasted her Chardonnay. "She gave the distinct impression that she was angry at me for hurting you."

"But you did hurt me," Freddie said. "Because I had hurt you worse. I wasn't honest with you."

"Does she know that?" Godiva challenged him with her eyes. "Absolute truth, Freddie."

He took another slow sip. "The absolute truth is that Sienna and I haven't been that close. Five months ago, after you and I split, I told her that you'd left me and I was devastated. Did she want to know details? Hell, yeah. Did I give them to her?" He looked at Godiva. "Hell, no. Last night, when I saw Sienna at our mother's house, she told me she met a woman fitting your description, with your name, working at Sage Earth Gifts. I was happy you'd come back into the land of the living. I wasn't so happy when I surmised what happened between the two of you."

Godiva thought for a moment. "Did she tell you what a stone-cold bitch she was?"

"Again, baby. That was evident, from what I deduced. I'm used to reading between the lines when my sister speaks. Been doing it all my life. I love her, but she's a challenging human being. Her husband loved her too. That's why it took him fifteen years to finally walk away. And I think what you saw was a textbook display of projection."

"I see. So I was kind of a stand-in for Sienna's estranged husband?"

"Something like that," Freddie said. "Wouldn't be the first time she's conveniently found a scapegoat when the person she really wanted to have it out with was unavailable. I know, baby, because I was often the replacement. Just like you were."

"I remember you telling me that she wasn't an easy person to deal with."

"That's a nice way to phrase it. Which is why I never took

pains for the two of you to meet."

"Oh," Godiva said, her guard firmly in place. "I thought maybe it was because she might have told me you were married."

"I'm gonna get to all of that, Diva. My divorce will be final any day now, and I was hoping to wait before I explained everything, but my sister's intervention kind of changed all that."

"Well," Godiva said, watching as a squirrel chased another up a tree, "you've had over five months to figure out to how to explain everything to me. You know, why leaving out that part about your marriage wasn't such a big deal."

"It's a very big deal," Freddie said, taking her hand again. "But I'm a man and I own what is mine. Good and bad." He paused. "I've been looking at your photos every day for months. But seeing you in the flesh just sends me right back to that place when I first laid eyes on you. I swear, the moment I looked into your big brown eyes, I already knew how good it would feel to make love to you." He smiled wickedly. "And you knew how good I'd feel the moment you looked into mine."

Godiva gulped as one memory after another overcame her. *Don't give in, girl.*

He took his hand away slowly. "I'm just going to tell you what happened and why. Okay? No bull. I promise."

"I'm listening," Godiva said as her thoughts of the past distracted her.

"You know I have a daughter," Freddie said.

"Jessica. Yes. You told me about her on day one. Sadly, you weren't as forthright about her mother."

"I'll get to that shortly." He took another sip, taking care to look into Godiva's eyes as he did. "My baby girl is eighteen now. She'll be nineteen in two months, and she's going to college in the fall. Got into Dartmouth. Couldn't be more proud."

"That's wonderful, Freddie."

He smiled. "Thanks. Now, getting back to us. When I first met you at the health club and asked you out for the next night, I had every intention of telling you my situation. *Exactly* as it was. But when we got talking, you told me your most recent relationship had just ended because the man was married. Very married."

"Yeah, that creep," Godiva said, remembering.

"And you said that you'd punch the next married SOB who lied to you."

"I did," Godiva said, glaring at him.

"Well, that night, I explained to you that I met Jessica's mother and dated her only briefly when she told me she was pregnant." He fiddled uncomfortably with his watch. "As I told you, it was a very intentional pregnancy. She had lied about being on the pill." He paused. "Of course, I should have prevented it on my end, but I didn't. Enough said on that. And hey, I love my daughter with everything I have, so I don't regret her coming into this world.

"Today, had that happened, I would have left her mother, supported the child, and been a father to her. But back then, when my father was still alive, there wasn't a chance in hell I could do that and keep his respect. And he was the finest man I ever knew. So I honored his wishes and I married her."

"I know every bit of this," Godiva reminded him.

"I know you do, baby. Let me get it together."

I hate it when you sound like Barry White. Godiva dug her nails into her thighs to try to keep pleasurable memories from coloring her good sense.

"I stayed with Brenda for ten years, and we raised our girl together. Now here's the part where I slightly changed the narrative."

"I can hardly wait," Godiva said, stone-faced as she fought to keep her emotions in check.

"Nothing could have surprised me more, but one night, my

father called and asked me to come over. Alone. He told me he was sick. And he told me that he knew how miserable I was with Brenda."

"You told me he gave you his blessing to get divorced."

"Yeah … that," Freddie said awkwardly.

"That wasn't the truth? Your father *didn't* give you his blessing?"

"It's the truth, Diva. He absolutely did. But what I didn't tell you was that he asked me to promise to wait until Jess was eighteen. And then, to my total surprise, he apologized for having been so tough, then explained in detail why he had such infinite respect for me." Freddie bit his lip. "I nearly cried on the spot. Hell, makes me want to cry now just thinking about it." He exhaled and took a moment to collect his thoughts. "Anyway, he told me that I needed to leave Brenda, get my own place, and find a woman that I could truly love." Freddie waved to a couple that walked by with their Golden Retriever. "Baby, I was blown away. I couldn't get out of there fast enough."

"If your father was okay with you leaving, why did he make you promise not to divorce Brenda until Jessica was eighteen?"

"Because he didn't want any kind of unpleasant legal proceedings to mess with Jessica's life while she was still in school here in Swansea. Jess is a sensitive young woman, and he was very concerned that a divorce in progress could profoundly affect her grades and destroy her chances of getting into a good college. He knew Brenda would make things miserable and drag our daughter smack in the middle of it. My father had the wisdom to know that if I didn't divorce Brenda at the time, she might stay in her lane, thinking there was still a chance we'd get back together. Yeah, I know that sounds crazy, because I never pretended to love her when I didn't. Ever. But my father was right about the hell she would have raised, and my priority was my daughter. Only thing I never did understand is why Bren was so insistent on staying with me. She knew I didn't love her and that I never really did."

"I guess she found you attractive," Godiva said, still refusing to reveal any emotion. "And hoped you might eventually come around and to feel the same about her."

"Ain't nothing attractive about clinging to someone who doesn't love you," Freddie said. "But it's everything to feel the blood pulsating through your veins when you know they do."

Damn, you get to me. "Go on," Godiva said.

"So, baby, when you and I met, I'd been on my own for a while. I knew I'd be getting a divorce, and I knew that my marriage had been in name only. I fell so hard for you … literally," he said, grinning, "that there was no way I could risk telling you that pesky little detail. You were still steaming mad from your last relationship, and me, having been stuck in a loveless marriage all of those years — well, I wasn't about to risk losing you." He sighed. "And if I hadn't been so sloppy with the divorce papers, you probably never would have known."

"And that would have been okay with you," Godiva said, her anger rising to the surface. "To have a big fat lie between us?"

"No."

"Then why did you just tell me that I probably would never have known?"

Freddie sighed. "Because I haven't quite been able to knock out all the stupid inside." He took a long sip of his Cabernet. "I would have told you, Diva. When everything was done. And I would have never proposed to you without putting the truth out there. And I mean that, baby. Never. Especially when you'd been so honest about your marriage and your divorce. And your son." He smiled. "How's Dylan doing, anyway? Hope he doesn't hate me too much."

"He's good. Still working in Chicago, for the time being."

She swallowed a lump in her throat. "I miss him. But my boy is a grown man now, and he's out there living his best life." She looked into his eyes. "Let's get back to us."

"I'd love to do that."

"You know what I mean," Godiva admonished him, mentally kicking herself for the inadvertent disclosure of emotion.

"There's not much more to tell," Freddie said. "You found those papers on the coffee table, and it was over. For a hot minute, I thought you'd take me back when the divorce was final. But then you made it very clear you were done with me. Forever. Because you could never trust me again."

"That's about how I remember it," Godiva said, stroking the stem of her wineglass. "So, here we are."

Freddie looked around at the crowds that had gathered. "Swansea's number one pick-up spot." He paused. "There's one more thing I need you to know. Not that it should have anything to do with us, but at this point, I don't want anything to get misconstrued."

"Hmm," Godiva said. "You sound like you think I'm taking you back."

Freddie smiled. "There's someone living in my guest house."

"Who is she?" Godiva said, making it a point not to sound jealous.

"He's a he," Freddie told her. "Benton Bradley. He's here from Australia for a couple months. He contacted me last year. He's about thirty, been in the business since his teens, and now he's got a small, but successful, line of apparel that features Australian animals. I won't bore you with the details, but we're in the process of merging parts of our businesses. He's a real animal lover and a sharp dude. Just wanted you to know. Last night, after seeing Sienna, I told him what happened at the store. I told him about you. Seems he had already known about the shop but hadn't had time to visit yet. He seemed really interested in stopping by. So, you'll probably meet him soon."

"Hmm," Godiva said. "I think he'd be most welcome. Might be able to cheer up my boss."

"How's that," Freddie asked.

"Not important now," Godiva said.

"Nothing is as important as you and me," Freddie said. "Can we go somewhere from here?"

"Literally or figuratively?"

"Both," Freddie said, his eyes hopeful.

"When your divorce is final, let me see the papers. Then, and only maybe," she said. She stood. "We'll talk. But right now, I'm going home and you're going wherever you're going. But we're not going anywhere together."

"Okay, Diva. I'm not going to push. I'm just happy you're even willing to give me that much. Can I have a hug?" He drank the last of his wine and stood.

She looked soulfully into his eyes. "Not today, baby. My thinking process is already out of whack. Hugging you would be like putting it through the shredder."

"I don't suppose I could walk you—"

"No walking, no hugging, no more talking. You just have a good night, baby."

CHAPTER SIX

"I still can't believe you came in so early," Sage said, looking at the new jewelry shipment Godiva had just fully unpacked and laid on the counter.

"I can't believe you made me leave early on my second day of work," Godiva said, picking up an amazonite necklace. "Oh, how my grandmother would have cherished this." She examined the necklace, then laid it down. "You have such a kind heart, Sage. And I'll never take advantage of that."

"I believe you. Even though we've known one another such a short time, I feel like we've been friends forever," Sage said as she attached a small price tag to an amber necklace and put it on display under the counter.

"Knowing that you were just burned so badly by your best friend, I am especially touched by that."

"Well, maybe the fact that I knew Carrie for such a long time — I let that cloud my vision." Sage sighed. "I'm still processing everything that Caleb said to me yesterday. And while I should be livid about all I learned, I'm just numb … in a way. And most of the anger I feel, well, it's at myself for not seeing what was right in front of my face. Last night, after you left, I thought about Carrie, and you know what?—the signs were right in front of my face. Looking back, for example, I can remember the inappropriate way that she used to look at Caleb and the strange, prying questions she would ask; I told myself it was my imagination. I let that best-friend label obfuscate the obvious." She twisted her face. "Too many O words?"

Before Godiva could respond, Sage continued, "I suppose I'm not the sensitive, intuitive person I thought I was."

"But you are. The fact that you gave Carrie the benefit of the doubt doesn't detract from that. You have such a big heart, Sage."

"Thank you," Sage said as her fingers traced the edges of a moonstone heart pendant. "But it's closed for business."

"No, it's not. You just said the most beautiful thing to me," Godiva reminded her. "Those words didn't come from a closed heart."

Sage laid the heart pendant down on the shelf. "I said what I did to you because I can see your goodness. And my heart isn't necessarily closed to friendship. It's just closed for romantic love."

Godiva picked up several pairs of earrings. "You said these belong in the wall display, yes?"

"They do. Thanks for double-checking. There's some space on the right."

"Like I told you yesterday," Godiva said, walking over to the display unit and opening the lock, "Caleb's not going to give up on you. He's bound and determined to win you back."

"He can be bound and determined to climb Mt. Everest or be the first marketing VP to walk on the moon, but that doesn't mean he'll succeed."

Arranging the earrings to her satisfaction, Godiva closed and locked the case, then walked back over to the counter and stood to face Sage. "You were so in love with him. You must still be. Those feelings don't just evaporate."

Sage looked into her eyes. "Even though you didn't take Freddie back yesterday, I can see that in your heart, you already have. I know it, you know it, and he knows it."

"But—"

"I've been on this planet for less time than you have," Sage told her, "but I still have the wisdom to know, and the eyes to see, that you're still crazy about that man. It's different with Caleb. It's far more complex." She paused to think. "And you know, there was something that kept nagging at me when I saw him. And it bugged me all through last night. I just can't quite put my finger on it. But it rattles me."

"If I found out that my supposed BFF roofied Freddie and took naked selfies with him, I'd be rattled too. And it would be a very loud rattle … like that of a snake. And that snake would have a bite that keeps on giving. So I get it, honey. But something made you fall hard for that man and want to spend your life with him. You can't just throw that away. Even if it takes time to figure out, well, then that's what you need to do."

"I don't want to be in love," Sage said. "I just want to look away from it. And I want love to look away from me."

"Why do those words sound so familiar?" Godiva asked.

"Maybe you know the song, 'Love, Look Away.' I'd never heard of it, but when I told Randy what I was feeling, he sang this song to me from the Broadway show, *Flower Drum Song*. I told him it was my new anthem."

"Oh, Sage."

"Trubs suggested I get a sign with those words and hang it next to the Private Property sign."

Godiva walked around the counter and put her hands gently on Sage's shoulders. "That's our Randy, isn't it? He wants to see you happy. He wants to see all of us happy."

"Maybe my happiness is just having the freedom to be myself—to enjoy my work, my animals, and my friends. Where is it written that I have to have a man to be happy?"

"You don't, honey. Lots of people are genuinely happier on their own. I just don't think you're one of them. Especially at twenty-nine." Godiva picked up Sage's ringing phone that was right by her hand and gave it to her.

"Hi, Adam … Sure. Yes, as soon as the store opens, the Rufster and I will be going for a walk." She smiled as if he were standing in front of her. "That sounds great. See you then."

"Now there's a genuinely nice man. And ruggedly handsome too."

Sage groaned, then smiled. "Let's talk about you for a moment. Tell me something. How are you so at peace with Freddie? I don't get the idea that you had a restless sleep last night as I did; rather, I'd guess you had some pretty nice imagery swirling around in your head."

Godiva smiled and rested the palm of her hand on the counter. "You *are* intuitive. I did. And I'll tell you why I slept so well. I don't like that Freddie wasn't honest, because my husband had lied to me … and cheated on me, and though I met some good men after my divorce, I unknowingly dated a not-separated-from-his-wife married man right before I met Freddie. And Freddie is right: if I had known he was married, even though he and his wife had been estranged for years, there were no circumstances where that would have been okay. And he and I would never have gotten to know one another. Ever. I was way too raw."

"And …"

"I learned something about him yesterday. He's a man of honor. I mean, I never doubted it, but now I'm sure. And here's a hard truth: a lot men I know, and women, would play around if they were stuck in an unhappy marriage. Not Freddie. He didn't see anyone—yours truly—until he was legally separated and in his own place. And that's rare. I still don't like that he wasn't entirely honest, but a part of me feels grateful things happened as they did."

"So what are you waiting for?" Sage asked.

"His divorce papers. Despite everything I know and feel, they're still important to me."

"What makes Freddie so special?" Sage asked. She laughed. "Aside from the obvious and multiple attributes which I took note of yesterday."

Godiva licked her lips. "He is one fine man, isn't he?"

"He is."

"But 'fine' isn't enough for Godiva Genevieve Jones. It's the entirety of a person. I have never felt the freedom to be more myself than I do with him. No matter what my mood, what the weather, or anything else." She picked up some price stickers and affixed them to the underside of a few cuff bracelets. "I don't mean to go all philosophical on you, but I'm a lifelong observer. And I believe that the people we love most in this world, Sage, whether they're friends or lovers, are always those with whom we feel free to let go of all of the many cloths that shroud us and the masks that we wear, even subconsciously, to disguise our emotions. With these people, we can embrace the freedom to be ourselves without fear of losing them." She thought for a moment. "Because even when things go way wrong ... so wrong that you want to throw everything away ... it's okay, because we know we have love worth fighting for, and we understand why that is so. We know we can fight without devaluing ourselves. Maybe that sounds hokey to you, but for me, that's what love is in every manifestation." She paused. "Of course, being comfortable with someone is not everything. There is that gray area where you can get into trouble."

Sage smiled ever so slightly. "Thank you, Godiva. I really ... um ... thank you." She called into the back room beyond the curtains. "Come on, boy. Walkie walk!"

"I haven't changed your mind. Have I?" Godiva asked. "You're not going to consider how good you felt being with Caleb and examine the reasons why."

"Doubtful," Sage said, grabbing Rufus's leash and harness from a wall hook. "As I said, there's something about my relationship with Caleb that's tweaked me. Maybe it's that gray area you just mentioned." She smiled. "I do appreciate what you had to say. You speak truth." She petted Rufus, who had just run over to her. "But I still want love to look far away from me. And I'm going to make sure it knows I don't want it around."

"How do you do that?" Godiva asked. "And I pose that question with all sincerity. I'm not being facetious; I promise. How do you tell love to look away?"

Sage kneeled to put Rufus's harness on him, then stood, looking at Godiva. "Okay, so I'm going to totally embarrass myself here, but I'll tell you. I think love lives in the sky … the night sky, somewhere between the stars and the moon. There's a reason it's been immortalized in song that way for so many years. Because even though other people probably don't visualize it as I do, their hearts feel it. For me, just visualizing love as existing somewhere, gives me a place to direct my innermost feelings. Nothing more, nothing less."

"I'm listening …."

"So, when I talk to love, I wait until the world around me is quiet, and I look upward and wait until I know love is listening, and then I speak to it. And right now, I'm telling it to look away from me."

"You think love is listening to you?" Godiva asked. "I mean, I'm sure it hears you, but it may be every bit as stubborn as you are."

"I hope not," Sage said, fastening Rufus's leash to his harness.

"Either way," Godiva said. "That's a beautiful way to communicate with love."

"It's my way," Sage said as she headed for the door. "That's all I know."

ళ   ళ   ళ

"Oh, how nice," Sage said, standing in the sunshine on the corner of Main and Hudson streets while Adam caught up to her. "You brought Invisible Toto to play with Rufus."

Adam laughed. "I did!" He gave Sage a hug and scratched Rufus on the neck. "Hey, thanks for meeting me," he said. "Okay if we walk down Main Street toward the park?" He offered a quick, but nervous smile. "I wanted to apologize for leaving so quickly yesterday. I think the world of you, Sage, and I didn't want to get in the way of your reconciliation with Caleb."

Sage looked down. "I think Toto might have a pebble in his paw. He's limping a bit."

"So he is," Adam said, bending down to help his nonexistent dog.

Without warning, a shadow obscured the sunlight. "And this is why your store should have never been allowed to open," said the tanned blonde wearing a bright-red linen dress. She glared at Sage. "Everyone who associates with you turns into some new-age kook."

"Naomi Hall-Benchley," Adam said, standing to face her. "So beloved in this town. Always a kind word for your fellow Swansea-ites."

"I have no idea what you were just doing, but you shouldn't be performing strange rituals on public streets. Not in this town anyway."

Sage tried not to giggle.

"I was removing something from my invisible dog's paw," Adam told her. "My friend here was kind enough to point out that Toto was limping." He turned to Sage. "Not a pebble after all. It was a dried burr. Or part of one."

"Oh," Sage said. "Ouch!"

"Ouch indeed." Adam looked down. "You okay now, boy?" He petted the invisible dog.

"What are you people smoking?" Naomi asked. She turned to address Sage. "If you're selling any kind of 'enhancements' out of that little shop of horrors you run, I'll have you shut down in no time."

"I do sell some unusual items," Sage told her. "But nothing illegal. I'm sorry that I don't sell senses of humor. I'd gladly donate one to you. I do like to give to the needy."

"How dare you speak to me that way," Naomi said. She turned to Adam. "And you, Mr. Canoga, opening a store for the 'hip and trendy man,' I hear."

"I am." Adam grinned.

"Jameson Clothier has everything the men in my life will ever need."

"Do they sell escape hatches?" Sage asked Adam.

Naomi glowered at Sage, then turned to address Adam. "You'll disassociate yourself with this whackadoodle immediately if you care about attracting the right people."

"If everyone I met were as wonderful as Sage Gordon, the world would be a better place."

"Ugh, she's contagious and you're infected!" Naomi huffed as she hurried away.

"Ah!" Adam said. "Nothing like a morning rebuke from Naomi Hall-Benchley to get one's blood pumping! Better than jumping jacks, don't you think?"

Sage laughed. "I feel positively invigorated."

"So," Adam said as they continued on their walk. "Getting back to what I was saying … um … sorry to be so hasty in my departure yesterday. I just felt I was in your way and didn't want

Caleb to get the wrong idea."

"Caleb has a lot of wrong ideas," Sage said, stopping as Rufus sniffed the base of a small tree. "And we did not reconcile, despite his public declaration in my store."

"I'm sorry, Sage. I didn't mean to imply that you took him back because that's what he wanted. I just remember how happy you were about your engagement, and I guess I wrongly assumed you'd be open to the possibility."

"I really meant what I said about not being interested in any relationship," Sage told him as they continued to walk.

"I'm not going to lie and say I wouldn't like to take you out, but please believe me when I tell you that I'm honored to be your friend. I have so much respect for you."

"Thanks, Adam. Now tell me, how is the store coming along?"

"Very well. I'll be in good shape for the pre-opening party in a couple of weeks. I'm waiting for a few deliveries, but I will be fully stocked and raring to go. Oh, and one other thing."

"What's that?"

"Well, I've been thinking. When I get the store up and running, I can adopt a flesh-and-blood brother or sister for Toto … from the pound, of course. I have to find a dog that has a good temperament for being in the store and meeting lots of people."

"I'm so happy to hear this, Adam. A real dog will bring so much joy into your life. I've never been without one."

"I wanted to adopt one when I worked at Jameson. But I didn't feel right leaving a dog home alone all day. Then, this past year, traveling to New York all the time and opening the store, well, that didn't work either."

"You'll know when the time is right. I'm just happy that Rufus will have a new friend he can actually see."

"Don't forget," Adam said, pressing the walk button at the

light, "invisible dogs have a lot of value as well."

"Give me an example," Sage asked, challenging him with a smile.

"Didn't you notice? Aside from Toto incurring Naomi's scorn, he also took a huge bite out of her leg. She was bleeding profusely down to her Salvatore Ferragamos and didn't even notice. I imagine by the time we walk back, the blood-spattered pavement, adorned with Ferragamo shoe prints, will be cordoned off with yellow crime-scene tape."

Sage laughed as the walk sign lit up, and they crossed the street toward the park. She noticed that her entire being felt lighter than it had in a long time, but admonished herself silently not to let the feeling linger.

୭   ୭   ୭

"What did I miss?" Sage asked, walking through the door with Rufus.

"Oh, not much," Godiva said. "Just that insanely expensive floral display on the counter. It was delivered about fifteen minutes ago."

Sage looked distraught. "I don't want flowers." She walked over and read the card aloud: "Bohemian baby, you are truly the love of my life. You and me ... until the end of time. Stay Zen. Kisses, Caleb."

Godiva pressed her lips together and said nothing.

"Thank you for not telling me that was beautiful or anything like that," Sage said, her eyes fixated on the arrangement, as if it had personally offended her.

"Believe me, honey, I wouldn't have dreamed of it." She paused. "Especially while that steam is coming out of your ears."

"Oh." Sage relaxed her shoulders. "Sorry." She refocused her attention on Godiva. "For one, I told him not to call me 'Bohemian baby' ever again. I hate that he intentionally disrespected my wishes. And the syrupy slop from the card is dripping all over my hands." She stared at the flowers with no expression. "Funny, he never sent me anything like this when we were engaged."

"Folks don't often know what they've lost until it's too late."

Sage raised an eyebrow. "So you're agreeing with me that it's too late?"

"I didn't quite mean it that way. I just meant that—"

"I'm putting these in the back room," Sage interrupted. "The last thing I need is the whole world coming in here and asking me what the special occasion is. And that, by the way, is exactly what Caleb wants to happen."

"Can't blame you there. Go ahead. I'll take the boy's harness off and hang up his leash."

"Thanks," Sage said as she picked up the arrangement, then went behind the curtains to hide the flowers. She put them on top of a file cabinet near her desk. She was just about to sit down and de-stress, when the bells of the front door clanged. "That better not be you, Caleb. Because this Bohemian baby will kick your butt right out."

Sage hurried back into the store, to see a gorgeous man with a huge head of tousled brown hair and a sexy two-day growth on his face. He was wearing a button-down blue-and-white checked cotton shirt, with three buttons undone and a pair of sunglasses hanging from the V neckline it created. His sleeves were rolled up to reveal three leather bracelets on his left wrist and a watch on the right. He wore khaki chino pants and ankle-high brown moccasins. And he had the biggest smile Sage had ever seen.

"G'day!" he said before she could greet him. He turned to see Godiva. "And g'day to you too."

"You must be Freddie's houseguest," Godiva said. "From

Australia."

"Benton Bradley," he said, taking care to make eye contact with both women before Rufus greeted him with enthusiasm. "G'day, fluffy mate. I reckon you and my Kelpie Matilda might enjoy a good pash."

"Is that short for 'passionate?'" Sage asked as she walked around the counter to greet him, her eyes bright and curious. "Hi, I'm Sage Gordon."

As Rufus finally settled on his mat by the meditation cushion, Benton took both of her hands in his. "Indeed it is, Sage. You're beautiful as."

Unnerved, but not put off by the intimacy of the exchange, Sage delicately pulled away. "Benton, you said, right?"

"I did." He winked. "You can call me Bent, but please, don't call me crooked."

Sage laughed, finding herself unable to avert her gaze.

He looked at Godiva. "You must be Freddie's lady, Godiva Jones."

"I am," Godiva said as she walked over to shake his hand. "Or I will be," she mumbled under her breath. "It's lovely to meet you, Benton." She winked at Sage. "I'm going into the office to finish those website updates we talked about."

Sage's eyes widened in surprise, then narrowed as if to playfully chastise Godiva. "Yeah, by all means, update my website. Seems like we've been talking about that incessantly … and nothing else."

"Don't I know it? Well, you know where to find me if the bells clang too much," Godiva said. She walked behind the curtains with a satisfied smile.

Sage looked at Benton while his eyes scanned the store with great interest. "Quite a place you have here. I like it." He looked at the sign above the counter. "What's that all about?"

"Oh, the Private Property sign. It's just there for decoration."

"I don't suppose you'd like to sell it. I've got a small farm, and that would be a welcome addition to my front gate."

"It's not for sale," Sage said. "Besides, you can't bring wood into Australia. They'd confiscate it at customs."

"No wood for me then," Benton said, laughing to himself.

Sage felt oddly tantalized by the stranger's words.

"That sign looks a good deal older than you."

"It is, I think. Or maybe it just ages faster. Besides, I use moisturizer twice a day. I don't think the sign cares about self-preservation."

"It could use a good oil rubdown," Benton said, grinning. "I'd be happy to do that for you."

"Oh … um, not at the moment. But if I … um, decide the sign needs a rubdown, I'll know who to call." She looked over at Rufus, who was taking a nap and therefore unable to provide the immediate distraction she needed. "So, is there anything here that I can help you with?"

"Possibly," he said, looking into her eyes. "I'm new in town. Rather, I'm on an extended stay. I'm working with Freddie Lamar. We're pooling our resources to kick arse on a new clothing line."

"You're in the clothing business?"

"Been in the manufacturing end for years," Benton told her. "But now I'm looking to sell my koala T-shirts, active wear, and other items."

"Oh, I get it. Quality T-shirts," Sage said. "With koalas on them."

"Exactly," Benton said. "Also quokkas, wombats, kangaroos, dingoes, wallabies and the whole lot of them. Have a line of jumpers … sweaters, as you call them … with animals embroidered on them. That's only the beginning."

"Is it a line for both men and women?"

"Absolutely." His eyes made another pass around the store. "Looks like you've got something here for everyone." He paused. "Or at least everyone who's got a spark of flair or individuality. I like that. I always …"

"You always what?" Sage asked.

"Oh, I was just going to say that I always admire people who aren't afraid to take the road less traveled."

"Hmm," Sage said. "Not that you look the part, but are you a loner?"

"Can be," Benton said. "All depends on what life throws at me. And trust me, I've had my share of surprises. I guess I'm good either way. My best mates'll tell you that. How about you?"

"I like people," Sage said. "I would never have opened a store if I didn't. But I'm far from being a party animal, nor do I remotely resemble a socialite. This town has a lot of both, and they're often one and the same." She smiled. "Must have been very different for you growing up in Australia."

"I lived in a rural area when I was a kid. Right before I started high school, my parents moved to Melbourne. I have a unit in Hawthorn, not too far from their house. I'm not a bushie, but I do own a small farm outside of the city in Pakenham. Best of both worlds. Not too much to whinge about."

"I hear you," Sage said. "I love being so proximate to New York City. It can be so electric and thrilling. But I like living in Swansea."

"So I take it you grew up here," Benton said, picking up a polished stone from the bowl on the counter. "Love You Forever. What a nice sentiment." He put the stone back.

Sage blushed. "I actually grew up in Bancroft. It's farm country, about fifteen minutes north. When I was a kid, during the summers, to give us a special treat, some nights my father would start a campfire in the backyard. Just for me, my mom, and my best friend who lived two doors down … for a while." She felt a rush of sadness in synchronicity with the memories that flowed. "Anyway, the campfire was the only thing we did that remotely resembled a rural life."

"Ah," Benton said. "Bush telly, as they say in the bush!"

"They do? Oh, that's hilarious," Sage said. "Anyway, when I went away to college in Massachusetts, my parents moved to a house in the Hudson Valley."

"So you had a good childhood?" Benton asked.

"Some of it was wonderful; the rest was okay. Good days and bad. You know, like you said before, life throws surprises at you."

"It does," Benton said, lowering his eyes. He looked at Sage, then immediately brightened. "So, I'd like to buy a prezzy for my mum. It's her birthday in two weeks, and it's doubtful I'll be home by then." He looked into the case under the counter, then at the display unit against the wall. "Looks like you have some lovely jewelry. Can you show me?"

"Sure," Sage said, walking around the counter to open the case. "We have a lot of beautiful stones. Is there any color or particular stone that you think your mother would like?"

"Mum loves pink stones."

"I have an idea," Sage said. She looked around and quickly put her hands on a beautiful pair of earrings with a pink stone and handed him the card with the earrings attached."

"Gorgeous," he said. "What is the stone?"

"Morganite. It can help balance the energies of the heart. It's also good for healing and releasing past traumas."

"I see," Benton said as he examined them. "Fabbo. Would you also have a thingy maggigy to put a chain?"

"You mean a pendant?"

"That's the one. Mum has some silver chains, and she enjoys wearing different pieces on them."

Sage pulled a pendant from the case. "Here you go. They make a beautiful set."

He looked into her eyes. "Indeed they do. I'll take them. Do you gift wrap?"

"Absolutely," Sage said.

"While you do that, I'll have a look at the cards."

Sage and Benton separated to handle their individual tasks. She had just finished wrapping his gifts when the bells clanged. Without seeing who had come in, Sage found herself resentful that anyone had.

"I need some lapis," an older woman said rather loudly. "My husband needs his third eye opened."

Sage saw Benton turn to look, grin, then turn his back.

"There are lapis stones over there in the bins," Sage said as she pointed.

The woman strutted over to the bins and grabbed a handful of stones, not even bothering to look at them. "Can you ring these up right away? I've got cash."

"Cash works," Sage said. "That'll be thirty-two fifty for the stones, including tax."

The woman slammed two twenties on the counter. "Here you go."

Sage noticed that Benton had turned around again and was enjoying the conversation. She rang up the sale and handed the woman her change."

"Thanks," the woman said, speaking far louder than necessary. "Let's hope this opens his third eye and closes his yap. He's as perceptive as a rock." She paused. "Can't miss the irony that I'm buying stones to remedy that, can you? See, my neighbor is a yoga teacher, and she told me lapis might help." She took the small bag Sage handed her. "I'm not into this hocus pocus woo woo stuff, but if you had a husband like mine, you'd try anything, believe me.

But for your sake, I hope you'll never have to. Marriage isn't everything it's cracked up to be." She paused, then mumbled. "The 'good egg' everyone was so happy I snagged is cracked beyond repair." She gave Sage a quick nod of thanks, then hurried out the door.

With a greeting card in his hand, Benton walked over to the counter and put it down. He smiled. "Well, this has been great. And speaking of rocks, do you mind if I rock up, you know, come by again soon?"

Sage nodded toward the top of the door. "… send not to know for whom the bell clangs, it clangs for thee."

"Clever you are. And literary too."

Sage reddened as she took both the greeting card and his credit card, then processed his purchase. Smiling, she handed him back his credit card along with a gift bag. "Thank you, kind sir, for visiting Sage Earth Gifts. I hope you'll come again."

"Soon indeed," Benton said. "Someone I know must be having a birthday … very soon." He laughed. "G'day, Sage. Tell Godiva g'day for me, please."

Her eyes followed him out the door and down the street, until he was out of her line of vision.

"Why do you look so sad?" Godiva said, coming back into the store. "Sounds like you had a lovely conversation. And excuse me, but he's burning hot."

"We did. And he is." She paused. "Not that his looks matter, seeing that I'm not in the market for love, and he lives in Australia." She sighed. "I don't know what's gotten into me. It's just weird."

Godiva gave her a sympathetic smile.

"Well, not as weird as that updating-my-website line that you came up with." Sage attempted a smile, determined to shake off the strange sadness she felt.

"Silly me. And I never even thought to turn on the

computer. Do you even have a website?"

"I do. And in the not-too-distant future, I will be updating it for real. I hope to sell some of my more unusual items online. A few months ago, I had a web designer come in for a consultation. He was pulling up some background images, and while we were waiting, the words 'fetching preview' appeared on the screen. He looked at me with his tongue wagging and said the preview wasn't the only thing that was fetching."

"Oh. Just no," Godiva said. "Bleccch!"

"You think? I never called him again. My momentum came to a crashing halt, especially then, when my breakup with Caleb was even more raw than it is now."

"Looks like you've got options, girl."

"Godiva Genevieve ..."

"Oh, scary. You sounded just like my mother."

"Good."

Godiva reached under the counter and picked up the spray bottle and the roll of paper towels she'd made friends with on the day she and Sage met. "I'm just going to take a stroll around the store to make sure everything is sparkling clean. You won't even hear the spray of cleaning fluid or the squeak of clean. I'll be so quiet, you'll barely know I'm here."

"Excellent," Sage said, laughing. "That's just what I need from you right now."

"But you'll hear me thinking," Godiva said devilishly as she scooted to the back of the store.

CHAPTER SEVEN

"So …," Sage said to Godiva, who was flipping through some product catalogs. "It's ten minutes after six, the boy is upstairs enjoying his dinner, and you've gone all afternoon without reminding me about the available men in my orbit."

"I'm sorry about that. I won't let so much time pass tomorrow." She laughed. "Seriously, Sage, I'll try to exact a bit more control over what comes out of my mouth. I really don't mean to be such a pain. When Freddie and I broke up, that was the worst agony I've ever felt. Worse than divorcing my husband, and almost worse than childbirth." She thought. "Well, maybe not, especially when I was rewarded with such a wonderful son. But the point is, I just don't want to see an amazing young woman like you become remotely like the tormented soul that I was."

"So why do I get the feeling there's more to this?"

Godiva closed the catalog and laid it on the counter. She turned to Sage, who was standing next to her. "Because you're so intuitive, it's scary."

"It's scary how intuitive I'm not," Sage lamented. "I'd have never gotten into such a mess with Caleb if I were."

"Like I said earlier," Godiva told her, "it's that gray area that got you into trouble. And it's not that you didn't feel something was up; you were so much in love that you ignored it."

"Which is exactly why I don't want to be in love," Sage said. "I'm glad you finally understand." She smiled. "But you were going to tell me why I'm so intuitive."

Godiva waved and said good-bye to two shoppers who had just come in to browse. "Can we pull up the purple thrones?"

Sage laughed as they each pulled an upholstered barstool toward the counter.

"I had a best friend," Godiva said. "Sheba Louise. She was one of the kindest people I've ever known. It hurts too much to talk about this, so I'm going to be really quick. Let's just say that when she was in her thirties, she got left at the altar in front of nearly three-hundred people. She was also short one bridesmaid. Yeah, you guessed it. The AWOL groom and bridesmaid had taken off together. A month later, they actually got married. Unbelievable." She shook her head in disgust. "Honey, talk about devastation. All I can tell you is that it wrecked my girl forever, not just the loss of the man — good riddance to him — but the humiliation in front of everyone she knew. Not to mention the financial devastation. She was never the same. Even after years went by, she was dead set against ever loving anyone again. It became a sickness."

"Oh, how sad."

"After several years, the loneliness ate her alive. She was too deep into her own world to come out of it and look around. And there were many men who would have loved her and treated her right. But she stopped caring about herself. She moved away, changed her number and her email address, and I never heard from her again. And it wasn't for the lack of trying, either. I didn't know what happened until her mama called to tell me she had died of cancer. And it was something that could have been easily treated, had it been caught early. But she just didn't care, felt she didn't matter in this world, and so she ignored the symptoms."

"That's tragic," Sage said.

"I'm not trying to sound like the Ghost of Christmas Future or anything, especially in the middle of the summer, but I guess I'm a bit sensitive to all of this. We're only nearing the end of my third day, and I know I've crossed the line a few times. And I'm sorry for that."

"It's okay," Sage said, gently touching her hand. "I know where your heart is, and believe me, I've appreciated the ear and the wise counsel. And I haven't stopped liking men or finding them attractive. I just don't want to be in love. Right now, that's how I feel. There's nothing anyone can tell me that will change that. I have to process my feelings and embrace them. Pretending to feel differently to keep others from worrying doesn't help anything. It will just make it harder." She paused. "I won't even ask you if you understand that because I know you do."

"Of course I do," Godiva told her. "Which makes me a bigger fool for acting as I have. And worse, I can't even promise I'll be able to stop. Unless you fire me."

"No way," Sage said. "You're the best person I could ever find to work for me. I'll take you as you are, okay?"

"You're amazing," Godiva said as she and Sage listened in unison to a text notification sounding on Sage's phone.

Sage picked her phone up from the counter and made a face. "Oh, no. Just as I feared: 'Sage, aren't you going to thank me for the flowers? I know they were delivered late this morning …' I can't even read the rest. It upsets me too much to say the words aloud."

"May I see?" Godiva asked while Sage held the phone so they could both read at the same time.

Before either woman could say another word, the door opened as the clanging bells almost sent the phone flying out of Sage's hands.

"What fresh skullduggery is this?" Randy said, seeing the

two women with their heads together.

A beautiful woman with shoulder-length auburn hair, who had accompanied Randy into the store, laughed.

"Not that I require enhancements," Randy said, "but bringing Molly Rose along does fill the air with something extra special."

"I'm glad you finally understand that," Molly said to Randy. She turned to face the counter. "Hi, Sage; hi, Godiva."

Both women got off the barstools and came around to give Molly a hug and get their kisses from Randy. As Rufus came rushing past the curtains and into the store to greet Randy, his tail wagged so hard it walloped Molly in the shin.

"How are you, Molly?" Sage said. "Were your ears burning this morning?

"I don't think so. Why? Were you talking about me?" She smiled as she watched Rufus and Randy interact. "That tail is a serious weapon," she said, laughing.

"It is." She paused to shift gears. "No, Molly, I wasn't talking about you," Sage said, "but I sure was thinking about you."

"All good, I hope."

"Well, more funny than good. Adam joined Rufus and I on our morning walk, and we had a run-in with Naomi."

"Did you bite her, boy?" Randy said as he scratched Rufus's neck."

"A close encounter of the she-devil kind, I call it," Molly said. "What happened?"

"Oh, Adam and I were joking about his invisible dog, Toto. Naomi saw him removing a burr from Invisible Toto's paw and went bonkers on us. Called me a whackadoodle and said that I was contagious, and Adam was infected. Among other charming things."

"Are you freakin' kidding me? I thought she had learned to

mind her own business. But then again, she-devils are incapable of allowing decorum to seep into their brains. It only seeps out. Considering how long it's been seeping downward, there's little left."

"And it all lands in a little puddle around her feet," Randy added. "And she slips in it every time."

Sage giggled, then rubbed the top of Rufus's head before pointing for him to go lie down. As usual, he looked at Randy to counteract his mother's command, but with no such luck, he headed to his mat and snuggled with his squeaky red snake.

"I know you've had your run-ins with Naomi," Godiva said.

"Head-on collisions," Molly corrected her. "And never because I deserved them, but only because I refused to let her manipulate me for her own purposes."

"Molly Rose has been Naomi's worst nightmare," Randy said.

"But all that is in the past, right?" Sage asked.

"The reprehensible matchmaking part," Molly said. "But she still tries to stab me with her pitchfork every time I see her."

"However, because of Molly Rose's brave and outspoken defense of herself, one of Naomi's pitchforks went somewhere she didn't intend it to," Randy explained. "And it has been there ever since."

"I'd love to see how that looks in an X-ray," Godiva said, chuckling.

"I would too, come to think of it," Molly said. "I'd frame that freakin' thing and hang it on the wall in my office." She turned to Randy. "Can you arrange that?"

Everyone laughed again, then stopped abruptly as the door opened, and Caleb came bursting into the store. His face tightened when he saw Sage was not alone. He looked at her. "Are you having a party in here?"

Randy spoke first. "Molly and I are here to buy a gift for our assistant, Ana. I hope that meets with your approval." He put his palm under his chin. "Hmm. On second thought, that's really not necessary, is it?"

Caleb looked angry. "Mind your own business, Randy." He turned to Sage. "Where are my flowers?"

"*Your* flowers?" Sage asked. "Hold on." She rushed behind the counter, pushed aside the tapestry curtains and went into the back room, then quickly returned with the arrangement in her hands. She pushed it into Caleb's chest. "Here are *your* flowers."

Caleb plunked the arrangement down on the counter. "I'm sorry, Bohemian baby. I just couldn't believe that you didn't thank me for them. Not even a text. Can you think for a moment how that made me feel?" He turned to Randy and Molly. "I know you people work for the *Swansea Herald.* I'd better not see any of this private exchange in the paper, because if I do—"

"First, don't 'you people' us. Second, we're not freakin' gossip columnists," Molly said. "And if we were, well, don't flatter yourself. The idea is to actually engage a readership in stories about cool peeps … or at least interesting ones."

"Score one for Molly Rose," Randy said, delighted.

Sage picked up the arrangement and shoved it back into Caleb's arms. "Really, Caleb? This is about what I've done to you and how you feel? Sheesh. I told you how I felt. That's why I went to Coffee & Teaz with you … so there would be no ambiguity. And I told you not to call me your 'Bohemian baby.' Twice! I feel nauseated even hearing that."

Randy mock frowned. "Sage is never in good spirits when she gets a case of the collywobbles."

Caleb wrinkled his forehead in confusion.

"Queasiness. Stomach pain," Molly explained. She looked at Randy. "Thanks to you, I have such a special vocabulary."

Caleb plunked the arrangement down on the counter for a second time, then looked at Randy. "Keep your wollycobbles, cobbler wolly, peach cobbler, or anything that wobbles out of my personal conversation."

"Oh, my!" Randy said, then gasped.

Randy, Molly, and Godiva tried not to laugh while Sage looked Caleb dead in the eyes. "You start a public conversation, then that's what it becomes. You don't get to make it private. And FYI, my friends are welcome to say whatever they want. Quite frankly, I'm very happy they're here."

"Your friends are laughing at me, Sage. Is that really okay with you?"

"Can you blame them, Caleb? You sound ridiculous!"

He nodded toward Randy. "How come *he* can say anything he wants, and you find it endearing?"

"Because Randy's words come from a caring heart," Sage shot back.

"You're *making* me say stupid things," Caleb told her. "Out of frustration. And I'm not stupid. I'm a marketing VP, and I make more than any of you. And I've got a higher education than any of you."

"Grrrr." Rufus growled from his mat.

"Keep going, honey," Godiva goaded him. "Keep going." She paused. "And to think, I told Sage to consider giving you another chance."

"You did?" His face fell. "Thank you. I'm sorry; I really am. I'm just so despondent. I didn't mean to offend anyone."

"Humph," Godiva mumbled.

He looked at Sage. "This is not me and you know it. The man you see in front of you is not the man you wanted to spend the rest of your life with."

"Don't I know *that*!" Sage said.

"That's not what I mean. What I'm saying is that the man you still love exists within me. He's there, Bohem ... more in love with you than ever. And when you're alone, think about the beautiful times we've had, the love we've professed for one another, and the plans we made for an incredible life. Remember how good you felt, and know that you can have all that back and more."

"Please take your flowers," Sage said quietly. "Please ... just go, Caleb."

"But—"

"Seriously," Sage said, her face tightening. "I need you to go ... now!" She nodded toward the flowers.

Caleb snarled as he picked up the expensive arrangement. "I'm going to take these to Swansea Hospital and make some old woman's day."

"A lovely thing to do," Randy said.

"Lemonade out of lemons," Molly added.

Caleb looked at Sage. "At least when I lay my head down at night, I'll know I've made at least one woman very happy." He paused. "Even if she's old. And for the record, one more time, I'm not giving up on you."

Everyone exchanged looks as Caleb and his flowers left the store. Rufus, content the threat was gone, put his head down.

"That ended well, I think," Randy said. He looked at Sage's face. "Let Randy give you a hug."

Molly looked at Godiva. "Maybe while they're hugging it out, you can show me where your mini fountains are. Ana's really been wanting one."

"Will you tell me a good Naomi story?" Godiva asked.

"Sure," Molly said. "Always happy to share the she-devil chronicles." She looked over at Sage and Randy. "I really hope she's okay."

"Me too," Godiva said. "Me too."

ও ও ও

"You're all dolled up with somewhere to go," Godiva said to Sage as she arrived at the store.

Sage, wearing a dusty-rose prairie dress adorned with beaded necklaces, a straw fedora hat with a black ribbon, and black-studded ankle boots, smiled as she finished straightening the votive candle display. "Thank you, Godiva. And you look pretty great yourself. Is that the amazonite pendant your grandmother gave you?"

"It is," Godiva said, laying her purse on the counter and lifting the pendant into her hands to show Sage. "Isn't it stunning? Today is my fourth day at Sage Earth Gifts. I thought it was about time I wore this. I just keep thinking how happy my grandmother would be that I'm working here, and that I'm using all of the knowledge she taught me."

"I think she knows," Sage said.

"I do too." Godiva smiled. "So, tell me. Is it my imagination, or are you dressed up extra special today?"

"My, my," Sage said. "Only in the door minutes and you're already suffering romantic delusions on my behalf."

"Your morning walk with Adam?"

"Actually, he's got a business meeting in his store soon. But he did ask me to lunch at the *Le Chat Noir*."

"Okaaaay …."

"It's not a date," Sage said.

"Okay. Not a date. But I do notice a blush in your cheeks."

"Really? Hmm. Nice to know the makeup I applied actually works."

Godiva laughed. "Okay, I deserved that. And I won't call it a date."

"Platonically speaking, it's a lunch date. Adam said he has some decisions to make about the store, personal decisions, and he asked me if I would lend him an ear." Sage smirked. "And yes, it's one of the nicest places in town, and I want to look good. And I'm not going to pretend I don't like Adam, because I really do. But what I'm wearing and what I just said don't change the fact that I'm not interested in a relationship." She looked at Godiva and saw she was trying to suppress a grin. Sage stuck out her tongue. "You can be as overjoyed about this as you want."

"Who, me?" Godiva said, picking up her purse and stashing it behind the counter. "I have no idea what you could possibly mean." She casually straightened the counter displays. "Seriously, I'm glad you and Adam have a nice friendship. I think that's great. What time are you meeting him?"

"Twelve thirty," Sage said. "Do you mind taking a late lunch?"

Godiva laughed. "Girl, you know you don't even have to ask."

CHAPTER EIGHT

"Oh, Sage, don't you look pretty," Adam said as the maître d' at *Le Chat Noir* led them to a table.

Adam waited until the tuxedo-clad man had left to speak to Sage. "By the way, not to ruin your appetite, but I just wanted to let you know that when I glanced at the reservation book, I noticed that a certain socialite is also having lunch here today. I'm afraid this is a regular haunt for her."

"Well, considering you didn't bring Invisible Toto, I'm sure she'll leave us alone. Especially in a place like this where she actually cares what people think." Sage smiled at the waiter as he brought them each a sparkling water with lemon.

"Have you taken a look at the menu?" Adam asked.

"I looked at it online last night," Sage said. "You know, so I wouldn't take forever making up my mind right now. It was easy. I'm going to have the Green Goddess salad."

Just as the waiter walked over to the table, Adam quickly opened and closed his menu. "The lady will have the Green Goddess salad, and I'll have the Salade Lynonnaise." He looked at Sage. "I'm going to have a glass of Chardonnay. Will you join me?"

"Why not?" Sage said. "Yes, thank you."

"I'm so glad you agreed to meet me."

"It's my pleasure." She took a moment to examine his face. "Are you okay? You look somewhat out of sorts."

"Can one be 'in sorts?'" Adam asked. "I've always wondered that, actually."

"I used to wonder about the word 'disgruntled.' You hear stories about 'disgruntled employees,' but never once in my life have I heard anyone talk about someone being gruntled. So I looked it up, and it's actually a back formation of the word disgruntled. Beyond that, I know nothing."

Adam laughed. "Interesting. And funny you should mention disgruntled employees, as that's one of the things I wanted to talk to you about."

"Oh, no. I hope you don't have one already. You haven't even opened your store yet."

"Exactly. And I'm trying to avoid that from happening. There's this woman, Joanie, who used to work at Jameson with me. Maybe you remember her. I think she's the only woman they ever hired, actually, and only because she's related to someone in this town with a lot of money. Anyway, we dated a few times after she left the store. I'm the one who broke it off. She's a nice person, but she didn't interest me at all. There was no spark. Anyway, the last time I saw her was a year ago when I told her in confidence I was seriously thinking of opening my own store. She asked me if I'd hire her if that ever came to be. And not thinking it through, I'm like, 'Yeah, sure,' figuring that she'd probably have a job by now, and I might not ever have the store. Bottom line, she put me on the spot, and I said yes on the spot." He laughed uncomfortably. "I could have used a big bottle of spot remover. And well, here I am. In a bind because of a spot."

Sage and Adam thanked the waiter as he put two glasses of wine and a basket of oven-toasted sliced baguettes on the table.

"And now she wants a job with you?"

"She does indeed," Adam said, raising his glass. "To your health and happiness."

"To yours as well," Sage said. "And to your success with Haber Dash."

As they clinked glasses, their eyes met. They both smiled uneasily, as if it didn't happen.

"And you want my advice on what to do?" Sage asked.

"I don't want to hurt her, nor do I like going back on my word," Adam said. "But one, I think she still likes me in a way I don't want her to. Two, she's a bit staid and uptight ... rather rigid ... and for some reason, unnerves me at times. I know that there was a lot about Margie that bothered you, but you never got rid of her. So I'm wondering if I should just keep my word and hire Joanie."

"I'll tell you something," Sage said, breaking off a piece of the toasted baguette. "I actually wanted to thank that crazy woman who came into my store with her melting ice-cream cone; she got Margie to quit. I really didn't like working with Margie, despite the fact that underneath her neuroses, she's a nice person most days. She wasn't, however, a good fit for my store or for me. Honestly, I should have let her go when she threatened to quit the first time. But after I contemplated what a hassle it would be to teach a new person, I let her stay. I swear, Godiva fell from the heavens at just the right time."

"Interesting," Adam said. "And you're right about Godiva; she's wonderful. A true one-eighty from what you were used to."

"You're not kidding! Margie got so crazy at times that I started developing anxiety. So much so that I even went to see my doctor."

"What did he or she say?" Adam asked.

"Thank you for not assuming my doctor has to be male," Sage said. "I like an enlightened man."

Adam blushed. "And what did *she* say?"

"My doctor is actually a he, but I like that you didn't assume that." She smiled. "He gave me samples of some anxiety medicine and told me to give them a try."

"Did they work?"

"Not at all," Sage said.

"That's a shame. They should have helped somewhat."

"If I had taken them, they probably would have." Sage laughed, then took a sip of her wine. "I hate swallowing pills. Or taking them. In the end, I used deep breathing and meditation techniques to get rid of the anxiety."

Adam laughed along with her. "A much better solution. You know, I've also found pharmaceuticals to be highly ineffective if not ingested. And wine is not nearly as delicious if not tasted," he said, picking up his glass.

"True," Sage said, then took a sip of her wine. "Honestly, Adam, my advice to you would be not to hire her. As uncomfortable as that may be, not hiring someone is way easier than firing them. It's the lesser of two evils."

"That's a really good point."

They both smiled and thanked the waiter as he served their salads.

"May I ask you a personal question?" Sage said.

"Fire away."

"This woman you're describing. She doesn't sound anything like someone that I see you with. I understand what you didn't like about her, but what attracted you to her in the first place?"

Adam sighed. "I'm embarrassed to admit this, but in my early twenties, I had a girlfriend named Tammy for a few years … a real party animal. At first, she was fun, but then I started to grow up and she didn't. In fact, she got more extreme with time. I had other relationships after her, but as Tammy was my first serious relationship, things that happened when we were together had quite an impact on me. For years, I would flash back to some of the outlandish things she did that made me cringe or turn ten shades of red with embarrassment. Not to mention the impact she had on my friends and family. So, I think when I met Joanie, I was sort of overcorrecting."

Sage's face blanched.

"What did I say?" Adam asked.

"I think you just … I'll tell you another time. I need time to mull over what I'm thinking, but I believe you just helped my life make a lot more sense."

"I sure hope so."

"Anyway," Sage told him, "sorry for the digression. All I can say is that you've worked so hard to get this far. Why start out with a thorn in your side when you can prevent it? I had no idea what Margie was really like until a few weeks into the job. I'd never have hired her if I even had a small clue she'd be so much trouble."

"You make a lot of sense," Adam said. "The last thing I want is a thorn in my side."

"Don't forget to ask for an invisible doggie bag," came the interruption.

"Speaking of thorns," Adam said, looking up at the intruder standing by their table. "Don't you have anything better to do, Naomi? Like eating lunch?"

"You're making a huge mistake being seen at an establishment like this with this voodoo priestess," Naomi said, looking at Sage.

Enraged, Adam stood. Before he could say anything, the maître d' came over, gently took Naomi by the elbow, rolled his eyes in a show of solidarity with Sage and Adam, then walked her to her table.

"I am so sorry about that," Adam said. "Voodoo priestess?

Really?"

"She has zero idea who I am or what my store is all about. Every time she sees me, she elevates me to some new, more bizarre status."

Adam was crestfallen. "I just feel so bad. You didn't deserve that at all."

"Hey," Sage said, putting a comforting hand on his. "I'm really fine. I'm quite gruntled actually." She laughed. "The only thing that's going to bring me down is if you feel guilty about something as ridiculous as what Naomi said."

He smiled. "If you put it that way ...."

"I *am* putting it that way." She smiled. "But it's very sweet that you wanted to defend me. Now, tell me what else is on your mind."

❧ ❧ ❧

"I have enjoyed every moment of this," Adam said, taking the leather folder from the waiter. "I can't thank you enough for meeting me, Sage."

"This was nice. I'm so glad you asked me. Thank you for this wonderful lunch."

"I was almost afraid to ask—"

"Don't be," Sage said. "We're friends." She stood. "Will you excuse me while I go to the ladies' room?"

Adam stood. "Absolutely. Oh, look who's coming this way: Molly."

"Hey, there," Molly said. "I saw the she-devil approach you earlier and get ushered away almost immediately. What was that all about?"

"I'm just headed to the ladies' room," Sage said. "I'll tell you there."

Molly laughed and looked at Adam, who had already sat down. "The favorite meeting spot for chatalicious women worldwide."

He smiled.

As the two women walked toward the ladies' room, Molly suddenly put her hand on Sage's arm to stop her from continuing and nodded to indicate the two women huddled together behind the large and leafy potted plant on a stand close to the ladies' room door. Molly put her index finger over her mouth and pulled Sage closer to the opposite side of the plant stand.

"It's lovely to see you, Mildred," Naomi said.

"And you too, Naomi." She took Naomi's hand in hers. "That is an exquisite ring!"

Naomi smiled as she admired her own ring. "Oh, this little bauble. It's a garnet cocktail ring with a diamond halo. I saw it in the window at Wortham Jeweler's and just *had* to have it." She laughed. "Nothing like a sparkling trinket to brighten one's day."

"Well, it looks stunning on you. If I look at it any longer, my eyes will turn green."

"We couldn't have that happen; I'd have to call the paramedics."

"Definitely not. Oh, by the way," Mildred said. "Speaking of things medical, I was just talking to Eleanor Salisbury. She said you were at Swansea Hospital last night and left an extraordinary arrangement of flowers for her daughter. She was surprised because Abigail was only recovering from an outpatient rhinoplasty procedure. She was in a private room because she didn't want to recover around 'other people.'"

"Of course not," Naomi said. "Horrors! I didn't realize she was there for an outpatient procedure. I just heard the nurses mention Abby's name and knew I had to do something special for her."

"How in the world did you get such a fabulous and expensive arrangement so quickly? And why were you at the hospital? Is everything all right?"

"I'll tell you the truth," Naomi said, lowering her voice. "But not a word to anyone. I'd be positively mortified."

From the other side of the plant, Molly and Sage looked at each other, both covering their mouths in delightful anticipation of whatever was to come.

Naomi continued, "An elderly woman, Beatrice, who my foundation has helped in the past, has been ailing. I made the obligatory visit, despite the fact that she's not a person I'd break bread with nor do we have a thing in common. But you know that I never let that get in the way of being charitable."

"Of course not," Mildred assured her. "Charity is in your blood."

"Yes. Indeed it is. Well, the nurse came in with this arrangement and told me that a young businessman in his early thirties had asked that the flowers be given to the oldest woman in the hospital. The nurse placed them on the tray table by Beatrice's bed and left. Knowing that a young vibrant woman like Abigail Salisbury was in the hospital, I didn't see any point in wasting such an arrangement on an old woman who was asleep and probably half blind when she's awake." Naomi smiled smugly. "And it was a perfect opportunity to score some points with the Salisbury family. And … since the flowers were not given by anyone who actually knows that unfortunate woman, I had nothing to lose. And everything to gain."

"You've always been a strategic genius," Mildred said, lightly squeezing Naomi's arm. "I want to be just like you when I grow up. That was brilliant."

Molly motioned to Sage to follow her lead.

"Are you freakin' kidding me?" Molly said loudly, revealing

herself and Sage as they came around the plant. "You took a sick and elderly woman's flowers and gave them to a young socialite getting a freakin' nose job? You are soooo lame and you are so busted."

"Oh, my," Sage said. "I'll have to share this with my fellow voodoo priestesses."

Naomi's tanned face turned a dark red. "Molly Hacker … or whatever your name is now! Don't you think about repeating what you heard, and don't you dare tell that obnoxious sidekick of yours."

"Don't tell her obnoxious sidekick what?" Randy said, walking over to the four women. "I'm sure I have no idea to whom you are referring."

Molly looked at Randy. "It seems after Caleb delivered the flowers to Swansea Hospital, Naomi pinched them from a sick old woman's room to score points with the Salisbury family, whose daughter was in recovery from a nose job."

"Well that's not right," Randy said, feigning shock. "I think we'll need to stop the presses. We've got a new headline."

"You write arts-and-leisure pieces," Naomi snarled. "You have no say in what makes the headlines. You idiotic entertainment writer."

"And this is not entertainment? Is it not about the idiotic?"

"I know the paper well, and you have no say in the headlines. Do I need to repeat that?"

"Don't be so sure, Naomi. Besides, do you think Molly's 'obnoxious sidekick' is averse to reporting a crime or alerting hospital security? Perhaps Mr. Caleb Dunlap will be interested in knowing what happened to his gift."

"You are three horrendous and vile peas in a pod. And Mildred and I will deny we ever had this conversation. You keep your mouths shut. Do you hear me?"

"I'm afraid most people in this restaurant can hear you," Randy said as he saw people from several tables looking in their direction.

"Don't worry," Molly said, gleefully pulling Sage toward the ladies' room. "We wouldn't think of doing anything to 'positively mortify' you."

"Meet you outside, Molly Rose," Randy said. He looked at Naomi, who was snarling at him. "Have a nice day." He winked. "You little headline-grabber, you!"

CHAPTER NINE

"I just *love* instant karma," Godiva said as soon as the last customer had left, and she locked the door. "What a busy afternoon we had. I didn't expect to have to wait until closing to hear what happened at *Le Chat Noir*. The suspense was killing me!"

I'm very glad it didn't," Sage said dryly. "That would have been difficult to explain to the authorities. And then there's the fact that I really like you."

Godiva smiled and put her hand over her heart. "Thank you." She thought for a moment. "When you told me you had a good story about your lunch outing, I wasn't expecting anything as delicious as what you just described," she said as she rounded the counter to sit next to Sage.

"I told you it was a good one."

"Naomi will think twice before she messes with any of you again."

"One would assume," Sage said. "But Molly told me karma has kicked Naomi's butt before, and she always lives to see another day and to fight another round."

"That is true," Godiva said. "I've heard the stories. Hey, who hasn't?" She fiddled with one of her braids. "May I ask you in a non-pushy way if you had a nice time with Adam? I promise not to be obnoxious or overly gleeful." She paused. "I mean that."

Sage laughed. "Good to hear. And yes, it was really nice. I gave him some advice about work-related issues, and then we just talked and laughed for another forty-five minutes. We really do connect. He's a wonderful friend." She paused to gauge Godiva's reaction. "And no, I still don't want to be in a relationship. There, I gave you a freebie. Here's one more. Yes, we're going to continue our morning walks, but that may change a bit once Adam opens Haber Dash. Like perhaps he'll join us for a walk later in the day. Anyway, it's a nice break for both of us."

"Wonderful," Godiva said, getting off her stool and straightening up the counter. "So, tomorrow will be my first Saturday and the end of my first week. Should I expect anything different on the weekend?"

"Perhaps," Sage said, also getting off the stool. "You don't get the people who work in downtown Swansea coming in on their lunch hours or after work. Saturday shoppers tend to browse more leisurely, and we actually get people from other towns coming to Swansea just to shop here."

"Sounds pretty much like the other places in Swansea I've worked. But this place is special."

"On the weird side?" Sage asked with a smile.

"No, silly. Special in the best way possible. I'm thrilled to be working here."

"And I'm every bit as happy about it as you are." Sage glanced at Rufus, who was lying on his mat. "Come on, boy. Walk time."

Rufus got up quickly and came running over to Sage. "Can you lock up for me?" Sage asked Godiva, grabbing the dog's harness and leash. "You know how to do everything, right?"

"I do. Go on. You're in good hands."

"Oh, and one more thing. For the record, I am going to meet

Adam now. Yes, for the second time today."

Godiva smiled. "Not saying a thing."

"Poor guy was at the table paying for our lunch when everything went down. I texted him that I'd meet him at his store after I closed up here." Sage laughed. "I don't want the suspense to kill him either."

❧   ❧   ❧

"I was really angry when Naomi called you a voodoo priestess," Adam said as he and Sage took a seat on a park bench. "Especially after interrupting our lunch for a bully session." He smiled and waved to someone he knew. "But that's a great story. I couldn't have asked for a better outcome. Are Randy and Molly actually going to do anything with the information?"

"No," Sage said, petting Rufus as he settled on the ground. "They're both consummate professionals. But they're really enjoying the fact that Naomi thinks they might."

"Grrr." Rufus watched as two bunnies hopped past him.

"Wufus, good boys don't gwowl at wabbits," Sage said in her best doggie talk. "Pway with Invisible Toto."

Rufus looked up at her as if to say, "You're nuts."

Sage looked at Adam and smiled. "So maybe it's a good thing that dogs don't actually talk."

"They don't?" Adam said with a straight face. "Toto and I chat every day." He laughed. "Hey, speaking of chats, I'm really glad we had that talk at lunch. I was going to call Joanie tonight to not hire her, but she showed up at the store about an hour after I got back. Really took me by surprise. I'm forever grateful that I had time to mull over the situation."

"How did it go?"

"Not well," Adam said. "But that's okay, because it

confirmed the fact that I'd made a good decision. For one, I was right when I said she wanted to get back together. Apparently, friends of hers, two eccentric ones, had told her she was too uptight. She's never been particularly comfortable in her own skin, so she went to therapy to try and morph into someone she's not. I think she was champing at the bit to try out her new-and-improved persona on me."

"Oh my," Sage said.

"She's still the same person she was before, only way more aggressive. And if I said before that she was nice, I take that back. Somehow, she lost that part of herself. Still, I didn't want to hurt her by telling her there was no spark for me. I just felt she was too fragile to hear it. But when I said I couldn't give her a job, she got really personal."

"I see." Sage bit her lip. "You don't have to tell me that part."

"I'd like to," Adam said, looking into her eyes. "Unless it would make you uncomfortable."

"No, not at all," Sage told him. "I just thought it might be uncomfortable for you."

"A week ago, maybe it would have. But not now."

Sage gestured with her hand as if to say, the floor is yours.

Adam leaned down to pet Rufus. "Well, Joanie went right for the jugular. She told me I was weak and I always would be. Her opinion is based on the fact that before she and I dated, albeit briefly, I was seeing a woman, Deborah, a designer, who I thought I really liked. We were dating for about three months when she dumped me, making it clear that she wanted someone with more edge and ambition. Apparently, my dream of opening a store and an animal sanctuary someday was not the least bit sexy to her."

"I'm sorry."

"Don't be," Adam said. "Deb wanted a guy who oozed testosterone out of every pore. She ended up marrying a bar owner who plays acoustic guitar in a heavy metal band, rides a Harley, and drinks too much. So, no, I really wasn't her dream man, and she was more interested in a kind of edge I'll never have and don't want." He sighed. "Anyway, before I ever dated Joanie, after Deb dumped me, Joanie told me that I should have gone after her, fought to get her back, and showed her the macho side of myself."

"That's not you," Sage said. "Never has been."

"Exactly. I don't have a macho side that I keep hidden. What you see is the real deal. I never tried to reconcile with Deb because she made it clear she didn't want to be together anymore. When a woman says no, I back off. Should I have been a bit more like Caleb's been with you? I don't know. Besides, I pretty much lost interest in her after she recited my 'shortcomings.' Not exactly an aphrodisiac, you know? As for Caleb and his aggressiveness in reclaiming your heart, his actions don't exactly seem to have changed your mind."

"Well, they might have," Sage admitted. "If I wasn't seeing a new side of him that I don't like. Maybe I would have wanted him to fight for me. But no, after what I've learned and how he's acted, I'm not interested."

Adam sighed. "Should I have pushed you when you said you don't want to date anyone? Because every instinct I have told me that I need to respect your wishes."

"I can't tell you how much that means to me, Adam. I don't exactly like it when people … men or women … take the attitude that they know what's better for me than I do. I've had way too much of that from Caleb."

"I really did disappear like a wuss when he showed up at your store." He looked at Sage. "Want to walk for a bit?" He looked down. "The natives are getting restless."

"Sure," Sage said. "Rufus, Toto, you heard the man. Up and at 'em."

Adam laughed as he stood. "So funny you should say that. I was sixteen when I figured out that saying. I always thought it was 'up and Adam,' and it never made any sense. In fact, it was just outright weird to hear my name in such an unusual construction."

"Don't feel bad," Sage said. "I never realized that what I heard as 'doggy dog world' was really 'dog-eat-dog world.' I was sixteen when I saw it written down, and I felt like an idiot."

"I thought the same thing," Adam said. "I'm betting there are millions who make the same mistake. Like all of those misheard song lyrics out there."

"Absolutely," Sage said, waving to some customers as they began walking. "And by the way, you weren't a wuss for leaving so quickly when you saw Caleb at my store. But you don't have to be that respectful. What I mean is, you're my friend, and you had every right to be with me. But most especially, to say good-bye."

Adam kicked a stone out of his way. "This is embarrassing to admit, but I have taken the easy way out at times. I hate the idea of being where I'm not wanted, so I tend to disappear before I can feel the sting of rejection."

Sage stopped for a moment. "I feel so bad I rejected you like that when you asked me out."

"You're not ready for a relationship now," Adam said. "You told me the truth. It's funny. With another woman, I might have become as invisible as Toto. But you and I have always had a good rapport, and I wasn't going to throw away a friendship. As much as the old me might have been tempted to do so."

"I'm glad you didn't," Sage said, stopping as Rufus and a French Bulldog performed a reciprocal butt sniff. "And our conversation at lunch was enlightening for me as well. As I told you earlier, you gave me something to think about."

"Which is nothing I should ask you about now," Adam confirmed.

"Exactly," Sage said. "But know that I appreciate your insight and sensitivity more every time I see you."

Sage didn't miss the gleam in Adam's eye that said, "Yes!" Nor did she miss him waving to a stranger, hoping she wouldn't see the huge grin on his face.

CHAPTER TEN

As they sat on the purple barstools behind the counter, Godiva took the lid off her coffee and added two creamers, while Sage let her tea steep for another few minutes.

"You look preoccupied today," Sage said.

"How's that?" Godiva asked with nonchalant elegance.

"Well, you've been here for twenty minutes, and you haven't asked about my non-date with Adam after work last night. Plus, you've got this eyebrow-knitting action in the works that screams to the world — okay, so maybe just to me — that you're engaged in some intense contemplation."

"I'm glad you ratcheted that down a notch. But, whoa. You are sharp as a razor this morning." Godiva took a sip of her coffee. "I'm impressed. I'll bet your parents named you Sage because they knew you'd be wise."

"More like because they've got a hippie vibe going, and they thought it was a cool name. They're different … which is probably why I am too. But they're wonderful down-to-earth people." Sage pulled the string of her tea bag until it was out of the cup, then dunked it again. "And you don't have to tell me a thing. I was just messing with you, because, well, you deserved it." She laughed.

"Okay. You got me. Turnabout is fair play," Godiva said,

smiling. "And actually, your 'non-date' was on my mind, but I spent last night wading through the Freddie swamp. He texted me around eight, and he clearly wanted to come by my house. I had to bite my fingers not to text him back an invitation." She exhaled loudly. "Baby, that man is hard to resist."

"I hope you won't have to resist him much longer," Sage said, taking the tea bag out of the cup and laying it on the saucer.

"I know he's as good as divorced now," Godiva said, "but after all we've been through, when we do get together, I want it to be a true celebration. I need to see those papers. And call me proud, but I need to stick with my plan."

"Any idea how much longer that might be?"

"He expects his divorce will be final any minute. Told me to hold on." Godiva shook her hands as if she were drying them. "I'm holding, but darned if my fingertips aren't sore from grabbing the edge of that cliff."

"Oh my. Look who's coming in." Sage took a quick sip of her tea. "Do you know Barbarino Leighton?"

"Tall lanky Barbie doll with attitude and cash to burn. Got married a couple years ago to Cal Leighton, that dorky billionaire. Oh, yeah, I know her. A regular in the health club. She's got a young teen daughter who used to tag along with her."

Dressed in white skinnies and a white sleeveless shirt, wearing black tie-up stiletto heels, the woman with the flowing blond hair made her grand entrance into Sage Earth Gifts and headed straight to the counter. "What do you have to get rid of people you don't like?"

Sage and Godiva shared a look.

"Well, um, we don't sell weapons here," Sage said.

Barbarino put her hands on her hips. "Do I look like I'm stupid enough to think this is a gun store?"

"Not at all," Sage said, smiling. "I was just wondering if you could elaborate on what you mean by 'get rid of?'"

"Use your temporary lobe, will you?"

Godiva stood and walked around the counter. "Hello, Barbarino. Long time no see. You look as stylish as ever. How about some crystals that ward off negative energy? Black tourmaline is a favorite, but I might also recommend tiger's eye, black onyx—"

"I want a doll that you stick pins into. You know, you zap the pin right where you want a particular dickweed or bimbo to feel the pain."

Sage stood and walked around the counter to join them. "We definitely do not sell voodoo dolls or anything remotely resembling them. I'm sorry."

"That's not what I heard," Barbarino told her.

"Naomi doesn't know what she's talking about," Sage said, looking right at her.

"How did you know—?"

"I'm omniscient," Sage said.

"I don't speak Weirdoese," Barbarino balked. "How about talking in something like, oh, I don't know, English?"

Godiva smiled. "Sage is speaking English. The word she used means 'all knowing.'"

Barbarino huffed. "Then next time, just say that. And for the record, Bimbo Naomi and I are *not* friends. I just overheard her tell my husband that voodoo priestess stuff." She sighed as irritation dripped from her brow. "I don't like the way she looks at him. I don't like her even talking to him. If I had one of those dolls, I'd paste her picture on its face and stab the stuffing right out of her." She seethed.

Sage spoke softly to Godiva. "The enemy of my enemy is my friend." She smiled at Barbarino. "Those crystals Godiva was telling you about are widely known to ward off negativity, though that's nothing we can guarantee. But you can buy them as stones or wear them as jewelry. Other than that, I don't know how to help you."

Barbarino thought, then jumped as the bells on the door clanged. "What the—"

Caleb, dressed in jeans and a gray T-shirt, wearing a face of contrition, walked through the door.

"Hell's bells, those things are loud. They could wake the dead." She looked at Sage. "By the way, Bimbo Naomi said it wouldn't surprise her if you had dead bodies in here. Or ghosts. Oh, yeah. And she said she's planning to shut you down for selling illegal condor's band."

"A condor's band? A group of birds that sing rock? Or like a ring around the leg of a vulture-like bird?"

"If that's what you're selling, she's planning to get you for it."

"Oh, contraband!" Sage said.

"Hello! Knock. Knock. Is anybody home? That's what I just said. And she's got it in for that Adam guy too." Barbarino took a moment to size up Caleb, then turned to Godiva. "Okay, show me those badass rocks. I want one I can wear. Give me something that says, 'I'm a size four and you're not; stay away from my husband or I'll kick your ass,' and 'Bitch, I'm sleek, fleek, and you just reek.'"

"We can most certainly do that," Godiva said as a sparkle danced in her eyes. Without hesitating, she led Barbarino away from Caleb and Sage. "I think you're going to love our selection."

"Caleb," Sage said. "Why are you back again?"

"To apologize for being a jackass. And just so you know, I called the *Herald* on Thursday night after I got home and left an apology voicemail for Randy and Molly. Can we please go upstairs and talk?"

Sage thought for a moment. "Actually, I've been thinking about you too. And I think a talk is in order. But we're not going upstairs. I'd appreciate it if you don't ask again. I have to walk Rufus now, so if you want to join me, we can talk in the park."

"But...."

"That's my final offer, Caleb. Take it or leave it."

"I'll take it. Beggars can't be choosers." He sighed.

Sage walked around behind the counter, pushed the curtains aside, and called for Rufus to come out. He rounded the corner to see who was there. Seeing Caleb, he went back behind the counter and looked at Sage, as if to ask her if a growl was in order.

"I need you to be a good boy," she said, putting on his harness.

"I will, Sage," Caleb said. "I promise. Believe me, I've learned my lesson after making an ass of myself the other night."

"I was talking to Rufus, but yeah, that works." She picked her phone off the counter. "I just have to send a quick text."

Once Sage had texted Adam to let him know she had to postpone their morning walk until the afternoon, she grabbed her sunglasses, then led the way to the door while Godiva still had Barbarino happily engaged in the wonders of black tourmaline.

༄ ༄ ༄

"You look like a movie star in those shades," Caleb told Sage as they walked. "Like a starlet from Hollywood's Golden Age."

"Gag!" Sage stopped walking and stood facing him. "I don't want to have to repeat this, so I'll say it just once. Lose the compliments, okay? They're having the exact opposite effect on me that you're hoping for. I can promise you that."

"But it's so difficult to look at you and not—"

While Sage stood there trying to reason with Caleb, she could not see across the street, where Adam was just about to cross to come meet her. Seeing her with Caleb, he stood and looked, needing to make sure that the bright sunshine was not playing tricks on his eyes. As disappointment swept over his face, he turned and walked back toward his store.

"I'm sorry," Caleb said. "It's alarming how quickly I can go into ass mode when I'm upset."

"Now there's a statement I can get on board with," Sage said as she continued to walk toward the park. "Come on, I need to give Rufus some time to do his thing; then we can find a place to sit and talk privately."

"Sounds like a plan," Caleb said.

Twelve minutes later, after finding the last unoccupied bench that was a suitable distance from Swansea crowd, they sat down. Rufus offered a warning growl to Caleb, then settled on the ground.

"I'm really glad that I'm not the only one who wanted to have a conversation," Caleb said. "I've handled all of this like a first-class jerk. My MBA certainly didn't teach me how to run my own life."

"They don't really have degrees for that," Sage said. "Just the one called 'Live and Learn.'"

"Yeah, don't I know it." He glanced over to see people walking through the park. "I'd forgotten how nice it was to spend weekends in Swansea with you. This park has a Zen vibe on Saturdays. Part of that is probably that I just feel so good not having to wear a suit." He turned back to Sage. "There's so much I want to say."

"I need to go first, Caleb. I hope you'll give me that. After our talk in Coffee & Teaz the other day, I've been going over everything in my mind. Yesterday, something clicked for me that I hadn't been able to put a finger on."

"What's that?"

"Well," she said, taking a deep breath, "laying aside Carrie's Machiavellian endgame, I keep going back to the beginning when she first tried to set us up." She paused to search for the right words. "I remember looking at your photo. I saw this exceptionally good-looking man, well dressed, who has a six-figure job and a great apartment on Manhattan's Upper West Side."

"I'm not sure I follow, Sage. Is there something wrong with that?"

"Not at all. And I don't want this to come out the wrong way, because my self-esteem is just fine. But I couldn't figure why this guy I saw in the photos, and yeah, who I checked out on the Internet, was so eager to meet Sage Gordon from Swansea."

"Because—"

"You need to let me get this out."

"Sorry. Go on," Caleb said.

"Nothing about it made any sense. Like I told you the other day, New York City is filled with amazing women from all walks of life. But Carrie told me this fantastic guy didn't want to know any of them; he just wanted to meet me."

"That's true. I did."

"Good. I want to make sure we're on the same page so far."

"We are," Caleb said. "But I don't see where you're going with this."

Sage exhaled. "I'll make it simple. Why me? Why were you so hell-bent on meeting *me* when you live and work in a city that is a virtual sea of available women."

"Because I was sick of that type."

"What type is that?" Sage asked, her voice heavy with frustration. "Because it would be ludicrous to paint all New York women with the same brush. They're as diverse as can be. I've been going to New York all my life. I have good friends there. I know."

"Well, you've got to remember that the women I work with are all corporate types."

"Really? So every businesswoman who works in New York

has the same basic personality and interests? They're just cookie cutter—"

"You know when I knew I would fall in love with you?" Caleb said. "When you first met me, you told me that you called Randy 'Trubs' for 'trouble' and that you were going to call me 'Corps' as short for 'corporate.' I pointed out to you that it sounded identical to 'corpse' and that wouldn't be the best nickname for a new boyfriend."

"I remember." Sage bent down to calm Rufus, who was overly animated as he watched a squirrel run up and down a nearby tree. "Perhaps that was prophetic of me. Maybe I knew the relationship would die a painful death."

"Oh, Sage."

"Please don't interrupt me, Caleb. You're getting me off track. I can't even remember where I was now."

"You were saying something about New York women not being cookie-cutter something or other."

"Right," Sage said. "Exactly. You're painting the women in your work environment like they're all clones of one another. So, even if you felt that way, your neighborhood, the Upper West Side, is as eclectic as it gets. Why were you hell-bent on meeting someone in Swansea, an hour's trip on a good day, instead of someone more proximate to you? Am I getting through to you at all?"

"Honey," Caleb said, reaching for her hand as she pulled it away. "I don't know where you're trying to go with this, but you're only proving my point. Even in a photograph, I could see something so special about you that it made me forget other women even existed."

"No," Sage said. "You didn't forget other women existed. You stereotyped them out of the equation."

"Yes, but …."

"Do you still think about Amanda?"

"Not if I can help it," Caleb said, his face reddening in anger.

"I'm guessing you think about her all the time."

"Then why the hell do you think I proposed to you?" Caleb said angrily.

Rufus looked up at him. "Grrrrr."

"Sorry, Ruf." Caleb took a moment to regain his composure.

"You don't have to ask me nicely," Sage said. "I'll answer the question."

Caleb sighed. "Good, please do. Because I'm really confused."

"You wanted me because you saw me as the polar opposite of your heiress girlfriend. Instead of taking the time to get over her or to deal with the disgusting way she broke up with you … not to mention the disgusting reason … you overcorrected as quickly as you could. You saw a picture of a free spirit who wears Bohemian dresses, crazy patched jeans, and funky hats, and you couldn't think of a better way to stick it to Amanda."

"That's not fair," Caleb said. "That's complete supposition on your part."

"Carrie told me that you were madly in love with Amanda and that you'd told her a million times that the two of you were destined to be life partners." Sage took off her sunglasses for a moment to remove something that had flown into the corner of her eye, then put them back on. "I know Carrie is a proven liar, but I don't think she was lying about that. Was she?"

"No." Caleb looked down at the heavy gold bracelet on his wrist.

"Oh my God," Sage said. "You're wearing the bracelet she gave you. I can't believe I didn't see it before. You told me you would never wear it again. And now look at you. You've probably been wearing it since we broke up. I didn't notice it the other two times I saw you because you were wearing a suit. Just wow. As my friend Molly likes to say, 'Are you freakin' kidding me?'"

"What can I say," Caleb said. "I really dig the bracelet."

"That's not the only thing you're digging."

"My own grave, you mean?"

"I meant Amanda, but yeah, that does the trick."

Sage shifted on the bench to face him. "Look, Caleb. I'll give you the benefit of the doubt and say maybe you weren't aware of what you were doing, although I think somewhere in your head, you were very aware. But you used me to get over the pain of losing her. That's why you wanted someone who was so different. Only that's not how you mend a broken heart. You don't go from one broken relationship into a brand new one. Especially when you are still crazy in love with the person who dumped you."

Caleb put both of his hands on his head. "You're making my head spin."

"I just thought of something," Sage said. "It makes more sense to me now that Carrie agreed to set us up. Yeah, I know all about the committee she forced you to be on, but she was looking at the bigger picture. She knew where your head was at, and she knew I was nothing but a bar lined with shots to help you get over Amanda. And when she figured I'd helped you to do that, then she'd be there to fill Amanda's designer shoes."

He sat on the bench and laid his head back while he soaked in the sun's rays. He said nothing for several minutes. Finally, he looked at Sage. "You just hit me out of the blue with all of this. I need time to think and I'll get back to you."

Sage stood in unison with Rufus, who was wagging his tail. "I don't want you to 'get back to me.' There's nothing you can say. This never would have worked. I love New York, but I don't want to live there, and you would never have wanted to live here. And your obsession with all things Zen is actually creepy. I'll bet you never used that word once before you met me. It's like you're trying to be someone you think I'll be good with. But it's not working. And the fact that you're wearing that gold bracelet only confirms what I've been thinking." She stopped to catch her breath. "I wish you a happy life, Caleb, but it won't be with me." She smiled and waved to some people she knew as they walked by. "I'm going to leave you here. I'll walk back to the store with my boy."

"Sage, if you'd only give me a day to process all of this."

"You can have the rest of your life to process it. But this is good-bye. And I think it's an excellent good-bye too because we both have a more solid understanding of what really happened."

"You have someone else, don't you?" Caleb snapped. "Nowwww we get to the meat on the bones. This is your way of rationalizing the demise of our relationship so you can fly into some other guy's arms." He grunted. "So, Sage, how does it feel when I analyze *your* motivations? Not a lot of fun, is it? Pot, meet kettle."

Sage looked at Rufus. "Do your thing, boy."

"Grrrrrrr."

CHAPTER ELEVEN

"You'll never believe this," Godiva said as Sage and Rufus came back into the store. She lowered her voice so the nearby customers couldn't hear. "Barbarino bought out the entire collection of black tourmaline jewelry. And, she wanted the stones as well. We're pretty much sold out of black tourmaline, smokey quartz, and ... oh, Sage. Here I am going on, and you look so devastated. What happened with Caleb?"

"I'll tell you later ... after I recover." She removed Rufus's harness, then walked around the counter to hang it on the wall hook, along with his leash.

"Excuse me," one of the customers said. "My sister-in-law wants to know more about vibrational healing with ohm tuning forks. Can you help us?"

"Absolutely," Godiva said with a smile.

"I'll be upstairs with Rufus for an hour," Sage said. "Call if you need me."

Godiva maintained her smile as she went to help the women, but the sadness she felt seeing the pain in Sage's eyes nearly overwhelmed her.

ço   ço   ço

"I'm so glad you shared everything with me, Sage. I wasn't sure if you'd come back down in an hour."

"No way I was going to fall apart in the middle of a workday again. I just went upstairs to talk with my mom. She's been really concerned about me. And Monday, her sister, my aunt Ruth, comes into work. I figured that if I didn't tell my mom what was going on, my aunt might say something to worry her, and I didn't want that to happen."

"Smart thinking. And speaking of smart thinking, everything that you told Caleb is smack on the money. I remember a few days ago when you said you didn't know if he'd gotten over his ex. I didn't know if you were serious or if it was a random thought. But it seems like you've really got a handle on all of this. I'm glad you had a chance to say your piece."

"So why do I feel like such an idiot?" Sage asked her.

"Why do you say that? Heck, girl, you stood up to the man like a champ."

"I did. That's not the part I feel idiotic about. Looking at Caleb now, I'm seeing him in a new light. And I don't like him very much. We really have nothing in common. And I was going to marry this guy! I thought my world had ended when he left."

"Little did you know it was just beginning."

Sage looked at her but said nothing.

"You can't beat yourself up because you realize that a man you thought you loved wasn't what you once believed. Be happy you didn't marry him and spend years learning the lesson. Honey, this is how people evolve. We get sharper and stronger as we endure. And as I told you this morning, you were aptly named."

"I told my mom you said that," Sage said. "It made her happy."

"Good." Godiva reached over for the bowl of engraved

stones and looked through them. She placed three in front of Sage. "Here you go: Trust, Love, Carpe Diem. These can mean whatever we need them to mean. Trust yourself, love yourself, and seize every day."

Sage picked up the love stone and ran her index finger over the word. "I hear you. I just can't understand how I could see the same man with completely different eyes in the space of less than six months. It really blows my mind."

Godiva pick up the "trust" stone. "This means that you have to trust yourself. I don't know about your relationships prior to Caleb. You only told me about that boy you loved as a child … um … the one who was going to give you a jeweled crown when you grew up."

"Jimmy Cole."

"Right. And you said that you didn't know why you were meant to love Jimmy or Caleb so much if neither was meant to be in your life."

"I did say that. And you told me that it was the universe just letting me know that love was possible, and that maybe I was interpreting the message wrong." Sage clutched the "love" stone in her hand. "I guess I needed to go through that to get where I'm going. Wherever that is."

"Exactly," Godiva said. "And you are moving toward love, even if you keep saying you want it to look away from you."

"I do want it to look away," Sage said with conviction. "I haven't changed my mind." She picked up her phone, swiped to unlock it. "Oh, no. I sent Adam a text this morning, to tell him that I needed to postpone our walk until this afternoon." She frowned. "He never texted me back."

"He's opening a store soon. Maybe he just got busy."

"If he was too busy to meet, then he would have texted *me*. But he didn't. And I was so wrapped up in this mess with Caleb that

I didn't even notice he hadn't texted me back. Now, there's no way I can call or text him about walking this afternoon."

"Why not?"

"Because I probably hurt his feelings somehow. If he needs space, I need to give it to him."

Godiva knew better than to say what she was thinking. *This is exactly what love looks like, baby. You're looking right at it, and it's looking at you.*

ço   ço   ço

"How was your walk?" Godiva asked as Sage and Rufus came back around two.

"Uneventful," Sage said. "At least I didn't run into Naomi, so that's a plus. But, I did walk past her friend Mildred and some other woman on the street and overheard them saying that Naomi has taken off for a friend's house in the Hamptons. She's probably mortified with embarrassment after Molly blasted her at *Le Chat Noir* the other day for stealing those flowers at the hospital." She sighed. "The whole town feels a bit lighter, being Naomi-free for a while."

Godiva smiled as a customer laid a silky yellow scarf with a sun design on the counter. "Will this be all?"

The customer smiled and handed her a credit card. Godiva quickly processed the transaction, then returned the woman's card along with a small shopping bag. "Thank you for visiting Sage Earth Gifts." She refocused her attention to Sage. "The Hamptons is the perfect place for a she-devil, as Molly calls her. She can tan in the hot sun and, it will feel just like the flames of home."

They both laughed.

"I'm so grateful you came along when you did," Sage said to Godiva. "I feel like you've been here for years."

"Hey, I'm glad you mentioned that because I wanted to say something to you."

"What's that?"

"Well, when I first told you about Freddie, I explained that I'd quit my job to help him manage the online part of his business, right before our relationship ended."

"I remember."

"So," Godiva said, fiddling with her amazonite pendant, "you might be thinking that once Freddie and I officially reconcile, that I'll be resuming my original plans."

"I did wonder," Sage said. "And I would understand …."

"Don't worry about that," Godiva told her. "Naturally, I'd be happy to help Freddie with something if he needs me. But I don't want to sit behind a desk on a computer all day. And I don't want my livelihood to be wrapped up in my man's business. Not at this stage of my life. Meeting you, working here — well, it's brought me a new kind of joy. It's brought me close to my grandmother again in ways I can't explain. I'm remembering things she taught me that had completely slipped away. It's made me grateful for all of the times I was able to pass on her wisdom to my son, Dylan. I feel like I have a new lease on life; this was all meant to be. I'm happy here, and I know that circumstances brought us together for a reason."

Just as Sage was about to respond, the bells clanged, and an exuberant presence filled the store.

"G'day, ladies!" He looked at Sage. "I'd sure be rapt if you could help me open my third eye. Guess I should take me sunnies off so you can see the problem."

Godiva's face registered surprise while Sage burst out laughing. "Hey, there, Benton." She turned to Godiva. "Benton was here the other day when that customer bought a handful of lapis stones in a desperate attempt to open her husband's third eye."

"Oh," Godiva said. "You had me going there. Oh, look, here

comes the boy. He's absolutely ecstatic."

Wagging his tail, Rufus came out of the back room and rushed over to greet Benton, jumping up to lick his face.

"G'day, fluffy mate!" Benton said, removing his sunglasses and putting them in his shirt pocket. "Sorry I don't have any treats for you." He took a closer look at Rufus. "I'm glad you're stoked to see me, but save that stiffy for the girls, hey."

Sage turned bright red. "Rufus!" She looked at Benton. "I am so embarrassed."

"No drama." He laughed. "Even the best of us can crack a fat at the wrong time."

Godiva tried not to laugh as she grabbed a folder off the counter. "I'm going to take this paperwork into the back room. Call me if you need me."

"Thanks, Godiva." Sage looked at Rufus, who was still greeting Benton. "Down, boy. Go to your mat or your bed. Give Benton a break, okay?"

Rufus looked at her, then at Benton.

"He wants you to counteract my wishes," Sage explained. "He does the same thing when my friend Randy is here."

"Can't go against your mum," Benton told Rufus. He rubbed the dog's neck with both hands. "Go on with you now." He looked at Sage. "My sister has three ankle biters. They're a lot more trouble than dogs, but a good kind of trouble. Guess one day I'll have some of my own."

Sage looked away.

"Sorry, Sage. Hope I didn't say the wrong thing."

"Not at all. My head is just too full. I wish I could just go inside my brain and take out all of the stuff I don't need, you know?"

"Defo. My head's been feeling that way since Freddie and I went to an after-work cocktail thingy in New York last night. Both of us wanted to bail, hey, but it can be that way in business. Worse than seeing rellies you don't like." He noticed the blank look on Sage's face. "Relatives, you know."

"Oh. Of course," Sage said. "So what happened?"

"We rocked up at five, and there were already about thirty people there. As soon as Freddie introduced me, they started swarming around me like mozzies after a summer rain." Benton put his hand up to pretend he was waving away mosquitoes. "This is what you call an 'Aussie salute.' Anyway, fair dinkum, before we left, I counted ten of them who wanted to 'keep in touch.' Yeah, I know the game. They're looking for a place to stay when they come to Oz, but this Aussie bloke isn't running a free hotel and travel service for bludgers."

"Nobody likes to be used," Sage said. "It can really take a toll on you." Her thoughts drifted away to Caleb, but she snapped back as Benton continued to talk.

"I was thinking of that Private Property sign you have up on the wall," Benton said. "I reckon I should hang it around my neck the next time."

Sage and Benton looked at the door as a regular customer walked in. "Hi, Sage," the woman said. "I just need some more essential oils and a crystal salt bar. I know where they are. I'll just snatch them up. I have an impatient husband waiting outside."

The woman quickly grabbed the items she wanted, paid for them with cash, then cheerfully left the store.

"I reckon I just figured out what it's like to hear my Aussie lingo. No clue what essential oils and crystal salt bars are."

Sage laughed. "It's amazing we can even have a conversation."

"Like we're both aliens and our spaceships broke down at the same servo," Benton added.

"I do feel like I'm from another planet some days. You're not as far off as you think. Where exactly in Australia were you born?"

"Not sure," Benton joked. "But I know me mum was with me." His expression turned more serious. "Say, tonight I promised to have dinner with Freddie's rellies. His aunt and uncle. They're headed to Oz for five weeks, all on their own. I offered to give them some travel advice, and they insisted that I bring a guest, their shout … to even things up. How 'bout it? Would you join me?"

"Um …."

"Bloody good then, Sage." He put on his sunglasses. "I'll be back here to pick you up at seven forty-five, if that works. Just going to Marcello's, that nice Italian place just a bee's dick from here." He flashed a huge grin. "See ya later."

Godiva came out from the back room as soon as Benton had left. "Pay no attention to this woman who was behind the curtains," she said with a smile so wide it threatened to break her face.

"I-I can't believe …."

"Believe it," Godiva said. "You've got a date!"

CHAPTER TWELVE

"Freddie's aunt and uncle couldn't have been nicer," Sage said as she waved good-night to the couple she and Benton had just enjoyed a meal with.

"They'll do right well in Straya," Benton said. "Very likeable people, especially for rellies, though I reckon everyone is someone's rellie." He nodded toward the bar. "If you're not too stuffed, care to have an after-dinner drink and a chinwag?"

"I've got room for a drink," Sage said. "I didn't eat that much."

"Oh, sorry, mate. Stuffed where I come from means tired."

She laughed as they walked to the bar. "Oh, good to know. I'd be mortified if you thought I ate too much."

"No drama. Did you see the plate of spag bol I had? Extra grouse, that was. I enjoyed every bite. Didn't mind that homemade bread and the cab sav either."

"Wasn't it all great? My linguine was delicious, too," Sage said. "But the biggest treat was spending time with the three of you. We made for a quirky quartet."

"And now we're a dynamic duo," Benton said. He winked as he pulled out a barstool for her. "What kind of grog do you fancy?"

"I'd like a bit of cognac."

"Right-o then." Benton spoke to the bartender, who had just put two cocktail napkins down in front of them. "Two of your best cognacs."

Sage smiled. "Your stories were so funny, Benton. Especially that one about that nosy neighbor you had when you were twelve. I was in the ladies' room and only caught the tail end. Would you mind telling the story again?"

"Oh, you wanna hear about that rough-as-guts sticky beak from the Banana State. Lived across the street from us. I reckon she had no life of her own. She lived two years in that house, every day in someone else's business but her own: hanging around too long in front of doors, stealing mail, having a natter with anyone who would engage her. As time went on, she got bolder and bolder. Would go to the neighbors' doors and pretend to be doing something or other while pressing her ear up against them. But we finally got her good. Stopped her cold that fateful night she came to our house, we did."

"How did you know she was outside of your door?"

"A neighbor rang my mum. Once we knew she was there, the four of us just started having a crazy row to keep her interested. Dad pretended to be as mad as a cut snake and pissed as a parrot. We kept it going for a good bit; then Mum tiptoed over to the door knowing the sticky beak thought we were all a safe distance away. Mum got into a good pozzy, her hand on the door, ready to go, and waited just a bit longer." He laughed. "Finally, Dad signaled Mum. She ripped open the front door, and the earwig fell right into our lounge room. Bashed her head on the floor and let out a scream like you've never heard. Bloody oath, mate!"

"Did she hurt herself?"

"Blood all over our floor. Dad had to call an ambo." Benton smiled at the bartender as he put their drinks down. "Ace! Cheers, mate!"

"Did she say anything?"

"Every last one of you can get rooted," he said, mimicking her in a crass, smoky voice. "That was right before they carried her away."

"I guess that means what I think it does," Sage said, then took a sip of her drink.

"You betcha." He winked.

"Was she okay?"

"Physically, I reckon she was just fine. But the jig was up. Moved away two weeks later."

"Sounds like you had a wonderful and colorful childhood," Sage said.

Benton's expression changed. "Things were balls-up in the early days. But it got better as I was heading into my teens."

"I don't want to be a sticky …"

"Sticky beak," Benton told her, then tasted his cognac. "And you're not. The day I met you, you said your childhood had some good and bad days too. Guess that's true of most people. It's called life."

"I never asked you. Is this your first trip to America?"

"Second," Benton said. "I take it you've never been to Oz."

"Nope. But I'd sure love to come visit someday."

"And I'd sure love to have you as my guest, unlike those bludgers I met in New York. Looks like your store sees its share of crazy, hey."

"My customers definitely keep things interesting. I never expected I'd see as much wacko stuff as I do. Not in Swansea. But I think my store brings out people's inner freak—plus, people come from all over to shop with me."

"I like to wear my freak on the outside," Benton said. "No surprises for anyone later."

"Are you sure?" She laughed.

"Now that you mention it," he said with a glint in his eye, "I might have a few tucked away."

"I hope so," Sage said, then turned crimson as she chastised herself for the unintentional come-on. "So, um, how did you get into the business you're in?"

"Well, since I was in my teens, I worked in my old man's business. He's in manufacturing. I learned it from the ground up. He wanted me to work with him, but I need to do my own thing. Love animals, I do, so I got this line going." He paused as he looked at Sage. "I'd love to show you our critters in person. Life will never be the same once a quokka smiles at you. We've also got super roos with springs in their feet. Hop right on over you, they will. The bushies call 'em leapsters."

Sage mulled over what he had said, then laughed. "No way on that last part." She hit him playfully on the arm. "How gullible do you think I am?"

"Just checking," Benton said. "You're one smart Sheila. Thought I had you there."

"Well you didn't," Sage said.

"But you took a hairy eyeball to it, didn't you?"

"A what?" She burst out laughing. "You're really proud of yourself, aren't you? I've never been to Australia, but I know kangaroos don't fly over people's heads."

"Well, that's not as far from the truth as you'd think. I hope you'll come see our super roos for yourself," Benton said.

"That would mean the world to me," Sage said. "I'm really having a much-needed and wonderful evening. I feel very comfortable with you. I'm glad I came." She offered a sly smile. "Not that I remember actually accepting your invitation. In fact, I'm quite sure I didn't."

Benton grinned. "No buts about it."

"Oh, really," Sage said, unable to stop herself from flirting.

"That's all you have to say for yourself?"

"When I saw you waiting for me at the appointed time," Benton said, "looking gorgeous as, that kinda said it all."

An hour later, Sage and Benton left Marcello's. Feeling a bit wobbly, she held onto his arm. While he regaled her with another humorous anecdote on the short walk home, she watched his animated face as he spoke. With her gaze only on Benton, she missed Adam, who was standing at the door to her shop, just about ready to slip an envelope under the door. When he saw the two of them, he grabbed the envelope, stuffed it in his pocket, then hurried away.

CHAPTER THIRTEEN

"Godiva! I haven't seen you in two days, and it feels like forever."

"Happy Tuesday, Sage," Godiva said, locking the door behind her as she entered the store. "Did you have a good weekend? I hope you don't mind, but I'm dying to hear about Saturday night with Benton." She put her bag from Coffee & Teaz on the counter. "Freddie texted me on Sunday. He wanted me to know that his aunt and uncle had a great time with the two of you. They're so happy I am working for someone so 'wonderful and charming.'"

"That's so sweet." She blushed. "I'm surprised you and Freddie text so much. You seem more like you'd be phone people."

"Totally," Godiva said. "Which is why I'm *only* allowing him to text. Hearing his sexy voice on the phone, well, one thing can lead to another *thing,* and all of that needs to wait until I see those divorce papers and hold them in my hand."

"You have great willpower," Sage said, laughing. She sat behind the counter and poured hot water into her favorite vintage teacup. "Good for you."

"Got to be that way," Godiva said, walking around the counter to sit next to her. "My self-respect and my sanity depend on it." She pulled out a barstool, then took her coffee and a bran muffin from the bag. "So, tell me, how was Saturday night?"

"I had the best time. Benton's a funny guy," Sage said. "Made us all laugh, and I sure needed it. And by the way, Freddie's aunt and uncle are very witty and way smart."

"Joseph and Kendra Lamar are brilliant, loving people," Godiva said. "They're a bit friendlier than his sister, Sienna, as I'm sure you noticed." She rolled her eyes. "Anyway, I adore them."

"I can see why. We both enjoyed their company immensely." She dunked her tea bag. "After they left, Benton and I went to the bar and had cognac."

"Is that when things took a romantic turn?"

Sage eyeballed Godiva with her best schoolmarm impression. "Did I say anything about that?"

"Nope," Godiva said, opening a creamer to pour into her coffee. "I just thought if it was difficult for you to do so, I might get things started. I can be very helpful that way." She pretended to duck for cover.

"Um, you can be a pain that way," Sage said with a smile. "No romantic turns ... just a lot of laughs. He told me funny stories about his childhood in Australia ... lots of silliness. We had some serious moments too, which were nice, but nothing too intense."

"And when he walked you home?"

"Well, Rufus was waiting for me at the door, so Benton offered to accompany us on our short walk. After that, we hugged and said good-night. And no, there was no thing to lead to another thing." She laughed.

"What a shame," Godiva teased. "That second thing can be so much fun." She broke off a piece of her muffin. "So that was it, Benton-wise, for the rest of the weekend?"

"It was," Sage said. "I went to the Hudson Valley with Rufus to visit my parents. My aunt took care of the cats on Sunday, then again yesterday when she worked in the store with my cousin Robin ... her daughter. I got back around eight thirty last night."

Godiva's expression changed as she took a sip of her coffee.

"Is the coffee bad?" Sage asked. "You have a weird look on your face."

"I just couldn't help but wonder if you and Adam ever made contact after that sort of mix-up you had on Saturday, when you had to cancel your walk after Caleb came by."

Sage lowered her eyes. "No. I really thought he would have texted or called. I thought about it all weekend. It just doesn't make sense that he would be angry over something like that. Adam is such a sweet and understanding guy. And if he never got the text, he would definitely have gotten in touch just to check and see if everything was okay. I just can't figure it out."

"I have an idea," Godiva said.

"What's that?"

"You could call the guy. You know? Quickest way to solve the mystery I can think of."

Sage sighed. "I just feel like he's upset and needs space."

"Maybe he's thinking the same thing about you. Nothing is going to get resolved if you both stay in this deadlock … impasse … or whatever it is."

"I can't think straight," Sage said, then took a sip of her tea. "Oh, look, it's nine fifty-nine. Time to open the store. And the boy needs to go for a walk."

"It's a lonely day, boy," Sage said to Rufus once they were out of the store. Sage did her best to wave to the people who passed her, but the heaviness in her heart made it impossible to smile at them. Once she had walked just a block from the store, she pulled out her phone to see if there had been any texts she might have missed. She sighed heavily and put the phone back into the pocket of her lavender floral prairie dress, then kneeled to give Rufus a loving squeeze.

"I'd sure like one of those hugs if you have another to spare."

"Adam!" she said, looking up. "Invisible Toto!" Making sure not to let Rufus's leash slip from her hand, Sage stood and gave Adam a hug, surprised at the fervor in which she did so and in which the hug was returned.

"I really missed you, Sage."

"I missed you too." She looked down. "You too, Toto." She met Adam's eyes. "Didn't you get my text saying that I had to postpone our walk until Saturday afternoon?"

"Yes, but not right away." He looked sullen. "Is it okay if I join you, and we talk in the park?"

"Of course! I'm so glad I ran into you."

Adam blushed. "Well, that might be less than coincidental."

Sage only smiled, but the light in her eyes said what she could not.

Fifteen minutes later, after Rufus had sniffed his way to the park and finished his business, Sage and Adam settled on their usual bench.

"Is it okay if I go first?" Adam asked.

"Absolutely," she said, petting Rufus on the head until he settled properly.

"This isn't easy for me, Sage." He looked over at the path to see a sixty-something man wearing a gray tweed cap, walking an Irish Wolfhound. "Hello, Mr. Conway; hello, Whiskey!"

Conway waved. "Top of the morning to you, Adam! And to the lovely lass."

Rufus stood on all fours and wagged his tail.

"And to you too, lad," he said. "Looking forward to the new store, Adam. The wife and I will be there for the party."

"Excellent," Adam said, waving as Conway continued on his walk.

"Lie down," Sage said to Rufus, who now had his eye on a Maltese.

"Cute little walking dust mop," Adam said.

"Aren't they?" Sage said, laughing. "I hear they make wonderful pets and are great watchdogs too."

"Interesting," Adam said. "So … before we wile away our time with small talk, I need to apologize."

"Oh, Adam …."

"Please," he said. "Let me get this out before I become hopelessly tongue-tied." He stopped to put his thoughts together. "On Saturday, when you texted, I was in the back opening some deliveries and had left my phone on a table in the main room. When it was time to meet you, I never thought to check for a text or missed call, and I just went on my merry way."

Sage's face dropped. "Oh, no."

"When I saw you headed to the park with Caleb, who looked so happy just to be with you, well, I thought perhaps you were going to give him a second chance." He looked into Sage's eyes. "I'm not going to say that I didn't feel hurt, because I did. And then, I got so angry with myself for acting like a jealous fool when you've made it crystal clear you're not in the market for a new boyfriend. But I thought maybe you had reconsidered taking an old one back."

"I-I just … um … no, definitely not."

"If my head had been on straight, I would have just texted you back, pretended I never saw a thing, and made plans for that afternoon. But no, I sulked like such an idiot. So much that even the contractor working in my store asked me what was wrong. He was concerned I was unhappy with his work. When I told him that wasn't the case, he said, 'Must be a woman then,' and he laughed when the look of mortification on my face affirmed the obvious."

"Oh, Adam. I'm so—"

"Please let me finish," he said. "Or I'll lose my nerve

forever." He glanced at the ground. "Don't interrupt me, Toto. You know this is hard." He smiled. "Toto feels my pain." He smiled awkwardly. "Anyway, after chastising myself all day and into the evening, I decided to write you a note of apology and slip it under the door to your place so you'd find it Sunday morning."

Sage scrunched up her face in pain as she anticipated what was coming.

"So, yeah. It was after eleven, and I had almost reached your store when I saw you walking arm in arm with this good-looking guy. Both of you were laughing, and I realized I hadn't seen you look that happy in a long time. I wasn't going to interrupt what I could see was a wonderful evening for you, so I hurried out of sight, then sulked throughout Sunday. I did pass by the store on Monday, but I saw your aunt and cousin working, so I assumed you were away ... probably with the man I saw Saturday night. And yeah, I know they usually work for you on Mondays, but that didn't stop my mind from taking me on a side trip." He made a fist and pounded his leg. "This is so hard, Sage. I feel like such a jerk. I'm happy to own my flaws, but I'm still embarrassed by this." He exhaled. "Anyway, I'm glad you're happy, even if it's not with me, and because we've been friends for years, I had to let you know what happened and tell you how sorry I am. If you want to stop our walks and keep your distance, I totally get it."

"Can I talk now?" Sage implored him. "Please."

"Sure. I think I've pretty much covered it all. I just left out the gory details. I figured the basics would do it ... no blood and guts."

"You're truly the sweetest man," Sage said. "And no, I certainly do *not* want you to keep your distance from me, and I love that we've been walking together. I was really down when I left the store this morning, thinking I wouldn't see you."

"You were?"

"I was. Why do you think I stopped to hug Rufus in the middle of our walk?" She stopped and twirled a lock of hair around her finger, then let it fall. "First, let me tell you about Caleb. He showed up unannounced on Saturday morning. He wanted to apologize for the ass he made of himself when he stopped by unannounced on Thursday night. Why did he show up? Oh, he needed to chew me out because I hadn't thanked him for that very unwanted and expensive floral arrangement that he'd sent Thursday morning. Aside from Godiva, of course, Molly and Randy were also at the store when he showed up. He acted very uncool … rude would be more accurate … to all of us.

"So, Saturday, he came to apologize. But that was only part of his reason for stopping by. He *still* wanted to make a case for getting back together." Sage gently touched Adam's hand. "It was thanks to something you said over lunch on Friday that made me very eager to talk to him. I'd finally figured out exactly what I needed to say … or, more to the point, what had been nagging at me."

"Really? What was that?"

Sage gulped, as she worried her words might have come out wrong.

"Do you remember when you were telling me all about Joanie — how she was really staid, and there was no spark between you?"

"I remember."

"And then I asked why you dated her in the first place?"

"Sure."

"Well, when you told me that you thought you were overcorrecting for your previous girlfriend … um …."

"Tammy," Adam said.

"Right, Tammy. You were saying how wild she was and that she just wasn't growing out of her crazy ways."

"Last time I ran into her, she was a mess," Adam said. "And from what I hear, she's content being that way. But yeah, I have no doubt that being with Tammy led me straight to Joanie, as short-lived as our relationship was."

"Right. Well, I realized at that moment that Caleb had wanted to date me because he was overcorrecting in an entirely different way. It was suddenly crystal clear that he wanted me because I'm the antithesis of his heiress ex, Amanda. And all of a sudden, it dawned on me how he was focused on everything about me that he saw as different from her, like the things I sell in my store, but not so much on who I really am. That was a major revelation to me."

"Wow," Adam said. "Glad I could unintentionally help."

"You did," Sage told him. "In a big way. Your self-awareness led to my own. As soon as you said that, a light went on in my head. I thought about it all night and the next day. So, when Caleb showed up and wanted to talk, I was all too happy to engage him and let him know that everything finally made sense to me."

"What did he say? If I may ask?"

"He listened," Sage said. "Then he decided to turn the tables on me. Said I was rationalizing everything so I could fly into another guy's arms without guilt."

"Saturday-night guy," Adam said.

"Nooo!" Sage said. "He wasn't specifying, and he knows nothing about him."

Rufus stood and let out a low growl at a gold-colored terrier mix that was barking loudly at him. The owner apologized as she hurried away with her dog. Still obsessed with Rufus, the dog turned and craned his neck to get in some last looks and an emphatic last bark.

"Grrrrrr."

"That wasn't your fault," she said to Rufus. "But be a good

boy for Mommy. This isn't easy." She turned to Adam. "Nothing like another good distraction to derail an awkward conversation. So … moving right along. The man you saw me with is Benton. He's from Australia. He lives in Melbourne and has a small farm in a more rural area. He's staying … temporarily … in the guesthouse at Freddie Lamar's place. They're working together on a line of clothing."

"I know Freddie," Adam said. "Godiva's ex. Really a good man."

"So I hear. Anyway, he's soon to be her current again, but that's another story."

"Actually, I do know about Benton," Adam said. "I'm going to sell some of the clothing line he and Freddie are working on. Just never saw the guy. I had no idea you knew him."

"Benton's been in the store a couple of times," Sage explained. "I haven't known him long at all. When he came in Saturday, he asked me if I'd go to Marcello's with him for dinner. Freddie's aunt and uncle, Joseph and Kendra, are taking an extended trip to Australia, and they wanted to meet Benton. They asked him to bring someone along, and well, it was sort of last minute, but he invited yours truly."

"Oh."

"We had a couple of glasses of wine at dinner; then Benton and I stayed and had some cognac at the bar. It was a bit more than I'm used to drinking, so I was holding his arm on the way home. He's a funny guy, especially with all of his crazy Aussie slang that I have to constantly decipher, but he's not my boyfriend. I did have a good time with him, though. And I had a wonderful time with you at *Le Chat Noir*."

"I liked seeing you laugh," Adam said. "I just wish I'd been the man on your arm."

"You make me laugh all the time, Adam. And I feel so

comfortable with you. And it's not only because we've known each other a long time. Just the time we've spent together this past week has been special. You're one of the most genuine human beings I've ever known."

"That's exactly how I feel about you, Sage. That and so much more." He stood and reached for her hand to help her up. "Are you okay with our friendship, knowing how I feel?"

"I am," she said, taking his hand.

He smiled. "This has turned out to be a much better day than I anticipated. Let's just hope we don't run into you-know-who on the way back."

"I'll make it an even better day for you," Sage told him. "Naomi went to the Hamptons to escape her public humiliation at the restaurant. There's still lots of summer left, so let's hope she stays for a very long time."

"Ah, wonderful. I'll have to get Toto a bone to chew on, now that I know Naomi and her legs are out of town."

"Too bad she can't always be as invisible as Toto," Sage said. "And that Toto can't come to life."

CHAPTER FOURTEEN

"Welcome to Sage Earth Gifts," Godiva said to the forty-something-year-old woman wearing a gray business suit and pink plaid shirt. "My name is Godiva. If I can help you with anything, just ask."

Sage looked up from the jewelry she was arranging in the display case on the wall and smiled at the customer.

"Actually," the woman said. "You can. I feel kind of silly about this, but well, here goes. I've been divorced for six years, and tonight I have a date with the first man I've really liked since I split with my husband. I've invited him over for dinner. This morning, on my way to work, I was listening to the oldies station in the car. When I heard that song 'Love Potion Number 9,' it got me thinking. I know this sounds totally nuts, but I wondered if you might actually have something here that resembles a love potion."

Godiva's face went blank.

"Well, we certainly don't have anything that a person would ingest," Sage said, closing the display case and locking it, "but we do have a love spray. You could just enhance a room or two with it."

"Oh! That's intriguing. What's in it?"

Sage walked over to a nearby shelf, reached up, and grabbed a bottle. "Rose geranium, Neroli ... here, take a look."

The woman took the bottle from Sage. "To bring in

compassion, love, and romance. I wonder if works. Does it smell good?"

With her back to the door, Sage didn't bother to look when she heard the bells clang, and continued to wait on woman. "I have a tester bottle of the love spray here. How about we give it a try?"

"Oh, please!"

Sage swapped the bottle for the tester and spritzed a small bit into the air. She did not see that Benton, dressed in lightweight khaki pants, with a black linen shirt that had three buttons undone, was watching the scene unfold.

"Love is in the air! Literally!" Benton said to Sage, removing his sunglasses and putting them on the counter, along with a bag he was carrying. "And you are the most beautiful Sheila I've seen in years. My ticker is beating like crazy. No question about it!" He walked up to Sage and grabbed her, then planted a slow, delicious kiss on her lips.

Godiva and the customer just looked at one other while Benton held Sage close and gazed into her eyes once the kiss had finished. Seconds later, Rufus came barreling into the room and jumped ecstatically onto Benton.

"I'll take two bottles," the woman said to Godiva. She lowered her voice and nodded toward Benton. "Heck, if he was available, I'd take him too."

᧞ ᧞ ᧞

Godiva quickly rang up the woman's purchase and put the two bottles in a gift bag. "Thanks for shopping at Sage Earth Gifts," she said as the women left the store with a smile. She looked at Sage and Benton. "I'll be in the back room."

Benton laughed. "I didn't even get to say g'day, Godiva. Hmm. That has a nice ring to it."

Godiva stopped. "G'day to you too, honey," she said, grinning at the still-stunned expression on Sage's face. She looked at Rufus. "Come on, boy. Into the back room with your auntie Diva."

Once Godiva and Rufus disappeared behind the curtains, Benton took a good look at Sage. "You look kind of gobsmacked, Sage. I hope I didn't upset you with that pash. I wanted to give that to you on Saturday night, but you kind of hurried inside."

"Yeah, I guess I did."

"You don't mind giving a bloke a fair go, do ya?"

Sage swallowed uncomfortably. "That was a really nice kiss. I haven't had one in a long time. But I'm not in the market to kiss anyone now. Can you understand that, Benton?" She looked at him, devoid of expression. "You know, we kind of talked about this. I'm not ready for love. I wouldn't have shared that with you if I wasn't serious."

"Sorry, Sage. I really am. I didn't want to disrespect your wishes. I mean that. I did hear you, but I thought maybe it was just the pain talking … and that was very wrong of me. But when I came in just now, well, it seemed like the perfect time to kiss you, with that love spray in the air. My ego gave me a bum steer, and I'm sorry." He smiled warmly. "Still mates?"

"Of course," Sage said.

He winked. "If things don't work out with my clothing line, I could always sell love spray, hey."

She laughed. "You're very good at that, for sure. But I really do think your line will take off."

"I'm feeling good about it." He walked over to the counter and grabbed his sunglasses and put them in his shirt pocket. Then, he reached into the bag he'd brought and handed a stuffed koala toy to Sage. "Hope you like this little fella. The red jumper he's wearing is a miniature version of the one I'll be selling. See the embroidered koala on his sleeve? That's our logo."

"Beautiful." Sage hugged the koala. "He is absolutely adorable! I love him so much. Thank you. Did you bring a lot of these koalas with you? Are these for special customers?"

"Just brought the one," Benton said. "Had a feeling I'd find a home for him in America."

"He'll be happy with me; I promise."

Benton walked over to Sage and gently led her toward the front of the store. When they were close to the window, he spoke softly. "One of the reasons I came by is because Freddie asked me to. He's planning to come by around six with a surprise for Godiva, but he wanted to make sure he doesn't do anything that will interfere with her job. Is it okay to give him the green light?"

"Absolutely. And we don't close until seven, but tell Freddie he can whisk her out of here as long as she wants to be whisked."

"She looks quite whiskable to me," Benton said.

"I think she is," Sage said. "And tell Freddie I can't wait to officially meet him. He was on his way into the store the first day I saw him, but Godiva rushed outside, and we never got to meet. We only waved at one another through the front window."

"I will. I've got some bizzo with him in an hour, so I'll get out of your way. Sorry again about that pash, Sage."

"We're good," she said. "And thanks for the koala."

"He's true-blue. You going to call him Benton?"

"Nope. I want to name him Jimmy. After a childhood friend who was … and is … still very special to me."

Benton stopped and looked into her eyes. "Very sweet. I like that. Sounds like an even better name for this little mate. See ya soon."

☙ ☙ ☙

"Whew!" Godiva said, looking through the bins of crystals. "It's five forty-five already. That day flew by. I think that love spray is more powerful than I thought. We sold a ton of rose quartz, not to mention several pieces of rose-quartz jewelry. My grandmother always told me, 'There's power in the stones.'"

"It did get crazy busy," Sage said, glancing over at Rufus who was lying on his mat. "Maybe it *was* the spray. Look. The boy is exhausted from greeting all of those people and spreading the love."

Godiva checked the last of the bins, then walked over to the counter, where Sage was doing some paperwork. "You look so down. You shouldn't be. You made up with Adam, and you got a kiss from a gorgeous hunk ... even if you didn't want it."

"That's exactly the problem, Godiva. I'm just so confused about everything," Sage said. "What's with Rufus? He's suddenly not looking so tired anymore."

Rufus jumped up from the mat and ran to the door. Within seconds, Randy came bursting in the door, wearing a top hat, and Rufus wasted no time in jumping up to show his affection and get some in return.

Randy smiled broadly, then burst into song: "Hey there, Sage, no need to grouse; Randy Goodrich is in the house. With all his charm, the store will be lit ..."

Sage watched with surprise. "And Randy Goodrich is full of ... it."

"Don't you curse and don't you frown; I hear Naomi ... is out of town. I'll make you smile; I'll make you laugh; I'll even give you ... my autograph. I know you don't sell anything voo-dah, but I'm here to buy ... Kyle that Buddha. Come here, my friend, I must be kissed; from lovely Sage who my heart has missed ...."

"You had me at that top hat," Sage said, hurrying around the counter to get her customary two kisses and a hug. "Where in the world did you get that?"

"From an interview I did at Alice Tully Hall in New York

years ago. It's a long story, but I was gifted this hat because of my grace and charm."

"Not for your songwriting abilities?" Sage said, laughing.

Randy made a face. "Darling, did you just hear my impromptu song? What do you think? And don't you dare answer that."

Sage looked down at Rufus, who was still begging for affection. "I think he's upset the song wasn't for him."

"I can remedy that," Randy said. He began dancing around Rufus and Sage.

"Ruf's a dog who's fine and dandy, and his best friend is a star named Randy. The Ruf protects his mommy Sage-O, when unscrupulous peeps cause her to rage, oh!" He slapped the palm of his hand against his heart for dramatic effect.

The bells clanged, the door opened, and in walked Freddie, wearing a tuxedo, holding a large envelope, and laughing heartily. "I don't know what's going on here, but don't let me stop you, brother."

Godiva gasped and put her hand over her mouth, her eyes twinkling as she saw Freddie standing there in gorgeous splendor.

Randy, not missing a beat, kept singing. "Freddie's here; he has arrived-ah, for his true love, La-dee Godiva." He looked at Freddie. "And he has got, wonderful timing, 'cause it's tough sometimes, always rhyming … interrupt Randy any time."

"Yeah," Godiva said as tears pooled in her eyes. "Interrupt Randy."

"Okay. But I really was enjoying the show," Freddie said. He hugged Godiva, who was now standing in front of him. When they pulled apart, he handed her the envelope. "Take a look inside, baby."

Tears now streaming down her face, Godiva opened the large manila envelope and pulled out a letter and a certificate. Her eyes scanned them quickly. "Oh, Freddie, it's really official. You're free and clear!"

"I have been for years," Freddie said, "but now it's legal."

"I'm so happy. And why are you looking so fine in this tux?"

Freddie nodded for Godiva to look out the window.

"Is that your limousine? I mean, did you rent that exquisite vehicle?"

"You don't think I would take my woman into New York, for what promises to be a very special evening, wearing anything less and being driven in anything less, do you?" He kissed her softly on the lips. "You know me better than that, baby girl."

Randy waved his hand up and down to mock fan himself while Sage and Rufus looked on.

"We're going into New York?"

"We are, Diva," Freddie said. "We definitely got our thing together."

Godiva put her hand to her throat, then turned to Sage. "He knows that Barry White thing makes me crazy."

"Randy can certainly empathize, darling." He looked at Freddie. "You do have Mr. White's voice down well. Your own voice isn't too far off."

"Never ever gonna give her up," Freddie said to Randy. He looked into Godiva's eyes while his hand stroked the side of her face. "Now, that limo driver is going to take you home to do whatever you need to do in preparation for the best night of your life. But you only have forty-five minutes; we've got a reservation for a very special table."

Godiva, still in shock, looked at Sage.

Sage laughed. "Get out of here. And don't worry; Freddie already alerted me. His Australian envoy came in here for a couple of reasons."

"You sent Benton in to ask Sage if I could leave early?"

Freddie looked at his watch. "Time's a wasting, baby."

Sage went behind the counter, grabbed Godiva's purse and handed it to her. "Here you go. And you were right; that love spray really works. So do the crystals."

Freddie extended his hand to Sage. "It's wonderful to meet you. I've heard nothing but exceptional things about you from both Godiva and Benton. And Randy, of course." He looked over at the koala sitting on the counter. "So Benton came bearing gifts, I see."

"He did," Sage said. "Possibly one too many."

Freddie wrinkled his brow.

"Forget I said that," Sage told him. "Have a wonderful time. I look forward to getting to know you … another time." She managed a laugh, then looked at Godiva. "Go on, get out now. Your chariot awaits."

Godiva looked up. "You were right, Grandma. About everything. I love you." Her face streaked with tears, Godiva hugged Randy, then Sage, then gave Rufus a scratch on the neck. "Bye, y'all. See you tomorrow. And thank you, Sage, for everything."

Randy and Sage watched them leave the store, then as Freddie opened the limousine door.

"Love is the beating heart of life," Randy said, taking Sage's hand and giving it a kiss. "You keep saying you want love to look away, but tell me, is there anything more beautiful than what you just saw?"

"No," Sage said, choking up. "I don't think so." She looked at Rufus. "Go lie down, boy."

"And what do you have to say to Randy?" he asked her.

"Um, let's look at the Buddha statues and pick out the perfect one for Kyle."

"Girlfriend," Randy said as he shook his head in dismay. "Sigh, sigh, me oh my. We've got some serious work to do."

CHAPTER FIFTEEN

Sage rushed to the door when she saw Godiva fumbling for her key on the other side. She quickly unlocked the door and gave her a hug. "Wow, you look positively radiant. You're glowing, and I don't think it's because of that full moon we're going to have tonight."

Godiva held up her left hand. "Isn't it beautiful?"

Sage held Godiva's hand in hers. "Blue zircon and diamonds. I love swirl rings. Absolutely exquisite! Freddie's taste in rings is as good as it is in women. Congratulations, you! I want to hear whatever you want to tell me. We still have time to chat before the store opens."

As Sage locked the door, Godiva put her purse behind the counter. "I can't believe it."

"What?" Sage asked, walking behind the counter to join her. "That Freddie was going to propose? You knew that was going to happen. Even Rufus knew that would happen."

"No, not that." Godiva laughed as Rufus bounded over to greet her. "I was so excited to show you my ring that I forgot to buy my coffee."

"I'm not sure you need it. You look electrified. Did you get much sleep?"

Godiva's smiled wickedly. "Well …."

Sage put her palm up. "I didn't ask that question. You're hearing things. I didn't say a word, and that being the case … or not, I think you're definitely going to need some coffee. I'll give the shop a call. They'll deliver. Do you want a muffin with it?"

"Kind of had a muffin when I got up." Godiva grinned.

"I didn't hear that either," Sage said. "Let me ask a different question. Would you like anything with your coffee?"

"A large coffee, some cream, and a toasted cinnamon raisin bagel."

Godiva picked up the landline behind the counter. "I shall place your order, madam."

As Sage called the coffee shop, Godiva kneeled to show Rufus her ring. "How do you like it, boy? Isn't it the most beautiful ring you ever saw?"

"Your order will be here in six minutes," Sage said. "When John heard it was for you, he said he'd be right over."

"Thank you," Godiva said, petting Rufus one more time before she stood. "Oh, Sage, I'm so sorry!"

"What in the world for?"

"What I just said to Rufus?"

"About your ring?"

"I wasn't even thinking. Here I am … over the full moon, and I didn't even think about the fact that you are coming off of a broken engagement." Godiva plunked down into the barstool.

"I'm really okay with that," Sage said, heating up her electric teapot. "I'm not in a good headspace regarding love, but I'm so glad I'm not going to make the mistake of marrying Caleb Dunlap." She looked at Godiva's ring. "As I told you, his ex broke up with him, via text, because the expensive rings he was looking at weren't nearly as pricey as she wanted. And it just occurred to me … the ring he bought for me was a fraction of what he planned to spend on her. That's another way that he overcorrected: he bought me a cheap ring because he knows that I'm not laser focused on things like that. But you know what?—it was a nothing ring because his heart wasn't in it, not because of what he paid for it. And that's what matters to me. I can't believe how clearly I can see everything now." She sighed. "So yes, your ring truly is the most beautiful engagement ring I've ever seen. And Freddie's face said it all when he walked in here. He's madly in love with you."

"I've never been happier in my life," Godiva said. "And as much as I want this kind of happiness for you, I'm really going to make an effort not to be so obnoxious about it."

Sage smiled. "It's all good. So, to ask the obvious question, do you know when you're going to get married?"

"We talked about spring. Neither of us had prior matrimonial situations that meant much, so this is like a true first marriage for both of us. We don't want to do anything over the top, but Freddie wants it to be a really special day that our friends and family can celebrate with us." She looked through the window, grabbed her purse, and hopped off the barstool. "My coffee and bagel have arrived."

As Godiva went to get her coffee, Sage heard a notification sound on her phone. She picked it up, looked at the message, and quickly texted back. The second she put the phone down, she saw Godiva looking at her. "Don't even think about—"

"I'm not asking," Godiva said, rounding the counter to take her seat again.

"That's good," Sage said as she poured hot water into her teacup. "But I'll tell you anyway so you don't have to wonder. Your thoughts are so loud that they puncture my eardrums."

Godiva pulled her coffee and bagel out of the bag and put them on the counter. "That bad, huh?"

"The worst," Sage said. "Anyway, that was Adam. He can't meet me this morning because he's got to go somewhere. He wants to walk later and share something very special with me."

"Intriguing," Godiva said. "I can hardly wait."

Sage laughed. "Drink your coffee, woman! Or you won't be awake long enough to find out, and I'll have to cancel because you won't be here to watch the store."

ೞ   ೞ   ೞ

"You need some Hollywood?" Godiva repeated back to the tall bearded man sporting a Nehru jacket.

"Holy wood," he mumbled. "Palo Alto."

Sage stopped what she was doing and walked over to the man when she saw Godiva's confused face. "Palo Alto is a city in Northern California. You must mean Palo Santo, which grows on a mystical tree on the coast of South America."

"I don't care if it grows in Swansea Square."

"I see," Sage said delicately. "Well, if you follow me to the wall, I can show you the different forms it comes in, and you can choose what's best for you."

"Just give me one of each. Quickly."

Sage made a point not to make eye contact with Godiva while she walked over to the wall and grabbed several different bags of the wood from the hooks.

"I'll take it from here," Godiva said as Sage put everything on the counter. "Will that be cash or charge?"

The man reached into his pockets and pulled out several crumpled bills. "Take what you need and be quick."

Godiva processed the transaction and handed the man a gift bag. "I hope you … uh, thank you for shopping at Sage Earth Gifts."

He looked at her. "Can't exactly get this anywhere else now, can I? Not like I had a choice."

He grabbed the bag and headed out the door.

"Well, wasn't he special," Godiva said, once he was gone. "Forget the holy wood. Holy full moon over Swansea! Have you ever seen him before?"

"I think," Sage said, "that he unloads trucks late at night for the supermarket. I've actually never seen him before, but I've heard him described. He only wears Nehru jackets, baseball tees, or flannel shirts. Go figure, because I can't. I don't want to, either."

"No. Me either. Too weird," Godiva said. "Speaking of strange people who I've never seen before, check out this woman coming in."

They both saw a Goth-looking woman with a long nose, sunglasses, and black hair down her back. She had black lipstick and wore a long, black cotton dress that came down to her ankles.

"Welcome to Sage Earth Gifts," Godiva said. "I'm Godiva, and I'm happy to help you if you have any questions."

Expressionless, the woman grunted, then walked past them both. For a half hour, she examined every product in the store, picking up objects to see them at every angle, peering into the display cases as if she were taking in every last piece of jewelry or crystals with her eyes. She spent ten minutes reading the spines of the books, then moved on the CDs. After a good half hour, she motioned to Godiva that she was interested in something from one of the display cases. "What's that?" she said, her gruff voice causing Godiva to shiver.

Godiva opened the case. "This," she said, picking up the object. "It's called a phurpa. You can read the card if you want. It's a Tibetan tool that some people refer to as a magic dart. Or a ritual knife." She looked at the woman, who averted her gaze. "There's more on the card."

"I'll take it," the woman rasped out. "Put it on the counter. I'm still looking."

"As you wish," Godiva said, walking away. She stood by

Sage, who was rearranging jewelry in the counter display, and softly whispered, "Did anything happen while I was in New York for the night that you forgot to tell me? Like an apocalypse."

Sage, noticing the woman was watching her, suppressed a laugh. "Could be."

The woman kept browsing for another ten minutes until she found a display of mortar and pestles on a lower shelf. She motioned for Godiva to come over again. "What's this?" she asked, picking up a mini cauldron.

"Well, it's really got many uses. Of course, it's made to look like a cauldron, but you can burn cone incense in here, mix herbs, or use it as a little jewelry box."

"I'll take it."

"Do you want me to put it on the counter with the phurpa?"

The woman nodded, then walked away to examine more items with intense concentration. After another ten minutes, she pointed to a glass charm with a blue cord, hanging on a wall hook.

Godiva, seeing that the woman was about to summon her, walked over to see what she wanted.

"What's this?" the gruff voice asked.

"This is an evil-eye charm."

"Hmm. What does it do?"

"Well, it's a curse or a legend, and it's believed to be cast by a malevolent glare. Gee, it's hard to explain."

Sage walked over to the woman. "It's usually given to people when they are unaware. But the eye also protects you from evil. I have literature that can explain it to you. We have necklaces and bracelets too."

"Just that," the woman mumbled, pointing to the large glass charm. "Those three things."

"Okeydokey, then," Godiva said. "I'll ring you up." She walked behind the counter and rang up the items while the woman dug into a large black hobo bag she was carrying. Pulling out brand new bills, she laid them down on the counter. Godiva counted the money, gave her change, then handed her a shopping bag. As she did, she noticed that there were now three other customers in the store, and they were all staring at the odd customer. "Thank you for shopping at Sage Earth Gifts," Godiva said cheerfully.

The woman grabbed the bag, lowered her head, and hurried out the door.

"She was lovely," Sage said. "I'll have to invite her for tea some time."

Godiva took several deep breaths. "She totally weirded me out. And just for the record, I've never said 'okeydokey' in my life. That was like an out-of-body experience. You okay? You look like you're in a trance or something. Hope she didn't cast a spell on you."

"No, silly," Sage said. "I'm just wondering what Adam's surprise is."

❧　　❧　　❧

"Are you freakin' kidding me?" Molly said as she walked into the store only moments after the Goth woman had left. "Seriously, what was *that*?"

"She's different," Godiva said. She gave Molly a hug. "Very different."

"I don't even want to know what her orbs look like behind those dark sunglasses. And I don't know what she bought here, but the stuff was heavy, and she 'accidentally' whacked me in the knees with her bag."

"Hey, Molly," Sage said, coming around the counter to give her a hug. "It might have been the cast-iron mini cauldron or the Tibetan knife. I doubt the evil-eye charm would do any damage."

"I'm not so sure of that. Like I said, two of them were looking at me behind the sunglasses, and now you tell me there was one in the bag. That's reassuring ... not! Cast-iron cauldron? Tibetan knife?"

"It sounds weirder than it is," Sage told her. "Her choices were—"

"Special," Godiva said. "There *is* a full moon out tonight. And I guess the store might be a magnet for those who choose the path less traveled, but in the best way possible."

"This store has always represented love, peace, and tranquility to me," Molly said. "And speaking of love, that's why I'm here. Randy may have told me something special happened last night and oh ... I see there's a stunning ring on your finger."

Godiva held up her left hand. "I love it. But it pales in comparison to the words Freddie spoke when he gave it to me."

"Congratulations!" Molly said, giving her another hug. "I'm so happy for you both. And this ring is exceptional. Honestly, if I just passed you on the street and didn't know you, this stunner of a ring would catch my eye."

"Molly Rose does like colorful rings," Randy said, coming through the door with a smile. "She can spot one a mile away. Zingy dingy ring radar, I call it. Let Randy see!"

Before Randy could look at Godiva's ring, Rufus came bounding out from the back, filled with love.

"Zingy dingy ring radar?" Molly repeated. She looked at Godiva and Sage. "He just made that up. I promise you, if I'd heard that before, well, let's just say it would be quickly banished from Randy's book of clever catchphrases."

"Well I think it has a zingy ding ring to it," Randy said, kneeling to show some love to Rufus. Randy stood, turned to Godiva, and took her hand in his. "Oh, my. Mr. Lamar has outdone himself. He is a man of impeccable taste." He smiled. "And the ring is lovely too."

"How sweet of you, Randy," Godiva said. "Thank you all for your beautiful words."

Molly turned to Randy. "Truth time: we do have to get back to work."

"Indeed, alas, we do. But I interrupt this gathering for some additional truth. Randy is a bit shaken. A strange creature in black, with a long nose unlike anything I've ever seen, passed me on the way here, and I must say, an odd need to purify every fiber of my being is, to say the least, overwhelming."

"At least she didn't hit you in the knees with her freakin' bag," Molly said.

"No, she didn't!" Randy said to Molly, his hand on his chest. "Oh, Molly Rose, I'm sorry to hear that happened."

Godiva turned to Sage. "She was the first customer I've ever given a logo-free bag to!"

"Smart thinking," Sage said. "Thank you."

"I have an idea," Godiva said. "That love spray worked miracles yesterday. Maybe some of the white-sage spray would help Randy's purification desires."

Molly laughed. "Careful, Godiva. You're sounding a lot like Randy."

"Miss Jones, soon-to-be Mrs. Lamar, could do a lot worse."

Everyone laughed as Sage reached for the white-sage spray tester bottle on the shelf. "Tell you what, Trubs, I'm just going to spray a bit into the room to purify the energy. Next, we all just need to fan ourselves with the mist, and that will cleanse our personal energy field."

"Great," Molly said, "and if that doesn't work, I'll go to my parents' house and borrow my dad's bowling ball. No doubt a twelve-pound swing into *her* knees will make us all feel much better."

CHAPTER SIXTEEN

"Oh, my goodness!" Sage said as she and Rufus ran down the street to meet Adam. "I can't believe my eyes!"

Adam, smiling broadly, stood on the corner, holding a leash with a flesh-and-blood dog at the other end of it.

"When you said you had a surprise," Sage exclaimed, "I never in a million years thought it would be a visible dog."

They both watched with joy as Rufus and Adam's dog sniffed both ends of one another, then began playing.

"I'm full of surprises," Adam said.

Sage looked down at the dogs. "Toto, you have a new ...." She peeked at the dog's undercarriage. "... sister!"

"Meet Vizzy," Adam told her. "It's short for 'visible,' but the whole world doesn't need to know that." He nodded toward the park. "Shall we?"

"You told me you were going to wait," Sage said as both dogs stopped to investigate the same tree.

"Believe me," Adam said. "That was my intention. But when I left you yesterday, you said something about it being too bad Naomi wouldn't stay invisible, and if only Toto would come to life."

"I did," Sage said as they continued to walk.

"I had zero intentions of getting a dog now, but what you

said made me want to go to the pound, visit with the dogs, make a donation, and just spread some cheer." They stopped at the light and Adam paused. "I'll tell you what happened as soon as we cross."

A minute later, they began walking into the park. "So," Adam continued, "I had only gotten as far as the reception area in the pound, when I saw this woman in there with Vizzy. Her name is Lulu, and she was crying her eyes out. Her mother had just died suddenly, and she was grief-stricken. Adding to her pain, Lulu lives in London and couldn't take her beloved mother's dog home with her. It was heartbreaking."

"Oh, that's so sad."

"Turns out Vizzy is only a year old, and she's fully trained. And when I saw she was a Cairn Terrier, just like Toto, well, it was like, I really believed that you and the universe led me to get her." Adam began to tear up. "I don't know what came over me, but I didn't even think about it. I just told Lulu who I was and that I was looking for a dog exactly like this one. I invited her to ask around town about me or look me up online, and promised her that the dog would have the best life I could give her."

"I'm going to cry," Sage said as Rufus and Vizzy stopped to fake psych each other out, their tails wagging.

"As luck would have it, the receptionist at the pound, Kathleen, remembered me from Jameson and then asked about my new store. She told Lulu I was very well known and respected in Swansea."

"How fortuitous!"

"It was. I gave Kathleen the lowdown, invited her to the pre-opening party, and assured Lulu that any dog I adopted would be with me all day at Haber Dash and not left home alone."

"That must have been so bittersweet for her to hear."

"It was. She said I would be the perfect dad for her mom's dog, and just asked that we exchange names, numbers, and email addresses, and that I promise to send photos now and again."

"Totally meant to be," Sage said. "By the way, you didn't have any issues with changing the dog's name to Vizzy?"

"Oh!" Adam said. "That was the other miracle. The dog was called Izzy, so I had no guilt in adding a V. And Vizzy loves being in the store. I put a bed for her in the back room, and I might eventually put something for her in the actual store. I'll play that part by ear."

"What an amazing story," Sage said, looking at Vizzy while she played with Rufus as if they were old friends. "And that was it?"

"It was. I paid the pound the standard adoption fee, then added the amount I'd originally planned to donate. It was kind of painful watching Lulu say good-bye to Vizzy, but she assured me that she was as happy as she could be under the circumstances, and that her prayers had been answered."

"Oh, look," Sage said. "Invisible Toto has a stick in his mouth, and I think his new sister is trying to take it from him."

Adam laughed. "And Rufus is trying to take it from both of them. Using his size to intimidate them. What a scoundrel."

"But a lovable one," Sage said as they kept walking. "Oh, by the way, speaking of size, you forgot to tell me your other good news."

Adam stopped on the path. "Okay, you've got me. I have no idea what you're talking about."

"You've lost more weight," Sage said. "In fact, it doesn't look like there's any more left to lose. I'll go one step further and say you look absolutely amazing."

Adam touched his face. "Am I beet red?"

"I'd prefer to say scarlet," Sage said. "I really detest beets."

"Me too. Thank you for noticing. I'm really happy. I finally reached my goal weight. And this past weekend, when I was in such an unnecessary and silly funk, I knew I was going to be okay, because my mood no longer affected what I chose to consume. Instead of eating too much, I worked out. I feel kind of proud, to say the least. And it feels pretty fantastic, actually, opening a clothing store and being able to look my best in what I sell."

"Even when you had extra pounds," Sage said. "That never changed the fact that you're an exceptional man. And, to me, you always looked good, and your smile brightened every space you were in. It still does. Losing the weight just makes your smile even brighter, because now you feel good about yourself." To her complete surprise, Sage stood on her tiptoes and gave him a quick, but soft, kiss on the lips.

Adam didn't say a word. He just radiated happiness, and nodded toward the path ahead.

ഔ   ഔ   ഔ

"You look like the cat who swallowed the canary," Godiva said as Sage and Rufus returned.

Sage grinned. "Perhaps that's an apt description, but animal lover that I am, I've always hated that expression."

"Yeah, come to think of it, I do too. Just like the one about killing two birds with one stone."

"Horrible," Sage said.

"Agreed." Godiva smiled. "Okay, let's rewind." She let a moment pass. "Hey, Sage, you have a mischievous glint in your eye. Looks like you're really happy about something." She checked to work out Sage's response. "Okay, so I'm trying to be nonchalant here, but I'm about to burst waiting to hear Adam's surprise."

"Oh, that silly surprise," Sage said. She took Rufus's harness off and hung it up.

"You're killing me, girl," Godiva said as she leaned on the counter. "And you're getting *so* much pleasure from it too."

Sage stood and smiled while Rufus went in the back room to drink some water, then returned to the store to lie on his mat. "Okay, I won't torture you: Invisible Toto now has a visible sister. She's a Cairn Terrier, just like he is, and her name is Vizzy."

"Tell me the whole … oh no, Sage … just no! If I had any doubt that the full moon can be a dangerous thing for a store like this, my doubts have just been completely erased."

"What are you talking about?"

"Here comes Sandra the Mooch! I wish she would take her frizzy red hair somewhere else. I hope she's still not looking for a reimbursement for that stupid ice-cream cone."

"Well," Sage said, "she was a blessing in disguise. You're working here because of her. And Margie is not. Maybe we should thank her."

With a scowl, Sandra pushed open the door, then shook it back and forth so the bells would clang extra loud. Her presence was immediately met with a low growl from Rufus, who stayed on his mat, but fixated his stare on her. She looked at the wall over the counter. "Still the same unwelcoming Private Property sign that was hanging here the last time."

"And you're here because …." Godiva asked, walking toward her.

"I'm here because the way I was treated a week ago last Tuesday left a bad taste in my mouth. It's tainted the entirety of downtown Swansea for me." She looked at Godiva. "Seems like you got a job out of it."

"Yes, and for that, I'd like to thank you."

Sandra narrowed her eyes and glared at her. "You told me to skedaddle. And you called me 'freckle cheeks' and made a disgusting little walking gesture with your fingers. I'm here to tell you I didn't appreciate that one little bit. And I think you're rude, so there's that too." She looked up at the wall again. "Just like that sign."

"What's your problem with my sign?" Sage asked, coming from behind the counter to stand in solidarity with Godiva. "It's clearly decoration; I told you that."

"It reminds me of my childhood. My father had signs just like it. I had already moved out when he put them up, but still … yuck."

Sage blanched. "Your last name wouldn't happen to be Simmons, would it?"

"Oh," Sandra said. "Miss Sherlocka Holmes has been checking me out! Snooping into my business."

"No. I haven't at all. And that's the truth."

"Liar! Sure you have," Sandra snapped. "Or you wouldn't know my last name: Sage *Gordon!*"

"What can I do for you?" Sage asked, her face tightening with anger.

"I want an apology and a fifty-dollar store credit for my pain and suffering. No, make that one hundred dollars."

"Does the name 'Harris Williams' mean anything to you?" Godiva asked.

"You mean the police chief?" Sandra asked.

"Yeah. Exactly."

"What about him?"

"Oh, nothing. Just that he and my brother Ken are besties. Went to school together. See, Harris isn't a big fan of harassment or extortion. If you don't believe me, I'm happy to give him a call. No doubt he'll come right over and verify what I've just told you."

Sandra sniggered. "All right. I'm going." She turned to address Sage. "And *you* can expect a visit from my father. We'll see how you like that, you little snoop dog! Oh, yeah!" She glanced over at Rufus. "Tell that thing to stop staring at me like he wants to attack."

"We're all entitled to our emotions," Godiva said, glancing at Rufus. "Bye now. Have a nice day."

"Grrrrr."

Sage and Godiva waited until Sandra had left the store and walked away to talk.

"Oh. My. God," Sage said. "She's the daughter of Chester Simmons, the grouch who put up the No Trespassing and Private Property signs. Remember, I told you about him? He's the guy who kicked Jimmy and I off his property and threatened to call the police on us. Jimmy stole one of his signs, and here it is … hanging on my wall." She exhaled. "I can't believe it!"

"Well, it seems like the apple didn't fall far from the tree." Godiva paused to reconsider. "With no disrespect to apples."

"I'm in so much trouble!"

"Why? Because of what Sandra said? She's a full-fledged whack job! Pay her no mind."

"But it seems like a given that she's going to tell her father about the sign, and obviously, she'll tell him my name as well. After all of these years, he'll know where his stolen sign went."

"There's a plus to this."

"Which would be what?" Sage asked. "Because I can't think of anything."

"Oh, I don't know. Just if the old man is anything like he used to be, after he calls the cops on you, he might send out a search team to find your lost friend Jimmy so they can round him up too."

"I'm totally freaked," Sage said. "And while it would be worth it to see Jimmy again, that won't happen, and I remain a one-woman freak show at the moment."

Godiva laughed. "Don't be rattled by all this. Really, it's all good. And I was kidding. You know that."

"Well, truth is spoken in jest all the time." Sage plucked the Love You Forever stone from the bowl on the counter and held it firmly in her hand. "I guess maybe I'm being a bit dramatic." She turned to Godiva. "But if I'm arrested for possession of stolen goods, will you bail me out of jail?"

"I will. Now, before the full moon sends another one of its disciples into the store, tell me why you came back with that smile on your face. I know you love dogs, but Adam's new dog was not what made you smile … not like that!"

"Well," Sage said, putting the stone back in the basket. "Adam and I were talking, about a lot of things, and all of a sudden, well, out of nowhere, I kind of kissed him."

"You did what?" Godiva's eyes doubled in size.

"I know! It just happened. And here I've spent so much time telling Adam I only want to be friends. And I do. But then I did that. I actually kissed him. It was only a quick kiss, but still. I'm not even sure why I did it. It felt really good, but I feel like such an idiot for giving him mega mixed signals. He's going to end up hating me."

Godiva put both hands on Sage's shoulders. "You need to realign your chakras or something. This full moon has you way out of sync."

"I know," Sage said. "I actually feel kind of sick."

"As the old song goes, Sage, 'You're not sick; you're just in love.'"

"I knew you'd say something like that, but really …."

"I know. It was that love spray from yesterday. Looks like you OD'd on it."

"That's probably it," Sage said, exasperated. "Well, at least I know the stuff works."

CHAPTER SEVENTEEN

"You are looking way better than you did when I left you last night," Godiva said as she put her bag from Coffee & Teaz onto the counter, then walked around it to stash her purse out of sight. "I'd go so far as to say that I see the faint trace of a smile on your lips. The corners of your mouth are turned ever-so-slightly upward."

Sage poured the kettle of hot water into her cup. "My aunt Ruth brought me homemade scones last night. Would you like one?"

"They look delish," Godiva said, eyeing the plate. "But I have a toasted bagel in this bag with my name on it. Can I tuck one away for tomorrow morning?"

"Sure thing." Sage broke off a piece of the scone on her plate. "I'm keeping them in the bread box in the office, right by the microwave."

"Good to know," Godiva said. "So, anything special that has you smiling this Thursday morning after full-moon Wednesday turned you into a 'one-woman freak show,' as I believe you called it?"

"I might be having lunch with Adam."

"And I might be marrying Freddie." Godiva laughed. "What time?"

"Around one. Oh, and my aunt is going to come over. She is so eager to meet you. She'll walk Rufus, and she can also cover the store if you want to go out. She's an amazing woman. I think you'll hit it off."

"I don't have any lunch plans, so we can spend that time getting acquainted. I'm looking forward to it. Where are you having lunch?"

"That little Greek place called Aesop's down on Hudson."

"It's a nice little hideaway," Godiva said. "Unlike *Le Chat Noir* where all of Swansea congregates on a daily basis." She took the lid off her coffee cup and poured some creamers into it. "Freddie and I used to go there. And look at us now."

የ   የ   የ

"I'm so glad you agreed to have lunch with me," Adam said after they'd placed their orders. He looked around. "This corner booth is perfect."

"Having lunch with you is not something I need to agree to do," Sage said. "It's an absolute pleasure."

Adam nodded thanks as the server put a bottle of sparkling water on the table, and poured some into their glasses.

"I was worried," Adam said, "that—"

"Wait," Sage said, reaching across the table and putting her hand on his. "May I say something first?"

"Of course."

"I'm just going to come right out with this: I'm not sorry I kissed you. It may have been spontaneous, or maybe even the same full moon that brought the crazies into my store, but I wanted to do it. And yes, I worried all night that telling you one thing and doing another is horribly unfair, not to mention confusing. And the last thing I want to do is mess with your head. So for that, I'm sorry.

Sorry for being so messed up."

Adam squeezed her hand. "I knew you were going to beat yourself up for that. And it's really sweet that you did. But I don't feel messed with in any way. To be honest, I think many men … and women … might feel differently, but we're unique human beings. I tossed my guide to being a macho man in the proverbial trash a long time ago. I know all too well that it's completely human to have conflicting desires happening simultaneously. I'm just happy that we can talk things out. And I'm happy that you felt comfortable enough with me to plant your beautiful lips on mine."

Sage took her hand away to make room as she saw the server standing tableside holding a basket of pita bread and a small dish of hummus.

"Looks delicious, thanks," Sage said to the server, then refocused her attention on Adam. "When I first met Godiva, she said something to me about how the people we like best are usually the people with whom we're most comfortable being ourselves. Every day, I see more truth in that. And while I hoped you'd understand, I couldn't rule out the possibility that you might not. I would never take you for granted, Adam."

"Being conflicted can suck," Adam said. He looked at the pita bread. "Two triangles is my limit. Conflict eliminated." He smiled. "You don't think I was conflicted when I saw you with Caleb, and then with the Aussie guy … Benton? I could have made my presence known, but no, I ran off. Only I'm still not sure I did the wrong thing, because showing myself would have just been awkward for everyone. But sulking all weekend and not getting in touch with you … no, that was bad. That was really bad."

"It was human." Sage took a pita triangle and spread some hummus on it. "How do you decide when to accept mixed signals and when to get angry instead?"

"It's all in a person's intentions," Adam told her. "If I feel someone is trying to purposely manipulate my feelings, I'm a very unhappy camper. But if a beautiful woman and longtime friend, who has just come out of a relationship, professes a need to stay single, but might just like me a little more than she used to, and I really like her, well, that's all good."

"Thank you, Adam." She blushed. "Now tell me: how is Vizzy?"

ço   ço   ço

"You must be Godiva. I'm Ruth Masterson, Sage's aunt."

"It's a pleasure," Godiva said, walking over to meet her at the door as Rufus followed.

Ruth scratched Rufus on the neck, waved hello to a customer who was browsing the bookshelves, then held out her hand to shake Godiva's. "First, congratulations on your engagement." She looked down at Godiva's hand. "May I?"

"Don't have to ask me twice," Godiva said, showing Ruth her ring.

"It's every bit as sparkling and gorgeous as you are." Ruth smiled, then made a sad face as she looked down. "Oh, no."

"What?"

"I just noticed that I have paint splatters on my jeans," Ruth said. "And these are my going-out-in-public clothes. You should see what I work in. Sometimes I think my jeans are more interesting than what I slop on the canvas." She laughed. "Oh, well, it's all good. But maybe I should hide behind the counter while I can."

"Sage did tell me you were an artist. I saw a couple of your landscapes in the office. They're breathtaking. I hear you have several pieces at the gallery here in Swansea."

"Seven," Ruth whispered. "But who's counting. And thank you for the kind words." She glanced at the barstools. "Shall we sit on the royal thrones?" She scratched Rufus on his head. "You go over to your royal mat, okay?"

As Ruth sat, Godiva rang up a book for the lone customer, then took a seat next to her.

"I must tell you," Ruth said, "I am ecstatic that you work here now. You're what this place has needed for a long time. Margie was so contrary to Sage's vision, and while Sage was too sweet to fire her, I would have painted that woman out of the picture a long time ago." She winked. "I like to use art terms when I'm tempted to use harsher language."

"I hear you," Godiva said. "I'll be forever grateful things happened as they did. It worked out well for everyone."

"Except Margie," Ruth and Godiva said in unison, then laughed.

"I'll tell you," Ruth said. "Sage won't tell you this, but Margie made everything in her life more difficult. Sage told me she confided more in you on the first day than she did with Margie during the entirety of her time here."

"I'm quite honored."

"I can see why Sage trusted you from the get-go. Margie, on the other hand, was infinitely pushing Sage to become her friend, bringing all of her family problems to work, and Sage had zero interest in anything beyond a business relationship. She told her that too. But that didn't stop Margie from yakking or prying, and when Sage and Caleb broke up, Margie tried to use Sage's pain to get close to her. I think that made Sage want to retreat even more from a relationship and everything that goes with it."

"Oh, no," Godiva said. "I think I'm guilty of the same. I've been nudging Sage, albeit playfully most times, to open her heart to love again. What makes me any different?"

Ruth put her hand on Godiva's wrist. "*Everything* makes you different. Halley's Comet could make two appearances, and I *still* wouldn't be finished answering your question."

"You're quite funny," Godiva said. "I hope you're right."

"Sage adores you," Ruth told her. "She wouldn't be listening to you otherwise. She's smart, and she knows who is good for her and who is not. Most of the time. I always felt there was something off with Caleb, but it was hard to nail down what … because 'on paper,' he ticked most of the boxes. But I'm not unhappy she got involved with him; I'm just happier that they broke up. Sage has had other relationships, but they never got as far. Frankly, I worried that she might never commit to anyone."

"Why were you so concerned?"

"Are you familiar with the term 'lovemap?' It was originated by a sexologist named John Money in the '80s."

"No, I'm not," Godiva said. "But I'm already fascinated."

"Well, without getting into it now, he studied how human beings develop their sexual preferences and their internal blueprint. I could talk about this for hours, but one thing about lovemaps is that they usually don't change once they are formed. I'm not necessarily talking about Sage in this regard, but what I can tell you is that her childhood love, Jimmy Cole, and his subsequent disappearance eighteen years ago, had a profound effect on her."

"No doubt," Godiva interjected. "She told me all about him."

"Speaking in totally nonscientific terms, I think the friendship they shared played a huge role in forming Sage's lovemap." Ruth scraped a patch of yellow paint on her jeans. "She's very aware of this, of course, but I always worried that she'd throw her youth away while waiting to find him again. That's why, when she met Caleb, I was happy at first."

"As I told Sage," Godiva said, "we go through the wrong relationships in our personal evolution process."

"Exactly!" Ruth said. "My goodness. I am so grateful you are here."

"All I can say," Godiva told her, "is that I truly believe Sage is going to be okay."

"I tell myself that too," Ruth said, "but I still don't believe that she's gotten Jimmy Cole out of her system. And quite honestly, between the two of us, that scares me."

CHAPTER EIGHTEEN

"Your aunt is a fascinating woman," Godiva said to Sage as the last of a midday rush of customers had left.

"We're very close," Sage said. "I adore her."

"I can see why. And how was lunch? Nice?"

"Very."

"Excellent."

Sage put her fist under her chin and pretended to study Godiva. "Hmm. That was quite short-winded of you." She walked over to the scarf display to fix a teal-and-purple scarf that was nearly off the hanger. "Ah, I get it. My aunt told you how Margie was always in my personal business, and that scared you. Am I right?" She laughed. "You don't even have to answer. I know I am."

"How did you know that?"

"My aunt *hates* Margie. You're lucky there wasn't time for her extended psychoanalysis of her." Sage walked over to Godiva, who was arranging jewelry in the wall case. "My aunt Ruth has a master's in psychology and an MFA."

"Oh, wow. She didn't tell me that."

"I know that too. Because she's very humble. But she did tell you how much she hated Margie. And I've got no doubt she adored you."

Godiva put her hand on her hip. "Well, am I not adorable?"

"G'day, adorable ladies! Lovely arvo, isn't it?" Benton turned to Sage. "Where's my fluffy mate?"

"He's upstairs. He fell asleep with the cats. After I took about fifty photos of them, I snuck down here. They're all so precious together."

Benton smiled at Sage, then made eye contact with Godiva and walked over to her. "Half your luck! Being engaged makes you even more beautiful. And adorable." He winked. "I've seen the ring, but not on your finger." He walked behind the counter for closer inspection. "Not too tatty. Very happy for you and Freddie both." He rounded the corner to see Sage, who was walking to the counter with something in her hand. "And being in my company makes *you* even more beautiful."

"Oh, really!" Sage said. She put a silver cat pendant on the counter as she spoke to Godiva. "I ran into a customer on the way back from lunch, and she asked me to hold this for her."

"What is it?" Benton asked.

"Bastet," Sage told him, "goddess of joy and protector of women."

"Can I have a squiz?" Benton said, taking the card with the pendant attached. "Doesn't look a thing like me, but then again, you did say 'goddess' and not 'god.' Looks like a cat, actually."

"It is," she told him as she put the pendant on the counter. "Meow. And you're a piece of work!"

"So my mum tells me," Benton said. "I'd better behave. A customer is on his way …."

Sage, Benton, and Godiva watched as a man in his late sixties, with a weathered face and old clothing, walked purposely into the store. His eyes swept over the room, then landed on the Private Property sign. He stared at it for a good while. "So that's where my stolen property went to. Been looking in every nook and cranny for that sign for damn near nineteen years." He looked directly at Sage. "Maybe you should cross out the word 'private' and change it to 'stolen.' What do you think, Miss Gordon?"

"Mr. Simmons," Sage said. "Um. Hello."

"Who have we got here?" he said, looking at Benton and Godiva.

"This is my associate, Godiva Jones, and my friend, Benton Bradley."

"G'day," Benton said, his usual charm absent.

"From down under, are you?" Simmons said. "Do they steal signs from neighbors there too?"

"We're a suss lot," Benton told him. "You name it. We do it."

"What kind of store is this, anyway?"

"It's many things," Sage said. "It's a gift shop, basically, with a metaphysical—"

"You were always different," Simmons said. "I saw you and the boy out there in the field, wearing that sparkly thing on your head, acting like royalty or something."

"Oh, well, we were just kids …."

"My daughter told you I'd be coming by, I take it. Told me she wants a hundred-dollar gift certificate because she doesn't like the way she was treated."

"I, um …."

"Don't bother trying to explain, young lady." He turned to Benton. "You look like you're about ready to burst wide open."

"I'm a protector of women," Benton said awkwardly.

"No one here needs protection from me."

"I can give you your sign back," Sage said, her eyes filling with sadness and a tinge of fear.

"After that Cole boy went to the trouble to steal it for you? Hell no, you keep it."

Sage's jaw dropped. "You knew that?"

"Saw him do it."

"Then why didn't you say anything? I mean, you threatened to call the police on us if we ever trespassed on your property again."

Simmons looked at Sage until she made eye contact with him. "I'll make a long story short. You met my daughter. She's a royal pain in the butt. And this is her father talking. I can only imagine what other people say about her. Her mother was almost as bad." He looked around as he collected his thoughts. "Ever see that movie called *The Bad Seed*? Well, Sandra didn't kill anyone ... not that I know about ... but she was pretty horrible. Still is. Back then, when I was hitched to her mother, I thought every kid was just like her. So when you and that Cole kid were playing on my property, I told myself you'd be as destructive as my own flesh and blood, and I needed to keep you out. Put up those signs to scare the bejesus out of you. But deep down, I knew you was good kids, and I guess ignoring sign theft was my way of making up for projecting my own kid's bad ways onto the two of you. I'll tell ya: having that girl underfoot turned me into a mean old grouch at the ripe old age of forty-eight."

"Oh, I never thought you were a—"

"Bull cocky! Of course you did!" Simmons told her. "You and that Cole kid hated my guts. Can't say as I blame you, either."

Benton looked blankly at him, then shared a look with Godiva, who was also at a loss.

"When Sandra ordered me, or so she thinks, to come in here and read you the riot act, I told her I'd be here the next day. What she doesn't know is that I was happier than a pig in ... well, you know, to learn where you were. I came here to apologize for being so awful to you when you were a kid. Sandra's my daughter and I love her ... I guess ... but I don't like her. Not one bit. Always trying to get something from me. Only time I give in is to shut her up, and I've pretty much stopped doing that." He glanced up at the sign. "I'm just glad that old piece of wood holds good memories for you. The way I treated you, I'd think you'd want to burn it."

"Oh no," Benton said. "Sage loves it. Right nice of you to want to square off with her."

"Well, I'd better get going. Got a new missus who's worth going home to."

"Mr. Simmons," Sage said. "Before you go … you don't, by any chance, know what happened to Jimmy Cole and his family, do you?"

He thought for a moment as an uneasy look settled on his face. "I know that Cole senior had a bad temper and a love affair with the bottle. Used to hear him yelling at the wife. And at the boy too. That's all I can tell you. Didn't want to get involved. Had enough of my own troubles back then."

Sage's face fell. "Oh, I didn't know that. Jimmy never said a word. He always seemed so happy."

"Sorry, I can't help you. I'm sure I was as surprised as your family was when the three of them disappeared." He managed a half smile. "Now, listen here. If Sandra comes by again, you tell her that I gave you my number and asked you to let me know if she bothers you." He pulled a business card out of his pocket and handed it to her. "Here you go." He looked at Benton. "Never met anyone from down under before. Tell me, you see a lot of kangaroos?"

"They have super roos there," Sage said. "Benton told me they have springs in their feet and fly over people."

"And they steal shrimps off the barbie," Benton said. "We've got quite a problem with that. It's epidemic, actually. Roos only eat grass and the like, but they bury the shrimps for the hungry dingoes to find."

"Sounds about right," Simmons mumbled as Benton's

humor sailed over his head. "You all seem like good people. Take care now."

Sage stared at the door long after the echo of the clang had gone silent. She watched as Simmons became but a dot in the distance, then vanished. But she kept looking.

"How ya doin' there, Sage?" Benton said, putting an arm around her. "Never seen such a long face on ya."

"I feel sick."

Godiva busied herself behind the counter, making a point to let Benton talk to Sage.

"I don't like to see you feeling crook, but a blast from the past can do that to a person. I understand."

Sage sniffled but said nothing.

"How about we go to that coffee shop? Sit in the corner and have a proper chinwag. Unless you'd rather go back to Marcello's and have a shot, but that doesn't seem like the best idea. I've got a good hour until I meet Freddie."

"I don't know."

"Can't stand in the middle of your store in a tizz. Especially if customers come in."

"He's right. Go on, honey," Godiva said. "I can handle everything here." She turned to address Benton. "And if you're running a bit late to meet the man, don't worry; I'll keep him occupied."

"Okay," Sage said, devoid of expression.

Benton squeezed her shoulder and led her to the door. "That's my girl."

৩৯   ৩৯   ৩৯

Sage took a sip of her chai latte. "I feel like I've been transported back to my childhood, but not in a good way. It's like I just found out that Jimmy was gone all over again." She lowered her eyes as she remembered. "That was the worst day of my life."

"Probably wasn't a good one for Jimmy either. You heard what the man said."

Sage pushed a lock of hair out of her face. "I can't believe his father was an abusive drunk. He never told me that. Ever."

"You have nice parents, yes?"

"They're wonderful," Sage said. "The best I could ask for."

"Sounds like Jimmy wanted to forget his home and pretend while he could that he was a part of a happy family."

"Maybe that's why he came up with the king-and-queen fantasy. Just to escape."

"Sounds right to me," Benton said. "Lots of kids use their imaginations to deal with tough times."

"Maybe he didn't like me the way I thought he did. Maybe my home was just a port in a storm or just some place to—"

"No way," Benton said. "You're a charmer. Speaking for myself, I wouldn't crown just any Sheila my queen to get out of a bad spot. And I wouldn't steal a sign for just anyone either. From everything you've told me, the boy cared every bit as much for you."

"I just wish I knew what happened to him. I wonder why he's never tried to find me." She looked at Benton. "Oh no! What if he's dead? What if his father …."

"Don't let your mind go there, Sage."

"It's like my life so far is this big puzzle, and it all comes together to form a picture, except for this big gaping hole in it from my childhood. That just doesn't make sense."

"I remember," Benton said. "When I was a kid, my mum bought a jigsaw puzzle for my sister and me. Bloody thing had five hundred pieces. We sat at the dining room table and worked on it for days. We put in the last piece we had, and wouldn't you know— there was one piece missing. After all that. My sister was cranky as!"

"Sounds like a metaphor for my childhood. Did you ever find the piece?"

Benton made an awkward face. "Oh yeah. Later that day, as a matter of fact."

"Where was it?"

"In the back garden." He grinned. "In the dog's business."

Sage smiled for the first time. "Oh, no! Your dog had eaten it?"

"He did. Boomer was the kind of dog who loved a snack wherever he could find one. Edible or not."

"So, um, I guess I have to ask. Did you finish the puzzle or leave it as it was?"

"Well, Harper—that's my sister—she wanted to chunder. But my dad just put a plastic bag on his hand, pulled it out, gave it a good wash, and finished the puzzle."

"How did Harper feel after he did that?"

"She said she preferred the puzzle better with the missing piece … rather than knowing where it had been."

Sage studied Benton's face. "That was very clever, that story."

"Fair dinkum. Bloody oath, mate!"

"Oh, I believe you. I didn't mean that you made it up, only that it was very clever to tell me that now. You're telling me that having the missing piece doesn't necessarily make the puzzle any better."

"Depends on how you see it. Harper hated the puzzle after that. But Mum and Dad loved it."

"And what did you think, Benton?"

"I could see both sides."

Sage took another sip of her chai. "I'll bet that Harper never did another puzzle after that."

"Hates them to this day," Benton told her, then took a swig

of his orange soda. "Hope her ankle biters don't want them when they get a bit older."

"I think she'll survive it if they do."

"We Aussies are made of tough stuff. And so are you, Sage."

"I don't feel very tough. I feel like I'm made out of glass, and I just shattered all over the floor." She looked at Benton. "I just hope that wherever Jimmy is, he knows that I loved him and always will."

"I'd bet on it."

"There's a good chance that he's married, I guess. Maybe he even has kids. And yeah, that would be a really good reason not to look me up. Unlike him, I'm easy to find."

"That makes a lot of sense. Could be anything. But I'd bet he'd want you to be happy."

"He would," Sage said. "I know that. I can feel him talking to me … as weird as that sounds. But I just wish I had that missing piece, no matter what or where it is. I just feel so incomplete without it. His disappearance has always bothered me, but seeing Mr. Simmons again, and learning what I did—it's just renewed my pain and elevated it to a whole new level."

Benton reached across the table and took her hand. "Not good, Sage. What can I do to make you feel better?"

"You've already done that," she told him. "Just by caring. Just by understanding."

"It'll all get sorted, Sage. You'll see. Just be happy. Life's too short to be anything else."

CHAPTER NINETEEN

"Ah, right on time," Freddie said as Sage and Benton walked into the store.

"You know I wouldn't hold you up, mate. Not that I want to see those bludgers in New York again."

Freddie chuckled. "They are rather transparently opportunistic. And spoiled."

"Aggro too. Wouldn't mind if a few of them chucked a sickie on meeting days. Sometimes I'm glad I live in another hemisphere." A wistful look came over him as he looked at Sage. "And sometimes not."

"Well," Freddie said, leaning on the counter. "If they were the kind of people to call in sick when they weren't, they wouldn't be people we'd want to work with."

"Fair enough. Can't argue with you there, mate."

"I think we've got the advertising end of things set to go for now," Freddie assured him.

Godiva studied Sage's face. "You're looking better than when you left. I hope that's not just my imagination. You had me concerned."

"Did you say I'm better looking than when I left?"

"*Looking* better," Godiva said with a smile.

"Don't think Sage could be any prettier if she tried," Benton said to Godiva. "But she does have more color in her face now. Nothing a few tunes on the old didgeridoo couldn't fix. Played it right there in the coffee shop."

Sage laughed. "Next he'll be telling you he had a chorus of wallabies singing to me."

"My backing vocalists," Benton said. He put his arm around Sage. "She'll be right. I'll make sure of it." He gave her a kiss on the top of her head, then said something softly in her ear.

As Benton did so, Godiva noticed the expression on Freddie's face change.

She gently nudged his arm. "What's up, baby?"

Absorbed in what he was thinking, Freddie didn't respond immediately. "Oh," he said. "Nothing, Diva. I've just got a lot on my mind. Just prepping for this last meeting in New York with the advertising team. Going over my mental checklist, making sure I haven't forgotten anything."

"Uh-huh," Godiva said. "Well, I can tell you what you forgot."

Freddie looked into her eyes. "Is that right? What is it, wise and sexy woman?"

"You forgot that your Diva knows when there's more to what you say than meets the eye. I hope you don't think those months apart changed any of that, Freddie Lamar."

He grinned. "You've got a customer, baby," he said as a woman who had been browsing in the back of the store put a box of tarot cards on the counter. "And Benton and I need to make tracks outta here." He gave Godiva a quick kiss on the lips. "New York traffic isn't kind to anyone."

"Ready when you are," Benton said. "Nothing like another ripsnorter with those bludgers to get my blood flowing." He put his arms around Sage and gave her a big hug, which she returned.

"We'll talk later," Godiva said to Freddie, unable to hide her attraction. "You know we will."

As the men left, Sage turned to Godiva. "I'm going to go upstairs and get the boy. Want to make sure Finlay and Babaloo haven't trapped him in the house. That actually happened once. They both decided to sleep by the doggie door, and Ruf didn't dare disturb them. The wrath of cats and all that."

"So you'll be upstairs?"

"Only for a few minutes. Then I'm going into the office to work on some orders. After we close the store, the boy and I are meeting Adam and Vizzy ... and Toto ... in the park."

"I'm glad to hear that," Godiva told her. "You look a bit better, but that doesn't mean I've stopped worrying about you."

"No need," Sage said. "As Benton said, playing that didgeridoo for me really did the trick."

"Oh, yeah, right. That." Godiva put a hand on her hip. "You sure seem to like men with invisible things."

"What?" Sage asked. She broke out laughing. "Think you might want to rephrase?"

Godiva put her hands over her face. "I can't believe I just said that." She laughed as tears rolled down her face.

"But you did. And for the record," Sage said, still laughing, "I prefer the visible ones. Every time."

ॐ   ॐ   ॐ

As Sage and Adam took a table by the kiosk in the park, a glass of Chardonnay in front of each of them, Adam reached into a canvas shoulder bag he was carrying. He pulled out a plastic dog bowl, put it on the ground, and filled it with a bottle of water, then took a few dog treats out as well.

"Don't want the kids to feel slighted," he said, reaching

down to hand each of the dogs a small treat. His expression turned serious. "I'm really glad you told me about what happened today with your unexpected visitor. I know it wasn't easy. I remember you telling me about your childhood friend Jimmy years ago. And I never forgot that story, nor how much his disappearance hurt you. When you started seeing Caleb, and subsequently got engaged, I figured you'd found a way to put the pain behind you."

"I did and I didn't. But what I failed to see was the new pain in my life … smack in front of me." She took a small sip of her wine.

"I suppose if we never made mistakes, it would be no fun fixing them."

"I can't say that fixing the Caleb debacle has been much fun, but maybe I haven't gotten to that part yet," Sage said. "Though I must admit, I did enjoy seeing the expression on his face when I told him how I'd figured everything out. He tried to throw it back at me, but I could tell: he knew I was on the money."

"You think?"

"He would have been in touch by now. Hopefully, he's turned on his self-awareness button and realized that I have zero interest in a reconciliation and that he needs to get his act together before jumping into another rebound relationship with the polar opposite of his true love." Sage made a face. "I had a dream the other morning that I was in a room filled with men who were all calling me their 'Bohemian baby,' and Caleb was shouting, 'No, she's *my* Bohemian baby. You can't have her.' Not kidding. I woke up in a cold sweat. It was horrible."

"Oh, no. What a way to start your day. Maybe it's good we had this talk," Adam said, lifting his glass to drink. "You know how they say that when you talk about something, your subconscious loses the need to dream about it."

"I sure hope so. Anyway, enough about Caleb. Tell me how the store is coming along."

"Beautifully," Adam said. He took a sip of wine and put his glass down. "I was worried about making the deadline for the party next week, but we're gonna be good to go. However, we almost had a bad mishap this afternoon. About an hour after I got back from our lunch."

"That's not good. Are you okay? What happened?"

"I'm fine," Adam said. "But Sam, my sales associate, almost fell from a step ladder. And while he was only three steps off the ground, he said it could have been a bad fall."

"Did he nearly miss a step? Slip on something?"

"Nope. Got spooked."

"Oh, no! I hope Invisible Toto didn't bite him. Or Vizzy!"

"My dogs are angels." He looked down. "Aren't you both?"

Vizzy started barking at a brown pit bull that was quietly walking by, spurring on Rufus to join in the racket.

"You had to go there, didn't you?" Sage said to Adam with a smile. She looked down and admonished Rufus to be quiet while Adam did the same with Vizzy.

"Ah, quiet," Sage said.

"Not sure what you're talking about. Toto's still barking up a storm."

She laughed. "Let him bark. Tell me what happened with Sam."

"Well, he was sorting dress shirts and putting them in the cubbyholes in the wall unit. He caught something in his peripheral vision, a figure all in black, and he said he thought Death had come for him, minus the scythe. Said it terrified him so much that it caused him to jerk forward, and he just missed landing splat on the floor."

"How terrifying!"

"Yeah, when he managed to take a second look, he saw it was a woman and thought it was his ex-girlfriend who's into Goth.

But when the woman turned sideways, he said that her long nose was nothing like his ex's. And she was taller as well."

"I know exactly who you mean," Sage told him. "That crazy woman came into my store the other night. She looked at every single thing I sell, carefully; then she bought a Tibetan knife, a mini cauldron, and an evil-eye charm. She talks like a three-pack-a-day smoker, but that said, she doesn't say much. Oh, and Molly crossed paths with her coming into the store as the woman was leaving. Goth Lady purposely swung her bag to whack Molly in the knees."

"Well that's creepy, to say the least. I hope Molly wasn't hurt. Sheesh, just what none of us need: a shrouded freak on the loose."

"Tell me what else happened at the store," Sage urged.

"Well, after Sam was lucky enough to avoid an ambulance ride to the ER and went back to sorting shirts, she started peering through the window. We couldn't see much, as she wears really big dark glasses, but it was clear she was giving the place a once-over. Then, what really upset me is that I saw her reading the flyer I have posted on the window. You know … about the party next week."

"She doesn't exactly seem like a social animal," Sage said. "But she is a nosy one."

"No clue what she is. But I don't want to find out." Adam raised his glass. "Here's hoping she'll phone home soon and return to her planet. They must miss her. Maybe if we can figure out how she got here, we can send her back."

"I'll drink to that," Sage said as they clinked glasses. "From your lips …."

CHAPTER TWENTY

The seventy-something-year-old woman, wearing a tailored blue dress and a string of pearls, her hair pinned up and sprayed into place, scanned the store as if she had been teleported somewhere that even her imagination couldn't conjure. She stood in front of the counter, her mouth opened in the same shape as her large clip-on pearl earrings. As she observed the other customers with an unconcealed disdain, the two women and one man, who had been browsing, stopped to return the scrutiny.

"Lord, give me strength," Godiva mumbled, then walked over to the woman with as much of a smile as she could muster. "Welcome to Sage Earth Gifts. My name is Godiva. Might I be able to help you with something?"

"What I won't do for my granddaughter," the woman said.

The other customers, seeing that her attention was refocused, continued to browse while still sneaking watchful eyes on her.

"Are you here shopping for your granddaughter?" Godiva asked.

The woman challenged her with a hard stare, then spoke. "Look at me. Do I look like someone who would choose to enter these premises without a very good reason?"

"I have no idea," Godiva said. "I don't stereotype people. I wouldn't know."

"Well maybe you should. It's a real time-saver."

Sage stepped around from the counter. "I'm Sage Gordon. I'm the owner. May I help you?"

The woman eyed Sage's olive-colored Bohemian dress accented with a large silver-and-turquoise pendant, then redirected her gaze to the leather cuff bracelet with a large turquoise heart in the center of it. After staring at the stone for several seconds, she glanced down the taupe lace-up espadrilles Sage was wearing. "Where in the world do you shop?"

"Hippies R' Us," Sage said, trying to keep her anger from showing. "What can I help you with?"

The woman huffed as she rifled through her handbag for a folded piece of paper, then opened it. "My granddaughter was in here last week, and she wants a ... 'yin- yang pendant' ... whatever that is ... the one with the black cord."

"I can help you with that," Sage said, noticing that Rufus was coming to say hello.

"I first want to know what the hell a 'yin yang' is." She looked at Rufus. "Is that mangy mutt going to attack me? I don't like the way he's looking at me."

Godiva, seeing the stress on Sage's face, motioned that she would take Rufus upstairs. As she hurried over to herd Rufus away, Sage continued, "In Chinese philosophy, yin and yang represent that what can appear as an opposite or contrary force may in fact be complementary."

The male customer, who was unable to focus on the book he'd been leafing through, walked over to them. "It's the concept of duality forming a whole."

"What language are you people speaking?"

The man turned to Sage. "I'll be back in later when this blue-blooded negative field of energy has dissipated."

"You know nothing about me," the woman snapped at him just as Godiva returned to the store.

"No, I don't, but I like to stereotype people. It's a real time-saver," he said as he headed toward the door.

Godiva and Sage shared a look while the two women customers turned their backs to giggle.

Sage walked over to the wall and grabbed the pendant with the black cord. She handed it to the woman. "This is exactly what you described. In fact, I remember a young woman, about fourteen, admiring it last week. Sounds like it was probably your granddaughter … pretty … blond hair … braces."

"That's her. So I'm to understand you allow young teens in here without parental supervision?"

"This is a place of peace and tranquility," Sage said. "At the very least, it's what it should be."

"How much is that thing?" the woman snarled.

"Fifteen dollars."

"Are you kidding me?"

"I'm sorry; that's the price."

"I don't buy cheap gifts. I've never spent less than a hundred dollars on any gift for my family. Fifteen dollars is disgusting."

"Gee, I'm sorry," Sage said. She looked at Godiva, then at the woman. "I can't believe I'm having this conversation. The pendants on the wall are not expensive. We have other items in the cases that are in your price range."

"But she wants *that* thing!" the woman said. "And I have no interest in what other horrors lie dormant in your display cases."

"We have lovely jewelry, not dissimilar to what you might find in any jewelry store. Now, what do you want me to do?" Sage asked as she noticed her aunt Ruth entering the store. "I'm not going to inflate the price of this pendant. If you want it, you can pay the fifteen dollars for it and buy eighty-five dollars' worth of gifts somewhere else."

"Hello, Marian," Ruth said. "Is there a problem here?"

"Finally, a sane person in my midst! I'm having a terrible time trying to communicate with this angry hippie in this unearthly emporium. All I wanted to do is buy my granddaughter a gift for a dignified price. I'm glad you're here, Ruth. For one, Leonard and I have been planning to talk to you about doing a commissioned painting of the LaFontaine-Griswold bungalow on The Cape, our precious summer home. He's there now, as a matter of fact. As Leonard says, 'there's no better landscape artist than Ruth Masterson, a true Swansea gem.'"

"Very kind of him." She put on a thinking face. "This 'angry hippie' is my gem of a niece. And this 'unearthly emporium' is a treasure. I myself work here on Mondays ... and other days when I'm needed." She smiled. "It renews my spirit. This is a very uplifting atmosphere." Ruth glared at Marian. "*Most* of the time."

"You ... um ..."

"Clearly," Ruth continued, "this isn't the place for you. I'm going to ask you nicely to leave. Furthermore, please tell Leonard that while I appreciate the kind words, I am definitely not the artist to paint your alternative residence. Cape Cod has a wonderful community of artists. I'm sure—"

"No, no, no! Leonard will be heartsick! He's counting on you, Ruth. He doesn't want some hippie artist ..." She took a moment to snicker at Sage. "You know what I'm saying. I won't demean myself with an explanation." She glanced at Sage's hand. "And I still need that black-and-white thing on a cord."

Ruth motioned to take the pendant from Sage. "Here you go, Marian. Consider it a parting gift. Do with it what you will. Now leave."

"Clearly," Marian snarled, dropping the pendant into her

purse, "spending time here has tainted you." She sighed, expelling a good deal of the hot air that inflated her. "The sacrifices I make for my granddaughter …."

Everyone watched as she hurried out the door. Ruth made a face. "Old biddy." She turned to Sage and Godiva. "I half expected her to say 'Well, I never.' Isn't that what angry battle-axes usually say in old movies when their dignity is affronted?"

Godiva chuckled, but Sage, on the brink of tears, hurried away and into the back room. Ruth followed her, while Godiva turned with a strained smile to help one of the customers.

"Sage, honey," Ruth said, putting her arm around Sage as she sank into a chaise lounge in the corner of her office, "I'm so sorry that horrid Marian came in here. Let me get you some tissues to wipe those tears."

"I feel like an idiot for crying," Sage said. "I handle difficult people all the time. I don't know why I picked today to fall apart." She looked at her aunt. "I'm so glad you're here, but I didn't expect to see you until Sunday or Monday."

Ruth smiled. "Well, it's your lucky day. I'm here on a Friday. And you saw me on Wednesday night and Thursday afternoon as well. Lady Luck has smiled down on you, hasn't she?"

Sage laughed through her tears. "Why are you always so good to me?"

"Because I love you with all my heart," Ruth said. "You've been a bright light in our lives since you were born."

"Thank you," Sage said. "I love you with all of my heart too. So really, why are you here?"

"To work," Ruth said. "Just for a couple hours. When we spoke on the phone this morning, there was tension in your voice that I haven't heard since the day you and Caleb broke up. I know you've got a lot going on. So, as my treat, I want you and Godiva to go somewhere and have lunch together. You need to be able to talk to a friend without having to wait on customers. And, I'm paying for that pendant too."

"No, you don't have to do that. It's worth it to be rid of her. And you don't need to buy our lunch."

"But I want to. The pendant and lunch are on me. I'm older than you, so I get the final word. That's how it works."

Really? Fascinating. Can I share that charming precept with your older sister?" Sage asked with a grin. "No doubt Mom would love to know you feel that way."

Ruth's eyes twinkled. "I'll deny it." She smiled and caressed Sage's hair. "Now you go freshen up, sweetie, and I'll let Godiva know she's got a lunch date. You can't hold in all of the pain and confusion anymore. I think Godiva can help you find some light in the darkness."

👁   👁   👁

"Your aunt is an exceptional human being, Sage. Just like you are."

"My aunt *is* wonderful," Sage said, taking a sip of her raspberry lemonade.

"Just like you are," Godiva repeated.

"I'm an exceptional wreck. But thank you. I feel like I've lost my ability to deal with anything. Like that stupid socialite … Marian whatever her hyphenated last name is. I don't even know what her game was: did she want me to charge her one hundred dollars for a fifteen-dollar pendant? Nothing she said made any sense."

"Oh, I had her number from jump," Godiva said. "Her game was to confuse you with a ridiculous complaint that you couldn't possibly resolve sanely. Trust me, honey, she doesn't spend a hundred bucks on every gift she buys. She's probably as cheap as a polyester suit. She wanted you to get so angry and frustrated that you'd give her the pendant for free to get her out of the store. A win-win for her: her granddaughter gets the pendant she wanted, and Grams didn't have to pay one cent to the 'angry hippie' in the 'unearthly emporium.' Her endgame is pretty close to Sandra's, actually."

"Ugh," Sage said, poking at her salad with a fork. "Of course. I've dealt with people like her before. So why did I need you to interpret the obvious?"

"Stress. It's a bitch. Messes with your mind in all kinds of ways."

"It sure does," Sage responded, then offered a weak smile to the server who placed two salads on the table. "Thank you." She looked at Godiva again. "I see it so clearly now." She pouted. "I wish my aunt hadn't given her what she wanted."

"But Marian didn't get what she wanted. She sure got more than she bargained for, though. She's fallen out of permanent favor with your aunt, and now she has to tell her husband he won't get his Ruth Masterson painting."

"True," Sage said. "I like that part. A lot."

"This dressing is divine," Godiva said as she finished tasting her first mouthful of salad. She looked at Sage, who was nearly inanimate. "It's especially good if you actually put it in your mouth. And eating it only further enhances the experience."

"So they say," Sage said, still poking at her food. "Godiva?"

"Yes?"

"How do I get back to *me*? Every day, I feel like I get further away from who I am."

"You sure you want me to have a stab at that question?"

"I do."

"I believe," Godiva said slowly, "that you were astute in figuring out that Caleb had overcorrected, but what you haven't been able to see is that you're kind of doing the same thing."

"Oh no. I have? How?"

"First, you were so hurt by the breakup that even though you no longer have any interest in Caleb, the whole experience has taken its toll. Because of that, you're insistent you have no interest in love while you're simultaneously developing relationships with two wonderful men. And if that weren't enough, you've resurrected feelings for a third man, Jimmy, who you only knew as a boy and who is a complete stranger to you. You don't think all of that is enough to wreak havoc in your head?"

Sage thought, then put a forkful of salad in her mouth. After a moment, she looked at Godiva. "You're right; the dressing is great. And yeah, you're right about everything else."

Godiva smiled and took a few sips of her peach iced tea. "I'm glad I'm getting through to you, but I'm even happier that you asked."

"So how do I even begin to fix things?"

"Stop fighting love. Spend time with Adam and Benton so you can find out what's in your heart... who's in your heart ... without pushing them away. Speaking of Benton, the other day, when he and Freddie met in the store to go to New York, I noticed Freddie seemed troubled after you and Benton came back from Coffee & Teaz. I asked him what was on his mind, but he wouldn't tell me. Then, last night I overheard him talking on the phone; I think Benton may be going back to Australia in a week. At least for now."

"Oh. I didn't know that. That really makes me sad, actually." She frowned. "So why would Freddie be upset? Is their business deal okay?"

"The business is better than fine. I think he's worried about you falling in love with a man who lives so far away."

"Are you?"

"Not really," Godiva said. "Because if you and Benton do fall in love, there are ways of arranging things. People do it all the time.

I think it's far worse if you don't find out how you really feel and let him go."

"And what else?" Sage said. "There's more that you want to tell me. Your expression gives you away."

"I need to work on my poker face," Godiva said, smiling. "I think that you're already in love with a man who lives in Swansea."

Sage said nothing.

"You look like a kid who's just been caught with her hand in the cookie jar," Godiva said.

"I do care about Adam. I like them both. I'm just so confused."

"What I said a few minutes ago, honey. Take that wall down and see how things feel. Nobody can push you into a relationship you're not ready for … so let that go. And one more thing, which may even be the hardest."

"What's that?" Sage asked, poking at her salad again.

"Let Jimmy go … with love. If you're meant to find each other, you will. Remember, he may have been the universe's way of letting you know how deeply you were able to feel."

"That's so hard."

Godiva took a piece of sourdough bread from the basket on the table and broke it in half. "I know it, Sage. It's always easier to see why someone else is hurting than to fix your own pain. Just try to take down the walls. If you live in the moment and let your senses respond to life as it is right now, I think you might see things in a different light … because it's not easy to see what's happening in front of you when re-runs of your past are playing behind you."

"I'll try. I've become very attached to my defenses. I know that. But for the sake of sanity … and love … I'll give it my best. But I'm not going to look into the night sky and tell love to look toward me. It's not that easy and I'm not that eager. Far from it. But I can see how my protestations have been messing with my head. I'll just do my best; that's all I've got."

"That's all anyone has got," Godiva said. "And I guess I should tell you; I might have overheard Benton say he was going to stop in to see you later."

"You overheard him? Did you see him?"

"Nope. But Freddie had the call on speaker while he was shaving."

"Thanks for letting me know." Sage raised her glass. "A toast to you and to my aunt Ruth … for knowing just how much I needed this lunch."

"Yes," Godiva said with a smile. "And no doubt she'd want you to eat it."

CHAPTER TWENTY-ONE

"You look like Sage again," Ruth said as Sage and Godiva returned from lunch.

"Who did I look like before I left?" Sage asked. She rounded the counter to put down her purse and pet Rufus, who had come out from the back room to greet her.

"Oh, I don't know. Like your own sad twin."

"I guess I did. Or maybe my angry twin, Rage."

"Thank you for lunch, Ruth," Godiva said. "It did us both good." She looked at Sage. "I had fun with Sage and Rage both. But when we were ready to go, Rage excused herself to the ladies' room and never came back. So, it's just Sage and me again."

"Good to know," Ruth said, smiling, giving Sage a hug, then Godiva. "Oh, by the way, I had the funniest customer earlier. She had a message for you both."

"Oh no," Sage said, leafing through the mail on the counter. "Do I want to hear it?" She looked down at Rufus. "Go to your mat, boy."

"Don't worry; it's a good message," Ruth said, petting Rufus as he brushed past her. "The store was quite busy when she came in, and before she left, she pretty much had everyone cracking up." Ruth grabbed her belongings and came around the counter to head out. "She said she bought several lapis stones from you recently. Apparently, her neighbor, a yoga teacher, told her they would help open her husband's third eye."

"Oh yes," Sage said. "She would be hard to forget."

"For sure," Godiva added. "She was a character. I was in the office when she came in, but I heard every word she spoke."

"Well, she wanted me to tell you that the stones appeared to have opened more than her husband's third eye. She said it opened eyes he didn't know he had. Apparently, they're all over every woman in town. She said she's divorcing the SOB, and she couldn't be happier. She was so thrilled with the lapis that she read the descriptions of some of the other stones we sell. She bought several of them, this time for herself. Said to tell you she'll be a regular customer."

"That's great," Sage said. "I do remember thinking she had a stand-up comic vibe."

"Indeed she did." Ruth smiled. "She sure stood up to her husband. Anyway, I had a good couple of hours. And as you will see, so did the store. I've got to get back to my studio. My landscape of Blue Heron Lake patiently awaits my magic touch. Good-bye, ladies. Good-bye, Rufus. I'll check in with you later, Sage."

As Ruth left the store, she nearly collided with Benton, who was just coming in. "G'day, ladies."

"Hey, there," Godiva said, waving as she disappeared through the curtains.

"Hi, Benton," Sage said, walking over to give him a warm hug. "It's really nice to see you."

"I reckon it would be," he said, chuckling, as Rufus rushed over to greet him. "G'day, fluffy mate!" He took a quick look at Rufus's not-so-private parts. "Glad to see the old fella's staying inside today."

"What does that … oh!" Sage said. She looked at him with a

crooked smile. "You're really *bent on* embarrassing me, aren't you?"

"No buts about it." He smiled. "Just having fun. Nice to see you, Sage. I came by to tell you that I'll probably be heading back to Oz in a little over a week. Freddie and I are just finishing up some loose ends at the moment."

"I heard."

Benton's jovial expression faded. "I'm a bit sad, mate. Not sure I'm ready to go."

"I hear you," Sage said.

"I'd sure be rapt if you'd like to have dinner with me tonight. Just the two of us. Afterward, I thought maybe you'd come with me to this rage. Just within cooee … about five blocks from here … some bloke I know from the tennis courts, Richard. He said his friends call him 'Dick,' or maybe I heard someone say he is a dick. Can't quite remember. Bloke's asked me to have a coldie with him a lot of times, but I haven't been interested in a mateship. When he heard I was leaving, told me he and the missus are having friends over for his fortieth birthday tonight. Gave me such an earbash I said I would try to make it. Don't have to stay long. Would you go with me, Sage?"

"I'd love to."

"Good onya, mate. That's what I wanted to hear."

"What time?" Sage asked just seconds before she saw Adam approaching the store with a bouquet of flowers. Her face dropped as they made eye contact through the window. "Um …."

"Whatever is good with you," Benton said.

Sage watched as Adam steeled himself, smiled, then walked into the store.

"G'day, mate," Benton said to Adam. "Are those for me?"

"If you want them to be," Adam said, tossing the play back to Benton.

"Aw, I'm a generous bloke. Let the lady have them."

Sage noticed Adam was working hard to keep the smile on his face as he handed the flowers to her. "These are for …."

"Oh, you didn't have to get me flowers," she said, trying to help Adam out of the awkward spot he was in. "I was glad to help you out."

Sage took a sniff of the flowers, beamed as she admired them, then put the bouquet down on the counter.

"Benton Bradley," he said, extending his hand to Adam with enthusiasm.

"Oh, yes," Adam said as they shook, pretending he hadn't known. "I figured as much when I heard the accent. I'm Adam Canoga. You're working with Freddie on the new line. I'm really glad to run into you. There's a good chance I'll be selling some of your merchandise down the line. You must've heard that I'm opening a new men's clothing store, Haber Dash. I'm wondering if you'd like to come to my pre-opening party the end of next week. I'd love to see you there."

"Ace, mate. I'll be there." He turned to Sage. "About seven forty-five, same as last week."

She nodded. "Sounds good."

"Ta-dah. See ya later then." He looked at Adam. "Next week for you."

Adam looked at Sage with a sad smile. "Guess the early bird got the worm."

"You calling me a worm?" Sage said, trying to lighten the mood.

"That definitely came out wrong. But you'd be the prettiest worm in the earth if you were."

"Thank you. Um … I don't know if you know, but Benton is going back to Australia in a little over a week. So I said yes to spending some time with him before he goes."

"You don't have to explain," Adam said, brightening a bit.

"We're friends."

"Would you have left if I hadn't seen you standing there?" Sage asked him. "With flowers in your hand."

Adam smiled at the customer who walked in. He stood in silence and watched her walk to the back of the store, then spoke, "I'd like to think I wouldn't have. That's all I can tell you."

"Thanks for your honesty."

"Would you be up for dinner with me tomorrow night? Not a date … you know, just two friends—"

"I don't mind calling it a date," Sage said.

His eyes sparkled. "And I don't mind telling you that makes me happy," he said.

"Hi, Adam," Godiva said as she came through the curtains and walked over to greet the customer.

"Hi, Godiva." He waited until she was out of earshot before redirecting his attention to Sage. "I hope you have fun tonight. I mean that." He started to walk away, then stopped to articulate a final thought. "But I hope you have even more fun tomorrow."

"Thanks again for the flowers, Adam. They're gorgeous."

"So are you, earthworm."

Sage watched as he left. When he was out of sight, she picked the bouquet up from the counter.

"Those are stunning," Godiva said. "I didn't know whether to stay in the office or come out here. Kind of a sticky wicket there for a moment."

"It was," Sage said. "But Adam handled it very gracefully. And so did Benton, although I don't know if he had a clue." She smelled the flowers again. "I'm going upstairs to put these in a vase on my kitchen table. Then, I'm going to take the boy over to my aunt's studio. I want to thank her again for today, and I'm really eager to see her newest painting. I'll be back before closing. I want to do something with myself before Benton comes back." She paused. "I don't know. What do hippies do to look pretty?" She glanced at the bouquet. "Maybe some flowers in my hair?"

"Don't let that horrible Marian live rent free in your head," Godiva said. "Banish her. And tell Rage to stay put."

"I'm working on it," Sage said, motioning for Rufus to come over to her. "I really am. Getting my head on straight isn't an easy task. Expect it to be crooked for a bit."

"You're doing just fine," Godiva said. She walked over to ring up a purchase. "We're all a bit lopsided that way."

ട്ട   ട്ട   ട്ട

"That was a fabulous meal," Sage said as she and Benton walked down the street. "I love Middle Eastern food. Not sure why I never tried that place before. I will in the future."

"Glad you liked it," Benton said. "Wish I'd be around to enjoy those future meals with you. Did I tell you how lovely you look tonight? You're gorgeous as, Sage. Even if you wore jam jars, you'd be."

"Jam jars?"

Benton made a circle with the index finger and thumb on each hand and held them up to his eyes.

"Oh," Sage said. "Like coke-bottle glasses."

"That'd be right," Benton said. "You Americans sure have some funny expressions." His eyes opened wide when an overly made-up woman wearing a black miniskirt and a low-cut neon orange top passed by. "Bet she bangs like a dunny door."

Sage laughed. "I don't even know what that means, but I can guess. I think you're right; she does. I've heard the stories."

"This must be the street," Benton said. "Hargrove. Don't think we need to look at the numbers. Must be where all of the music is coming from. Richard said there'd be live musos."

"I find they play much better that way," Sage said with a straight face.

He looked at her.

"When they're alive," Sage said.

"Oh, gotcha." Benton laughed. "Sounds like a real bash in there, doesn't it?"

He took her hand as they walked up the path to the house. The front door was open, and there were several people, all holding drinks, standing in the living room.

"Party's out back," one woman yelled. "That's where the band is."

Benton laughed and looked at Sage. "Did she say the party's in the outback?"

They walked through the dining room, then through the kitchen to the back door.

"There must be eighty people here," Sage said to Benton. "At least."

"My man, Benton!" The man in the white pants and the navy polo shirt, with a glass of whiskey on the rocks in one hand, rushed up to him. "Glad you could make it, buddy." He eyed Sage. "I've seen this lady before. You walk your dog around town. Sure, I know who you are." He took a large swig of his drink. "Well, ashually, I don't have a clue. I just see you. I'm Rishhard."

"Sage."

"Parsley, sage, rosemary, and thyme," Richard sang loudly over the rock music. "Tell me, Sage, are you going to Scarborough Fair?"

Sage winced and said nothing.

"I reckon she's heard that one before, mate. Probably a few hundred times."

"What's your poison?" Richard said as he slapped a guy on the back who was passing him. He returned his attention to Benton.

"Cashhhh bar, right over there." He pointed to the man he'd just slapped. "That's my brother-in-law, Steve-oh. Owns a fleet of limos. Think he owns some trucks too." He put his arm around his wife, who had just sidled up next to him. "Steve owns trucks, yeah, sweetie doll?"

"How do you forget six trucks, you crazy birthday boy?"

"With six drinks, I guess." He took a step closer to Sage and Benton. "So yeah, Steve owns limousines and six trucks. You might say he's a guy who likes things on wheels. Even my sister has a couple of wheels. That's why he married her."

Richard and his wife laughed while Sage and Benton exchanged looks.

"I like wheels too," Richard continued. "But not enough to go on the wagon."

He and his wife laughed again while Sage and Benton looked blankly at them.

"Hi, I'm Nancy, Richard's wife. Do we know you?" She took a gulp of her vodka martini.

"This is Benton. Swansea's visitor from Australia," Richard said loud enough for several nearby people to hear. "The guy I know from the tennis court."

"Oh," Nancy said. She looked at Sage. "Who's this?"

"Parsley, Sage … uh, yeah, this is Rosemary. She walks her dog."

"Nice to meet you, Rosemary," Nancy said, looking Sage up and down. "Are you a paid dog walker? Because we could use someone to take our Moochie out when we're not here? Does five dollars per walk sound good?"

"No, actually. It doesn't. And I'm not a paid dog walker," Sage said.

Benton looked at her as if to apologize. "They got the wobbly boot on," he said in her ear.

"Hey, hey, hey," a large man in a tailored plaid shirt holding a bottle of beer said. "It's the man from the land of down under." He grabbed Benton by the arm and gripped him tightly. "I'm Walter Widgdale. Been wanting to ask a real live Australian this: is it true there's a guy named Goober Petey who lives underground in Australia?"

"Ah," Benton said. "You're thinking of a town called Coober Pedy in northern South Australia. It's the opal capital of the world."

"Waaaait a minute," Walter said. "You just said it was north; then you said it was south. Make up your mind there, fella."

"South Australia is the name of a state," Benton explained with a not-so-polite edge to his voice. "And Coober Pedy is in the northern part of it."

Walter turned to Richard and Nancy. "This is what happens when you live in another hemisphere. You don't know north from south or east from west."

"I know my directions quite well," Benton said.

"How about this Goober guy who lives underground?"

Benton turned to Sage. "Wish this Goober did." He paused before answering Walter, who was eagerly awaiting a response. "Coober Pedy, the town, has some blazing heat in the daytime. So they built homes underground."

Richard nudged Walter out of the way. "Nancy and I are thinking of visiting Australia in the winter when the seasons are reversed. Switchy witchy, we call it." He smacked Benton on the arm. "Think you could put us up, mate?" He laughed raucously.

"Full as a boot," Benton mumbled to himself.

"Hey, I was gonna ask him the same thing," Walter said.

"So this is your fortieth," Benton said to Richard as he put a protective arm around Sage.

"I see what you're doing there," Richard said, pointing a finger at Benton, then wagging it.

"Was just going to wish you a happy birthday, mate."

"You're changing the sud-jeck," Richard said. He downed the last of the whiskey left in his glass as a caterer handed him a fresh one. "Hey, garçon! Drinks for my Australian host-to-be. Start a tab."

Benton looked at Sage, then waved him off. "No thanks. We're good."

"Shhhure you're *good*," Richard slurred. "But you could be betterrrr. So come on, tell us how we can contact you. Bet you're famous there, huh?" He turned to Nancy. "The wizard of Oz is gonna be our host."

"I'll tell you what, mate. Look up a place called the Bludger Inn. It's been in my family for generations, and I'd be real happy to put you where you belong for an extra-special mate's rate. We're usually chock a block, but we'll make room."

"What's that name again?" Walter said, trying to type it onto his phone.

"Bludger Inn," Benton said. "In the state of Porky."

"Whoa, slow down," Walter said. "I've got chubby fingers."

"Oh, bloody hell," Benton exclaimed, pointing in the distance. "That's not right! What's going on over there? Somebody better stop those people before they get away!"

As everyone within earshot turned to look, Benton grabbed Sage by the hand. "Run like the wind, chicky." She laughed, and holding on to him, they ran out of the crowd, along the side of the house, until they were back on the street.

"I'm out of breath," Sage said, once they were several houses away. "Brilliant move there, Benton. Because I, I mean Rosemary … ugh … can't believe he called me that … was seriously going to punch those people in the face."

"I was almost ready to have a blue with him. Those people were paralytic," Benton said. "Damn pack of bludgers. I'm really sorry, Sage. Like I said, Richard isn't my kind of mate, but he's less of a scumbag sober. I was just trying to be nice and make an appearance. Didn't have a clue he was tight as a fish's arse and a bludger in disguise."

"Who the heck has a cash bar at their own birthday party? That's crazy cheap. Did you hear what their dog's name is?"

"Sailed by me, that one."

"Moochie."

"That's the one," Benton said. "Poor dog. How about we go get a drink?"

"Oh, yeah," Sage said. "I thought you'd never ask."

ço   ço   ço

"Cheers," Sage said as she and Benton clinked their brandy snifters. "Those were awful people, but that was so much fun. I needed that."

"I didn't expect to have much in common with Richard or his mates, but I didn't think we'd have to shoot through like that."

"It took me back to my childhood," Sage said.

"How's that?" Benton said, taking a small handful of peanuts from a nearby bowl.

"Well, when Jimmy and I would hang out in Mr. Simmons's field, we'd always be half looking for him. And there were a couple of times when we saw him coming that Jimmy took my hand, just like you did, and we'd run for our lives. And it was scary because we were young enough to believe he could have had us thrown in jail. But at the same time, it was a rush."

"Ah, I can well imagine." He took a sip of his drink to wash down the peanuts. "I wasn't going to listen to that dipstick's earbash much longer," Benton said. "Especially when he was stonkered. If you need that much grog to have a good time, something's not right with you." His eyes twinkled. "I was going to tell him to knick off;

then I remembered it was his house. It felt great to escape, especially with you at my side."

Sage smiled. "I wonder if they even noticed we were gone. Which begs the question: do we care?"

"Exactly, mate! I'll tell you this much: I won't be going back to the tennis courts again."

"No, I wouldn't think you'd want to, especially with only a week left." She frowned. "I've kind of gotten used to you being around and brightening up my day. I'll miss the many moments when my brain is scrambling to figure out what you're talking about."

"You think I can understand Americans that easily?" Benton said, then laughed.

"Yeah," Sage said. "I think you can, actually."

Benton's countenance became serious. "I understand your words, Sage, but I don't always know what you mean by them. Bloody oath, mate."

Sage touched his arm. "I'm not trying to play games with anyone. I promise. And if you haven't understood something, it's because I haven't either."

"That bloke who brought you flowers is in love with you."

Sage's mouth fell open. "Oh, wow. I wasn't expecting you to go there."

"You think I couldn't see that?"

She blushed and said nothing.

"What I can't see, however, is how you feel about him."

"Um ...."

"I'm heading back to Oz soon. Can't say I haven't thought about what it would be like if you came with me."

Sage could see the sadness and the hope as he looked longingly into her eyes. Unsure of how to respond, her eyes mirrored what she saw in his.

Benton tapped his fingers on the bar. "I don't mean next week, of course. But I'll definitely be back in these parts, and I couldn't help but wonder how things might go down the road if our mateship develops."

"I-I just don't …."

"Then again, there's every possibility you might be happy just to give me the flick."

"No, not at all," Sage said. "I'm trying to figure out my feelings. I'm just not being very successful."

"If I'm not in the race, you can tell me that too."

"Oh, Benton," Sage said, making an exaggerated pout, "it's nothing that simple." She rubbed three fingers on the mahogany bar as she stared at it. "I just noticed this gorgeous wood."

"The bar likes you, hey."

Sage's face went blank. "What?" She looked at the gleam in Benton's eyes. "Oh, you!" she said, punching him. "You need to stop with that."

"Sorry, Sage. You can take the Aussie out of Oz, but you can't—"

"Exactly," Sage said, then laughed. "You're hopeless. And if you don't behave, I'm going to send you back to Richard and Nancy's house. He's probably on his tenth drink by now. Or passed out."

"I'd rather drink with the flies than ever see those mongrels again," Benton said. He stroked a lock of her long brown hair for a moment before taking his hand away. "You really are quite extraordinary, Sage. And I'm really sorry if I pressured you to give me answers to things you haven't figured out yet. I'd just never forgive myself if I didn't tell you how I feel."

৯   ৯   ৯

"This was a really great evening," Sage said, taking the keys out of her purse as they reached her store. I enjoyed the dinner, our great escape, and our time at Marcello's. Very special."

"I'm packing this memory and taking it home with me, but I hope to make a few more before I go. Do you need a late-night escort on my fluffy mate's last walk of the day?"

"Nope," Sage said. "My aunt texted me earlier that she was going to stop by the store to pick something up, and she'd walk him for me."

They both looked down to see Rufus excitedly circling on the other side of the door.

"But please come in and say good-night to him," Sage said as she unlocked the door and pulled it open.

"Evenin' mate," Benton said, giving Rufus a vigorous rub of the neck. "Gets lonely here when your mum's gone, doesn't it? Can't blame a bloke for wanting to take her out now, can you?" He looked at Sage and grinned. "Says he doesn't blame me at all."

"Oh, really," Sage said. "So now you can communicate telepathically with my dog?"

"Didn't say that," Benton told her. "It's all in the tail. See, it's like this: I learned tailspeak from the dingoes in the bush. There's an entire language in the way they use their tails. That's why the bushies called them waggers. Spend enough time around a wagger slash dingo and you'll be able to interpret every swish and swash, every flip and dip."

Sage punched him playfully in the arm. "You are totally full of it." She laughed. "And I have no idea what a flip and a dip of the tail even means." She thought for a moment. "And actually, neither do you, for that matter. You totally think you can just make up anything at all, tell me it's Australian, and get away with it."

Benton laughed. "Thought that was a pretty good effort, hey." He followed Sage over to the counter as she laid her purse down. "Bet those bludgers at the bash would have believed me."

"Being heavily intoxicated tends to muddle one's thinking."

"Don't I know that," Benton said, his tone more serious.

"You okay?" Sage asked.

"All's good," he said, putting his hands on her shoulders.

Sage smiled, and before she knew it, his soft lips were kissing hers, his arms were around her, and she kissed him back as if she had loved him forever.

ço   ço   ço

As Sage walked upstairs with Rufus behind her, she felt a warm rush of happiness she had feared might elude her forever. Her smile was so big that she could feel the way it changed her face.

Everything felt right within her world. Even Finlay and Babaloo seemed to sense her happiness. She felt as if she were glowing …. She must be, if her cats had come to greet her with such uncharacteristic enthusiasm.

She looked at Rufus. "Hey, fluffy mate, what do you think of our friend from Australia?" Rufus wagged his tail, and Sage laughed, remembering Benton's tall tale about Australia's bush. But as she glanced at the counter, which separated her kitchen from the living room, she felt her face drop … with a thud. There, the bouquet that Adam had brought her earlier just seemed to look at her with sad but colorful eyes. Don't forget me, it seemed to say.

"Oh, Adam," Sage said as she let her purse fall to the floor. "Why do I feel like I've just cheated on you?"

CHAPTER TWENTY-TWO

"Hey, Trubs. What a treat to see you on a Saturday."

Before Sage could greet Randy, Rufus made it clear who was more deserving of Randy's immediate affection.

"I know how you feel, boy," Randy said as he scratched Rufus on the head and let the dog give him a few kisses. "I get it; I do. Every time Uncle Randy looks in the mirror, he sees the reason for your euphoria."

Sage laughed, then walked over to greet him.

"Where's Godiva," Randy said, scanning the store.

"At lunch with Freddie," Sage said, petting Rufus before he headed to the back room.

"The future Mr. and Mrs. Lamar do make a beautiful couple," Randy said, picking up a few white stones in his hand. "When they broke up, it pained me. I always knew they belonged together, and I'm just glad everything worked out before anyone else could come along for either one of them."

"They love each other something fierce. I think it would have been quite a while before a third person could have gotten in the way."

"I do agree, though I've seen more shocking things happen." Randy held out his open hand. "What magic powers might these stones possess?"

"Oh, the howlite," Sage said. "It's a very calming stone. Good for high-energy people who work at newspapers, write on deadlines, and yet still have time to admire themselves in the mirror."

Randy put a hand to his chest, as if to calm heart flutter. "Surely the choice of that description is coincidental, having no relation to actual persons, past or present."

Sage laughed. "Oh, yeah. Total coincidence." She looked at the stones in his hand. "These are also good for those nights when your brain is working overtime, and you can't get to sleep."

"Excellent," Randy said. "As long as they don't put anything else to sleep that I wish to stay woke."

"I can't imagine," Sage said with a grin.

Randy walked over to the counter and put four howlite stones down. "I'll take these, but the reason I came in is because Kyle came into the *Herald* office and saw the fountain that Molly Rose and I bought for Ana. He would like something similar for the reception area at his new business."

"I can help with that," Sage said, walking him over to a display. "We just got in a brand new fountain that I haven't sold yet. It's a Balinese-inspired tabletop fountain with green bamboo containers. It's also got dual water flows. If you don't like it, I have seven other models that you might prefer, and I can order pretty much anything at all if I don't stock it."

Randy pulled out his phone. "I'm going to snap a few photos and let Kyle decide." His expression changed. "Speaking of decision-making, how was your evening with Benton? Have you come any closer to deciding who to insist you're not in love with?"

Sage smiled as one of her regular customers walked in and headed for the jewelry displays. "And you know I was out with Benton last night because ....?"

"Because Kyle and I were having a late dinner at Marcello's

and saw the two of you come in and head to the bar."

"Oh," she said, walking behind the counter to ring up some votive candles and incense for a male customer. "I see. I wish you had made your presence known."

Randy didn't say anything until Sage finished with the transaction. "No way. I know Mr. Bradley is headed back to Australia, and neither Kyle nor I wanted to interrupt your precious time together."

"Well, to save you from wondering if there might be another chance discovery tonight, I should tell you that I have a date with Adam. For dinner."

"Miss Sage! Your snark is showing."

"It's about time then, isn't it?"

Randy leaned on the counter. "Can you tell your good friend Randy if there are any feelings developing for these men?"

"Maybe," Sage said, straightening some catalogs behind the counter. "It's not easy. There are different things I like about each man."

"Such as?"

"Well, they both make me laugh, but Benton does so in a way that makes me want to punch him sometimes … lovingly, of course. Being with him takes me back to the carefree childhood days I spent with Jimmy. I feel safe around Benton. I'm not going to lie and say that I don't find him insanely attractive too, because I do."

"Randy understands. And Mr. Canoga?"

"Adam touches my heart in so many ways. He's not afraid to tell the world he's a flawed human being who can be as insecure as the rest of us. And at the same time, he's proud, gracious, intuitive, funny, caring, loyal, and yes, a sexy teddy bear. And he works hard every day to be a better person. I have so much respect for him."

Randy handed Sage some cash to pay for the stones. "Too bad you can't take some features from column A and some from column B."

"I hear you," Sage said. "But in a way, all kidding aside, that's kind of creepy. I'm not looking for perfection. The thing is, if I do fall in love with Adam, I don't want it to be because Benton has to return to Australia. And I don't want to dismiss Benton because he's not geographically proximate at the moment, but it's also way hard to forget that he lives over ten thousand miles away." Sage handed Randy a small brown bag with the stones inside, along with his change.

"A good reminder how lucky I am to have found my Mister Right," Randy said, putting the bag and change in his pocket. "Oh, speaking of Mr. Canoga, I almost forgot!"

"What's that?"

"I was on Hudson Street earlier, and I saw that Gothic long-nosed horror who whacked Molly Rose in the knees with her bag. The creature was headed right for Adam's store. I stepped out of sight so she wouldn't see me watching her."

"Oh, no! Did she go inside?"

"No. But she took a really good look in the window before making her way down the street. Just talking about her makes my pampered skin crawl. How about another squirt of that spray bearing your name to purify the air that surrounds? Would that be too much for Randy to ask?"

Sage laughed as she came from around the corner and grabbed the tester bottle of sage spray. "On the count of three, get ready to fan the mist."

Randy waved his hand in the air while she sprayed. "Thank you for the purification. I feel better already. Well, I must be on my way. I'll get back to you about the fountain." He thought for a moment. "Have a good night. Try not to overthink it all. Just let yourself feel. You can do it, Miss Sage."

༄   ༄   ༄

Sage radiated happiness as the host seated her and Adam in the white tufted-leather booth. The moment they sat across from one another, the warmth between them flowed, further augmented by the candle in the amber glass holder that intensified the heat.

"I had no idea you were bringing me into New York," Sage said. "Especially not to this beautiful place. This restaurant is breathtakingly gorgeous."

"I see 'breathtakingly gorgeous' as well," Adam said, the light from the candle flickering in his eyes.

Sage blushed. "There are only a million restaurants in this city. How did you come to choose this one?"

"Remember all of the time I spent in New York getting ready to open my store? Well, I was here for a business lunch one day. And even though you and I hadn't seen one another for a long time, it was kind of hard for me to focus on designer suits that day. I kept thinking how much I'd rather be here with you. For dinner."

"Oh, Adam."

"I've cared about you for a long time, Sage. But I never thought our being here together would be a reality. Well … you know, because …."

"I was engaged to Caleb." Sage made a face as if she had just tasted a bitter herb.

"Yeah. But it didn't stop me from visualizing this moment. Funny, I'd thought about you so much before, but never allowed my mind to carry me to the place it did that day."

"Do you happen to remember exactly when you were here?"

"I'm guessing," Adam said, "that it was a couple weeks before Valentine's Day. Yes. That's right. I remember now because the guy I was with told me he was bringing his girlfriend here for a special evening."

"Oh, really," Sage said. "That's right around the time Caleb and I broke up. Maybe your visualization had something to do with it."

"Interesting," Adam said. "Maybe I shouldn't have restrained myself from fantasizing … I mean 'visualizing' sooner." He looked at Sage as the waiter approached their table. "Do you still prefer white wine with your meal?"

"I do," Sage said.

Adam opened the wine menu and looked at the waiter. "What would you suggest in a dry white wine?"

"We have an excellent Australian Chardonnay. It's got a smoky, citrusy flavor and is one of our most popular."

"Hmm," Adam said.

The waiter pointed to the menu Adam was holding. "Another popular choice is this Chardonnay from the Napa Valley. It has—"

"The California wine will be perfect, thank you," Adam said, closing the wine menu and handing it to him. "And we've yet to make any decisions about dinner."

ço   ço   ço

"The chef is quite the artist," Adam said as the waiter placed Sage's meal before her, then his. "Thank you."

"The salad was delicious," Sage said to Adam after the waiter had left. "This shrimp and crabmeat dish looks like it could grace the cover of *Bon Appetit*." She picked up her dinner fork. "So tell me, how is the store coming along? I missed our walk today. Rufus has gotten used to being with Toto and Vizzy; he was looking everywhere for them." She smiled. "And I've gotten used to spending that time with you as well."

"I missed walking with you too," Adam said, trying not to let his face reveal how much Sage's comment meant to him. "But knowing that I'd see you tonight was a great impetus to keep working so we could have this time together. To answer your question, I'm right on schedule and couldn't be happier about it. I'm really pleased with the people I've hired." He took a bite of his food, then a sip of wine. "There was one small hiccup today, though. I'm just hoping it doesn't turn into a whooping cough."

"Oh, no, Adam. What was it?" Sage laid her fork down. "Wait, don't tell me you saw Goth Lady looking in your store window."

"You knew?"

"Randy saw her." Sage crinkled her forehead. "I hope you're not upset that I didn't tell you. I thought that if you didn't see her, I might let it go and not upset you. Of course, if I heard that she'd done anything *but* just look in the window, I would have said something."

"She hasn't come back to your store, has she?"

"Nope," Sage said. "But she was in there long enough to look at every last thing we sell, so I'm guessing she got what she wanted. The question is: why did she want it, and what is she going to do with it? Honestly, that was the first time I was weirded out by a customer buying anything I sell. But a mini cauldron, an evil-eye charm, and a Tibetan knife … well, I don't know. I guess I wouldn't have given it a second thought if she were remotely normal. I know you might think my store attracts anything but …."

"Actually," Adam said. "I think your store attracts a lot of wonderful people. I've always gotten a good vibe in there. Before we move on, I should tell you that I have an idea about who that woman might be."

"Please!"

"Well, remember when I told Joanie that I wasn't going to hire her, and I said that she went right for the jugular?"

"Sure."

"I'm thinking that woman is likely one of her eccentric friends who's spying on me for reasons I hate to consider, and is possibly doing the same where you're concerned … as we have been seen together a lot lately. In Joanie's twisted mind, maybe she thinks she'll find out something at your store to turn me against you. That might explain why that woman spent so much time there."

"Unfortunately," Sage said, "that makes more sense than I'd like it to."

"Yeah, I know," Adam replied. "I wish it didn't. And, if you want the whole truth, I'm concerned that she might show up at the party. I just hope she isn't planning to cause a scene as payback for me not hiring Joanie … or worse … for not taking her back."

"That would be awful, Adam. But try not to worry. Your friends will all be there to support you if she tries anything." She paused to savor another taste of her wine. "I'm glad you told me. And if she comes into my store again, I'll be sure not to have even the slightest bit of personal conversation when she's nearby." She paused. "Not that I would anyway."

Adam smiled and thanked the waiter as he took the wine bottle out of the chilled holder and filled their glasses.

"Oh," Adam said. "Speaking of unusual women, we had an arrest in Swansea last night."

"No way," Sage said. "For what?"

"Prostitution."

"Get out of here."

"I'd rather stay." Adam smiled. "I'd like to finish my meal and look at the gorgeous woman I'm with." He took a sip of his wine.

"That's so sweet," Sage said. She leaned slightly forward and lowered her voice. "Tell me about the arrest."

"I forget the woman's name, but she's in her forties and

walks around in miniskirts most of the time. I have no doubt the story will get out, but it's on the down low at the moment because the guy they caught her with was Roland Everest Hall, Naomi's older brother. A friend of mine happened to be at the police station when they brought *her* in and let *him* go. You know how it is: money talks and then it walks." He thought for a moment. "Maybe he'll join his sister at her *Hall*-of-shame hideaway in the Hamptons."

Sage laughed. "Good one. The family can't be happy about Naomi's public shaming at *Le Chat Noir* for stealing flowers at Swansea Hospital. I guess the good news is that Roland's arrest will take some of the negative attention away from Naomi."

"For sure. And Roland is married, so his wife … and his family … won't be happy campers when they find out he was with another woman … doing what they were doing. Ahem. Especially *that* woman."

"No, they won't be," Sage said. "I actually saw her out walking last night. It had to have been before she and Roland hooked up. I was with … um …."

Adam reached across the table and took her hand. "It's okay to say Benton's name. I know you were with him. His name isn't taboo." He squeezed her hand, then took his away.

"Thanks for that." She smiled. "How about if I just tell you that Benton took a quick look at her as she passed us on the street, and he said she looks as if she 'bangs like a dunny door.'"

Adam laughed. "Whatever a dunny door is. That's quite amusing."

"He told me later that a dunny door is an outhouse door. Like the ones they have in the bush."

"Oh, okay. That makes sense. Benton's a very likeable guy. I just like him better when he's not with you." He twisted his lips. "Is that terrible of me?"

"No," Sage said with a sheepish grin. "Especially since I'm pretty sure he feels the same way about you."

Adam nodded as if to indicate he understood. "I've always liked you, Sage. And those feelings have only intensified over time. I really believe that what is meant to be will be. I'm not so pumped up on testosterone that I'm going to pull some crazy macho stunts in the hopes of winning your affection. If I did something like that, I would only be acting out some character I created. And he wouldn't be the real me. And that's especially important because what I've always liked most about you is that you're comfortable in your own skin. Your smile is authentic and your spirit always shines through. You're like a gorgeous wildflower that stands out in a row of perfectly planted flowers. You've got petals that Mother Nature created just for you, and your leaves sway gently in the breeze, while all of the other flowers stay rigid and still." His face reddened slightly. "Too much?"

Sage lowered her eyes for a moment. After taking a breath, she looked at him. "No. Not at all. Thank you for seeing that in me. You know, from the time I was in junior high, I used to watch the other girls get all silly and flirtatious with the boys. Now, when I see women put on that kind of a show for men, I wonder how it's going to all work out when the glitter rubs off. You know? And if a man pumps himself full of machismo, I'm less than impressed. Anyone who gets any sense of me at all knows that's not what I want." She took another bite of her food, then met his gaze. "I just feel really grateful that I've always been okay being me."

"You're more than okay," Adam said. "You're the most special woman I've ever known."

৯ ৯ ৯

Adam took Sage's hand as they walked down West Forty-Sixth

Street toward Times Square.

"So many theaters on this block alone," Sage said while theatergoers brushed past her with rolled-up *Playbills* in their hands.

"There are. And I hope someday we can see a show in every one of them. I don't think I've been to the theater since I was a teenager."

"Me either," Sage said, turning her head to watch a group of tourists eagerly greeting a well-known actress the moment she exited the stage door. "I hope she isn't in a big hurry. Her fans have her surrounded. Everyone wants a selfie *and* an autograph."

"Little do they know," Adam said, "that the biggest star in the galaxy just walked past them."

"Who's that?" Sage asked, turning her head to look. "Oh!" She blushed. "You're too nice."

"I'm just the luckiest guy in New York tonight," he said as they approached Times Square. He looked around. "A real flickering spectacle of lights and quite the mass and mix of people, isn't it? Time Square is too touristy for my taste, too crowded as well, especially on a summer night, but it was too close to pass up having a quick adventure here with you."

"I agree on all counts," Sage said. "This is quite the change of scenery from our usual walks. Oh, no. Look over there. Elmo looks a bit upset with those tourists he just took a photo with. I don't think that couple realizes that these characters are here for one reason only … and it's not to enhance the New York experience for out-of-town visitors for only a smile."

"Exactly," Adam said. "There have been several unfortunate incidents with people who didn't know you're supposed to tip. Of course, most people figure it out, but there are always those people who simply don't want to give up the cash. Not good. But, for those who can't get tickets for a Broadway show, if they hang out here long enough, they can see characters fighting with each other for prime spots and other things. I was passing through one night, and Spiderman was being less than chivalrous to Wonder Woman. Turned into a physical altercation."

"I hope Wonder Woman wasn't hurt."

"Actually, Wonder Woman turned out to be a man, and to everyone's surprise, there was a woman inside of the Spiderman costume. And yeah, she pummeled him. I saw the cops show up, but I didn't stick around to see what happened."

Sage looked up at a movie trailer playing on the side of a building while an electronic billboard displayed a clothing advertisement next to it. The second she looked down, a man eating a hot dog almost collided with her.

"Sorry," the guy said, rushing away.

"At least he apologized," Adam said, laughing. "But I think he's going to really be sorry when he figures out that he used too much mustard, and he's wearing it now."

"Yeah, I saw that yellow stripe on the front of his suit. I'm just glad I'm not wearing it too." She smiled and snuggled closer to Adam.

"I wish we could spend more time in New York before we drive back to Swansea," Adam said as they walked through the crowds. "I'll be working all throughout Sunday to be ready for the party and the opening, so I suppose I should get some sleep. How about you?"

"I'm going to see my parents again. I'll be back sometime Monday. Probably later in the day."

"I miss you already," Adam said. "Hey, before we go, let's do something touristy."

"Like what?" Sage asked. "I hope you don't want to take a photo with Elmo. He's in a bad mood."

"Nothing like that," Adam said. He nodded toward a large

souvenir shop in front of them. "How do matching T-shirts sound?"

"Like the best possible souvenir." Her eyes sparkled as she reached up and kissed him on the lips.

He grinned. "That's the second time you've done that. Not that I'm counting or anything."

She smiled and pulled him toward the store. "Let's go look at the shirts. I hope we'll be able to agree on a color."

"That could be a problem," Adam said, his eyes smiling. "Not everything goes with my hair or my brown eyes. In fact, there's only one color I can think of that goes with matches me without question."

"What color would that be?"

"Just a certain shade of green I'm partial to …."

"Um, lime green? Hunter green? I hope not, because New York tees don't come in those colors."

"Sage green," he said as they entered the store. "Sage is so pretty."

"And you're so sweet. Unless you want to get a white shirt and dye it, which you hardly have time for, you're out of luck. There is one more option, though."

"What's that?" Adam said, opening his eyes wide in playful surprise.

"I could change my name to Blue, Gray, or Black."

"I'm just glad you didn't change it to Dunlap," Adam said. He stopped to look at her and ran a tendril of her hair through two fingers. "You don't need to change a thing."

"Can I change my *mind* about something?" Sage asked.

"What's that?" Adam said as they entered the souvenir shop.

"After we get these shirts, let's go back and get our photo taken with Elmo. I've got a five-dollar bill in my purse for a tip. I kind of like the idea of a photo to help me remember this magical evening with you."

CHAPTER TWENTY-THREE

"Amazing," Godiva said, taking the last sip of her morning coffee. "I haven't seen you in two days, and you have more news than the *Swansea Herald*. Darn, woman, when you finally agree to go on dates, you don't mess around."

"I did have two wonderful evenings," Sage said. "But I haven't always been so lucky." She laughed. "A couple of years ago, Molly and I had dinner together, and we spent hours comparing disastrous date stories."

"And you won?"

"No way! Molly beat me by a mile. The thing is, though, she never let her bad dates keep her from looking, but they did make her highly selective ... or, as she says, 'picky.' I pretty much withdrew from even thinking about love until I agreed to meet Caleb. And well, we all know how that turned out."

"Yes. You withdrew again," Godiva said. "You stonewalled love in epic proportions. But now you're getting to know Adam in a brand new way ... and you've met Benton. It's all good, so don't ever regret the relationship with Caleb. You grew from it in so many ways."

"I know what you're saying. I just get sick thinking about him. But I guess we all have to have a past with some substance to have a future with the same. Right? And isn't it kind of a necessary cliché to have an ex that we're glad to be rid of?"

"That is how it works, I think. Some days, anyway." Godiva smiled, put her coffee cup into the bag, got up, then walked over to throw it out. She sat down again and turned to Sage. "Did I tell you how much I loved hearing how you and Benton escaped from Richard and Nancy Klapper's party? Not only are they known around town for being heavy drinkers, but they're incredibly cheap. They're both stockbrokers and do very well, but, yeah, it doesn't surprise me in the least that the guy had a cash bar for his fortieth."

"Why are people like that?"

"Don't know, Sage. Just that they're so afraid of being taken advantage of because they're rich that they take advantage of everyone else."

"But their friends all looked like they were rich too."

"No doubt," Godiva said. "They wouldn't have it any other way. But that doesn't stop them from being cheap. More money to spend on booze and bigger numbers in their bank accounts to assuage their fear of being poor, I suppose."

"Benton apologized for not having known the kind of people they are. But the only time he's ever seen the guy has been at the tennis court, early in the day."

"I'm glad he didn't know; it made for an exciting adventure. *The Great Escape*, starring Sage Gordon and Benton Bradley."

Sage laughed as she broke off a piece of banana bread on the small plate in front of her. "I did feel like I was in a movie for a moment." She reached over for her phone. "Oh, I almost forgot to show you this."

"What's that?"

"The photos of Adam and me with Elmo in Times Square."

Godiva took the phone and smiled as she looked at the photos. "Oh, Sage. These are so special. You both look absolutely joyous. What a beautiful way to end your official first date."

Sage blushed.

"Oh," Godiva said. "Yeah. I guess your date didn't actually end until you got back to Swansea."

"No, it didn't. And our date ended with a kiss so beautiful I can still feel his lips on mine."

"Okaaaay. So why do you have that funny look on your face? Like something is torturing you?"

Sage dunked her tea bag. "I don't know. Maybe it's because my date with Benton kind of ended the same way."

ം ം ം

"Did I miss anything while I was gone?" Sage asked as she and Rufus returned from their morning walk.

Godiva, who was standing by the wall display case with a wire basket on her arm, had just finished placing some new jewelry pieces on the shelves. "Well, I had a customer offer … or should I say beg, to buy the Private Property sign."

Instinctively, Sage looked up to make sure it was still on the wall before she bent down to remove the dog's harness. "I don't know why so many people want to buy my sign. It has great sentimental value to me, but it's not like you can't go to a hardware store or a sign maker and get one."

"I actually suggested the woman do something like that. But she said it wasn't easy to find something with a 'rustic, nostalgic feel to it' like this one has."

"True," Sage said. She looked at Rufus. "Go drink some water, boy." She walked over to Godiva and reached her hand out. "I'll put the basket back for you."

Rufus greeted a customer who had just walked in. After a few exuberant tail wags, he hurried behind the curtains into the back room.

After Godiva said hello to the same customer, she led her to the bookshelves toward the back, then returned to Sage, who was now behind the counter. She looked up on the wall. "Do you think that having this constant reminder of Jimmy might be making it harder for you to move on?"

"No," Sage snapped. "It means something to me, okay? It's my store, and I like it just where it is."

Godiva reeled back. "Oh, Sage, I'm so sorry. I really overstepped. Please accept my apology." She put her hands over her face. "Can we rewind just one minute so I can keep my big mouth closed?"

Sage sighed. "No need. I'm the one who is sorry. I didn't mean to go off on you." She waited a moment until the customers were out of earshot. "Seriously, I'm sorry, Godiva. I know this is going to sound really stupid, but being on those wonderful dates made me feel guilty. Like I was giving up on ever finding Jimmy. Like I was betraying him somehow. I know that's insanely stupid, or maybe just insanely sentimental, but I felt in that second like you were reading my mind and chastising me for my thoughts. And of course, you weren't. And I apologize."

"I couldn't be happier that you've opened your heart, and here I am like an idiot, putting you on the defensive. And it's not as if I don't understand why the sign is so comforting to you."

Sage grabbed the pile of mail on the counter and began leafing through it. "Well, sometimes I don't understand myself. So how can I expect anyone else to do so?"

"Did you and Adam just have your morning walk?"

"No," Sage said. "He's going crazy trying to get his store ready. He's got the rest of today, Wednesday, and Thursday to be ready for Friday's grand opening. Most people who are coming will be there after seven, when most stores in Swansea have closed. He's expecting a big turnout. Oh, and he has a very good theory about who crazy Goth Woman is. I'll tell you at lunch."

"I'm intrigued! I've been wracking my brain and haven't come up with a thing."

"I just hope she doesn't cause a scene. I have a bad feeling about her."

"Well, if she or anyone else even thinks about it, Adam will have lots of friends there."

"That's what I told him. But hopefully, she'll have the good sense to stay away."

"Well, try not to let her worry you," Godiva said. "It's all very exciting. Adam is such a great guy … a real hard worker. I couldn't be happier for him."

"Me too," Sage said. "By the way, while Rufus and I didn't walk with him today, we did go over to the store to get Vizzy and Invisible Toto. I took them for a walk since Adam is too busy to get away."

"Impressive," Godiva said. "Walking three dogs isn't easy."

"Yeah," Sage said. "It's not. But it really helps when the one of them is invisible. Easier to pick up after Toto too."

"Or not," Godiva said.

"True," Sage said, laughing. "I'm going to be in the office paying some bills. If it gets busy, just call me, okay? I'll be done by lunchtime."

"Sure thing," Godiva said. She smiled as a customer placed a blue scarf and a book about shamanic healing on the counter. "And trust me, everything will have a way of landing right where it belongs."

৯   ৯   ৯

Benton, dressed in khaki pants, a navy blue V-neck shirt, sporting sunglasses, and holding half a submarine sandwich in one hand, hurried through the door, causing the bells to clang less gently than normal.

He smiled, took a big bite from his sandwich, chewed it, then looked at Sage, who was behind the counter, and at Godiva, who was carefully cleaning some crystal singing bowls nearby.

"G'day, ladies." He took another bite of his sandwich.

"Hi, Benton," Sage said. "You look … um … hungry!"

"Hey, Benton," Godiva said. "I thought you and Freddie had one last meeting in New York."

He took a moment to finish chewing. "Sure am hungry. Only had a dingo's breakfast. Been taking care of a lot of last-minute details and didn't get to eat." He turned to Godiva. "Meeting Freddie here in an hour. Wanted to see my girl Sage before we go."

He took off his sunglasses and hung them on his shirt. "Sorry, didn't mean to keep my sunnies on indoors," he said just before another large piece of the sandwich entered his mouth at warp speed. He chewed voraciously, still managing to smile as he did so, glancing. Seconds later, Rufus, overjoyed by his presence, came bounding over to him.

A couple of women, who were looking at the display case of jewelry, smiled to each other as they eyed the handsome Aussie with the dog standing on two legs to greet him.

Benton looked at Sage. "I'll be finished in two shakes of a lamb's tail." He took another bite, then reached down to pet Rufus with his free hand. Proud of his multitasking skills, Benton smiled, averting his attention just long enough for Rufus to grab the last bite of his sandwich and take off through the curtains with it. Sage, Godiva, and the nearby customers burst out laughing.

"Fluffy mate!" Benton called after him. "Never figured you to nick the last of my lunch." He looked at Sage. "Sorry, hope there's nothing in there that will make his tummy hurt."

"Not likely," Sage said. "He steals bits of food here and there and never seems worse for the wear. I totally saw that coming, but Rufus sprang into action before I could warn you."

Benton walked over to Sage and gave her a hug. "Would you mind going for a short wander with me? I'd just like to talk to you about something in private."

"Oh, sure," Sage said. She looked over at Godiva. "I won't be long. Just going for a walk with Benton." She hurried behind the counter to grab her purse.

"No problem," Godiva said, walking over to the counter to ring up a customer. "See you soon."

Benton smiled, put his sunglasses back on, then held the door open for Sage as she rejoined him. "We can walk," he said, "or stop at that sidewalk café around the corner for a cuppa or whatever you'd like."

Sage looked into his eyes. "You look like you have something weighing heavily on your mind."

"Yes, I do. Very much so."

"Then why don't we go to Bremer's? They make the best lemonade. Perfect for a hot summer's day like this. And it's better that we sit and talk."

They walked for two minutes until they reached Bremer's Café. They sat under the yellow-and-white striped awning, at the table farthest away from everyone else. As Benton ordered their drinks, Sage reached into her purse, put her sunglasses on, then edged her chair slightly closer to him to avoid the sun's glare.

"Hope you don't mind that I ordered a basket of chips," Benton said. "I'm still hungry. I could blame it on your boy, but it's my fault for missing brekkie."

"I think I can forgive you for having an appetite."

Benton smiled. "So you went away again this weekend?"

"I did," Sage said. "Took Rufus and went to see my parents

on Sunday. Got back early on Monday night."

"Ace. Cheers, mate!" Benton said to the young man who delivered drinks to their table. He waited until they were alone.

"You look nervous," Sage said. "Does that mean I should be too?"

"I booked my return flight," he said. "I'm leaving on Saturday. I guess your mate's store opening will be my last bash in America for a while."

Sage felt the corners of her mouth turn down as if they had a mind of their own. "I think I'm really going to miss you." She tasted her lemonade. "I feel like I've known you much longer than two weeks. You have this way of filling up a room when you enter it. In a good way."

"And you have a way of making every day meaningful. Even on the days when bludgers and mongrels get the best of me."

Self-conscious that she was blushing, Sage looked into her frosty glass and poked at a cube of ice with her straw.

Benton looked up as the young man delivered his basket of fries. "Ace! Nice and crispy. Got some sauce to go with that, mate?"

Seeing the dumbfounded look on the server's face, Sage translated. "Ketchup."

"Oh," the young man said, embarrassed. "Sure, I'll be right back with that."

Benton picked up the saltshaker and lightly sprinkled his fries. "Thanks for that, Sage."

"We don't call it sauce here, but I couldn't imagine what else you'd be asking for." She smiled. "I'm clever that way."

"You are," Benton said, offering thanks as he took the bottle of ketchup and poured a large dollop in the corner of the basket. "Help yourself, Sage." He dipped a fry into the ketchup and ate it. "I've been thinking. All bloody weekend, actually."

"About?"

"About how I'm not ready to go back," he said. "But my business is nearly finished here, and I have no reason to stay. But I was wondering if you'd come with me, Sage. Just for a holiday, you know. My shout. For as long as you'd like." He dipped another fry and ate it. "Have to be in Tassy for a meeting at the end of next week. Thought I'd show you around, and then we'd head back to Victoria, where I live. After that, New South Wales, Adelaide ... wherever your heart desires. Just as mates. No pressure."

"Oh, Benton!"

He took a few gulps of his Coke as he tried to work out Sage's reaction, her eyes only revealing shock. "Whaddya say, Sage? I know I mentioned you coming to Oz down the line, but when I got to thinking about everything, well, now just seemed like a better time."

"Oh, Benton, I just ...."

"Of course it's winter there now," he said, dipping another fry, "but it's not too bad. A nice break from this heat." He looked at her, still trying to read her face. "I promise, Sage. I won't force you to try Vegemite toast or watch bush telly."

"I would love to try Vegemite toast," Sage said. "And I love campfires. They remind me of my childhood. It's not that. I've always wanted to see Australia, and since I've met you, it's beckoning to me even more."

"I sense a big old but coming," Benton said, lowering his eyes.

"I just can't leave with you," Sage said. "Not on Saturday. Not any time soon." She reached for a fry and ate it without ketchup. "We'll stay in touch. And who knows—maybe I will be able to come over one day. But now, I just can't. I'm so sorry, Benton. As tempting as your generous offer is, I have to decline. But I can't thank you enough for wanting to bring me to your country."

Sage gulped as she saw Benton making every effort not to

tear up.

"We can video chat," she offered.

"Ah, flat friends," he said.

"No," Sage corrected him. "Friends who just live far away and keep in touch when they can't be together in person. Nothing flat about that." She drank some more of her lemonade. "You said you'd be back. We'll see each other again. I just know it. This may sound silly, but I don't think we would have become such fast friends if the relationship was only going to die when you went back home."

Benton look wistfully into the distance, as if his mind was as far away as the land he lived in. After a moment, he made eye contact with her again. "No worries, Sage. I reckoned you'd probably say what you just did. I just hoped I'd be wrong."

❧   ❧   ❧

Freddie checked his watch. "Back with ten minutes to spare," he said as Sage and Benton returned to the store.

Trying to lighten the mood, Benton put an arm around Sage. "Just went for a little chinwag. Not too far."

Godiva looked at Freddie, just in time to notice a familiar unsettling look cross his face.

"Hey, fluffy mate," Benton said as Rufus ran over to him, then began sniffing. "Hope you're not looking for sweets to go with that piece of my lunch that you nicked." He knelt down to talk to Rufus at eye level. "Don't you have some kind of favorite doovealacky to chew on? How about that red snake I've seen you carrying around?" He scratched the dog's head. "You're a cute little bugger, hey. I sure am gonna miss you and your mum." He stood and addressed Freddie. "Well, guess there's no time like the present to make our way to the Big Apple."

Freddie put his arms on Godiva's shoulders, then kissed her quickly but soulfully on the lips. "I love you, Diva. And don't let me forget. There's something I need to talk to you about tonight."

She looked at him curiously. "Okay, baby," she said, caressing his arm. "Believe me, I won't. Drive safely."

"Don't you know I will," Freddie said as he winked at her. "Until tonight." He looked at Sage. "If I don't see you before, I'll definitely see you on Friday night at Haber Dash."

"You will," Sage said. "Take care, guys."

Benton hugged Sage and gave her a kiss on the cheek. "I'll come by tomorrow," he said softly. He paused long enough to let the look linger before following Freddie toward the door.

Godiva took one last look at Freddie, then turned to Sage. "You all right?"

"Sure," Sage said flatly as she walked over to straighten some elephant charms hanging on the wall. "Everything good here?"

"Something's up," Godiva mumbled to herself. "The Diva gut tells no lies."

"Are you talking to me?" Sage said.

"Oh, no," Godiva said. "Just reminded myself I was in the middle of sorting stones when Freddie came in and need to get back to work."

Sage stopped and gave her a hard stare. "Nah, don't think so. That's okay, though. You're entitled to mumble every so often. Just be careful. A little more volume and I would've caught every word."

"So noted."

"Come on, Rufus," Sage said. "Let's go see how Uncle Adam's store is coming along."

CHAPTER TWENTY-FOUR

"It's amazing how much this place has progressed since this morning," Sage said to Adam as he greeted her at the door of the yet-to-be-opened Haber Dash.

He gave her a hug, holding her just a second or two longer than usual. "I'm still in awe of it myself. The crew that came in after you left this morning was one of the most efficient I've ever seen."

"I can see that." Sage looked around the store. "I love the vibe you've got going on here as well. If I haven't said it before, this black-and-white interior is so hip and classy. Love the track lighting and the contemporary carpet design. Very cool."

"I'm so glad you approve," he said. Adam led her toward the middle of the store. "Can't remember if I told you that I worked with a designer in New York to help me get the look I envisioned."

"Seriously gorgeous," Sage said. She smiled to see Vizzy come running over to greet Rufus with almost-contagious enthusiasm. "It's so different from the staid, mahogany atmosphere that is all-pervasive at Jameson. And the layout is spacious. Very free-flowing."

"Thanks for noticing. There will be a table in the center of the room … with stock shelves underneath," Adam said. "I'm going to start by displaying summer shirts there, but I'll be changing that up. I won't be putting that unit into place until after the party. Right now, for tomorrow, I'm going to use that space for a large table where all of the food will go; I'm having a bar set up over to the left. One of the bartenders from *Le Chat Noir* is going to be working it. It's his day off, and he knows pretty much everyone in town. The sound system is up and running, and I'll be playing jazz."

"I'm super proud of you," Sage said. "Your vision has turned into something really special."

"Just as yours did when you opened Sage Earth Gifts."

"Thanks," Sage said. She looked down at Rufus, who was socializing with the wrong end of Vizzy. "Her butt still smells the same way it did thirty seconds ago, boy. You can stop sniffing now."

Adam laughed. "She doesn't seem to mind, but Toto is feeling left out." He noticed that Sage's attention seemed to drift away.

"Oh, yeah, right," she said as she realized Adam had said something.

"You okay? You suddenly seem distracted."

"I don't mean to be," Sage said. "I guess I have a lot on my mind today. Sorry."

"I don't suppose I can help, can I?" he said, studying her absentminded expression.

Sage, lost in her thoughts again, made a quick recovery. "Oh, no. Um, anyway, I guess you still have a lot to do before you open."

"Pricing mainly," Adam said. "What a laborious job. But we've got to get it done."

"I hear you," Sage said. "Not fun. But I'll be happy to take Vizzy for a walk. And Toto too."

"That would be great," Adam said. He frowned. "But not as great as if I were able to walk with you myself. I'll go get her harness and leash."

As Adam hurried into the back room, a replay of Benton

asking her to go to Australia filled her mind as her memorable Saturday night in New York with Adam competed for attention.

"I really appreciate this," Adam said, kneeling to put Vizzy's harness on. "I know you're not opening a store, but you've still got one to run." He bit his lip. "Oh, I do have something to tell you."

"Oh, no. It's nothing good," Sage said as she looked at him. "Your face is a bit crooked."

"Yeah, it gets that way sometimes," he said. "Joanie called this morning. She asked me if I'd come to my senses about hiring her. She said her friends were horrified that I'd gone back on my word."

"Horrified?" Sage asked. "Isn't that a bit extreme for something you said casually … when you were put on the spot, no less … long before you knew this store would be a reality?"

"You think?" He clipped Vizzy's leash to her harness, stood, then handed the loop to Sage. "It would have been bad enough if she alone were 'horrified,' but the fact that she brought her friends into it not only sounds like a thinly veiled threat, but it also makes my suspicions about that strange woman feel all the more genuine." He paused. "I don't like this. Joanie is casting a pall over something I've worked hard to do for a very long time."

"Don't let her do that!" Sage said, taking a firm grip on Adam's forearm. "Seriously. Do not let her do that. This store is stunning, and you have knocked yourself out to put all of this together. There's nothing Joanie and her friends can do that your many loving friends cannot take care of for you. We'll all have your back." Sage took her hand away. "Hope I'm getting through to you. It will be an unforgettable and spectacular opening. You'll see. Anyway, I've got to get going so I can walk these guys and get back to my store. "Don't worry!" She reached up and kissed him on the cheek. "And by the way, you are looking like a lean, mean muscle machine."

"I've lost all my weight and have been working out every other morning. I've never felt better."

"Well, you look amazing," Sage said. You *are* amazing."

"Thanks. There's nothing anyone could say to make me happier than what you've just said. I'll take everything to heart. Promise."

"Good. I meant every word about every *thing*." She smiled. "So you won't worry about Joanie?"

"Joanie who?"

Sage smiled. "See you in a bit."

ço   ço   ço

Sage put Vizzy's leash in her left hand for a moment while she adjusted her straw fedora to block out the sun, then continued to walk with one leash in each hand.

"And you said you weren't a dog walker," the voice said.

Sage turned to see Nancy Klapper, dressed in a pale-blue pantsuit, wearing rimless aviator wrap sunglasses, and carrying an oversized Louis Vuitton bag, giving her the once-over. "Oh, it's you. From the party."

"From *my* party, yes. At *my* house. Remember … the one where you and that rude Australian crashed and dashed." She glanced down at Rufus and Vizzy, then looked at Sage. "Gives new meaning to the phrase 'dashing foreigner,' don't you think? No, wait. I don't care what you think. But you clearly said you weren't a dog walker. Is that why you have two dogs sprouting from the end of the two leashes you holding? Because you're *not* a dog walker?"

Sage stopped. "We didn't crash your party. And as for my vocation, I don't owe you any explanations. Not a one."

Nancy laughed. "It's quite hilarious that the duck who said she wasn't a duck is quacking and waddling. I can't wait to tell

Richard. It will make his day."

"Too bad you can't do that on your own."

"What's that?" Nancy asked.

"Nothing. You know, you were actually nicer when you were drunk," Sage said. "Have a nice day."

"Quack, quack," Nancy said, laughing to herself as she strolled away.

"Are you freaking kidding me!" the second voice said.

Sage turned around. "Molly! Where did you come from?"

"My mother," Molly said, grinning as Rufus excitedly greeted her.

"Funny. No, seriously. Where were you when I needed you?"

"I was only a few yards away," Molly said, petting Rufus, then Vizzy. "I heard the whole exchange. I would have said something, but I had just run into one of the owners of the *Herald*, and I had to act like a professional for the entire two minutes she was talking to me."

"That long?" Sage asked.

Molly laughed as she adjusted the strap of her laptop bag on her shoulder. "Yeah. Let me tell you: it wasn't easy." She looked around. "I know the Klappers, and if it weren't for that she-devil Naomi, they might be my least fave peeps in this town, but they're definitely in the top ten. What was that all about anyway?"

"Oh, nothing much," Sage explained. "Benton knows Richard from the tennis court, and he took me to the guy's fortieth birthday party because he was sort of pushed into making an appearance. We were only there a super short time. They were all smashed. Richard, who doesn't know me at all, said he recognized me from walking my dog, and she asked me if I was a dog walker. I said no. So just now, she was harassing me because I have Vizzy with me, along with Rufus, and she thinks I was lying out of embarrassment or something."

"Knowing Nancy, snob that she is, she's upset because she thinks she had someone as lowly as a dog walker mingling with the Swansea elite at her house, drinking her wine or whatever you had."

"That makes more sense. I think you nailed it. But we didn't have a drop or a taste of anything," Sage said. "We wanted to leave from the second we got there. Oh, and they had a cash bar. And they were all drunk. We hated them, and Benton created a distraction so we could run away … not too long after we arrived."

"That part sounds like fun," Molly said.

"Totally. It was a real rush for both of us."

"Hey, I'm headed back to the paper," Molly said. "I was just out interviewing someone for a story; then I stopped in a coffee shop to write it because the ideas were fast and flowing, and I couldn't wait. Translation: I'm ahead of schedule. Do you want me to walk Vizzy with you for a while?"

"That would be great," Sage said. "But you're already carrying your laptop bag and your purse. Plus you're wearing heels. Are you sure?"

"Totally," Molly said, taking Vizzy's leash from Sage. "Life is a continuous balancing act."

"It is. And thanks for offering. Walking two dogs isn't as easy as it looks. They both have completely different paces, and it's tough when they each go in a different direction. I have a newfound respect for actual dog walkers. It's an acquired skill."

"Figuring out my cat's moods is an acquired skill too," Molly said. "But I love my Captain Jack. My furry ginger protector."

"Your husband isn't your biggest protector?"

Molly laughed. "He's the joy of my life. But a man can't protect you the same way a cat can. They can't growl and hiss nearly as well. When we moved to our house, the real-estate agent, Bruce, was scared to death of my boy. But not enough to lose the commission."

"Of course not," Sage said.

"Which way do you want to … oh em freakin' gee!" Molly said.

"What?" Sage looked down the street a bit to see the Goth woman walking their way. "Oh, no!" She turned to Molly. "By the way, Adam thinks she's one of his ex-girlfriend's wacky friends who's out to stick it to him for not hiring her and to me for being his friend."

"So she whacked *me* in the knees with her bag?"

"I guess that's the price you paid for being my friend," Sage said.

"Your friendship is worth much more than that," Molly said, "but this lunatic better not mess with me. What is that red thing she is carrying along with that massive black purse?" She watched while the woman continued to walk toward them. "A bag of apples?"

Rufus stopped suddenly on the sidewalk as the woman approached. "Grrrrr." Even Vizzy, taking a cue from her older-and-wiser friend, froze as she analyzed the oncoming threat.

"Ugh," the raspy-voiced woman said. Before Molly or Sage could respond, accidentally on purpose, the woman let the bag of apples fall onto the sidewalk. Molly, with commendable dexterity, managed to just miss the apple that rolled up to her Jimmy Choo, threatening to take her down, while Sage got hit in the espadrille with two apples bumping her ankle. Meanwhile, both dogs started to chase the apples that came rolling at them, wildly yanking both Molly and Sage respectively in opposite directions.

"No, no, boy," Sage said to Rufus, watching the apples roll away. "They go, you stay."

"You too," Molly said to Vizzy, tugging at her leash until she gave up the chase.

The woman hurried along, making no effort to recover her

apples or the red mesh bag they had been in.

"No freakin' way, you despicable trying-to-murder-us crackpot," Molly yelled. Handing Vizzy's leash to Sage, laying her laptop bag and purse on the sidewalk, she picked up two apples and rolled them, like bowling balls, toward the woman's spiky black heels. As soon as she had done so, she picked up two more and repeated the process. "How do you like these apples, you walking mutant?" Molly shouted as the second two apples hit their target, felled the woman, and partial contents of her purse tumbled out onto the sidewalk.

Sage's mouth dropped open. "Oh, Molly. You are the best! Look at her. She's down for the count, and her face smashed into her black leather bag. Oh, and look, the heel of one of her shoes broke off."

A look of smug satisfaction rested on Molly's face. "Score one for Team Molly and Sage!"

The woman's deep guttural groans wafted pleasantly to Molly and Sage's ears. As the woman scrambled to get up and pick up items that had fallen, she grabbed something and clutched it in her right hand while trying to stuff her now-useless shoes into her purse. She then put her right arm over her face and hurried away.

"Too ashamed to show her vile visage," Molly said. She looked down the street and yelled, "Hope the sidewalk doesn't burn your witch paws!"

"Well that was instant karma," Sage said, reaching down to grab Molly's bags. "Guess we should pick up these apples so nobody gets hurt … or poisoned."

Molly laughed. "You got that right! If you can hold both dogs and my bags for just a minute, I'll take care of that."

Within a minute, Molly had picked up all of the apples, put them back in the mesh bag, then disposed of them in the nearest trash can. Putting her laptop and her purse straps back on her shoulder, Molly took Vizzy's leash and they continued on their walk.

"Gee, such an uneventful afternoon," Sage said with a grin as they walked on toward the park.

"Isn't it, though?" Molly said. A smile still played on her lips. "Hey, in all of the excitement, I forgot to ask you how things are going."

Sage nodded toward the park. "Want to go sit for a few?"

❧   ❧   ❧

"Because we both have to work to get back to," Sage said, plunking down on a bench in the shade, "that was the abbreviated version of everything that happened since last week."

Molly took the seat next to her. "Two amazing and completely different men. Benton looks like he could be on the cover of *Outback Studs*, even though I know he didn't live in the outback, and there is no such magazine … I don't think … and Adam, did I mention how he's hunk-tified himself. He could be on the cover of *GQ*."

"They are two good-looking guys with even better personalities."

"That goes without saying," Molly said. "Gee, that sounded way more shallow than it was intended to be."

Sage laughed. "So that was meant to be a *little* shallow?"

Molly cracked up. "For a journalist, I'm really batting a thousand, aren't I?" She bent down to pet Vizzy. "I may not be articulating as well as I should, but my investigative insights have concluded that you're not as happy as you could be."

"I wish I could hide my emotions better."

"Oh, Sage. You don't need to do that when you're with friends."

"I just wonder if I wasn't better off when I was avoiding love like the plague."

"No. You weren't. For one, like you, I've known Adam for years," Molly said. "He's a superior human being. And even before he hunk-tified himself, he was still adorable. Always has been."

"I know."

"I can see that you have some strong feelings for him. But you're not without feelings for Benton."

"No," Sage said. "And I've only known Benton for two weeks and change. I shouldn't be upset that he is going back to Australia, but I feel like I'm losing much more than a new friend. And when he asked me to go with him, a huge part of me wanted to say yes." She looked at Molly. "Please keep this between the two of us. I don't even want Trubs to know because I haven't confided in Godiva. Not because I don't trust her; I just don't know what I'm feeling and well ... I'm too upset to really discuss it."

"I hear you," Molly said. "If it means anything at all, I foresee a happy ending."

"I don't know," Sage said. "Godiva said things have a way of landing where they're supposed to. That sure was true for her and Freddie, but as for me, I'm not convinced things will work out as well in my world."

"Any particular reason you feel that way?"

"Just a feeling I can't shake," Sage said, looking down at her lap. "You know, as if I'm sabotaging myself while simultaneously trying to find happiness. What kind of person does that?"

"A flawed human being with a brain."

"That leaves me out," Sage said. "At least the last part."

"Don't be so hard on yourself," Molly said. "And before you give Vizzy back to Adam, think about Goth Woman falling. It will put a smile on your face. And when you tell him what happened, he'll be smiling too."

"He will," Sage said, "but he'll also worry even more that she's going to disrupt his party."

"Oh, no," Molly said. "Maybe I shouldn't have done what I did."

"She tried to kill us with a bag of apples," Sage said as she stood. "You fought back. You're my shero!"

"And I'll be right there if she ever tries it again," Molly said. "But hopefully, Goth Woman has learned that evil can backfire when you least expect it."

CHAPTER TWENTY-FIVE

"Good morning," Sage said as Godiva came through the door, carrying her usual bag from the coffee shop. "I was going to say 'Happy Hump Day,' but since you work on Saturdays, I guess Thursday actually fits the bill, not Wednesday."

"It's a joy working here," Godiva said. "I'm actually a little sad at the end of the week, but not too sad, now that I'm back with Freddie." She walked around the counter, pulled up a barstool, and took a cup of coffee and a blueberry muffin out of the bag.

Sage, sitting down, sipped her tea. "Hey, I was wondering how the final New York trip went for the guys last night. I haven't talked to Benton yet, but he said he was stopping by later today."

"Oh … they saw a completely different group of people, but I think someone did try to hit Benton up for a place to stay in Australia. I don't really know." Godiva took the lid off her cup and watched as the steam rose into the air. Without saying a word, she broke off a piece of her muffin and ate it.

Sage watched curiously. "So, um, this is the most quiet I've ever seen you. Not that you need to talk or anything. I'm just observing."

Godiva put her cup on the counter as a pained expression took over her face. "I have something to tell you. I'm just not sure *how* to tell you."

"Oh. You're going to quit, after all. You're going to work for Freddie, aren't you?"

"No! Nothing like that," Godiva told her. "Hey, I just told you how much I love working here."

"Statements like that are often followed by a 'but,'" Sage said.

"True. They are. But … I mean, however, that's not the case here."

"Can you please tell me?" Sage asked. "Because just seeing the agony on your face, I'm not feeling up to a game of Twenty Questions."

"Okay," Godiva said as she twirled her engagement ring. "So, going back to the day when Freddie showed up here in a tux … that wonderful day when he took me into New York to propose …."

"Yeah, that was a joyous day for you both. But what else about that day do you want to tell me?"

"Well, before Randy and Freddie arrived, Benton had paid you a visit."

"And?"

"And he brought you a toy koala in a red sweater."

"He did. And you are really dragging out whatever it is that you don't want to tell me."

"I'm sorry," Godiva said. "I'll try to speed it up. See, when Freddie arrived, before we left, I introduced the two of you, and he immediately said something to you about how he saw Benton had come bearing gifts."

"Yeah, I remember." Sage put elbows on the counter, then pressed her hands to either side of her head and squeezed. "You are really torturing me. Yes, Freddie noticed the koala. So what of it?"

Godiva broke off another piece of her muffin, but instead of eating it, she let it crumble between her fingers, then dropped the pieces on the wrapper it came in. "I thought Freddie had kind of a weird look on his face, but I let it pass."

Sage, her eyes wide open, looked incredulously at Godiva. "Did he think it was a real koala?"

"Of course not," Godiva said. "Even though I know you're being facetious."

"This is fascinating." Sage looked at Godiva. "Still being facetious." She sighed. "Let me make sure I've got this down: Freddie was weirded out because his business partner gave me a souvenir from their business, and you noticed Freddie's odd reaction but you didn't say anything." She sighed. "Am I missing anything? You've never been more riveting, Godiva. Seriously. Sheesh!"

"I know! Sorry, sorry. Anyway, moving on, it was on a Thursday afternoon when Freddie and Benton met here in the store for a last conference with the advertising people in New York. You and Benton were at the coffee shop when Freddie arrived, and after you came back, you two were joking about Benton playing a didgeridoo and there having been singing wallabies."

"You are killing me!" Sage said.

"Sorry again. Don't mean to. So anyway, I noticed that once again Freddie looked upset seeing the closeness between you and Benton. I was going to ask him what was up, but I never did because I thought I'd figured out what the problem was. I assumed he was upset at seeing the chemistry you two have, knowing Benton is going back to Australia. Freddie is a really sensitive man, and I just knew he didn't want you to get hurt."

"Yeah, I think you mentioned that."

"I wasn't wrong. But I was only partially correct," Godiva said. "See, last night, when the guys left, that was the third time I saw Freddie get that troubled look, but this time, he said the two of us needed to talk when he got home." She looked at Sage. "Guess it's kind of obvious I stay with him most nights."

"No kidding," Sage said, sarcasm piercing her tone. "Just go on."

"Several hours later, when he got back, I asked him what was wrong. He told me. Flat out. And this is the part I have to tell you but really don't want to tell you."

"Is there a silver lining to this bomb you're about to drop?" Sage asked.

"You could look at it that way, if you were so inclined."

"Just tell me. And who cares if there is or not."

Godiva took a few sips of coffee to fortify her nerves. "There's a woman in Benton's life. He told Freddie about her before he ever set foot into this store. Her name is Rita. I don't know anything about her, and neither does Freddie. All he knows is that Benton has mentioned her several times, but only once since he's been in this country, and that was apparently on the first day. He said something about how he's always loved her and that his life will be complete when they're together."

"Rita?"

"Yeah, Rita. I don't know her last name or anything about her. Freddie isn't the type to pry into another man's personal business. He said he figured if Benton wanted to tell him more, he would have by now. So, yeah, I was right about Freddie being concerned that you two were getting close, but I didn't realize that Benton has a girlfriend. I'm so sorry, Sage. I know he's going back to Australia, and that probably doesn't even matter, but nobody likes to be played."

"Benton has a girlfriend named Rita?" Sage repeated, unable to believe the words she spoke.

"Yes, honey. I'm afraid he does. Freddie said if Benton had only mentioned it once, then maybe he'd think he got it wrong. But Benton really loves this woman."

"I don't understand," Sage said. "Why in the world would he

ask me to ….."

"Ask you what?"

"Nothing," Sage said. "Just wondering why he kept asking me out and why he acts like he really cares about me? Did I seriously just let another guy pull a Caleb on me?"

Godiva shrugged. "I don't know. You said he's coming by later. Why don't you ask him?"

"No!" Sage said sharply. "I don't want to know. It seems pretty clear. Rita is obviously in Australia, and maybe she got upset with him or something, maybe even broke up with him, and so he's been using me as some rebound thing just like Caleb did." She dropped her face into her palms for a moment, then looked up. "So why doesn't that feel remotely right? How could I feel so much affection from a guy … never mind. I was engaged to Caleb and remained clueless until everything hit the fan. It's already been established how stupid I am."

"You're not stupid," Godiva said. "Not even close."

Sage stood. "I'm going upstairs to hug my animals. Then I'm bringing Rufus down and taking him for a walk." She bit her lip as her eyes welled with tears. "You know what really sucks even worse than Benton having a girlfriend? I feel angry with Adam now, just because he's a man. And that's ridiculous and unfair." She looked at Godiva. "So that silver lining you mentioned. Were you thinking that I wouldn't have to choose between Adam and Benton any longer?"

"Yes. That's it exactly," Godiva said, her eyes filled with sorrow.

"I really do want love to look away," Sage muttered as she walked toward the back room. "I shouldn't have caved on that. Life is much easier without it."

"But not nearly as beautiful," Godiva said, long after Sage could hear her.

❧ ❧ ❧

"I'm so happy I stumbled into this store," the twenty-something-year-old customer said to Sage. "This azurite pendant is just the something special I've been looking to buy my mom for her fiftieth birthday."

"I hope she'll love it and wear it in good health," Sage said, handing the customer the wrapped gift in a small shopping bag.

"When I saw that exquisite fountain in the window, I knew I had to check this place out." The customer glanced at the window, then fixed her eyes on something beyond it. "You know, you not only have an amazing window display, but I'm really digging what I'm seeing on the sidewalk. Hello, hotness!"

Sage looked out the window to see Benton, who waved at her upon making eye contact, then made his way into the store.

The customer's face lit up, but dimmed upon realizing that Benton's broad smile was meant for Sage. Dropping mumbles of barely audible regret, she left the store.

"G'day, Sage," Benton said, removing his sunglasses as he walked over to greet her.

Sage barely smiled, returning his warm embrace with a perfunctory hug. "Hi, Benton."

Unsettled, he pulled back, hung his glasses on the V of his shirt, and with a light grip on her shoulders, studied her face. "You don't look too chuffed to see me." He looked over Sage's shoulders to see Godiva, who was helping a customer at the back of the store, turn away as if she hadn't seen him. "In fact, you're both kind of acting like I just flogged something from the store."

"Sorry," Sage said. "Guess we're just having a busy afternoon. I'm tired, I think."

Benton released his hands and watched Sage walk around

the counter as Rufus came bounding out from the back room. "I've never seen you look knackered at this time in the arvo." He looked down at Rufus. "Hey, fluffy mate, glad you're still happy to see me." As he returned Rufus's affection, he bit his lip, then spoke. "Thing is, Sage, you not only don't look chuffed to see me, you look kind of cranky, like you're ready to spit the dummy."

"I'm not sure what that means, but I'm fine."

"And that'd be okay," Benton continued, pretending he hadn't heard her denial, "because we all get angry at things, except I feel like I'm the cause. Now, I'm thinking I shouldn't have rocked up at all. I guess you remember I'm leaving on Saturday." He paused, looking at her with wishful eyes, as if he were hoping she'd fill the void with her words, but she didn't. "While my rellies back in Straya are stoked about that, I've been wishin' I could linger a bit. I thought maybe you felt the same way, but now I reckon you'd like to give me the flick." He took another look at Godiva, who half-heartedly waved, then began straightening books on the shelves. He scratched Rufus on the head. "Glad someone still loves me."

The customer, who Godiva had been helping, walked to the counter with three books and laid them down.

"Do you need these gift wrapped?" Sage asked, brightening.

"Nope. They're all for me. I'm reading everything I can find on astral projection."

Benton frowned, watching Sage motion for Rufus to return to the back room before he could even say good-bye.

He straightened himself, smiled, and turned to the customer. "Last time I tried to astrally project ... I was beside myself."

"Oh, funny," she said. "Hey, you're an Aussie, right?"

"True-blue."

"I didn't know they had astral projection in Australia." She blushed as she handed Sage her credit card while looking only at Benton. "That was really stupid. I can't believe that I just said that.

What I meant was that I'm surprised you've heard of it." She smacked her forehead. "I didn't mean that, either. It's just that you look like a rugged outback type and … not that I really know what a rugged outback type looks like … and um … I'm going to keep my mouth shut before any more stupidity escapes."

"My stellar good looks seem to have you flustered," Benton said with a grin.

Sage stared at the register longer than necessary to hide the jealousy on her face.

The woman's eyes opened wide. She looked at Benton, then cringed. "I'm so embarrassed. No wonder my family calls me 'Obvious Ophelia.'"

"That's your name? Ophelia?"

"Oh, no," she said to Benton. "It's Susan. Ophelia is just an alliteration thing. You know, like being a Nervous Nellie."

"Ah!"

"Here you go," Sage said, handing a gift bag and credit card to Susan. "Thanks so much for shopping at Sage Earth Gifts."

"Oh," she said, taking the bag. "I guess that's my cue. I didn't realize you two were um …. Oh, I'm sorry." She looked at Sage. "He's a keeper, for sure."

"Sure wouldn't know it today," Benton said loudly, embarrassing both women.

"Bye now," Susan said, hurrying out of the store.

"Well," Sage said, straightening up some papers that were already neatly stacked, "that was kind of unnecessary."

"So is what you're doing now, Sage," Benton said. He put his hand gently under her chin and raised it until their eyes met. "You want to tell me what's going on?"

Before she could respond, Godiva walked up to them. "Hey, if you need to step outside for some privacy, I've got you covered. Looks like we've got a lull now if you want to take advantage of it."

"It's so nice to see you, Benton," he said to Godiva.

"Sorry. I was distracted, and I seem to have misplaced my congeniality. It *is* nice to see you, Benton," Godiva said.

"You'll probably find it wherever Sage lost hers."

Both women looked at him with blank faces, then shared a look.

"Yes, thank you, Godiva," Sage said. She took some slow breaths to calm the oncoming panic she felt. "I would appreciate it if you take care of things while I step outside."

Sadness filled Benton's eyes. "Okay, I hear you," he said, putting his sunglasses on. He gestured toward the door. "After you."

As soon as they were on the sidewalk, Sage walked over to a spot under the awning that blocked some of the sunlight.

"We're just going to stand here and talk?" Benton said. "Not even over to the café for another lemonade and a Coke?"

"I don't have time," Sage said. "I've let my personal life take me away from the store a lot lately. I just can't keep letting Godiva carry everything."

"The store is empty now, Sage. You know that."

"It could get busy," she said as her body filled with self-loathing.

"You just escorted me out of your store ... to give me the flick on the bloody footpath. You'll excuse me if I'm having a problem here."

"I'm sorry," Sage said, her eyes filling with tears. "I just realized that you're going back home, and I think it would be virtually impossible for you not to have women in Australia who are very attracted to you, just the way my last two customers were. We live more than ten thousand miles apart, Benton. Getting closer to one another is just going to make everything more difficult. I don't see how prolonging this is good for either one of us."

"How about a little dance to commemorate this occasion?"

Benton said with an edge to his voice Sage hadn't heard before. "Let's call it the 'Footpath Flick.'" He put his hands on his hips. "You kick with the left," he said, making a sweeping gesture on the sidewalk with his left foot. "Then," he continued, shifting feet, "you kick with your right, until it lands straight on the arse of the person who gets the flick. In this case, me."

"Oh, Benton!"

"C'mon, Sage," Benton said, putting his hands on his hips again and motioning for Sage to copy him. "I reckon you can do this."

"No, I can't."

"How about if I make up a song to go with it: when a bloke makes you sick, you give him the flick." He thought for a moment. "No, we need a true-blue Aussie version. How's this: when a bloke from down under, makes you wanna chunder …."

"Please, stop," Sage said. "You're killing me."

"Is this because I asked you to come to Oz with me?"

"No, Benton. Believe me. I was flattered. This isn't a punishment for anything," she lied. "I just don't think that we should get any closer."

"Bloody hell, Sage. I thought if nothing else happened, we'd have a lifelong friendship."

"Benton, I just don't …."

"I don't either," Benton said. "And I have no idea how you planned to finish that sentence. So this is good-bye?"

"No, of course not," Sage said. "I'll see you at the party on Friday night."

"Oh, swell. You'll see me at a business function given by the bloke who's got a permanent stiffy for you? And that's it? Have a nice life, Benton?"

"No! I just think you should go back to your …."

"To my WHAT?"

"Your home. Your home in Australia … without leaving behind the ties that bind."

"I get it," Benton said. "You make me mad as a cut snake so I take off, and then you can put that on me while you choose stiffy man."

"Don't be crude," Sage said. "Really, Benton. Enough already. You're better than that."

His face blank, Benton stood in the hot sun as tears pooled in his eyes. He took a long pause before speaking. "And you're better than this, Sage. Way better."

Sage looked down at the pavement and tried to muster up a response. She could feel her stomach churn and her heart breaking. "Benton, I'm so sorry. I didn't mean—" she said to no one at all. As tears ran down her face, she glanced in every direction, hoping he was still nearby. But he wasn't.

Godiva opened the door and stepped out onto the sidewalk. "Oh, honey. I'm so sorry. Please come back inside."

Without saying a word, Sage hurried into the store. Rufus, hearing her sobs, came out from the back room to comfort her.

"I'm an idiot," Sage said to Godiva. "I was horrible to him. And now he's gone. Just like Jimmy was gone when I was ten."

Godiva rushed behind the counter and grabbed some tissues. "Here, honey."

Sage blew her nose and wiped her tears as more fell.

"I know it must feel like the same kind of loss to you, Sage. But you know Jimmy didn't choose to leave in the middle of the night. As for Benton, he's still around. And Freddie told me Benton is definitely going to be at the party on Friday. If for nothing else, it's business and he has to show up. And if you don't want to wait forty-eight hours only to see him in public, well, you can call him tonight or tomorrow. Or right now, for that matter."

"The only person I'm going to call now is my cousin Robin,

Ruth's daughter. I'm going to ask her to come over and help you in the store, and to walk the boy later. I'm completely useless in my present condition."

"I'm so sorry," Godiva said. "I should have kept my big mouth shut."

"No," Sage said as she went around the counter to grab her purse and some folders. "You were right to tell me. Benton having a girlfriend is about as necessary as information gets."

"I know. That's why I told you. But now I'm—"

"I'm going upstairs," she said, walking toward the curtains. "I'll see you in the morning, Godiva. And yeah, once again, I'm wussing out, just like I did after seeing Caleb. Only Caleb doesn't matter to me. But Benton matters a whole lot."

"Are you sure you don't want to talk?" Godiva said.

"No, I'm not in the mood. I need to think this through. Besides, I'm hardly going to be seen crying like an idiot in my own store or anywhere else, for that matter," Sage said. "Come on, boy," she said to Rufus, but he had already gone behind the curtains, into the office, and was halfway up the stairs to their home. Sage looked at Godiva. "Oh, and you'll know Robin when she gets here. She looks a lot like my aunt and is every bit as nice."

"Rest well, Sage. And I really hope we can talk in the morning."

CHAPTER TWENTY-SIX

Sage, sitting behind the counter reading the *Swansea Herald,* looked up in surprise to see Godiva unlock the front door an hour and a half before the store opened.

"You're way early," Sage said. "It's only eight thirty. I'm usually done with the paper by the time you get here."

"Anything interesting in our delightful little town?" Godiva asked as she walked toward her.

"Oh, just something Adam told me during dinner in New York. That Naomi's brother, Roland Everest Hall, was arrested for procuring a prostitute. Even their money couldn't keep this out of the paper forever. The family must be furious," Sage said.

"Well that's good news," Godiva said. "Maybe the added embarrassment will keep Naomi away for even longer."

"One can hope. This article is really going to get her blood boiling," Sage said. "And the main reason won't be because her brother was arrested."

Godiva put her purse and bag from the coffee shop on the counter, then walked around it and took a seat. "Really? Why is that?"

"Because Molly wrote the story," Sage said, laughing. "That's akin to getting a barrel of salt and pouring it into Naomi's wounds.

She must be seething. Especially knowing this isn't the kind of story Molly usually writes." She looked at Godiva. "Again, you came to work so early because …?"

"I thought that would be obvious," Godiva said. "I'm really worried about you and wanted to make sure we get time to talk before the store opens. Where's Rufus?"

"Upstairs with the cats," Sage said. "He just had breakfast. And that's very sweet of you to care so much. Don't let my amusement over this Roland-Hall nonsense fool you, though. I'm a wreck. But before we get into any of that, business first. What did I miss after I went upstairs yesterday?"

"Well," Godiva said, reaching into the bag for her coffee and muffin. "First, your cousin Robin is a doll. I was glad to finally meet her after working here almost three weeks."

"I knew you'd love her. She and my aunt have been there for me in so many ways."

"Robin said you've been there for her your entire life."

"That was sweet," Sage said. "And it's nice to hear, especially now when I'm feeling kind of bad about myself. Like I'm hurting the people I care about. When Adam called me last night, he could tell I was down, but for obvious reasons, I couldn't tell him what happened. I just hated to worry him. Especially when he's so close to opening his store and realizing his dream. I made a half-hearted attempt to hide my mood, but he's so tuned in to me."

"When people love you, they usually *are* tuned into you. Just as you are to them," Godiva said. "And you're a ray of sunshine. There's nothing hurtful about you."

"Thanks," Sage said, shooing away the emotion. "So what else did I miss?"

"Well, Randy and Kyle came by at the end of the day. Kyle bought the Balinese fountain. They were really sorry you weren't here. And of course, Randy was concerned about you."

"I know," Sage said. "Trubs texted me last night. I hate worrying everyone." She got up to grab her electric teapot and pour more hot water into her teacup. "Is that all the news?" She paused. "Benton didn't come back, did he?"

"No, honey," Godiva said. "He didn't. And I hate telling you this, but that crazy Goth woman did. Well ... sort of. We saw her peeking in the window."

Sage scrunched her nose up. "Yuk. She has some nerve showing her face after she tried to kill Molly and me with a bag of runaway apples," she said, returning the teapot to the counter, then taking her seat again.

Godiva shifted in her barstool. "Speaking of her face, maybe it was just the way the sun was hitting her, but she looked slightly different ... but not really. I can't figure it out. That said, I don't want to figure it out. She gives me the willies. But there is a fun part to this story."

"Really?"

"Sure is. When Randy caught her staring at him, he put his hands up in the air, like a bear getting ready to pounce, and then lurched forward with this clawing gesture as he stared back. Like this!" Godiva re-enacted Randy's comical moves. "He actually scared me ... well sort of." She laughed. "But he spooked her so bad that she left in quite a hurry. I think she would have come in otherwise."

"Oh, my! That's hilarious. One more thing I have to be indebted to Randy for. He really is such a great friend. But I'm seriously glad she didn't step foot inside again."

"You and me both," Godiva said, delicately breaking off a piece of her muffin. "So, without being a royal busybody or a pain in your butt, is it okay for me to ask how you are? Did you do any thinking about the situation with Benton?"

"That's pretty much *all* I did. I thought about Benton,

Adam, and of course, because I haven't stopped since I was a child, my mind went back to Jimmy because he's a perfect example of how unresolved relationships can haunt you forever. I don't want it to be like that with Benton. But I feel like my actions yesterday are going to result in the same thing happening." Sage dunked her tea bag, staring at it as it bobbed up and down. "Am I a case of someone unwittingly forcing a situation to repeat itself because it's how a person, meaning me, is used to responding?" She paused to mull over her own question. "I guess it's like wearing a pair of hideous and worn-out shoes because they're comfortable to walk in."

"An astute observation," Godiva said. "And yes, it can and does happen. Human beings are creatures of habit, even when they know the habit is a bad one. I had a friend who dated four abusive men in a row. She didn't mean to do it, but she was being drawn toward what was familiar to her without realizing what it was. Even before the abuse began. Her story isn't uncommon, either. I'm happy to say she finally figured things out and is now happily married to a great man. But self-awareness is so vital, Sage. So the fact that you're asking yourself questions is a very good thing."

"Glad to hear that. Benton has been nothing short of wonderful to me. Even if he does have a girlfriend, that's no excuse for acting like I did." She stopped to arrange her thoughts. "But maybe he stopped mentioning her because they broke up."

"I wondered about that too," Godiva said. "But last night Freddie went over to the guest house to see Benton about business." She hesitated. "Well, he made up an excuse because after I told him what happened, he was concerned and wanted to check on the guy. He said Benton was packing his bags and feeling really down."

"I hate hearing that. I wonder why he would feel so sad thinking about me if the love of his life is waiting for him at home? Seriously, maybe Benton and Rita *did* break up."

Godiva shook her head. "Well, Freddie said he had written

her name on a legal pad. Over and over. That doesn't necessary mean they're together, but to me, it means that he really loves her."

Sage exhaled. "Oh. Well, it's all for the best. I guess. I went back and forth about contacting him before tomorrow night's party, and while I really want to do so, I don't know how that would actually work."

"What's stopping you, honey?" Godiva said before taking a slow sip of her coffee.

Sage looked around with despair on her face. "Everything is stopping me. For one, I have pretty mad feelings for Adam. And just because he's been crushing hard on me for years, that doesn't mean I should take it for granted that he'll be there when I'm ready. Because if I choose another man, I don't think Adam will be able to continue with our friendship, even if a part of him wants to. He's a proud man, and I think even with profound regret weighing him down, he'd walk."

"He is proud," Godiva said. "I saw that from the time he first came to the health club, but I'd say he's a lot more self-confident now, and it shows."

"Yeah," Sage said, fidgeting with the spoon that rested on the saucer. "So there's that. And really, I don't know how to deal with the fact that I'm drawn to Benton. Yes, he's a charming and gorgeous guy, but that's not it. It goes deeper. I wish I could explain it. So if I contact him and ask him to see me, I feel like I might hurt him more if the two of us reconcile and get closer. That's what I mean by feeling like I'm no good for anyone. Maybe it's just best that he's goes back to Australia, marries Rita, and forgets about me."

"I wish Freddie knew more about Rita," Godiva said. "Maybe all of this would make more sense. Or not."

Sage laughed, but the humor was absent. "At one point, I even told myself that maybe Rita was his pet kangaroo. And yeah, I know how stupid that sounds. Even if he did have one somewhere that a person can actually keep a kangaroo, from what Benton told Freddie, Rita is definitely a woman."

"One-hundred percent," Godiva said.

"So," Sage said, putting down her spoon after a sudden awareness that she was rattling it on the china saucer, "while I wore my brain out thinking, I didn't come to any real conclusion. I just hope that I can be friendly to Benton at the party and show him there are no hard feelings. But somehow, even that falls very short of what is right. He's a very special guy, and I just hate myself for having hurt him."

"Hmm," Godiva said, lowering her eyes. "You know, you're not the only one who hurt Benton. I wasn't exactly my usual ebullient self with him, and he noticed that immediately. So what's my excuse … anger by proxy? Even if he believes that you freaked out solely over the prospect of your relationship progressing right before he leaves, how does that excuse *me* being kind of a bitch to him?"

Sage twisted her face, as if she were testing its elasticity. "I thought about that as well. Though I didn't use that word. I just thought about how confused the guy must be that we both kind of turned on him."

"The Diva brain can come up with some kind of reason," Godiva said. "How about if I apologize to him?"

"Maybe it's better just to leave things as they are," Sage said. "It might be awkward to apologize without an honest explanation. Just be friendly to him at the party, the way I'm going to be. So that he can leave feeling good." She frowned. "Who am I kidding. I don't even know if that's even possible." She took a sip of tea. "I'm sorry to be such a downer."

"You're not," Godiva said. "And it's very healthy to acknowledge your emotions. What's not healthy is to choose which ones are cool to feel and which ones to stuff away. Because when a person does that, well, the things you stuff away come back to hit you with a vengeance. I learned that from my grandmother at a tender age: when you face your emotions, you work through your emotions. So don't apologize for doing just that, okay?"

"Thank you," Sage said. "And there is something else I should tell you. I didn't say anything when it happened because I just didn't want to talk about it."

"What's that?"

"Well, Benton asked me to come to Australia with him when he leaves. Just for a vacation, but he wanted me to come all the same."

"He did? That's major. Oh, wow!"

"Yeah. Oh wow. That's one reason I reacted as horribly as I did when you told me about Rita. I thought I was being played. And I couldn't help but be reminded of Caleb, you know, actually asking me to marry him when he still loved someone else. That's why I was so upset."

Godiva took a few sips of her coffee. "That makes so much more sense. Unfortunately, now I'm even more baffled about Benton and his girlfriend down under."

"Me too," Sage said. "But I may have to live with the mystery. It wouldn't be the first one."

৽ ৽ ৽

"Thank you so much for walking Vizzy … and Toto," Adam said as Sage returned to Haber Dash. "My parents were confused about why I decided to adopt a dog at such a hectic time in my life, but—"

"It was serendipitous that you went to the shelter when you did. Vizzy was right there and she needed a loving home. She was meant to be yours; that's all there is to it."

Adam smiled while he pointed to some boxes that an

employee was frantically looking for. "Why weren't you there to explain that to my parents for me? I was far less succinct and way more rambly. Is that a word?"

"It is now," Sage said.

"Right," he said. He motioned for an employee to take Vizzy into the back room. "Yeah, so the kid in me emerged in my thirty-two-year-old body. But you know what?—my mom and dad are very happy for me. I guess we are never too old to feel good when we make our parents proud." He gestured to a man carrying several cartons of water. "Those go in the back room, to the left of the fridge. I can sign for them when you're ready."

"I know what you mean. My parents were not only ecstatic that I opened my store, but they were so happy that I did something to bring Swansea into the twenty-first century," Sage said, noticing that Rufus was becoming unsettled by all of the frenzied activity.

"I hope I'm continuing in your tradition," Adam said.

"You have to be," Sage told him, rubbing Rufus's neck. "You're making some people angry. Especially Naomi and her associates. But word around town is that people are thrilled with this store. Men and women."

Adam took the clipboard from the man who had just delivered the water. He signed his name and handed it back to him. "Thanks." He looked up to see two men carrying a large table with the legs folded up. "That will go right here," he said, pointing to the center of the store.

"The Rufster and I are going to leave you to this controlled chaos," Sage said. "Oh, and I meant to tell you that your sign exceeds my expectations. It's fantastic."

"Thank you!" Adam said. "I was worried it wasn't going up in time, but that's another story." He looked over at an employee who was unpacking some folded dress shirts from a box. "Those still need to be priced."

"Okay, I'm going," Sage said. "But just to let you know, Godiva and I are leaving the store two hours early tomorrow, so we'll be here around five. Robin is going to handle the last two hours for me. And she'll call you about helping with Vizzy if I'm too swamped to get over here. So don't worry; we've got you covered."

He looked into Sage's eyes. "Thank you, beautiful."

"Hey, Adam," an employee yelled. "The Mistress of Death was just outside having a staring contest with your new sign. But don't worry, the sign won. She stormed off."

"Just what I don't need," Adam told Sage. "And I'd gone the whole day without thinking about her. I know she's up to no good."

CHAPTER TWENTY-SEVEN

"G'day," Benton said as he walked into Sage Earth Gifts carrying a small shopping bag.

"Oh, hi," the brown-haired woman with blond highlights said. "You must be Benton from Australia. I've heard wonderful things about you."

"Well I'll be buggered," Benton said. "That's a surprise."

"I'm Robin Masterson," she said, extending her hand. "Sage's cousin." She looked quizzically at him. "Nothing to be surprised about. Sage thinks the world of you. I'm so sorry you missed her. She and Godiva left a while ago for Adam Canoga's store opening."

"I know," Benton said, his face uncharacteristically serious. "I purposely waited until they were gone." He held up the bag he was carrying. "I have something very important for Sage. A prezzy. But I don't want her to get it, under any circumstances, until the party is over or until after eight thirty."

Robin smiled at a customer who just walked in. "Hello! Welcome to Sage Earth Gifts." She turned to Benton. "I don't think you need to worry. She won't be back until then. I'm sure of it."

"Well, just in case she was in a tizz when she left and forgot something, and then comes back for it, please don't tell her about it."

Robin smiled warmly. "I understand. I won't let you down." She nodded to indicate the bag. "If you want to give that to me, I'll hide it on the bottom shelf of the cabinet on the right ... behind the counter. Sage rarely uses that space, and she can't look in there if she's not here, right? I promise I'll do exactly as you ask, unless you change your mind. Please don't worry; I'm sure she'll be way too engaged in things to come back here before the party ends. Just so you know, I'm taking Rufus home with me and bringing him back around that time. So I'll make sure to give her the message personally, okay?"

Benton handed her the bag. "No doubt she'll be flat out like a lizard drinking," Benton said, mostly to himself.

Robin giggled. "No idea what means, but Sage told me you were funny even when you weren't trying to be. Will you be at the party?"

"I'll be there," Benton said. "Adam will be carrying the clothing line I'm working on with Freddie Lamar. So, I've got to show my face before I head back to Oz tomorrow. How about you?"

"I've already stopped in and made my appearance," Robin said. "I'm a doctoral student, and I'm afraid I'm going to be a bore and go back to working on my dissertation tonight. My boyfriend is coming back from a trip to London tomorrow, and I want to work hard tonight so I won't be a bore tomorrow." She winked. "There's this drive-in movie theater that was just restored and re-opened, and we're eager to see it."

"Ah, you're going to a passion pit! Hope you have fun."

"For sure!" Robin reddened. "That was a bit TMI, wasn't it? But we will, thanks."

"You mentioned my fluffy mate a minute ago. Where is he?" Benton said.

"Oh, Rufus? He's upstairs. My mom is doing some work in

the office. She put him up there because a bunch of older socialites came in, and they don't take to dogs in stores. Even one lying peacefully on a mat. They call that 'lying in wait.' And knowing some of them as I do, that may be exactly what Rufus is doing."

Benton attempted to laugh. "If you wouldn't mind, Robin, could you bring the boy down here? I've grown quite fond of him and never got to say a proper good-bye. I'd be most appreciative."

Ruth stuck her head out from between the curtains. "I was just coming out to grab something off the counter and I heard your exchange. I'll go get Rufus."

"Thanks, Mom," Robin said, noticing that a customer was walking over to the counter with some merchandise. "I've got to help this lady, but please, Benton, rest assured that if I'm not here when Sage gets back, I'll leave her a note. I won't let you down."

"That makes one of you," he mumbled.

"Sorry, what's that?" Robin said as she walked behind the counter.

"Nothing," Benton said. A smile appeared on his face as Rufus rushed in to greet him, turning three circles in excitement. "Ah, fluffy mate. You'll make everything right in my world. If even for a minute."

ço   ço   ço

"To Adam and to Haber Dash," Kyle said, raising his wineglass in a toast. "Classy guy, classy attire!"

Randy turned to Kyle. "Stop, I'm blushing. This is supposed to be a toast about Adam, but you're describing moi."

Kyle, Molly, Sage, Godiva, and Freddie laughed.

"I wasn't done, my precocious," Kyle said, giving Randy a mock side-eye. "Here's to Adam! May he have great success with Haber Dash." He raised his glass in synchronicity with his friends.

"Impressive party," Freddie said. "The man knows what he's doing, and I couldn't be more honored to have our clothing sold here."

"I'm honored to do business with *you*," Adam said, sidling up to Freddie. He lowered his voice. "We're going to kick some Jameson butt."

"Ah, there you are," Freddie said. "We were just toasting you."

"Jameson'll wish they carried Freddie's line," Godiva said. She looked up at Freddie. "They'll be sorry they turned you down three years ago, baby."

"A blessing in disguise," Freddie said. "No, I wasn't happy that I couldn't sell in my hometown, but to be exclusive at Haber Dash was worth waiting for. And from what I'm hearing through the sour grapevine is that they're already sorry. Oh well, and all that."

"Amen," Godiva said.

"I'll second that," Molly chimed in. "The she-devil seems so sure that the town doesn't need another men's clothing store, but I know she-devil speak, and her protestations only mean she's afraid of her buttoned-down little world being burst wide open like a piñata." Molly looked at Sage. "Same reason she fought your store."

"And lost," Sage added. She smiled, but her thoughts were elsewhere.

Kyle turned to Freddie. "When do you expect your joint endeavor with Benton to happen?"

"It'll be at least six months for the Australian line," Freddie said. "Just hope it doesn't take that long for my partner to show up at this party. He's not here yet, is he?"

"No," Sage said, looking around the room. "He's not. I've been checking the door." The moment she spoke, she gulped, realizing how her words sounded to Adam. "I ... um, know he's leaving tomorrow, and I just hope he gets here so he can say his good-byes to everyone."

Godiva shot her a sympathetic look but didn't say anything.

"There must be seventy-five people here right now," Molly said. "How many people came by before we arrived?"

"Maybe a hundred and fifty in and out," Adam said. "But the best people are here now." He smiled at his friends, his eyes landing on Sage with an extra twinkle in them.

"Mini crab cake?" the server in a tux said as he walked past everyone with a tray.

Randy, Kyle, Molly, and Godiva took one off the tray and offered thanks.

"The food and the service is fabulous," Godiva said after finishing the bite-sized treat. She glanced around. "Seriously, Adam, you couldn't have choreographed a more fluid team of caterers. Everything is spot-on. And your food and wine choices are heavenly for the Diva palette."

"Glad you approve," Adam said, moving closer to Godiva. "Unfortunately, the wine is a bit too tasty for some people."

"Like the Klappers?" Molly asked. "They need to 'Klap off.' I can't help but keep an eye on those parasites, and they've each had at least three glasses of the Cabernet within a half hour. You'd think we were in the freakin' Sahara here, in triple-digit heat, and someone was handing them glasses of water. Red water."

"Yeah, they're guzzling, all right," Adam said. "But not much I can do about it."

"Randy can think of some things to do," Randy whispered to Molly and Kyle.

"Ah, here's my business partner now," Freddie said, looking toward the door.

Benton, steeling himself to face the crowd, walked in with half a smile on his face. Before he could reach his friends, Richard

Klapper, an unknown number of sheets to the wind, approached him. "Soooo, the dasssshing Aussstralian has come to Haber Dasssh for another dasssh." Richard gave Benton a dirty look. "I had your nummmer from the gecko."

"The gecko, huh?" He pretended to mull over Richard's slurred words. "Ah, so you've spoken to some of my reptilian mates, have you?" Benton said, his disgust obvious. "Good many of them from Western Straya and the Banana State, but we've got the Marbled Gecko where I live."

"Huh?"

"Did the gecko give you my mobile number or my house phone? Didn't happen to get names did you, Drongo?"

"Wass a drongo?" Richard asked.

"Figure it out, wacker."

Nancy approached Benton. "I don't know what you're saying to my husband, but it doesn't sound nice and I'm quite sure it isn't."

"Ah, the ball and chain wants to give me an earbash!"

"You're a sexist pig," Nancy scolded him as she wobbled slightly to her left.

Benton ignored the admonishment. "I'm surprised you're drinking so much, seeing how Adam is running a tab on everyone."

"Wasss that?" Richard said.

"You heard me," Benton said. "He's not going to collect cash at a store opening. Too complicated. But that fancy wine you're drinking is gonna cost you twelve dollars a glass. You'll get the docket when you leave."

Richard turned to Nancy. "Did you know thissss?"

"He's gotta be lying," Nancy said as she grabbed her husband's arm to steady herself.

"Nope," Benton said. "Told him all about your party, and he thought charging for drinks was an ace idea to keep bludgers from taking advantage of his good nature."

"Drink up!" Richard said to his wife. "Let's get the hell out of here. I'm not taking any chancessss."

"Pisspots," Benton mumbled under his breath. "Hope you're not driving," he said to Richard.

"Hell no," Richard said, turning around. "You crassshed our party. You know where we live. Only carrr I'm driving tonight is one like Fred Flintstone had. It only moves as fast as my feet will carry me." He looked at Nancy. "Come on, Wilma! Yabba dabba do!"

"How about you yabba dabba don't show your faces here again," Benton said.

Across the room, Adam turned to his friends. "I don't know what Benton just said, but I think I owe him one. It looks like the Klappers are about to leave."

"Good," Molly said. "Richard's not a prospective customer anyway. He's Jameson through and through. And even they probably have trouble shaking loose the bucks from his money tree."

"Good riddance," Sage said.

"Spectacular party!" a man said to Adam.

"Hello, Mr. Conway. I just saw your wife …" Adam turned to his friends. "Excuse me, everyone," he said, walking away with the man in the tweed cap, as the two engaged in conversation.

"Our host knows how to charm the whole town," Godiva said. She looked over at Sage, but she was watching Benton, who was still engaged with Richard.

"Ya know what, Outback Man? You can pay our tab," Richard snapped at Benton. "Since you crassshed our party and didn't spend a dime."

"You've gone troppo," Benton said.

"Thankssss for the drinks," Richard said gleefully, as if he'd gotten away with something.

Benton watched the miserly, intoxicated couple hurrying to the door.

Across the room, Molly also watched the Klappers leave, but her joy was short-lived. "Are you freakin' kidding me? Holy Gothic nightmare!"

Randy, Kyle, Sage, Godiva, and Freddie all looked at the door, unhappy to see the Goth woman stroll into the party as if she owned the place, bumping into the Klappers on their way out.

"Oh, poor Adam," Sage said. "He's going to be so upset. He had his fingers crossed that she would stay away."

"Randy will get rid of her."

"No," Kyle said, grabbing Randy's arm. "Don't be so impulsive. Especially when it's not your party. She hasn't done anything yet. Just play it cool."

Randy looked at him. "I hate when you're right."

Kyle smiled.

"Which isn't often," Randy said loudly so his friends could hear.

"Puh-leeze," Sage said. "You're a piece of work, Trubs. Kyle is often the voice of reason. Though I do thank you for that imitation of a bear you did to keep her out of my store the other day."

Randy smiled. "You're welcome, Miss Sage. I take it Miss Jones gave you an accounting."

Nearby, Barbarino Leighton, dressed in another all-white ensemble, turned to her husband, Cal. "You see this freak in black?" she said, nodding toward the Goth woman. "Don't you be chatting her up if you want to share my bed tonight."

"Wouldn't think of it, my little spitfire," Cal said as he put his trademark goofy grin on display. "My angel of seduction …."

"Freak scavenger," Barbarino muttered, rubbing her black

tourmaline pendant as she watched the woman help herself to food. She looked at her pendant. "Ward off this evil. I paid good bucks for you."

Sage watched while two women stopped Benton in his tracks. They were clearly attracted to him, barely unable to keep their hands to themselves … chattering and fawning before him … despite the lack of any reciprocal enthusiasm on his part. Sage knew they were ignoring his body language—which was impatiently tolerant at best. Realizing she was staring, her gaze quickly shifted to Adam. A look of horror swept over his face upon noticing the Goth woman, who was still helping herself to food. Sage made eye contact with Adam, an apologetic look on her face, as if she were somehow responsible for the woman's presence.

Adam regained his composure, said a few more hellos to his guests, then rushed over to Sage, who gave him a hug. "I'm so sorry she's here, Adam. Hopefully, she's just trying to psych you out and won't do anything."

"I hope not," Adam said, revealing worry lines on his forehead. "I didn't get a chance to tell you, but Joanie came by with some friends earlier. When she saw what I've done with the place, I could tell she was even more upset that I didn't give her a job. She said a few things I won't repeat, but then she left. There was a tall woman with her, and I was hoping she might be Goth Woman out of her black garb, and that I'd seen the last of her, but I was fooling myself. They didn't look anything alike, for one. It appears that Joanie was waiting until the end of the night to stick it to me. You know, lull me into a false sense of confidence."

"I know I'm the worst person to give you this advice," Sage said, "being as emotional as I am, but if you let your discomfort show on your face, that's not only a victory for her, but she may be encouraged to actually do something. Seriously. Try not to react. Besides, this is your night, your show. You've worked so long for this. Don't let anyone take it away from you."

"And I thought I was the voice of reason," Kyle said. "Sorry. I couldn't help but overhear." He looked at Adam. "Sage is absolutely right. And if she tries anything, she's not going to get far with Molly and Randy in the house."

"Word!" Randy said as he joined the conversation. He handed Kyle and Sage a fresh glass of white wine.

"Thanks, Trubs."

Molly walked over to Adam. "You aren't serving apples by any chance, are you?" She put the palm of her hand up. "I know— it's a pretty stupid question."

"Molly Rose wants to poison one if you do," Randy said.

Adam smiled. "Sage told me everything that happened the other day when Goth Woman dropped that bag of apples on the street. I'm happy to report there is only cut fruit on the table, along with some red grapes by the cheese display. And my staff is very aware of that woman's presence, as is the catering staff." He sighed. "So I don't know why I'm still so concerned."

Godiva and Freddie, each with a fresh glass of Cabernet in their hands, made their way over to the huddle of friends.

"Don't worry, Adam," Godiva said. "It's all good." She took a sip of her drink. "By the way, where's Vizzy?"

"Believe it or not," Adam said, "sleeping. She wore herself out with all of the excitement today. But I suspect she'll be waking up soon."

A half an hour later, several people had left, but even more people had come in. Benton, having finally extricated himself from the clutches of the female desperadoes, hurried over to talk to Sage. Happy to extricate herself from an exchange of pleasantries with some Swansea locals, she smiled before turning to go. "It was so nice to meet you all. Hope to see you again. If you'll excuse me …."

Now standing face to face with Benton, Sage gulped, each of

them longing for the right words to say to one another.

"I'm so glad you're here," she said, politely waving off the server who offered them a selection of hors d'oeuvres on a tray. "I feel so bad about what happened, Benton."

"Maybe I'm just thick as a brick, Sage," he said. "But I still don't know what actually did happen. We've had such an ace relationship since the day we met, and suddenly, you wanted to take a piece out of me. Not sure what I did. Not a clue." He frowned. "Well, I do have a clue. I think it was my invitation to Oz that did me in. Or did you in. I asked for something you couldn't give me and pushed you away in the process when a 'no thank you' would have done just fine."

"No, Benton. The invitation didn't do me in. I was really flattered."

"So why do you want to wipe me from your life?"

"I don't."

"That's a pretty wonky denial, Sage. You don't want anything more to do with me. That stands out like dog's balls."

She smiled. "I'm sorry. I'm not laughing at the situation. Only at the dog's balls."

"I'm sad," Benton said, straight-faced. "I feel like a zonk."

"What's a zonk?"

"Like a bloody idiot," he said, his voice getting slightly louder. "Is that better?"

Sage covered her face for a moment, then took her hands away. She shifted as she stood so that it was impossible to see Adam from the corner of her eye, only that didn't stop her from feeling his eyes on her back. "I can't bear for you to leave like this. Everything turned out all wrong on Wednesday. I handled everything horribly, and if we don't sort things out, I think we'll both regret it forever."

Benton bit his lip before speaking. "On Wednesday, when you lowered the boom on me, I asked you if you were going to give me the flick on the footpath, or if maybe we could go back to that café for some drinks and a chinwag. And despite knowing I was leaving tomorrow, what did you tell me, Sage?"

She tried to speak but he kept talking.

"You told me you'd already taken too much time away from the store. And that was bloody it."

"We have to talk, Benton."

"How's that going to work?" he challenged her. "Your mate would be devastated if you left this bash, and I know you don't want to do that. But unless you're into astral projection, like that lady at your store the other day, you can't be two places at once. And I'm flying home tomorrow. I had all the time in the world to talk, Sage. But you weren't interested."

"Oh, Benton. I'm so sorry." She noticed that he was looking at something across the room. "What's going on?"

"That crazy Goth lady just moved a whole lot closer to your mates. Looks like she's trying to earwig."

Sage turned to see the woman inching closer to Godiva and Freddie, while Molly, Randy, and Kyle stood behind her, watching every move. To their left, Barbarino stood watching, her eyes fixed on the woman, as her admiring husband stood by her side, blissfully drinking a glass of Cabernet.

Sage watched, feeling a thud in her chest when Molly covered her mouth in shock. As the two women made eye contact, Molly motioned for her to hurry over.

"I'll be back, Benton. I promise. Something's happening."

Sage excused her way through the crowd, finally reaching Molly, who was standing with Randy and Kyle. "What is it?" she mouthed, realizing that Molly's discovery had to do with the Goth woman.

Molly pulled Sage, Randy, and Kyle away, not realizing they were now right next to Barbarino. "Her ring!" Molly said. "Oh em freakin' gee! It all makes sense now! I can't believe I didn't figure it out before!"

"Figure what out?"

"Remember that day in *Le Chat Noir*," Molly asked. "When we were eavesdropping on Naomi and Mildred?"

"How could I forget?"

"Well, right before Naomi admitted stealing flowers in the hospital, she was bragging to Mildred about her new 'bauble,' a garnet cocktail ring with a diamond halo. And that woman is wearing that same exact ring. And that woman has the same manicure Naomi gets. And that woman is Naomi's height. And that woman *is* the freakin' she-devil. In disguise! Her ring gave her away."

"No way!" Sage said.

"Yes, way!"

Randy laughed. "Miss Sage sounds just like Little Miss Muffet when she was only served curds. No whey?"

Molly laughed. "Well, that's a new one on me."

Randy smiled. "An oldie but goodie. I just don't have occasion to use it that often." He looked at Sage. "But thanks for the opportunity."

"You're a piece of work, Trubs."

"What did Randy tell you in the store recently about Molly Rose having zingy dingy ring radar? Does this not prove Randy correct?"

Sage laughed while Molly put her hands on her hips and looked at him. "Is this really the time to gloat? I mean, really?"

"Guess not," Randy said. "But this is a delicious dilemma."

"His mouth is watering," Kyle said.

"No freakin' wonder she whacked me in the knees with her bag. And hello, should Sage and I be surprised she tried to murder us with apples?"

Barbarino, who had heard everything, glowered at Naomi, then turned to her husband. "See that woman in black? That's Bimbo Naomi!"

Sage turned to look at Barbarino. "Yeah. It is. I remember you don't like her very much."

"I don't dig bimbos who are trying to steal my husband and his money. Do you remember what else I told you?"

Sage screwed up her face. "That you wished we sold voodoo dolls?"

"Get with the program!" Barbarino barked. "I told you she was gonna try to shut you down for illegal condor's band and that she had it out for your friend Adam too."

"That's it!" Sage said. "Thank you. Seriously, thank you, Barbarino." Sage turned to Molly and Randy. "That's why she bought the weird things she did. She thinks I sell contraband. She's trying to prove I'm into witchcraft or something. And that's why she's here. She wants to destroy Adam's business too, because he stuck up for me … and because the Jameson brothers are her friends, and she sees Adam as a threat to her and to her vision of this town. And because she has nothing better to do."

"The she-devil is in the details," Molly said, her eyes filled with excitement. She looked at Barbarino. "Never thought I'd thank you for anything, but thanks."

"I hate the bitch more than you do," Barbarino said.

"That's debatable," Molly said, "but nothing we need to prove one way or the other."

"So what do we do?" Sage said. Adam, seeing their heads together, hurried over.

"What's going on?" he said as he caught up to everyone.

"Goth Woman is Naomi!" Sage said. "Molly figured it out when she recognized her ring."

Adam turned away and muttered some curse words. "I was

so fixated on her being one of Joanie's weirdo friends that I didn't see what was as plain as the nose on my face."

"That's it!" Sage said. "That long fake nose! Changed her whole look."

Molly looked at Adam with pleading eyes. "I know this is your party, but do you mind if I confront her? I don't want to make a scene at this amazing event, but I know this she-devil, and she's planning to disrupt the festivities. I need to get to her first."

"It's my store," Adam said. "I don't want to put you in that position, Molly. I should be the one to do something."

"Oh, believe me, you'd be doing me a huge favor. I was excited to bust her at the restaurant, but this is even better. Way better. She was never in the freakin' Hamptons. She was here all the time, wearing that fake nose and black wig, floating around town like Death, plotting her evil schemes."

"Well," Adam said, a smirk on his face. "I never did hire any live entertainment. I thought playing jazz on this amazing sound system would be just what this party needed. But maybe something more memorable is called for."

Sage noticed that Godiva and Freddie were on their way over.

"What in the Sam Hill is going on here?" Godiva asked. She looked at Sage's confused face. "It's slang that my grandmother used to use. It's sort of a euphemism for the devil."

"Couldn't be more appropriate," Molly said.

"Goth Woman is Naomi!" Sage told her.

"Hot damn!" Godiva said. "And we know and she doesn't know we know, right?"

"Slow down, Diva," Freddie said. "You're getting all wild-eyed and crazy on me, girl."

"This is exciting," Godiva said to Freddie as she reached into her purse for her phone. She turned to Sage. "How did you figure it out?"

"Molly Rose figured it out," Randy said. "She recognized Naomi's ring. Remember that day we came to see your ring? What did Randy say? That Molly has zingy dingy ring radar!"

Molly swatted Randy on the arm. "You're too much. I figure it out and you're still trying to ride the zingy dingy radar wave."

"He's incorrigible," Kyle said, his eyes smiling at Randy. "Oh, look, Adam, here comes your dog."

"Hey, Vizzy," Adam said as the Cairn Terrier ran over to him. "Looks like someone had a refreshing nap."

"Okay," Molly said. "Gather 'round, troops." She looked at Barbarino. "You too."

Barbarino smiled and dragged Cal over to the huddle.

"I'm going to approach her," Molly continued. "I just need you all to form a protective barrier behind me, in case she has some kind of weapon in that big black bag she's carrying. Let me expose her. We'll play the rest by ear."

"Or nose," Randy said. "Go for it, Molly Rose."

Molly, visibly seething with contempt, walked over to Naomi like a wild cat stalking its prey. She took one last look at the group, then walked around to look Naomi in the eyes.

Alarmed to see her so close, Naomi took a step back.

"Someone's not in the Hamptons, is she?" Molly said loudly.

"I-I …" Naomi stuttered. "Let's take this outside, Molly."

"Are you freakin' kidding me?"

"Please," Naomi pleaded. "I won't ever bother you again, I promise."

"You're no match for me, Naomi," Molly said. "You should have thought twice: First, before you whacked me in the knees coming out of Sage's store. Second, when you tried to make Sage and me fall flat on our faces on the sidewalk with those freakin' apples. You would have been happy to kill us both."

"How much do you want?" Naomi said, sweat forming on her face.

"Oh, please! You know I don't want your money," Molly said, turning up the volume on her voice. "What I do want is for everyone here to know that Naomi Hall-Benchley never went out of town after being busted for stealing an old woman's flower arrangement ... out of her *hospital room*. No, she promptly disguised herself to be the beautiful creature you see before you."

Molly paused to look around the store. Everyone had stopped talking, and at least eighty people were staring in her direction. Only assorted gasps and whispers could be heard floating through the crowd. Realizing that all eyes were on her, Naomi put her hands to her face.

"Take your hands away from your plastic-surgified face, you fake-nosed freak!" Barbarino shouted. "Let the whole town see you for the bimbo you are!"

Livid and hopelessly exposed, Naomi tried to uncover her face to have it out with Barbarino, but only her left arm fell to her side. Flustered, she changed direction and tried to leave, but she was surrounded.

"OMG! Is your ring stuck in your nose?" Molly asked, unable to keep from smiling. She turned to her friends. "Someone's garnet ring with the diamond halo is stuck in her freakin' fake nose."

Enraged, Naomi ripped her hand away, her long prosthetic nose now on her ring finger, while chunks of sticky nose putty stayed behind, refusing to budge. Naomi touched the tacky remains and winced in horror, then gasped as she saw the nose had attached itself to her ring finger.

"My, my," Randy said. "Gives new meaning to the term 'nose ring.'"

Meanwhile, Vizzy, who had been sniffing around, jumped

up and began frantically pawing at a pocket on Naomi's long black dress.

"Get off me, you stupid dog," Naomi said, but Vizzy became even more determined to uncover what her real nose told her was there. "Naomi reached into her pocket and pulled out a large wrapped wedge of expensive cheese. "Here, you wiry little monster, is this what you want?"

"Are you freaking kidding me? First you steal flowers at a hospital and now expensive cheese from a party? I'm surprised you didn't steal any of the deviled eggs, but admittedly, they'd be hard to pocket. And you only like them *she-deviled!*"

The laughter that had rumbled through the crowd was now explosive.

"Get this dog away from me!" Naomi screamed. "Whose dog is this, anyway?"

Adam winked at Sage. "Watch this." He walked over to Naomi. "This is my dog, Naomi. This is Toto. You've met Toto on the street several times."

"You can't be serious!" Naomi said. In absolute despair, she looked out at the sea of faces for some sympathy. "This dog used to be invisible!"

Adam's guests were now howling with laughter, as at least forty people had their cell phones up in the air recording, including Godiva, who had caught the entire scene from the beginning.

"I'm not kidding," Naomi insisted to the crowd. "I ran into this dog on the street several times, and it was always invisible. I know it sounds crazy, but it's true!"

Godiva nudged Sage. "Didn't you say that she fell down on the street the other day and walked away holding her face?"

"Yeah," Sage said. "I did. She must have been holding her smashed fake nose."

"Exactly," Godiva said. "And remember when I told you she

looked slightly different when she was looking in the window?"

"Yes!" Sage said. "She must have fixed her nose but couldn't get it back the way it was."

"Uh-huh," Godiva said, still recording the mayhem. "I knew something was off." She turned to Freddie. "I've got it going on, baby. Your Diva is one sharp cookie."

Freddie laughed and draped his arm around her. "Don't I know it, honey."

"I swear the dog was invisible," Naomi said, yanking off her wig and throwing it on the floor. Red-faced and enraged, she reached into her bag before turning to the crowd of people laughing so hard that tears were streaming down their faces. "And Sage Gordon is selling witchcraft supplies at her so-called gift shop." She reached into her large black bag and pulled out the mini cauldron. Not missing a beat, she held it up high for the crowd to see. "Look, a witch's cauldron! Where witches cook up evil brew."

The laughter only intensified.

"I've got one of those," a woman said. "Isn't it adorbs? I burn incense in it. My home smells so nice."

Furious, Naomi dug into her bag until she came out with the evil-eye charm. She held it up to the crowd. "Tell me this isn't witchy. It's an evil eye! Sage Gordon is trying to cast a curse on this entire town!"

"That's for protection *against* a true evil eye. It was created to ward off curses. It's a good thing," a man called out.

Sage turned to Godiva. "That's Ivan, the same guy who told off that socialite in the store. He's a regular customer."

Naomi threw the evil-eye charm into the crowd, then reached into her bag for the Tibetan knife. "This is a ritual knife," she screamed. "Who knows what evil purposes it's used for!"

"Ooh, that's pretty!" a woman called out. "I'll have to stop at Sage Earth Gifts."

Sage walked over to Naomi. "Thanks so much for the live infomercial. That's so nice of you." She whispered to Naomi, "By the way, got to give you credit. That raspy voice really threw me off. I thought for sure you were a three-pack-a-day smoker."

"Oh, shut up!" Naomi said. Her nose still attached to her ring, she angrily pushed her way through the laughing crowd, finally making it to the front door.

"Well," Randy said. "That ought to teach her!"

"But you know it won't, Randy. Nothing stops Naomi. Tearing down others is her *raison d'etre*."

"True," Randy said. "But it'll be a while. There are many wounds to be licked."

Barbarino walked over to Godiva, caressing her pendant. "You weren't kidding! This black tourmaline kicks butt! I'm glad I bought out the store."

"We aim to please," Godiva said, bursting with glee.

Freddie looked at his watch. "It's eight forty-five already." He turned to Adam. "What time does this gala end?"

Adam shrugged. "It was supposed to end at nine. But now I'm thinking it ends whenever people are ready to leave. It's so joyful in here now. I hate to tell a happy crowd that the party's over."

Sage looked around the store, panicked. "Benton. I can't find him. Does anyone know where he is?"

"He left a good half hour ago," Freddie said.

"Is he back at your guesthouse? Getting ready to leave tomorrow?"

"Oh, no," Freddie said. "Benton took everything with him this morning. Packed it all in a limo that my friend Rick owns. Rick's taking Benton to JFK. Benton is staying in a hotel there tonight and flying out tomorrow."

"But he didn't say good-bye," Sage said. "I can't believe he didn't say good-bye!"

"Calm down, honey," Godiva said, trying to comfort her. "Maybe he's not gone yet. He might be waiting for you at the store. If Robin or Ruth are still there, maybe they let him in."

Molly turned to Randy and Kyle. "I've never seen her this distraught. This is way worse than when Caleb left. I'm really concerned. We've got to go with her to the store."

Randy, Molly, Kyle, Godiva, and Freddie all looked sympathetically at Adam, whose once-joyous face had turned to pain and heartbreak.

Godiva walked over and touched him tenderly on the arm. "She just needs to say good-bye to a friend because that's the kind of wonderful person she is. Don't give up on her, honey."

Adam didn't say a word, but just nodded in response, and they all rushed out behind the woman he loved.

CHAPTER TWENTY-EIGHT

Breathless, Sage hurried into her store, with Godiva, Freddie, Molly, Randy, and Kyle only a few paces behind her.

Robin, who was just taking Rufus's harness off, looked up at her while Rufus squirmed to get to his mom.

"Hey, boy," Sage said, hugging the dog. She looked at Robin. "Have you seen my Australian friend, Benton Bradley?"

Randy motioned to Rufus to come over to him as Sage spoke to her cousin.

"As a matter of fact," Robin said, "I did. He came in here maybe a half hour after you and Godiva left for the party."

Sage turned to look at all her friends, who were paying rapt attention to the conversation, then back to Robin. "No way! Why would he come here when he knew I'd be at the party?"

"Well … ." Robin said with an uneasy smile. "He kind of did that on purpose. He said he waited until you and Godiva had left."

"For what earthly reason?" Sage asked. Her face dropped and her breathing became labored.

"I don't know. But he left a present for you," Robin told her. "And he was really adamant that you didn't get it until the party was over or until after eight thirty."

"Well, it's nearly nine o'clock," Freddie said, looking at his watch.

Randy made a loud aside to Kyle. "Mister Lamar loves to look at that watch."

"That's because his beloved Diva bought it for him," Godiva said. "Now hush!"

"What she said!" Molly whispered to Randy.

"Where's the present?" Sage asked.

"It's in a bag, on the bottom shelf, in the right cabinet behind the counter."

Sage hurried around the corner, rushed to the cabinet, and opened the door. She pulled out a small shopping bag. Taking a deep breath, she looked inside, then pulled out a small gold gift box decorated with rhinestones. She looked up at everyone. "Why I am so afraid to open this?"

"Randy will do it!"

Kyle playfully slapped his hand. "Randy will not do it," he assured Sage. "Open it when you're ready."

Sage took the lid off the box and gasped. Her mouth dropped and she froze in stunned silence.

"Ruff," Rufus said, feeling everyone's anticipation.

Sage remained frozen in place.

"It's okay," Randy said to everyone. "She just blinked." He turned to Kyle. "Before you hit me, darling, I was just assuring everyone she hadn't petrified."

Molly whacked him on the arm. "This is no time for a joke."

"And Randy isn't joking, Molly Rose."

All eyes turned back to Sage, who was trying to form words. "I-I can't believe it."

"Oh Lord have mercy," Godiva said loudly. "Give her strength to take the mystery item out of the box before they find our bodies strewn across the floor after we all die from curiosity."

Slowly, Sage pulled a small golden, jeweled crown out of the box and held it up for everyone to see. "I don't understand," she said, looking at the large red, blue, yellow, and green stones that were placed evenly around the circumference.

Godiva walked over to inspect the crown. "This is what you said Jimmy was going to give you someday. And this is how you described it. Did you tell Benton about that?"

"Yes," Sage said, sobbing. "I did. I told him this is what Jimmy wanted to give me when we were old enough to be king and queen."

"Oh, honey," Godiva said. "It looks like Benton wanted to help fulfill Jimmy's childhood wish, knowing how it's haunted you all of those years."

"Nothing else makes sense."

"It's a very sweet gesture," Godiva said, "though I don't quite understand why he would want to fulfill another man's promise, even if that man was a boy when he made the promise." She turned to Freddie. "Benton really cares about Sage. Which makes this whole mess about his girlfriend, Rita, all the more puzzling."

"It does," Sage agreed.

"Diva, her name isn't Rita. It's Riva. Rhymes with Diva."

"Really? I could swear you said Rita," Godiva mumbled. "Not that it really matters."

"What's her last name?" Sage asked Freddie, her heart rate accelerating again.

"Roper," Freddie said. "Riva Roper."

"OH MY GOD!" Sage screamed. "There's no way!"

Everyone exchanged shocked looks. Sage walked around from behind the counter, then grabbed onto to it, just before she lost her grip and slid down to the floor.

Godiva and Randy hurried to help her up. Noticing she was about to slide to the floor again, they held her tight.

"Are you all right," Robin asked. "Should I call Mom?

Should I call an ambulance, for that matter? And why does that name sound vaguely familiar to me?"

"I've got to go to the airport," Sage said. "Now! I can't believe I forgot that name. I thought I remembered everything, but that was in the way back of my brain. Now I remember how he used to call me that."

"What are you talking about?" Molly asked. "Sage, I'm so freakin' worried about you."

Sage pointed up to the **Priva**te **Proper**ty sign. "It's in there. It's in the sign."

Molly looked up at the sign in unison with everyone else. "Look at that! Take off the 'P' at the beginning of Private, then the 'te' at the end, and you've got Riva. Then, take the 'P' from Property and the 'ty' at the end, and that gives you Roper. Riva Roper." Molly, blanching at the unexpected revelation, looked at Sage. "This is Jimmy's name for you, Riva Roper?"

"Yes," Sage managed to say. "He said my queen name was hidden in the sign."

"Are you freakin' kidding me?" Molly said. "Does this mean what I think it means?"

"Of course!" Robin said to herself. "I remember now."

"Yes," Sage said. "I don't know how, but Benton is Jimmy Cole! And now that I know that, I can see Jimmy so clearly. I just never thought to look for him in this charming Australian man who grew up ten thousand miles away. But they're one and the same, and I've got to find him. Now!"

"You can't drive like this," Godiva said. "Freddie and I will take you." Godiva looked at her fiancé. "Where exactly do we take her?"

"I know what hotel he's staying in," Freddie said. "I was there when he made the reservation."

"Thank goodness," Sage said. "But even if you didn't know,

I'd search every single hotel until I found him."

Molly turned to Randy. "Can you drive Kyle and me in your car? And Robin, if she wants to come?"

"At your service," Randy said.

"I'll take Rufus home with me," Robin said to Sage. "Just let me know when you want me to bring him back." She looked at everyone. "I wish I could come, but I've got to finish this chapter of my dissertation. Going to be a long night for me."

"Absolutely, Miss Robin," Randy said. He looked at Freddie. "Do you have an address I can plug into my GPS?"

Freddie pulled out his phone and swiped to unlock it. "Gonna look it up right now. C'mon. I'll give it to you outside."

Everyone but Godiva rushed to the door.

"Hurry, Godiva," Sage said.

"Yeah, shake those pretty tail feathers and dance on outta here," Freddie said.

"Two seconds," Godiva said, pulling her phone out of her purse. "My brother texted me earlier and it's urgent. Just got to respond. It can't wait. I'll be right there."

Freddie looked at her oddly, then with a gentle hand on Sage's back, escorted her out of the door.

CHAPTER TWENTY-NINE

"Your destination is three tenths of a mile on the left," the GPS said.

Godiva looked at Freddie. "I'm glad she got us here, but I need to turn this digital beeotch off. She gets on my last nerve."

"You jealous, baby?" Freddie said with a grin. "That she can take me to places you can't?"

"She so cannot," Godiva said, her eyes sparkling. "And no, I'm not."

Sage, oblivious to their conversation, looked at the large imposing four-star hotel with a tinted glass façade ahead of them. "What if they won't tell me what room he's in? They don't usually give out room numbers, do they? And even if I can get them to ring his room without telling me the number, Benton will probably guess that it's me and not answer."

"Did you try calling him, honey?" Godiva asked.

"He's turned off his phone. It goes straight to voicemail."

Freddie spoke over his shoulder to Sage, who was sitting in the back, "I can let you off at the door while I park, if you want. Randy was behind me, and he just pulled into the parking lot."

"Yes, please," Sage said.

"I'll go in with you," Godiva said. "Just so you're not alone. Freddie can catch up with us, or me, after he parks the car."

Freddie drove slowly through the circular drive to the front doors. Before he could get out and show off his chivalrous side, a doorman opened both car doors for Sage and Godiva.

"Thank you so much, Freddie," Sage said as she stepped out. She turned to Godiva, who was next to her. "I feel like I'm about to slip to the ground again."

"Hold steady, girl." Godiva turned and blew a kiss to Freddie. "Call me when you're not driving." Refocusing her attention on Sage, she walked with her toward the hotel.

"I'm a wreck," Sage said. "I have no idea what to do now."

"Not a problem," Godiva said as they passed through the main doors into the lobby. "Let me put my thinking cap on."

"Please," Sage said. "I'm too distraught to make use of mine."

"Well," Godiva said. "We don't know exactly when Benton left the party, but you do know the last time you spoke to him. And it wasn't that long before everything went down with Naomi. So, my guess is that he couldn't have gotten here much sooner than we did. Maybe he beat us by thirty or forty minutes. An hour at best."

"Why does that even matter?" Sage asked, tears in her eyes.

"Because it's very doubtful the man had time to eat dinner before he left. He was probably too upset to eat, but by now, he must be hungry. So, before we try to find out his room number, I think we should check out the restaurants."

"Your phone," Sage said, looking down.

Godiva reached into her purse and swiped to answer her phone. "Yeah, baby. We're in the lobby. Just gonna check the restaurants first. When you get here, just wait in the lobby by the red couches on the round Persian rug. And please let the others know … Thanks, baby. Love you too."

"There's a coffee shop over there," Sage said, pointing. "Can you come with me just until I find him … hopefully." She wiped a few tears away. "I don't even want to think about not finding him."

After they hurried over to the coffee shop, Godiva explained to the hostess standing at the podium that she and Sage were just looking for a friend. Without hesitation, the hostess smiled and ushered them in. As Sage and Godiva carefully walked through the room, they checked out every single table.

"He's not here," Sage said. "We've looked at every table … twice."

"Wait, I have an idea," Godiva said. She walked back to the hostess. "Hi, we aren't able to find our friend. Do you happen to remember seating a very good-looking Australian man? About thirty?"

"I'm sorry," the hostess said. "I would remember someone who fit that description … even if it were a week ago. If he's here, he somehow escaped my notice. You might try The Aviator. It's our upscale restaurant. It's to the right of the registration desk, across the lobby and down the hall."

"Thank you," Sage said as she grabbed Godiva's arm and hurried away.

As they re-entered the lobby, they saw Freddie, Molly, Randy, and Kyle, all waiting in the designated spot. Godiva held up the palm of her hand, to ask them all to wait there while she and Sage navigated their way down the hall.

"There it is," Godiva said. "The Aviator. Looks like a nice place … such soft romantic lighting. "

"I feel like my heart is going to burst through my chest and splatter all over these shiny floors. It's already mush inside of my body."

"Hold steady, honey." Godiva led her toward the maître d', who was standing on the left side of the large archway entrance. Sage stopped suddenly as she surveyed the lounge to the right of the restaurant.

"Look, he's in the bar," Sage said. "Do you see him? He's all the way at the end in the last seat." She blew out a loud puff of air. "I'm a wreck!"

"You can do it, Sage. Just remember. That man loves you, and he has for his entire life. He'll be happy to see you. He didn't leave you that crown because he doesn't care."

"Maybe he left it because—"

Godiva put a hand on Sage's shoulder. "Now why in the world would you want to stand here and speculate with me when the answers are sitting right down there?"

"I don't know," Sage said. "Because I'm not afraid of you?"

"Bad answer," Godiva said, giving her a you-know-better look. "We'll be waiting in the lobby. Go on, now. Godspeed. Even though you're only going to the end of the bar, you need all of the love and protection you can get."

Before Sage could respond, Godiva headed off to the lobby, leaving her standing alone in the bar, wearing her lavender floral prairie dress, her fringed ankle boots, and a purple scarf around her neck. Aware that people were noticing her, she walked purposely to the end of the bar. Reaching Benton, she stood behind him for a few moments, watching as he stared mournfully into his drink.

"Benton," she whispered, lightly tapping him on the shoulder.

He turned to look at her, his face streaked with tears. "Oh, Sage. You found me."

"I did," she said as her own tears began to roll.

"Guess we've both got our eye taps turned on," he said.

She looked blankly at him for a moment. "Oh, the tears. Yes, we do."

A well-dressed man in his fifties, who had been sitting next to Benton, quickly assessed the situation and got up. "Please, take my seat," he said to Sage.

"Thanks, mate," Benton said as he motioned to the bartender to buy the man a drink.

Sage sat down and looked into his eyes. "I can see you now, Jimmy. You've been right there the whole time."

"I have been," he said, taking both of her hands in his. "I didn't know if I should tell you who I was. I was afraid if I did, you'd never get to know me for the man I am today. Took me some time after I arrived in the states to even come into your store. Nothing about this has been easy." He looked up as he saw the bartender standing before them. "What would you like, Sage?"

"Just some Italian sparkling water," Sage said to the bartender. "With lime please." She looked at Benton. "I had wine at the party. Besides, I need to be clear now. I'll get drunk later if I have to."

Benton just looked at her.

"I'm kidding," she said. "At least I think I am. I don't like being drunk."

"That makes two of us," Benton said. "I never want to be like that pisspot Richard and his wife. Or my old man."

"Have you eaten?" Sage asked.

"Just had a sanger … a sandwich … and some chips."

"Good," she said as the bartender placed her drink and a bottle in front of her. "Thank you."

"Cheers, mate," Benton said to the bartender.

Sage looked at him. "I don't even know what to call you."

Ever so slightly, the corners of Benton's mouth turned upward. "That first day we met … well, that we met again, I handed you my credit card when I bought that prezzy for my mum. I wondered right then if you noticed the name on it."

"I just remember seeing Benton Bradley on the card," Sage said. "I always look. It's habit when you own a store."

Benton reached into his wallet and pulled out a credit card

and handed it to her.

"Oh! J. Benton Bradley," Sage said, reading the card. "I never noticed. Not that I would have thought twice if I had."

"Only showing it to you because I want you to know my legal first name is still James. But I go by Benton these days."

She handed the card back to him. "Before we talk about anything that happened between us, you have to tell me how you went from being Jimmy Cole who lived in a farmhouse in Bancroft … to becoming Benton Bradley from Australia."

"A minor detail, hey," Benton said. He took a sip of his whiskey. "You know, that night Chester Simmons came into the store, I'll tell you, it took everything in me not to reveal myself right then. At one point, he looked at me and said I looked like I was ready to burst wide open. He was right. I was. I mumbled something about how I was a protector of women, but I wanted to tell him who I was in the worst way. But I wasn't ready to tell *you*. And I just about died when he said he saw me steal the sign."

"I remember," Sage said. "And yeah, that last part totally blew me away."

"Do you remember what he said about my old man, being an abusive pisspot?"

"I do," Sage said. "That's why you left, isn't it?"

"It is. I'll tell you everything I remember. I know this may be hard to understand, but Mum *never* talks about those days. I'm the only part of her life from that time that still exists. So, I've only got my memories to go on. I'll do my best to explain to you from there. Okay?"

"Of course," Sage said. "I can totally understand why your mother wants to leave the past behind. Please, tell me what you remember."

"First, I should apologize for never telling you how horrible my life was. You were my salvation, and I guess even at that age, I didn't want the horrors of my home tainting the best part of my life. And I was afraid that if your parents knew, and tried to help, he'd hurt them … and you. I couldn't take that risk, but more than anything, I wanted to pretend that my family was happy and normal. Just like yours was."

"I never had a clue," Sage said. "And we were so close. I feel like I should have known, even at that young age."

"No, you shouldn't have. I hid it well. A couple of times your mum asked me if I was all right, and that worried me. So after that, I tried even harder to keep my pain tucked away. Not just when I was at your house, but at school as well."

"I guess you succeeded," Sage said. "Tell me more."

"Well, as bad as things were, we couldn't just up and leave. No telling what he would have done. Mum knew that, and planned our escape a long time before it happened. But she never said a word until right before we left. My father's mother, my grandmother, who lived in Indiana, was dying. She'd been sick for a long time. Mum always knew that when the end got near, he'd go there to say good-bye. So, when the time did come, he got himself a ticket to Indianapolis, and we drove him to the airport. Mum was very quiet on the ride back. When we got home, she called the airline to make sure the plane had taken off on schedule. Then, she looked at me and said, 'Jimmy, we're leaving tonight. But we've got to go after midnight, when everyone who lives near us is asleep … when every window in every house is dark. Nobody can see us leaving with our suitcases. We're going to have a new life very far away.'"

"Oh," Sage said. "I'm feeling the pain of your disappearance all over again."

"Me too, Sage. The only thing I cared about, when my mum told me we had to go, was you. I cried and cried. I begged her to at least let me call you the next day to say good-bye. She said she knew how sad it was for me to leave you, and that she knew you'd be really sad too, but that it was way too dangerous for us to be in touch. Then she promised me that one day, when we were older, we'd see one another again."

"I wonder how she knew," Sage said.

"She knows her son," Benton said. "She knew what you meant to me, and she knew then, just like she knows now, that I take care of what is important to me."

Sage lowered her eyes, then looked up at him. "What happened after she told you it was time to leave your home forever?"

"Well," Benton said, "that night, her friend Angela came just after one a.m., picked us up, then drove us to her home in Jersey. Mum just left the family car in the driveway so nobody could track us. Also, she didn't want anyone to notice we were gone until we were far away. I remember we stayed with Angela maybe three days, then flew to Australia, where Mum had a good friend, a boy she'd gone to high school with."

"Australian?" Sage asked.

"True-blue," Benton said. "Carter only lived in the states two years, when his dad had a short-term contract for work, but he and Mum secretly kept in touch, just as friends. After she got together with my father, they'd write to one another using my grandmother's address. Mum knew my old man had a jealous side, but it took a while before she learned how abusive he was. I guess that's a good thing, or I never would have been born. Anyway, her friend Carter lived in The Wang, Wangaratta, nearly three hours outside of Melbourne. His wife had died, and he invited us to live with him and his daughter. Mum knew it would be the perfect place for me to grow up. She told me that she would be calling me Benton from then on, but James would still be my first name." Benton smiled. "James is my grandfather's name. She didn't want to change that ...

and I guess she wanted me to still have a piece of my original self. But she said that in order to stay safe, we should never talk about life in America again, and from that moment on, I should call her 'mum' and not 'mom,' and learn to talk like the people around me as quickly as I could."

"I remember how you used to imitate cartoon characters," Sage said. "You were so good at that. You made me laugh; you still make me laugh. I'll bet you sounded Aussie in no time flat."

"I reckon," Benton said. "Mum had a lot more trouble."

"So I guess you changed your last names immediately."

"Yeah. Mum had us take on the surname of her friend Carter Bradley." He smiled. "She knew it was only a matter of time before she married him, and he became my dad. Got an older sister in the deal too. Harper. Love her to pieces. Poor thing lost her mum to cancer when she was only seven. But Mum loves her like she was her own."

"That's wonderful," Sage said. "And it explains why I could never find you or your mother. But how come I could never find your father? How come he never came back home if he didn't know you had left? And how did your parents get divorced if he had no idea where you were, and your mother never wanted him to find out?" She sighed. "Sorry for all of the questions. I know I'm all over the place. So much is whizzing around my brain at warp speed." She paused to take a breath. "I searched a million different ways and never did find a 'Harold Cole.' At least not one who remotely fit your father's description."

"That's okay. I'll get to everything. First, I guess it shouldn't surprise you that a mongrel who regularly abused his wife might lie about his name. See, he was on the run from law enforcement when she met him, but of course, she didn't know that." Benton finished his drink and motioned to the bartender for a refill. "He was as cunning as a dunny rat. Mum met him when she was only eighteen

… in a local boozer. When she asked his last name, Nat King Cole was playing on the jukebox, so he flogged the name Cole right there on the spot. Mum was sharp enough to notice the supposed coincidence, but it wasn't until years later she figured out what had happened. By that point, she wasn't the least bit surprised he flogged the name of a famous singer, seeing how he'd flogged a whole lot of other things. I think his name was actually Howard, not Harold. I'm not really sure; I don't really care. Oh, and as for their divorce, I never knew this until I had become Benton Bradley, but they were never legally married. The old man gave her a bunch of reasons why he couldn't marry her, but the truth turned out to be that he already had a wife somewhere … and was lying about his last name and everything else."

"Holy secret life," Sage said. "What a blessing they weren't legally married."

"You're not kidding," Benton said. "Mum never told me while we were still in America because she didn't want me to feel ashamed for any reason."

"Where is he now?" Sage asked.

"Dead as doornail," Benton said. "Died in prison."

"Oh, I see. How did he finally end up where he belonged? In prison, I mean. And don't forget to tell me why nobody in our neighborhood ever saw him again. I always thought the three of you left together." Sage tried to refill her sparkling water, but her hand shook so that the water splashed and landed in a puddle on the bar. "Oh, I'm so sorry! Did I get you wet?"

"No worries," Benton said. "I'm as dry as a dead dingo's donger."

Sage laughed as the bartender quickly wiped up the spill, then refilled her glass. "Please go on. Back to that night when you left … the night you left Bancroft."

"Well, we didn't all leave together, but I guess we were all 'gone together.' But first let me answer your question about why nobody ever saw my old man again. From what Mum told me, when I didn't show up for school, and Mum's friends couldn't get in touch with her, the cops were called. They found the note Mum left on the dining room table saying we were gone forever. There was some brief speculation at first that she may have been forced to write the note and that he might have taken us, or worse, so the cops were looking for him just to get things sorted and make sure Mum's note was for real.

"Harold … Howard … whatever … had left his number in Indiana with his drinking mate across the street. He was the one who alerted him that we were gone and that the cops were suss and looking to question him. You'd think the abusive pisspot would have wanted to clear himself of any suspicion right away, but Mum reckoned he was afraid she might have figured out he was a wanted man and if that were the case, that she'd have had a mind to ring the federallies before we left. She didn't, though. She learned about him being a criminal later, after it all came out and we were living in The Wang. I only know this because I heard her on the phone talking to her friend in Jersey, about how she'd called the police after they found him, to let them know we were okay, and that he hadn't killed or kidnapped us, despite probably being capable of it. That's how Mum came to find out how he actually got arrested. She told her friend the whole story. I remember hearing Mum say she wasn't surprised by any of it. Not really. Said everything finally made sense, and it was time to close the book on him." Benton bit his lip as he reflected on what he had just said. "I'm glad I played earwig that day, because Mum never spoke about him again, and I never had to ask."

"I don't remember that part of it," Sage said. "About people thinking he'd done anything to you and your mother. For one, I was too young to understand everything your disappearance entailed.

And I was far too distraught over your being gone to remember much else. That's not the kind of information my parents would have shared with me. They were trying to calm me down, not get me more upset than I was. All I really remember is hearing that your family disappeared." She took a sip of her water. "Do you mind me asking how he got arrested? Did you hear the entire conversation?"

"Oh, yeah," Benton said. "Seems he flipped out and went to some fellow mongrel's house, a couple of hours away from Bancroft, to lay low. But the next night, he went into town there, drank all of the grog he could get his hands on, and got some kind of rotten. He was a real root rat and tried to shag the wrong Sheila. Boys in blue got called, took him in, and it didn't take them long to figure out his name wasn't Harold Cole and that the law had been after him for twelve years."

"This is all so mind-boggling."

"It is, Sage. But that's the reason my old man never went back to the house. And that's why nobody ever saw any of us again."

"What an amazing story," she said as she watched the bartender put a fresh drink in front of Benton.

Noticing, Benton looked at her. "I hope you've figured out by now that two or three drinks is my limit. Like I said earlier, I never want to be—"

"I know," Sage told him. "You don't owe me any explanation. Besides, if there was ever a night you really needed another drink, this would be it." She took a sip of her water. "It's totally bizarre that you're actually an American."

"Jimmy was an American," he said with conviction. "Benton is Australian. The only thing they both have in common is you. In fact, you're the only reason Jimmy still exists at all."

"Well, I know it was Jimmy who left that beautiful crown for me. How did you ever find one so much like the one we'd envisioned?"

"I've worked in manufacturing for years. It wasn't difficult to find a mate who could custom-make that for me. But deciding whether to leave it for you ... well, that was tough. Real tough. Especially after ...."

"I'm so glad you did; I'll treasure it for the rest of my life." She sniffled, then reached into her purse for a tissue. "It would have been tragic for you to leave, and for me to never know. There were a few times—I swear—I saw Jimmy's eyes when I looked into yours. But I thought that my unresolved past was playing tricks on me. And I've had enough tricks played on me, so I never let those passing thoughts stay longer than necessary, and I never shared them with a soul. But now that I think about it, it's not impossible that I might have looked at our childhood photos and figured it out. I can't even imagine what that would be like ... now that I know you as an adult ...for you to have left for the second time. I'm so glad it didn't happen that way."

"Me too," Benton said. "And thanks to me, it almost did."

She looked down and played with the fringe on the end of her scarf. "I guess we just had the easy part of our conversation ... not that there was anything remotely easy about the ordeal you and your mother went through." She paused for a moment to collect her thoughts. "Do you mind if I speak first ... about us? There's just so much in my head, and I want to get it out before it evaporates into another solar system."

"Sounds like an ace science-fiction plot." Benton laughed, then quickly became serious. "Go for it," he said, pulling her scarf gently out of her hands to help her eliminate the distraction.

"First," Sage said, "I can't apologize enough for the way I treated you. You see, after you invited me to Australia, I was really torn, for a lot of reasons, but I didn't lie when I said that I was flattered. But the next day, when Godiva came to work on

Wednesday morning, she told me that you had a girlfriend named Rita."

"Riva," Benton said.

"Yeah, I know, but Godiva heard 'Rita.' It wasn't until we got back from the party tonight, after I saw the crown, when Godiva wondered aloud why you would give me such a gift if you were in love with a woman named Rita. That's when Freddie corrected her. And when he said the full name, 'Riva Roper,' I became overwhelmed in a way unlike anything I'd ever experienced. I'd completely forgotten that my queen name was hidden in the sign that I'd been cherishing all of these years … the sign that I look at every day. In the instant, it all came together and I had to find you. After I got up off the floor."

"You mean that metaphorically, right?"

"Nope," Sage said with an embarrassed grin. "I was in such shock that I literally collapsed onto the floor."

"Hope you weren't hurt."

"No. But it was just the most surreal moment of my entire life."

"I have a confession to make," Benton said.

"Really? There's more?"

"Not exactly. Just that on the day I met you and saw that sign, as much as I would have liked to have it, I wanted it to stay with you. But I asked you if you'd sell it to me because I needed to know just how much meaning it held for you."

Sage looked into his eyes. "The fact that it was hanging in my store should have given you a clue."

"It did. But I needed more."

"I can't blame you. I think I would have done the same thing."

"Thanks for that, Sage."

"No worries. And as much as I detest thinking about last

Wednesday, I need to finish what I was saying. Right before I went full freak on you, Godiva had told me about 'Rita,' and I couldn't believe you were playing games and inviting me to come to Australia with you when you were in love with someone else. And coming on the heels of Caleb's deceptions, I just felt like I was every man's fool. I'm so sorry. And yeah, I might have felt angry." A self-conscious smile played on her lips. "Not that you could really tell."

"Oh, not at all," Benton said with a twinkle in his eye.

"Didn't think so."

"Well, geez," Benton said. "Finally something makes sense. No wonder you wanted to bail out like you did, giving me the 'Footpath Flick' and all. I just wish you'd told me."

"I considered it very carefully. I can't even tell you how many times I examined the situation from every conceivable angle. And maybe," Sage said delicately, "if the thoughts in my head were only about you and me, I would have done so." She looked down. "But they're not."

"I had some stiff competition," Benton said. He reddened, suppressing a smile. "I didn't mean it like that. Not that you'd believe me, the way I've been cracking onto you … saying the things I said about Adam. He's a good bloke, your stiffy man."

Sage tried not to laugh. "You really need to stop calling him that. Luckily for you, it doesn't have the bite it would have if you Americanized it."

"I know," Benton said. "I get away with a lot, putting on the Aussie."

"You do," Sage said. Her visage turned serious. "You were such a big part of my life, Benton … Jimmy. Knowing and loving you as a child influenced everything I ever did in my life … every decision I ever made. You were unfinished business. Your friendship, your love … it all made such an impact on me."

"That night we had to shoot through the bludgers' bash, you

told me you felt like a child again, running away from Old Man Simmons with Jimmy. I almost told you that I felt the same way. The words came so close to falling out of my lips, but I stopped them. Bloody hell, Sage, I hope you don't ever think this was easy on me. That I was playing you by not telling you who I was."

"Did you want me to figure it out?" Sage asked.

"Yes and no. I know that's not a good answer, but what I really wanted was for us both to end up where we belonged. I had always wondered if you'd forgotten me," Benton said, "but almost from the beginning, after meeting you again, I knew you hadn't. I knew I had a place in your heart like you've always had in mine. What I didn't know is if we were right for one another … now … as adults, and even if we were, if we could make it work."

"Oh, Benton," Sage said, gently touching his arm. "Everything you're saying resonates with me more than I could possibly explain."

"No drama," Benton said. "I truly believe, my sweet, that we both got what we needed."

Sage sniffled again. "What's that?"

Benton gently stroked a tendril of her long hair, then pulled his hand away. "To know that what we shared as children was extra grouse … that it will always be a part of us. That we can love different people for different reasons, but that we need to find the person who we can really build a future with … and for reasons that go far beyond sentiment." He exhaled. "Bloody hell. I've never been this choked up in my life. And it's not like I've got the wobbly boot on or anything. Everything's just got me right here." Benton swallowed and touched his chest. "You'd think I was American or something."

Sage burst out laughing. "I think you were meant to be Australian. It suits you."

"It does, doesn't it?"

"One thing I'm curious about," Sage asked. "How is it that you came to work with Freddie? There's no way that could be a coincidence."

"No, not exactly. Thing is, I really wanted to bring my line to America. And I wanted to find the best partner. I thought I might find someone in the New York area and eventually make my way to find you. But when I found Freddie, right there in Swansea, and learned what a stellar reputation he had, I kinda thought it was meant to be. I contacted him, asked if he might give me a fair go and see what happened from there. The rest of that story you already know. But it was just sheer luck that Godiva had started working for you. Never counted on that."

"I guess it was meant to be. You and Freddie, I mean."

"He's not my type," Benton said with a glint in his eye.

Sage smiled. "Why can't this be easier? Saying good-bye is so hard."

"Then how about if we just say, 'Until next time.'"

"I like that better," Sage said. "Because I truly believe there will be a next time. I hope we will always be friends … real friends who are there for one another."

"I want the same thing; I really do. We'll make that happen."

"And I promise I'll never act so stupid like I did on Wednesday. I'm so sorry."

"You need to focus on what you have. Because Adam is a good bloke … and he loves you. And you love him back."

"I do," Sage said. "But I don't think he'll want anything to do with me, the way I ran out of the party to look for you. The thing is, when Adam feels unwanted, he just sort of slinks away."

"And you want him to be a bit more aggro," Benton said. "To go after what he wants, no matter who's there or whatever seems to be in his way."

"I haven't quite thought of it like that, but I guess I do," Sage said. "Is that terrible of me? I truly don't want to change him; he's so wonderful just as he is. I just need to know he loves me."

"My suggestion is that you go ask him," Benton said. "Right now."

"I don't understand."

Benton nodded toward the entrance to the bar. As Sage turned her head to follow his gaze, she saw Adam. With tears in his eyes, he stood there, looking at her, with more love than she had ever seen. Behind him, Godiva, Molly, Randy, Kyle, and Freddie looked on, as if something or someone had turned them into a glob of sentimental mush.

"Go on," Benton said, fighting the tears. "Go to your man."

Sage got up from the barstool and hugged Benton as hard as she could. "Let me know when you're home safe, you hear? And I'll always love you, Jimmy Benton Bradley." She paused to take a last look at him. "Until next time, my friend."

"See ya, Sage, and tell my fluffy mate not to forget me. I'll miss you both more than I can say. And tell your parents 'Jimmy' says hey, and please thank them for being such a port in a storm for me. All of you saved my life, and I'll always be grateful. Next time I come for a visit, I'd love to see them again." He smiled through his tears as he pushed her toward Adam with a wave of his hand.

Sage stood in place and looked at Adam. She beamed as she had never done before. With everything she had, she made sure Adam would know that the love shining in her eyes was all for him. A moment later, they rushed toward one another. When they finally embraced, the entire bar, including Benton, applauded.

"I love you, Adam," Sage said. "I love you with all my heart. I'm sorry I had to work through so much to get there."

"I get it," he said, stroking her hair. "I do. I don't regret any of it. I wouldn't want you any other way."

"I am so glad you're here. I never thought you'd …."

"You never thought I'd come for you, right?"

"I didn't."

"When you ran out of the party to find Benton, I was devastated. I'm sure if you had eyes in the back of your head and could have seen me standing there, you'd never in a million years have seen a man that was going to fight for you. But I was hosting eighty people in my store and didn't know where to go. But as soon as I figured it out, I left my store in the good hands of my staff and my family, and ran like the wind."

"How did you find me here?" Sage said, seeing that everyone had now gathered around them.

"I believe a certain Diva might have texted her 'brother,'" Freddie interjected, making air quotes.

"You were texting Adam?" Sage asked Godiva. "To tell him where I was headed?"

Godiva put her hand up in the air. "After my stupid mistake caused so much trouble, I had to do my best to make things right." She sighed. "So yes, guilty as charged. Forgive me?"

"Of course she does," Randy said, putting his arms around Adam and Sage.

"I'm so glad you're both getting the happy ending you wanted," Molly said. "I got mine, and it's the best feeling in the world. I swear, I'm happier every day I'm alive."

Freddie put his arm around Godiva at the same moment Kyle put his arm around Randy.

Adam leaned in and kissed Sage as if no one was watching. When he finally pulled away, he looked down at the end of the bar. "I need to thank someone," he said. "I'm not sure I'd be the happiest man on Earth without a helping hand from one of the most decent guys I've met in a long time."

Sage watched as Adam walked down to Benton, and the two shared a manly hug. She didn't know what they were saying, but she knew it was eloquent, gracious, and beautiful.

"You were right, Sage," Godiva said. "Jimmy Cole was the key to your happiness, the missing link. Miracles do happen. I'm so happy you found each other and got the closure you needed. I just hope he finds someone as special as you are."

"He will," Sage said. "Riva Roper will see to it."

"Excuse me, everyone," Randy said. "Not to disturb this touching repartee or anything, but I just got a text from Miss Robin Masterson. Miss Sage, she wants to know if she should bring Rufus back to your place tonight?"

"Um ..." Sage said, turning around to find Adam standing there.

"Would it be presumptuous of me to ask that perhaps Robin might keep Rufus for the night," Adam asked.

"I don't know," Sage said with a grin. "Would it?"

Adam shrugged. "Hmm. Not sure. I guess no more presumptuous than it was asking my sister to take Vizzy home tonight."

Sage blushed. "You did?"

Adam nodded. "Uh-huh."

"Work it, Miss Sage! Work it, Mister Canoga!"

"They know what to do," Molly said, whacking Randy in the arm.

"You two go on ahead," Godiva told Sage. "We're going to stay here and have a proper good-bye with Benton."

"Oh," Adam said, "I completely forgot! Can you tell him I said thank you for getting rid of the Klappers? Whatever he did, it worked like a charm. I think I can open a second store with the money I saved on wine."

"Will do!" Freddie said. "Now go on, you two. Go find your bliss."

Kyle put his index finger to his lips to silence Randy, who

was dying to say the final send-off words.

Sage and Adam, arm in arm, walked out of the bar into the lobby.

"I'm smiling so much," she said. "I think I might break my face."

"I already broke mine," Adam said, pointing to his grin. "Now, where should we go to start our new adventure together?"

"You mean you weren't presumptuous enough to book us a room somewhere?" Sage asked.

Adam looked into her eyes. "Never," he said. "Never ever. I'll never take you for granted, Sage and—"

"Good. I'm so glad you didn't, though I am happy that you asked your sister to take care of Vizzy. I just needed to know. Everything is perfect. I couldn't be happier." She paused to take a breath. "Sorry, I didn't mean to interrupt you."

Adam smiled. "I'm glad you did. I want you to know who I am … in every way. And I want to say that I'm very grateful that Benton came into our lives. Of course, admittedly, I didn't always feel that way, but the fact that he was there and that in the end, you still saw your way clear to me, means everything."

"I feel as if I've really grown up," Sage said. "I know I've finally evolved into the woman I was meant to me. And that's why I was able to finally love the man I'm meant to be with."

Adam put his hands on her shoulders and smiled as he drew her close. "I never thought I could be this happy. I'm so glad you found your way … and I'm glad I found mine. I lost the weight I needed to lose, and found the wisdom and strength I needed to gain." He laughed. "Would have been pretty disastrous the other way around, you know?"

The light in Sage's eyes danced. She took a step toward Adam, then kissed him on the lips. "You know, Godiva Genevieve Jones, who I have only known for three weeks, is always by my side with her pearls of wisdom. The other day, she shared something with me that her very wise grandmother told her: 'When you face your emotions, you work through your emotions.' And that's what I did. I think it's what we both did." She looked up at Adam. "I just need to walk over to the window and look out at the night sky. By myself ... for just a moment. Do you mind?"

"Of course not, sweetheart," he said.

A feeling of warmth surged through her body. Sage walked over to the large plate-glass window. Above her, in the night sky, she saw a plane take off and watched it disappear into the clouds, imagining the sound of its jet engines as it vanished out of sight beyond the soundproof glass. Once the plane was gone, she watched the clouds move ever so slightly. Then, somehow spotting exactly what she was looking for, she smiled as her eyes focused on two twinkling stars. "Love," she whispered. "It's me, Sage. I hope you can hear me. I just need you to know, you don't have to look away anymore. I'm good. I'm real good."

THE END

LISETTE BRODEY was born and raised in the Philadelphia area. She lived in New York City for ten years and now resides in Los Angeles.

She is the multi-genre author of eight novels and one short story collection. Her books include: *Crooked Moon; Squalor, New Mexico; Molly Hacker Is Too Picky!*; The Desert Series: (*Mystical High; Desert Star; Drawn Apart*); *Barrie Hill Reunion; Hotel Obscure: A Collection of Short Stories; and Love, Look Away.*

Additionally, in January 2013, the author edited and published a book of her mother's poetry (written 50 years earlier) called *My Way to Anywhere* by Jean Lisette Brodey.

She has also published two short stories in an anthology called *Triptychs (Mind's Eye Series, Book 3).*

Website & contact: lisettebrodey.com
Amazon author page: Author.to/lisettebrodey
Twitter: twitter.com/lisettebrodey
Facebook: facebook.com/BrodeyAuthor
Instagram: @ca_lisette
Pinterest: pinterest.com/lisetteca/